The Chosen One's Substitute

The Jagged Sword Chronicles, Volume 1

Suzie Nicks

Published by Suzie Nicks, 2026.

Table of Contents

The Chosen One's Substitute (The Jagged Sword Chronicles, #1)....... 1
Prologue........ 5
Chapter 1........ 12
Chapter 2........ 23
Chapter 3........ 29
Chapter 4........ 38
Chapter 5........ 48
Chapter 6........ 60
Chapter 7........ 69
Chapter 8........ 77
Chapter 9........ 88
Chapter 10........ 97
Chapter 11........ 108
Chapter 12........ 118
Chapter 13........ 127
Chapter 14........ 137
Chapter 15........ 146
Chapter 16........ 160
Chapter 17........ 166
Chapter 18........ 177
Chapter 19........ 185
Chapter 20........ 198
Chapter 21........ 207
Chapter 22........ 218
Chapter 23........ 227
Chapter 24........ 232
Chapter 25........ 244
Chapter 26........ 257
Chapter 27........ 269
Chapter 28........ 278
Chapter 29........ 294
Chapter 30........ 303
Chapter 31........ 309

Chapter 32 317
Chapter 33 320
Chapter 34 323
Epilogue 327
Pronunciation Guide 331

suizienicks@protonmail.com

Cover art and Map by NBoar Art
ISBN (paperback) 979-8-9949904-0-7
ISBN (eBook) 979-8-9949904-1-4

ANITARIS
GREATER ANITARIS
Pacatus's Family Home
CAIRNGROM RANGE
Inglerhio
Cairngrom
ILE OF CHE
TANGGULAN
Andeireahd
Carados
Faioloa
MEDITULLIO
PAKAHARI
Ados
Domum Commercia
Pekeatu
ILE OF QUAL
KORETAKE
TREBRI ILES
Ogatotonu
HADRUMENTUM
Tipasa
Dragon Rider's Fortress
LESSER ANITARIS

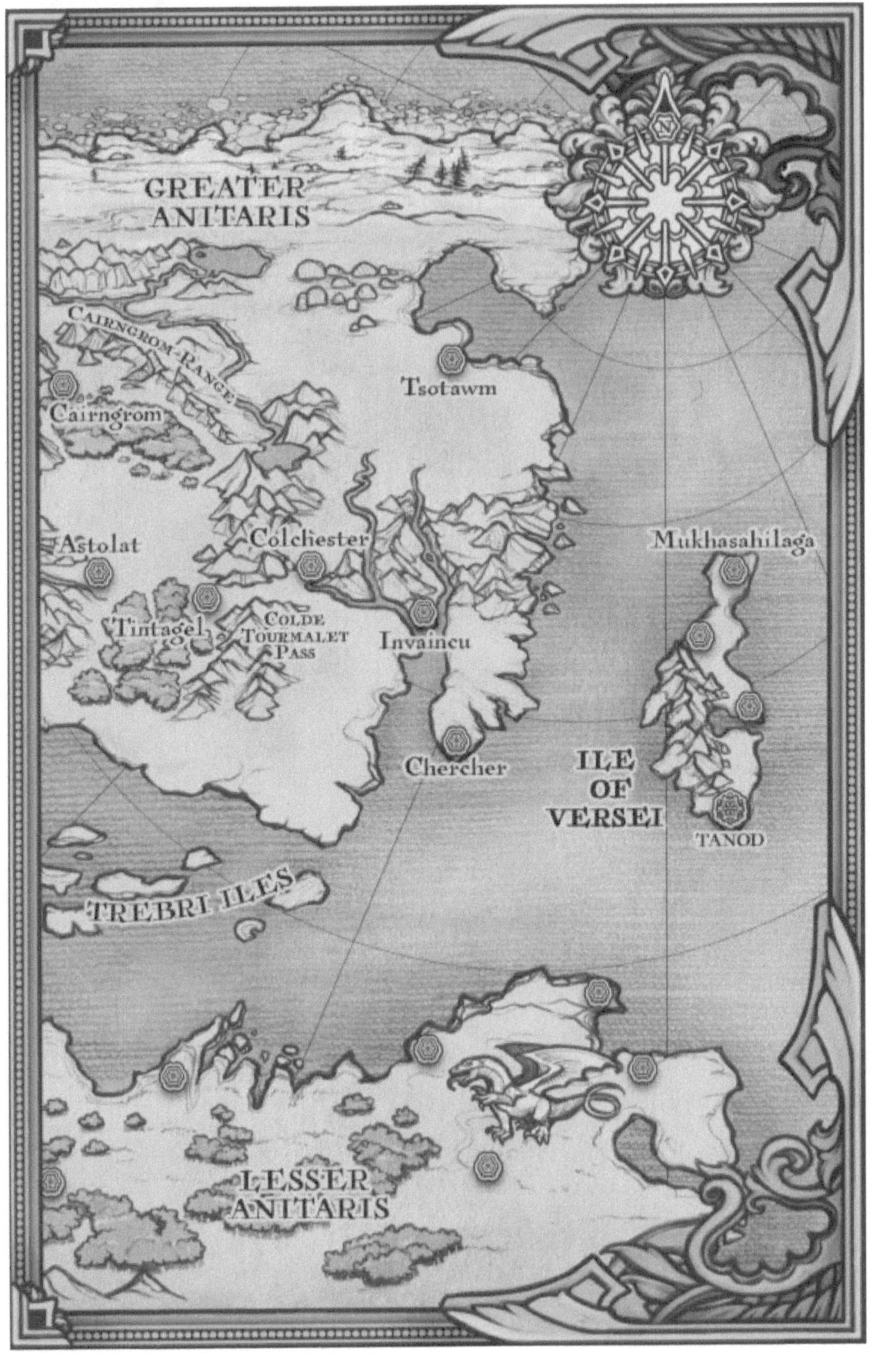
GREATER
ANITARIS
CAIRNGROM RANGE
Cairngrom
Tsotawm
Astolat
Colchester
Tintagel
COLDE
TOURMALET
PASS
Invaincu
Mukhasahilaga
Chercher
ILE
OF
VERSEI
TANOD
TREBRI ILES
LESSER
ANITARIS

To my husband, Tony. The love of my life, brainstorming partner, biggest fan, combat realism inspector, spellchecker, panic attack calmer, and financial supporter (at least until I become a millionaire author😊)

Prologue

Mago

As Mago walked slowly down the line of female captives, he contemplated the meaning of mercy. He was a benevolent master. His whores were never beaten. He ensured that they were always well-fed, sheltered, and protected. They were even permitted to drink (as long as they didn't get too drunk to perform) and to appeal to his mistress if they objected to a particular client. Not that she let them out of the task without a good reason, but it was better than they would be treated in most other brothels.

As he continued his line of travel, he was certain that the trembling, battered, shackled women wouldn't see it that way. They would, after all, still be whores if he chose them, no matter how he treated them. And since the Warlords and any of their warriors who got a hold of spare coin were his primary clientele of late...well, the freshly brutalized women would be unhappy to see such men again.

His sandals squished in the mud, reminding him that the interlude of sunshine caressing his face would not last long in the wet season. Metal quietly clinked as the girl he passed—barely sixteen if he were any judge—trembled with relief. Should she be relieved? He supposed that was also a matter of opinion. Those he didn't choose wouldn't be set free. The best she could hope for was slavery in her own home and her own trade, sending valuable tribute to the Dragon Riders. The worst? Well, at least whores got paid.

Brightly colored robes swished as he stopped in front of another girl (woman? maybe?). She was pretty, despite the bruises and scrapes. Full chest and hips, but not full in the waist. She was tall, with long, slender legs exposed by her torn linen skirt. Her warm almond skin was light enough to be considered exotic, but her matted, bloodied hair was enough of a rich, tightly curled black to be familiar. She was not the type of girl he could pass by without raising suspicion.

"This one." He affected an uninterested tone as he pointed at her, continuing his slow march. "Her, too." He gestured to the shorter but likely older girl standing next to her. She had a rounder face but shared enough features that they had to be related. Neither of them could be more than twenty. The shorter one cursed at him and tried to run, earning herself a blow from the warrior-turned-guard who staggered her. He had enough self-control not to flinch as he heard it land.

He didn't like this method of increasing his harem, or den, or whatever this tribe called a group of women for sale, or more accurately, for rent. When he started, he had only solicited women already working in the trade of flesh. He had enticed them with better conditions and marginally better pay. They had chosen to join him. No, he hated this method. One should have a choice if they were to enter whoredom. But the stronger he forged his ties with the Dragon Riders, the more generosity they showed him. It hadn't taken long for their kindness to escalate from promises to golden trinkets to first pick of female prisoners. No matter his personal opinion of this method, he would not—could not—sever those ties now. Too many people would die without so much as a warning.

"This one also." He gestured to a strongly built woman of about thirty with skin the color of roasted cocoa beans and equally dark hair twisted in knots. She had probably born children and no doubt had the marks to prove it, but some men liked that. Again, she was too pretty to overlook, and he would treat her better than a slave, whether she believed it or not.

He finally reached the end of the line of captives, smiling to cover the grimace that the smell of the guard's body odor brought to his face as he spoke his respectful farewells.

"Come, Gisco," he said when they were just far enough away to not cause offense. "I would like to get back to our own camp before they finish rounding up the children."

Gisco held the chains of the three women in one enormous hand, his other hanging easily by the club tucked into his belt.

"Yes, master. As would I. Seen it once. Not eager to again."

Mago nodded and kept his eyes forward. He wanted to reassure the women that the club was not for them, but then they might try to run or fight, and that would cause delay. Reassurances would have to come later and would probably be better received if they came from his existing whores, not himself.

"Mago!" a familiar voice rang out from behind him. *Bomilcar.*

Damn. There would be no avoiding delay now. He turned toward the voice and saw Bomilcar striding toward him. His helmet was tucked under his arm, and his half-plate reflected the sunlight as a smile stretched across his broad, dark face. The Warlord's son was in an excellent mood. But then, why wouldn't he be?

"Bomilcar, my friend! What can I do for you?" He mirrored the younger man's cruel happiness.

"I was going to help you get your pick of new girls, but it seems you already did." He chuckled and ran the back of a gauntleted finger down the tall, almond-skinned girl's exposed arm. She whimpered and pulled away, stepping too close to Gisco for him to effectively use his club. Her fear only encouraged the man, and he nearly purred, "Don't cry, beautiful. I'll be gentle."

Mago knew that wasn't true. Bomilcar had never tried to strike the whores, nor did he have any unusual appetites, but he was anything but gentle, often leaving them sore and walking with wide steps the next day.

"I have already finished, as you see. The victory celebrations do require a bit of planning. I wouldn't want to bore you with such trivial details, but I didn't wish to waste any time. Besides, I'm sure your quartermaster has plans for the women who didn't interest me."

"Oh, indeed. But as you say, I am bored by such trivial details."

The Warlord's son wanted something else. He still rode the post-conquest excitement and always seemed to find Mago when he sought calm or distraction. Oddly enough, the young man didn't always seek him out for the company of his whores. Sometimes, it appeared that he genuinely wanted a friendship with their master, which suited Mago's purposes just fine, even if it always felt like sharing a table with a snake.

"Gisco, get these women to Sophonisba to be cleaned up. It seems I have other business."

The hulking eunuch grunted his acknowledgement and led the women away toward their camp.

They fell into step and Bomilcar unconsciously guided them toward the center of the army's camp. As they weaved among the slaves setting up wood-framed tents and preparing cooking fires, Mago kept silent. He had learned the effect calm silence had on most people and waited until Bomilcar decided to reveal his true reason for seeking him out.

But Bomilcar was comfortable in the silence; perhaps he had grown so accustomed to time with Mago that he no longer felt the awkward pressure to fill it. Mago listened to the rhythmic thuds of mallets driving stakes into the ground and the soft crunch of the long, matted grass under their feet. Then another sound reached his ears: Crying. Children crying.

They emerged from the forming alleyway between tents into a large open area with the rapid construction of the Warlord and his family's tents on one side and a wide, grassy knoll on the other. Mago fought down a jolt of fear. He had been tailing the Dragon Riders' army for months, serving them in their southwestern canyon fortress for at least a year. But the sight of the dragons still gave him the intense urge to run and hide.

Half a dozen dragons lounged atop the knoll, necks and tails lolling out, all four legs tucked under them like cats, and mighty wings spread across the ground, thick green scales soaking up sunlight after a long day of aerial combat. Mago still marveled that such a large beast could fly. They were as big as elephants, though much leaner. The thick, scaled flesh was only a few shades darker than the grass they lay atop. The gold-plated bridles caught the light and threw it in all directions, giving them a slightly ethereal look, which did nothing to quell the fear they inspired.

The Warlord, Bostar, sat atop the seventh dragon in the open area, as regal and composed as a king on a throne. Mago supposed that in his own way, he was a king. Kings often started as Warlords who amassed support and power. What was more powerful than a man who had the support of dragons?

Rather than overseeing court, the Warlord watched one of his riders, a daughter by a concubine. Dido examined all of the children of the newly subjugated tribe and sorted them into groups. Each child was forced in front of her, where she stared at them with glassy, unseeing eyes. Then she would instruct the warriors into which group to put them.

Bomilcar shifted beside him, his greaves clinking as they flexed, but he didn't look away from the spectacle. To look away would be weakness, and the Warlord's eldest son was not weak. Bringing a friend along, though...that would not be seen as weakness. So, that was the purpose he had for seeking out Mago's company.

"What is she looking for?" Mago broke the silence, hoping to exchange honesty for honesty.

"Something to do with their futures. I don't know. I think she's smoked Gnome shit. But Father wants to cull the dangerous ones."

"She can see their futures?"

Bomilcar chuffed. "She claims to be able to see if they are dangerous to us or not."

"How dangerous can children be?" Mago continued to mirror the other man's disbelief.

"Exactly my point, but she objects that they will be someday, and that's what she claims to see in their futures. I think she's just trying to get Father to rely on her more. She's just sorting them at random."

Mago considered that. He couldn't be sure that Bomilcar was correct in his assessment, but none of the other family members were forthcoming. It wasn't as though he could ask the Blind Seer herself, just in case Bomilcar was wrong, and she could see that he was dangerous to the Dragon Riders.

"She is her mother's seventh child, is she not?" he asked quietly.

"I suppose so. I don't keep track of how many babies my father's concubines squeeze out."

"And were they all girls, or a mix?"

"I don't know; most of them are dead. The living ones are all girls, but I still think she's a liar."

"I trust your judgement." Mago bowed his head with the words. Deference was almost always effective at soothing away offense with the Warlord's son. The young man flashed white teeth in a feline grin that quickly fell when his half-sister bowed to the Warlord, indicating she was finished.

Two of the three groups of captive children were shuffled off to the side of the open area, just a few paces next to where Mago and his companion stood. The third group was kept in front of the Warlord.

Bostar shouted a command. Mago probably should've tried to remember it, but his mind rebelled in that moment. What did it matter anyway? Who else could command fell beasts, let alone dragons? The dragon shifted its feet underneath it, not unlike a cat preparing to pounce. It drew in a great breath, and its chest glowed between its scales. Mago looked away. He was a whore master; he didn't care if they thought him too weak to watch.

He could turn his eyes but not his other senses, and that was almost worse. The rush of air, the roar of fire, the screams that started and cut sharply off, all these still reached him. Air around him suddenly heated and drew beads of sweat along his dark skin. The acrid, stomach-churning scent of charred flesh, hair, and bone. It was over in an instant, but the memory would linger in his mind. He closed his eyes as terrified shrieks and sobbing started from the children to his right, followed by yelling and blows from their captors to keep them in line before they were herded off to rejoin their parents as captives or vassals.

Mago inwardly renewed his vow to keep this carnage from the shores of the Empire by whatever means necessary. Then he turned to his companion, who, despite being a hardened warrior, looked a bit pallid.

"Have we met your obligation? Or must we witness the slaves clean away the charred remains?"

"I imagine we have." The young man shrugged. "I don't want to keep you from your trivial preparations, but if I had to watch..."

It was as close to an apology as he could expect. So, he accepted it with false grace and bowed to excuse himself. He hurried to his own camp, just outside of the army's camp but close enough for convenience. His small cluster of tents was already up, and fires were alight. The tempting scent of sheep and various fowl roasting over them was not enough to block out the recent memory of the children's execution.

Several of his eunuchs climbed into empty carts to gather more supplies from the nearest winehouse. He hailed them and climbed atop the foremost one. It might've been a bit odd that a whore master fetched his own wine, but he could always pretend that he simply didn't trust his eunuchs with that much coin.

Nearly an hour of bumping roughly against the wooden seat later, he stepped into the winehouse.

"Picking up, master?" the brewer asked him.

"Aye. I'll need six barrels, I think, and one or two smaller casks of that imported ale if you have more."

"I do, indeed." The other man's eyes widened at the recognition of the code words. He hoped that the Dragon Riders would move on from this place soon; he didn't need his cover blown because this contact was so obvious. "Will you be wanting me to order more?"

"Yes."

The winehouse owner nodded briskly and went into the backroom. He gave some instructions to the eunuchs who had followed him in, and they began loading the indicated barrels onto the wagons. When they were occupied, he brought a parchment and quill to Mago, who quickly scribbled his cyphered note. He didn't have much time, but he knew the cypher as well as he knew the common tongue.

Then he handed it over to the winehouse owner, along with coin, and received back a signed receipt for the wine, which he tucked into the pouch that hung from his belt. "Make sure you dip it in wax to be sure it survives the crossing."

"Yes, yes, of course," was the man's flustered reply. "Will you be returning soon for another order, master?"

Gods, he hoped not, but he must be prepared for such an eventuality. "I cannot be certain; my camp will move when my Lord does. As long as you see Dragons in the sky, you can look for my business." Mago said, then he strode out and back to his waiting cart.

Chapter 1

Asha

Asha's sword moved so quickly, the swish of air was drowned out by the clangs of her strikes against the post quintain. High, high, low, high again, a simple combination. She had practiced it enough that her arm could have accomplished the task without her mind attending it, which was likely why something was moving in her left periphery.

Her left arm rose without further thought and she clenched her fist, filling the shield bracelet on her wrist with mana as she did so. The small spherical object that her sister had thrown at her hit the red haze that shimmered in a disc around her torso and exploded back in the direction it had come. Shrieks and giggles pierced her ears as she gagged at the smell of burning mule dung. More mule chips followed the first into the air from several directions. Great Uncle Luca had enlisted at least three of her younger sisters for this surprise attack.

"Keep striking. That fellow isn't going to stop attacking you just because you're defending," the grizzled and gray old man scolded in his characteristic monotone. "Quite the opposite, in fact. Situational awareness, lass."

Asha clenched her sharp jaw and forced an exhale out of her aquiline nose. Tendrils of her auburn hair had pulled free from her braid and tickled the corners of her gray-blue eyes, adding to her distraction. She repeated the combo, keeping her shield arm raised, shifting it slightly to better deflect the dung that still flew at her.

"Does mother know you let them throw shit?" she said to him as she practiced a feint into a lunge at about throat height.

"She doesn't, but since she doesn't know you use that word, I say we call it even." He hadn't moved or changed expressions. "Besides, you'll be dealing with far worse training methods where you're going."

Where she was going... Her sword tip drooped as her heart skipped a beat.

"Steady on that guard." Great Uncle Luca never missed a thing.

Finally, the rain of shit stopped. She struck the post quintain again and again, the force of her blows increasing. Her great uncle might have encouraged her five-year-old baby sister to pick up and throw mule droppings, but he wasn't trying to rip her away from her family.

Asha's shield blazed brighter, and heat rose in her sword hand as she repeated the combo in rapid succession.

"Enough! Drop that sword in the water barrel before you melt it," the old man shouted at her. He rarely shouted, but lately it seemed that when he did, it was always at her.

She pulled the mana out of the bracelet, dropping her arm, and complied. The sword hissed, which meant she had ruined the heat treatment. Her uncles and aunts in the family armory would be very annoyed with that. But it was still sword-shaped, so she had caught herself early enough this time. Or rather, he had caught her.

"Ye can go back and clean up for supper," Great Uncle Luca said to her, then turned to her three youngest sisters. "You three as well. But wash up in the creek before you go to the house."

"No thanks," she mumbled as she pulled her whip from her belt and walked out into the middle of the dirt training field.

The old man didn't say anything but came to stand by her left side as she drew small bits of mana and flicked the whip out. Runes woven into the braided leather of the whip channeled her spells and projected them, so she didn't have to worry about melting it. She targeted dirt clods and tufts of grass trying to grow out of the dry, frosty ground with fireballs and tiny explosions.

"Is the Order's training really that bad?" she asked after a while.

"Not officially. But it will depend on who your instructors are, and your preceptor. You would be surprised at how much unofficial wrongdoing gets overlooked based on the rank or bloodline of the transgressor."

"We could just ignore the summons," she said petulantly as she continued to cast.

"No, we cannot, Asha. You know that or you wouldn't have agreed to go in your sister's stead." When he spoke like that, she remembered that he had once been a commander of an outpost for the Order of Holy Heroes a very long time ago. It wasn't that his voice or words changed, but something in his shoulders or the set of his jaw.

"We have you, two Seers, an entire armory, and over a hundred of us are full Mages!" She turned on him, letting the whip hang slack. He pivoted slowly and met her eyes. She was a little tall for a woman, around average for a man, but he was a good head taller than her. "We have walls, water, and plenty of food. Our winter stores are nearly gone, but the first spring harvest is near. We would be untouchable here! It would take an army to get Dendra away from us by force!"

"You don't think they would send an army?" His quiet question took the wind out of her. "You think that the Order of Holy Heroes, the richest, most politically powerful order in the entire Empire, would allow us to ignore a summons for a seventh daughter of a seventh daughter of a seventh daughter, by a seventh son no less? And endure the insult that a non-noble family refused their lawful order?"

"She's only five!" she shouted, as if convincing him would change anything. In her heart, she knew it wouldn't and she couldn't. "She can't even access mana for another two years. Nine until her first Iulru', seven more after that before she is a full Mage. What could they possibly want with a little girl?"

"Seers are rare. A triple-generation Seer, by a Void father." Great Uncle Luca sighed. "I think your baby sister is the only one in existence, Asha. I don't know why they would summon a mere child, but I know that they will not be ignored. And they have the power to enforce their will. If they convince the Emperor that ignoring a summons amounts to an insurrection, even a thousand Mages may not be enough. If we kept them out, what then? Hmm? Make an enemy of the very Empire we owe our allegiance to?"

Asha's shoulders dropped, and she hung her head. "They were always going to come for her. This is kidnapping!"

The old man squeezed her shoulder with one large hand. "Legally," She snapped her eyes up at his playful tone. "it's not, unfortunately. But perhaps, you can buy her enough time to grow into an adult by going as substitute. It will spoil their fun to have a first daughter instead of a seventh. And they cannot prosecute us for refusing a summons." He clapped her on the back. "You're just getting nervous, lass. You are close to being well-trained." He gave her a rare smile; he usually saved those for his wife, Verna. "And have a good head on you. I think you can hold your own in the mighty Order of Holy Heroes. Besides, you are powerful enough that they won't refuse your service."

"And if they do? Then will we fight them?" she asked as he steered her back toward the family dining hall.

"I don't think so, but your grandmother has sent inquiries regarding becoming an official order ourselves."

Asha nearly tripped when she heard that. "But I thought the legal strings that came with such protections and exemptions were too great a risk to the family."

"It is, but not greater than being labeled rebels against the crown. That's why it is so imperative that you convince the Order to accept you as substitute." His light brown eyes bore into hers.

"I understand," she whispered and squared her shoulders.

"Come on. Better not to let your final family supper get cold." He took the whip, still dragging in the dirt, from her hand and coiled it for her as they walked back to the courtyard.

Asha strained to read the summons again by the flickering candlelight. It didn't say anything different than it had the night before, or the day before that, or the day before that when it had first arrived. But she had awoken long before dawn; she hadn't thought she would sleep at all. Fortunately, she had, but it had been short-lived. She didn't have a name for the feeling buzzing in her chest and electrifying her limbs. It wasn't fear; it wasn't that intense. Worried? Not quite. She needed to do something, to act, to move.

Her urge was to walk out the door and not stop walking until she was at the Capital.

She couldn't do that. Her family would never let her leave without farewells, gifts, and blessings. Furthermore, she didn't even know the way. It wasn't as easy as 'just head south'. Her uncles—or rather the first cousins once removed who she called uncle because that was too much of a mouthful for daily use—Jetti and Jolli had said something about a river barge for one leg of the trip and danger of pirate raiders along the coast.

Instead, she rose in the wee hours and made her final preparations. It hadn't taken long for her to dress in her soft linen undergarments, sturdy wool riding habit, and runed leather boots. The runes were simple enough but invaluable. They would protect against small things like snakes or spider bites and ensure solid footing for the wearer. A broken ankle or snake bite had killed more than one relative before their family had learned the value of 'small' artifice. But that was before she was born. Most of her maternal line was comprised of natural Mages, with some healer and weather Mages. One great aunt and a few aunts had married Artificers, and the family hadn't realized the holes in the armor so to speak until they were patched. Her paternal line, she didn't actually know anything about her paternal line, other than her father.

She drummed her fingers on the small bedside table, frowning again at the parchment summons. Her father was a Void; his type of mana stopped other Mages from being able to use their own. The Order of Holy Heroes was particularly fond of Voids and employed many. Great Uncle Luca was right. It may be suicide to try and take her sister by force with anything less than an army. Yet the threat remained, written between every beautifully scripted line of prose and emphasized by the Imperial seal. The threat of what would come if they had refused to send Dendra. Because the Order had an army, a very powerful one.

In order to convince the Order to accept her instead, she must think of what to say. Some fine speech to keep that army away from her home. Her thoughts raced and only became more muddled. Sometimes she wished she was a Seer like her mother and grandmother, not a Destructive. Such decisions would be easier if she could see the future. Of course, anytime she had said so, she got either a lecture on accepting who she was as the

Gods made her or reminded sternly that that was not how Seer mana worked. Seers didn't see the future exactly; they saw a person's next action or decision and could infer the consequences of it. They could follow that chain into the future, but the further from the present moment they went, the more uncertain it became. Dreams were different. More like warnings, and easier to follow without the conscious mind to get in the way. Still, knowing how the Order's Counsel would react to her words before she said them would help. Not that it mattered. She was a first daughter; only seventh daughters could be Seers.

Soft footfalls echoed in the halls outside her door. One pair was unmistakably small, Dendra. Probably Mia and Mya with her, avoiding the breakfast preparations. She couldn't see any light around the shutter of her window shut tight against the cold spring nights. But based on how much candle wax had melted since she lit it to pack her saddlebags and bedroll, it was nearly time to go eat.

Sure enough, the handle on her door turned without knocking or asking permission, and her youngest three sisters entered. Normally, this annoyed her, but today, her heart ached for missing them. She hadn't even left yet.

Asha tucked the summons in a small pouch on her hip in front of her runed whip, which she wore in the place of a sword on her dominant side. Then she turned on the stool in time to nearly knock her chin on Dendra's forehead as she launched herself into Asha's lap. The ten-year-old twins weren't wearing their characteristic grins. Dendra squeezed her as hard as her tiny arms could manage.

"You can't be mad about the poo we threw at you," Mya declared.

"Oh, can't I?" Asha squeezed Dendra back until she giggled.

"No, because none hit you. 'Sides, you're not allowed to leave mad." Mya crossed her arms triumphantly.

"Well, I guess that is that." Asha chuckled and held Dendra more loosely. Dendra leaned on her.

"Want help with your hair?" Mia said, holding up a boar's-hair brush.

Asha nodded, then stood, tossing Dendra onto the bed, who shrieked more in joy than shock. Then she turned around and plucked out the simple braid she had fastened herself.

She sat in silence while the twins brushed her hair, gathering mana and weaving the spell as they plaited. They had natural and healer mana. Animals and plants responded to them in ways Asha didn't understand. Coaxing hair fibers to grow this way or weave into this shape came easily to them in ways it never did for her. It was a simple enough spell, mostly to keep her hair free of tangles and secure on her head. The spell also kept the hair cleaner and wouldn't need to be redone as often. Pretty handy when traveling. Sometimes she wondered how Mundanes managed without all the little magic. Tripping on sticks with spiders in their boots and hair in their face, she supposed. The image made her smile.

Her thoughts drifted back to her father. "Is Father coming today?"

"Of course, he is! Where else would he be, foolish sissy?" Dendra started to jump on the down mattress.

"Stop that. You'll break it," she snapped, harsher than she meant to.

Dendra didn't seem to notice, but she did stop. "You're not going to be sleeping in it, so what if I do?"

"Someone else might. Besides, I won't be gone forever." She hoped.

Asha really didn't want to see her father. Did he know why Dendra was summoned by the Order he had once been a part of? Would he try to stop Asha from going and send Dendra? That was absurd, but he had a loyalty to the Order that she never understood, so she couldn't rule it out. A nagging voice in the back of her mind told her she didn't understand because she had never tried to. If she were honest, she didn't want to understand the man who had left her, her mother, and all her sisters. She could never say so because her sisters all disagreed, but she thought it was worse that he was still around and would visit from time to time. Why couldn't he have left and started his new family in a far-off village, so she didn't have to smile and make small talk with his wife and her half-brothers every month or so?

"Finished!"

Mia's declaration saved her from feeling guilty for that uncharitable thought. It wasn't the boys' fault that their existence was a knife in her heart. Asha reached up and touched the four small braids, two on either side, between her temple and ear, perfectly symmetrical running back to join the larger braid that started at her crown and fell just between her shoulder blades.

"Thanks, girls. Run along to eat. I'll be right behind you." All three beamed at her and skipped from the room, linking arms as they did.

After a fairly normal (i.e. loud and chaotic) breakfast of porridge with dried fruits and bread with cheese, Asha grabbed the last of her things from her room that would go in her small pack behind her saddle. The burdens for the pack animals had been prepped for days, her uncles and cousins adding and removing and bickering and repacking. That happened every time the family shipped wool and various textiles to the Capital. An outsider might wonder how on earth her family got anything done at all. But an outsider wouldn't understand the deep love and respect that ran through the family. Bickering and teasing and nagging and even shouting, her family could move mountains because somehow the chaos flowed together like a hundred tiny streams and became a (relatively) orderly river. There was nothing her family couldn't do if they really wanted to.

Even mighty rivers could be dammed, the anxiety living in her head whispered. Nonsense. Woe onto anyone who tried to harm her family. There were over three hundred people in her family, and nearly two-thirds were Mages. It wasn't as if the Mundanes of the family were dunces, either. Most Mages were quite condescending to folk who weren't blessed with mana, but they had never seen her uncles and cousins in action. She hoped they would never need to. Peace ought to remain in the valley she called home. The desire to leave nearly choked her. All this waiting was making her very nostalgic and entirely too melancholy.

She turned away from her room for what would probably be the last time in quite a long time, if not the very last time, through the kitchen and dining hall, past the great fireplace with all its happy memories, and out the door into the sunshine. The frosted grass crunched under her boots.

If she had ever doubted how many people loved her, she certainly didn't at that moment. No less than three hundred people stood outside waiting for her, their collective body heat warming the air in the courtyard to a more comfortable temperature. They were all massed to one side with her uncles, Jetti and Jolli, on the other. She went to stand next to them, and the murmuring of chatting relations ceased. The five second cousins who were also going on the trading journey stepped away from the ponies, and the party stood facing the rest of the family. Her great aunt, Verna, the family matriarch, and her great uncle, Luca, stepped out of the crowd and stood directly in front of the travelers. Asha's grandmother and mother moved to the front of the crowd but didn't separate from it.

"We bless you travelers." Great Aunt Verna's voice was loud and strong, ringing across the courtyard.

"Walk with purpose."

"Purpose!" the crowd of loving family echoed in a shout that shook Asha to her core.

"Look with wisdom.

"Wisdom!

"See with kindness.

"Kindness!

"Hear with compassion.

"Compassion!

"Act with strength.

"Strength!

"Live with courage.

"Courage!

"And return in peace.

"Peace!"

After the blessing, Great Aunt Verna and Great Uncle Luca stepped in to hug each of them. Great Aunt Verna didn't say anything else, but she squeezed Asha so tight, she couldn't breathe for a moment.

Great Uncle Luca whispered in her ear as he hugged her. "If peace is not an option, strike with swiftness. Remember that most battles are won by the one who commits the most violence the quickest. Not by whom is most moral. Remember our lessons. Trust your mana in dangerous moments."

Her mother sniffled in her ear. "I'm so proud of you, my dearest. I am not ready to let you go but know that is my heart and not a reflection of you and whether or not you are ready."

Grandmother took her face in weathered hands and pressed their foreheads together. "Common sense, child. Though after this journey, I won't be able to call you that, for you will be a woman grown and tested. Just remember your good sense. It is far more valuable than any spell. "

Easy for a Seer to say.

The rest of her massive family filtered through and gave hugs, wise words, and well wishes. She received them all and trinkets from her cousins, spells on paper scraps, small homemade artifices, herbal sachets, and a small stuffed sheep from one of her youngest second cousins once removed. At the very end of them all was her father and his new family.

First, four of her half-brothers, aged ten through four, gave her awkward hugs and told her how much they would miss her. Then her stepmother, Jessa, stepped in front of her. She awkwardly fished out a small ring around the grabby hands of the twins secured to her by a tight wrap and handed it to Asha. It was made of silver that had been carved to appear as though it were twisted like a hemp rope. There was a beautiful simplicity in its appearance, though she was sure it had not been simple to create.

"It'll glow to warn when an evil creature is near," Jessa explained with a tired smile.

Asha wanted to say that a creature couldn't be evil. Creatures just were; they didn't have intent or motives like people. But she bit her tongue. This was a gesture of kindness from a minor Artificer with the best of intentions. Instead, she forced a smile she hoped looked grateful and said thank you as she slipped it on her left forefinger. It fit just right, but she had expected nothing less. Jessa came from a family of jewelers, and she could size someone for rings or bracelets and such just by looking at them.

Her father's wife returned the smile and went to follow her other sons, wherever they had run off to. All that was left was her father.

He stepped up to her and took her right hand in his, the one without the shield bracelet. "I would hug you, my dear, but I don't want to undo any of your fancy spells or damage your artifices. I know that your family has many—" he hesitated and smiled tightly— "strong opinions about the Order. Don't let that cloud your views of them. They do much good in this world. Even if your grandmother can't see it"

"There is nothing good about stealing a five-year-old," Asha shot back and started to pull her hand away.

He held her hand tighter. "Asha," he warned. "There is more to life than this valley. More people in this world than this family. I'm in agreement with your mother that it is too soon, but in time, your sister will have obligations to that world and those people. The Order is not wrong about that."

"Don't speak to me of obligations," Asha practically hissed and this time, successfully jerked her hand free.

A sad look crossed her father's face. "Someday, Asha, someday when you are older and wiser, I would like to explain myself to you. Maybe when you return, you will be ready to listen."

Asha huffed and turned away. *Why do all the adults treat me like a child and speak of the wisdom they think I lack? I am twenty-two, an entire year past adulthood.* She fumed as she collected her pony and mounted it. They couldn't even wish her farewell without implying she was foolish.

Her uncles and cousins were already mounted and waiting.

"Ready?" Uncle Jetti called.

"Ready," she answered, and the company turned their ponies and exited the courtyard. It was so final and yet very much like a new beginning, leaving the only world she had ever known. She thought of the planting soon to come, of the seeds that must be buried if they were to spring forth and grow. Was she a seed? Was the tightness in her chest and burning behind her eyes the soil that must cover her before she could become something larger, stronger, and better than she had been?

Chapter 2

Bernard

Commandant Bernard Paynes didn't appreciate the surprised look on Master Louis Fulk's face as the servant announced his arrival in the sitting room. A quick glance around the brightly decorated room explained his superior's shock. While Bernard was never late to meetings of the High Council, he was rarely early and was never the first to arrive. Then again, he almost never had his lovely wife on his arm, and she was a stickler about being early.

The most powerful man in the Order of Holy Heroes recovered quickly and rose to extend his greetings, the finely woven fabric of his civilian doublet sliding up as he did so. Bernard saluted him, now conscious if his own doublet would shift around as he did so; he much preferred his well-worn arming doublet, but that would have been inappropriate for an evening tea that was really a meeting. His wife's hand arrested his slight forward bow, still resting in his left elbow. She likely didn't realize that she was tugging against him.

"Welcome, welcome," Master Fulk said as he stepped closer. "None of that formality now, Bernard. You are in my home, not the garrison. Let us act as friends here."

"Certainly, sir. Your sitting room is far more comfortable than the garrison's meeting hall," Bernard answered. "Have you met my wife, Helena?"

On cue, she gave a small informal curtesy. "We have met several times, in fact." She shared a confidential smile with Master Fulk. "As you can see, keeping track of acquaintances falls to me in our marriage."

"As in mine," said Lady Fulk as she breezed in the room, perfectly poised in credit to her aristocratic blood. "As in most marriages I believe."

A servant announced the Order's Treasurer, Martin Redin, his wife, and the Hospitaller, Isabella Navarre and her husband. *Ah, we aren't that early.* Greetings and salutes were exchanged. The Master repeated his dismissal of formalities, and yet as the remaining members of the High Council arrived with spouses in tow, all of them gave the formalities just the same.

"Now that we are all here," Master Fulk raised his voice only enough to cut through the polite chatter. "My elegant wife has laid out tea in the garden for all of our better halves. I am afraid I must monopolize my officer's time."

"I am delighted with your companionship while my husband has yet another meeting," she purred as she made her way toward a side door. "I hardly ever have company in the evenings."

Most of the wives echoed her playful complaint as they all filed out of the sitting room and into the garden beyond. Bernard was gratified that he had insisted his wife wear her thick wool shawl, even though she whined that it was the wrong shade of blue for her richly embroidered evening gown. The warmth of the spring afternoon would fade quickly now that the sun was setting. Although Lady Fulk was an experienced hostess, perhaps she had arranged for a warming fire outside.

"I don't wish to waste any of your, or your spouse's time this evening," Fulk began as servants arrived with imported wine, Imperial ale, various cheeses and dried fruits, and enough tobacco and pipes for the entire Council. Ironically, no tea was served, calling it an evening tea must have been merely a formality. "I assume everyone has read the latest reports from the South. That warlord from the Western coast of that God's forsaken continent is doing very well in his endeavors. How are preparations coming along?"

"The nobility are quite resistant, sir." Grand Commander Alonso Fernandez answered first. "They see no reason to fear this warlord over the others, but most have been pressured by His and Her Majesty to return to court early and keep their children close to, if not in, the Capital."

"Aye, what about taming Dragons, the most feared of all fell beasts, is unusual? Nothing at all, nothing at all." Ramon Despuig, the Order's Marshal, shook his head.

"Being unusual doesn't mean that the skirmishing savages will be any threat to us," retorted the Order's High Priest, Hadrian West.

"That takes care of the noble children, but what of the powerful but poor youngsters?" Master Fulk moved on before an argument could derail the meeting. "We summoned several I believe."

"Yes, sir," Isabella Navarre said. "I have about two dozen incorporated into the hospitals and almshouse. Though I am not certain all of them will have enough mana to be seen as a threat, should an invasion come."

"Better safe than sorry," Emery Ponte, the Harbinger, replied. "I have added roughly the same number to inventory and the weaver's circles."

"Indeed," Bernard took advantage of Emery's habit of long pauses between thoughts to seize an opportunity. He might not get a chance if the Harbinger started on tallies of weapons, armament, and other supplies that were being stockpiled. "Proper planning prevents piss poor performance." His quotation was met with several eyerolls and an equal number of approving nods. "Speaking of planning, have we established what to do with the young Seer we summoned from the North? Where should she go? Who will hold her wardship? She is very young yes, not even able to access her mana?"

"I suppose you think she ought to be in the academy," West did not openly sneer but his distaste was evident, nonetheless.

"I would not close the academy doors to her," he maintained a pleasant expression as he replied. Professional bearing was his goal, the fact that it would needle the priest was only a benefit. "However, I believe that a child so young and powerful ought to be placed directly in a noble family. I'm certain the infirmaries and weaving circles are taking excellent care of the children that they have but how many more can they handle? And a third generation Seer is not the child we want to fall through the cracks."

"It is a good point but without disseminating reports of the Dragon Rider's murdering of powerful children, it would be very difficult to convince a high-ranking family to accept a merchant girl from the North."

Richard Beaumont spoke for the first time that evening. "Does she have any relations in Meditullio?"

All eyes turned to Alonzo, who was not only the master's second, but also the head of all intelligence gathering, legal and otherwise. "None whatsoever," he said. "At least not outside of the working class, there is a distant connection to the head of a smithing guild, but not a drop of aristocratic blood in the girl."

"Why the Gods bestow such gifts on the lowly born, I have not the wisdom to divine." West muttered. Then louder he said, "I could take her into the temples. We have plenty of priests and no cracks for her to fall through."

"That would provide her family with a legal avenue to dispute her summons, Hadrian." Master Fulk sighed. "We cannot compel anyone into priesthood. The best place for her would be if one of us here accepted her as a ward. Fully legal, and no one who is not already privy to our intelligence needs to be made aware."

Heads nodded and agreement was murmured, but no one volunteered to take the girl, not even the High Priest. He might want a win over Bernard, but it seemed not enough to take lawful parentage of the young Seer. This did not escape Fulk. After a few quiet moments he turned sharp brown eyes on Bernard again. "You said that you would not close the academy. What of your home?"

"I would have to discuss it with my wife," he answered. "But I do not believe she will object. However-"

"However, that will undermine whatever it is that you truly wanted to ask us for, hmm?" Fulk interrupted, his eyes narrowed but he was grinning. "Out with it, man. My wife looks especially ravishing in that dress, and I prefer her company to yours."

A net cast for a minnow is also cast for a dire pike. "I wish to form a new type of ballast." Bernard stated.

"New how?"

"I think that we are wasting the most powerful of our allies. I wish to experiment with bonding all three races into a ballast." Bernard kept his voice confident and his face neutral, knowing the objections to follow.

At first everyone was silent, then half-articulated thoughts burst out of several mouths.

"Preposterous! Bind with foreigners-" Despuig bellowed.

"Not even the Gods mixed the races' blood-" hissed Hadrian.

"The surf-riding Elves will never agree to-" scoffed Admiral Matilda Tewkes.

"At Ease!" Master Fulk did raise his voice to a shout this time. "A blood bond is no experiment, Commandant. Good Mages will be soul-tied unless one of them perishes. Why do you think that this would be a good idea?"

"As our marshal pointed out, we are facing an unprecedented threat," Bernard answered quietly. "The three races working together would be far more powerful than merely side by side. Think of it! We have the strongest and most diverse mana, but the way an Elf can weave a wind spell after three to four hundred years...or the mastery of a Dwarven Artificer. All three together, pulling mana as one...that would take down a dragon."

"Even if you convinced us," Ponte finally had closed his gaping jaw just before speaking. "It won't be covered by the Alliance, and our treaty with the Elves is far less tenable."

"The Alliance includes military aid," Beaumont said. *That is one on my side.* "I don't think that a few Artificers for a ballast would be that large of a step from the Trade."

"A blood bond is in fact quite a large step from exchanging healer's service beside the rock-tunneling army for Artificer apprenticeships under Dwarven smiths." Hadrian's face was schooled, but the nasally octave of his voice had gone up. *One firmly against.*

"The Elves would likely go for it, if only so that they can wiggle out of any further commitments," Tewkes said dispassionately. "Can't go a league without sighting their traders but help with pirates has been few and far between. They like to keep their storied marines scattered and far from us." Bernard noted her as neutral.

"Who would pay their wages?" Redin asked and everyone chuckled. Another neutral.

"I don't know, Bernard," Fulk leaned back in his seat. "I see your point about skill and specialization that unfortunately humans are too short-lived to achieve. But we have fought every other war just fine without intermingling, fighting alongside even, but never that. Can not the distinctly human ability to cross cast or the diversity, as you put it, to access all seven types of mana do far more than that?"

"Perhaps it can, the Seventh did bless us with more mana, but then the Sixth punished us for our hubris with fell beasts." Bernard spoke slowly, focusing on making eye contact with the quiet, undecided members. "I think it would be wise to approach this fell beast differently than we have in previous wars. Binding to the other races would show that we will not repeat our ancestors' mistakes and trade anything for power. We become stronger together without losing our humility and humanity."

His words were met with grumbles and muttering, but no more outright dispute. He let it stretch. Referring to the War of the Gods might have been cheating but he truly believed his words. He hoped that they understood that.

"One," Fulk finally said. "You may experiment with one ballast. I leave the negotiating for members and training to you. Assuming you can work out who will pay them." He smiled and Bernard returned it.

"Thank you, sir. This will work. I have faith."

"Now, if you have no more requests?" Fulk's patience had finally run out, and Bernard shook his head and then bowed it in deference. "Tall tales or hair-brained schemes? Good, now Emery, tell me more. What are the numbers of dry stores? Richard, Ramon, how are the smiths handling the increased quotas for spears, cuirasses, horseshoes, and such? We may or may not be facing a war, but I will certainly be facing a fate worse than a troll den if this takes all night."

Chapter 3

Asha

The party skirted the compound and picked up the herd of thirty sheep with its two herding dogs and the twelve pack mules laden with textiles. It was a relatively small number of packs, but then it was early in the year. Under normal circumstances, the Pacatus traders wouldn't have made this journey in the fifth week of the second month. The earliest trip Asha was aware that they had made was the first week of the third month, and that had been an unusually warm spring. It had only been twelve weeks since the new year feasts. Asha was grateful that her family had arranged an early trading trip rather than just putting her on a boat out of Inglerho. She wasn't ready to be truly alone just yet.

As had been explained to her, the sheep were going as commission from some noble on the outskirts of the Capital. He had sent inquiries about the best breeding stock that the family was willing to part with, specifying that the sheep must be herded down the continent, not placed on a ship. This nobleman had some strange notion that a sea voyage would impair the sheep's fertility. Sheep did have delicate constitutions, but none of the Pacatus shepherds had heard of such danger. Nevertheless, this noble was willing to pay more than enough to make it worth the excess travel time. As long as they arrived in one piece.

Hooves crunched on the frosted, freshly sprouted grass. Saddles creaked, and great puffs of fog lifted into the air every time a pony or mule snorted. The peaks that hemmed them in were especially beautiful that morning, standing starkly white with stubborn snow halfway down. Asha loved springtime. *Were there mountains down south?* She scrambled her mind for her geography lessons. There had to be. How did anyone live far from mountains?

The party angled south and east, out of the valley that the Pacatus family controlled and toward the river that cut through the middle of it. Asha's family did not own the entire valley, but it seemed like they did some days. She had never been to the far side of the river. That side was plagued by raiders and fell beasts from the mountains that did not belong to either the Empire or the Dwarves. The river was wide, shifting, and embedded into glacier silt, making it as effective a barrier as the wall visible in the far distance.

They rode in a loose circle around the sheep and pack mules, with more space between riders at the front than the back. Uncle Jetti rode at the front eastern side, guiding the party. Uncle Jolli rode parallel to him on the western side. Asha rode behind Jetti. Across the herd from her was Alaric (who was married to Jetti's eldest daughter, Adelaide). She normally rode in Asha's position, but she had given birth to her fourth child only a few weeks prior. Behind Asha was Erika, Jetti's second daughter. Fanning out to the west, holding the rear, was Jolli's three oldest sons: Arne, Bard, and Crispin.

The two herding dogs caught her eye as they ran back and forth behind the herd, nipping and nudging, keeping all the animals that weren't being ridden moving in the same direction and tight enough together to be easily led by Jetti. Slender, dark brown dogs that were the very picture of canine speed and agility. They seemed to never tire, though she supposed that this was only the first day of travel. The herd moved at a quick walk, but the dogs were trotting constantly.

As it turned out, the herding dogs did tire, but not before Asha did. As the evening shadows began to fall, it took all her strength to hold herself properly in her saddle. Her back and knees ached, and her buttocks was tender in the saddle. She was pretty sure she could have fallen asleep right where she was, but she was not going to be the first rider to slouch or ask for a break. Luckily for her, Uncle Jetti called for a halt shortly after.

"Best get a camp set up before it's dark," he called entirely too cheerfully after a day's ride. But then again, he'd made this trip often, and even at home, he was entirely too cheerful.

They had crossed almost all her family's lands and set up camp about two miles inside their border.

"Is there a reason we aren't pressing on to the village?" she asked Erika as the group began their assigned tasks to set up camp. Theirs was to strip the saddles and packs from the ponies and mules and tether them out to graze.

"Gotta travel slower with the sheep. Hard travel will make them lose weight, which will make bartering at the Capital harder. They're also more likely to go lame," Erika responded as she stripped another saddle. "Besides, the village isn't likely to have accommodations large enough for us where we can also watch over the herd. We would have to camp out and post guards on the livestock. Might as well do that on our own lands."

"Surely no one in the village would try to steal from us!" Asha exclaimed.

"To my knowledge, no one so close has tried, but you can never be sure. The only thing you can trust a thief to do is try to steal."

"I guess that is fair enough then." Asha had been expecting to sleep in a bed or at least on a pallet mattress that night. She had been warned that they would be sleeping out most nights, might as well start now. Asha turned to stake out another mule.

Supper consisted of pottage and seasoned, dried meat. It wasn't fancy, but it was nourishing and warm against the cold of night that had settled in as the sun set behind the mountains. Asha went to her bedroll as soon as she was sure that nothing else needed to be done around the camp. She fell asleep listening to Jetti and Jolli bickering about the best way to stew salt pork. Jetti preferred a hard, quick boil, but Jolli insisted that it was more tender when it simmered long and slow. Jetti was questioning the practicality of slow simmers at the end of a long travel day when Asha crossed into a deep, exhausted sleep.

She awoke to someone lightly kicking her boot. Stars shone brightly as she blinked her vison clear. *It can't be my watch yet. I've barely slept.* She opened her mouth to complain, but Crispin covered her mouth with his hand. Starting, she inhaled a foul, rotting stench. Crispin motioned for her to be quiet, then removed his hand.

"Ye got any bright light spells?" he whispered close to her ear. "Something unnatural to scare our unwelcome friend but won't scare the sheep?"

"Unwelcome—" she sputtered and cut off at a snuffing sound, accompanied by scratching in the dirt. She sat up and turned toward the sound.

A large creature with thick black fur was circling the camp. It lingered near the hole they had dug to bury food scraps and other bits of waste. The head was similar to a bear in shape and size and was set on hulking shoulders that were stooped to scrape at the ground with its massive forepaws.

"How did a cave yeti get past our barrier spells? Aunt Cora and Nora took a party along the mountains to refresh them only two weeks ago," she whispered in a rush.

Crispin shrugged. "Don't know, that's Mage business. Got a light spell or not? I'd rather just frighten it off, but if it gets any closer, we lose that chance."

The cave yeti was bent down now over the refuse, not hungry enough to go after fresh meat from the sleeping sheep. Solitary scavengers that preferred caves as the name suggested, yetis were nocturnal and therefore sensitive to light.

"Not a light spell, but I have something for it," she said, reaching for her whip. She shook it out and drew up a quick spark of mana. The cave yeti scratched the ground again. She flicked a fireball out of the tip of the whip right in front of its paw as the eight-inch claws scraped the ground again. The beast jumped back and harrumphed. She flicked out three more small fireballs, hoping the frost on the grass would keep it from catching.

The cave yeti retreated a few steps, rising to stand twelve feet high. She flicked out another fireball in front of its nose. It snorted and swiped its claws near its face as if it could bat away mana. She wondered if the rumors of opposable thumbs to open feed bins were true as she prepared for another flick, but the beast turned away, evidently deciding the trash pit wasn't worth a singed nose. Asha sighed, grateful they hadn't had to fight or kill the beast. She watched the shambling, unnatural steps of the shorter hind legs as it retreated.

"Since you're already awake..." Crispin grinned at her in the pale starlight.

"Yeah, yeah, yeah." She rolled her eyes and pulled on her clothes to take her watch early.

A few hours later, the pale light broke across the sky, turning the mountaintops pastel pink and orange. Asha lit the cooking fire with a tiny fireball as the others rolled out of their blankets and dressed.

The party made quick work of cleaning up, saddling ponies, and remounting packs onto the mules. Several stubborn sheep were not interested in being roused from their makeshift paddock, but once again, the herding dogs did most of the work to convince them they couldn't stay and chew their cud.

It didn't take long for the party to cross the remaining family lands. They were spotted by the large, white guardian dogs that patrolled the inside of the family's border wall. The guardian dogs were hostile and barked ferociously. It cut through the quiet birdsongs, making Asha's ears ring until one of the guards on the wall gave them a command. He then accompanied the dogs to inspect the party with a firm grip on the loose skin at the back of its neck. The dogs settled and even played with the herding dogs a bit after they recognized the party was, in fact, allowed on their territory.

Asha had seen this many times; everyone in the family was introduced to any new guardian puppies and periodically reintroduced to trained dogs. But the dogs couldn't be expected to instantly recognize everyone in a family so large. That made the stand-down command and a proper and cautious approach imperative. Even being familiar with the process, the change from 'I will rip you open if you take another step' to 'belly rubs, pretty please, and ear scratches' was jarring.

After the dogs were properly patted and rubbed down, they exchanged greetings with the wall guards. Then they crossed the bridge that went over the stream running through the wall and exited through the only gate. They skirted several other smaller families' holdings before entering the village, at which point, they tightened their formation around the herd and commanded the herding dogs to bunch the sheep as tightly as possible without inhibiting movement. Luckily, the mules were strung together on a line, one behind another, and needed no rearranging.

The party kept off the main street of the town that would have gone through the square and the market. They followed the side streets along the eastern side of the town, stopping only to pay respect, which also meant taxes, to the magistrate. Despite the formation change, the party still took up the entire street as they passed, which made polite navigation nearly impossible, but they did their best to limit inconvenience to the villagers. Finally, they arrived at the ford at the village's southeast edge.

At this point, the ford master instructed them to split into three groups to cross. First, Jetti and Alaric with the mules. Then, Erika, Bard, and Crispin with half the sheep and one herding dog. Lastly, Asha, Arne, and Jolli with the rest of the flock and the other dog. As the large raft was tugged across the great river, Asha realized this was the farthest she had ever been from home, and the journey was only just beginning. She wondered how long it would be before she would be this close to home again. Loneliness squeezed her heart, and anxiety sunk her stomach. She was grateful for the light breeze that rose with the warm, midday sunshine.

After regrouping, the party turned south once more, but this time angled west toward the inlet and the trade city of Inglerho. The rugged, looming peaks of the Cairngrom range grew closer with every passing mile. Asha remembered her uncle's brief of the route and that the nearest pass was over a hundred miles inland and would have made them journey twice that, backtracking west to get to the Capital.

The plan to hug the coast and skirt the mountains by way of the beaches didn't seem much better to her. She had been assured that this was, in fact, the better trade route and that they would join a larger caravan in Inglerho. Larger caravans had more booty but also more weapons and Mages. Most pirates or raiders wouldn't take that gamble. Erika also warned that the plains of the interior between the pass and the Capital were not free from danger and had fewer caravans to join.

She would have to trust their judgement. Her branch of the family was much more involved in growing, nurturing, and healing the animals and plants that became the livestock, fodder, and textiles her family traded. Jolli and Jetti's branch were the traders, travelers, and merchants. After a long day of riding, she once again fell asleep almost as soon as she laid her head down and pulled her bedroll over herself.

The following day went much the same as the previous afternoon, rising and breaking camp with the first traces of dawn. Saddles creaked and hooves crunched on the barely frozen grass until the spring sunshine warmed enough to melt it and loosen chilly limbs.

They had turned fully west now. In the late afternoon, the party crested a large hill, and Asha got a glimpse of the outskirts of Inglerho on the horizon. She urged her mount to catch up to Uncle Jetti.

"Close yer mouth, or you'll catch flies," he teased. "'Sides, that will seem a small hick town when we get to the Capital."

"Will we camp on the outskirts, like when we approached our village?" Asha asked, trying to redirect attention away from her face before he noticed her blush.

"No. No need for that. Being a dandy port city, Inglerho has what they call 'tradesman accommodation'. You can get rooms for a whole party overlooking a neat little paddock for yer stock, for an upcharge, of course."

"Oh, of course." She nodded, looking forward to a bed and a washbasin.

"I will insist on a stock guard though." Uncle Jetti looked serious for a moment. "We'll take shifts. Can't be too careful, even in 'tradesman accommodation'." Just as quickly, the jovial look returned. *Aunt Vesha really should have named them both Jolli*, Asha thought. It suited them both. She fell back into her proper place in formation for the remaining miles until they approached the city gates.

No matter what her uncle said, the city was huge. It took them nearly two hours to cross from the eastern gate to the inn they would stay at near the southern docks. The going was slow, herding so many animals through the crowded streets, despite using the tight formation they had utilized back in the village.

There were so many people, more than she had ever seen in her entire life, all packed into one crowded street. No one touched her; they wouldn't dare, but their presence pressed into her skin. It made her feel trapped and like she couldn't breathe. Not to mention the smell—sweat and mud and feces all mingling together.

"Don't look at the people!" Arne shouted at her to be heard above the din of the street, noticing her distress. "Focus on something else. The colors of the venders' tents, or the hairs in your mount's mane."

Bard reached into his saddlebag and tossed her a small pouch. He mimed that she should smell it. As the pouch opened, soft lavender, lilac, and valerian tickled her nose. She inhaled deeply while silently counting all the colors and patterns of the venders' tents. The calming spell hit her, and muscles she hadn't realized were clenched relaxed at once. She continued to take small sniffs every few steps while they navigated the city.

Tradesman accommodation at the inn were indeed comfortable. Well, she probably shouldn't have referred to it as 'the inn'. Unlike her home village, Inglerho had more than one; she had counted four on their trek across the city, and surely there would be at least that many more.

The Pretty Pike was a large structure compared to the rest of the city, rising two stories high and one hundred feet long on the side they approached. They passed through the open, heavy timber gate, and the scent of hot food tickled her nose. A glance showed her that the buildings flanking the gate were the kitchen on the bottom floor to the left, with servants' quarters atop it, and a bathhouse on the bottom floor to the right, with what had to be the innkeeper's quarters above that. The gate side was the shorter side of the rectangular courtyard, with halls containing rooms for rent half again as long.

They were met by the stable hands and the innkeeper. Fees were discussed, and their animals were led off to the stable on the right. The ponies and mules would be grouped together in standing stalls, with the sheep and dogs in a pen in front of the stalls.

Then they were led by another servant to the rooms directly across from the stables. They passed the cheaper public accommodations on the bottom floor and climbed the stairs to the private rooms on the second. Asha was glad not to rent space on an open pallet along the wall. She shared a room with Erika, and the men were split into the flanking rooms, three a piece. After setting down her bags and removing her cloak, she looked out the slit that passed as a window. Sure enough, as Uncle Jetti had said, their livestock was visible across the courtyard.

Erika hurried her out of the room and back down the stairs, over to the fourth and final building that made up the inn, the dining hall. It was equally tall as the other three, but instead of a second story, it had a high vaulted ceiling. Tables were aligned in rows with stools along them. On one end, there was a great fireplace, and on the other, a stage of sorts where a small band plucked their instruments above the low roar of guests chatting and eating. The food was good, a hearty chowder with potatoes, leeks, and the catch of the day, fresh honey wheat rolls, and stewed, spiced apples. While the meal was delicious, she was most interested in a bath. Jolli had assigned her the last shift before dawn, so after a quick trip to the bathing house, she went straight to bed.

When she roused for her shift, it seemed like the entire world was asleep. She relieved Crispin and sat at her post next to the two slumbering herding dogs. An hour into her shift, Erika brought her a large breakfast roll stuffed with eggs, ham, and cheese.

"The others will be out soon," Erika said to her as they ate. "I didn't think anyone mentioned that this inn provides food at all hours. I figured you probably hadn't eaten."

"Must have slipped their minds. Thank you. It would have been a long day on an empty stomach." Erika nodded in acknowledgement.

Once the rest of the party joined them, it was quick work to gather the animals and place packs and saddles. Then, they moved to a staging area at the southwestern side of the city, where they met up with the rest of the trading parties traveling to the Capital. Just past dawn, the streets were not nearly so crowded, and the cold dampened the foul smell. The trapped, panicky feeling hadn't hit her on the way over. It started to rise again in the arena, but this time, she was able to quell it with deep breathing and thoughts of home. She was making progress, both toward her destination and in herself.

Chapter 4

Asha

Jetti and Jolli stayed at the main gate of the staging area to meet with the other parties' leaders, while the rest of them herded their animals to an open space on the far side of the arena. Asha surveyed the group.

The caravan totaled ten parties in all, the Pacatus' being the smallest. There was a party of eighteen goatherds from the foothills of the Cairngrom range, with at least a hundred goats on the hoof and as many pelts loaded on their mules. She found it off-putting that they wore skins of their goats as their outermost garment, but perhaps they thought the same of her woolen clothes. Though, sheep didn't need to die to produce wool, so she felt justified in her unsettlement.

Next, there was a party of twelve architects returning to the Capital from diplomatically directed repairs to the docks and bridges of Inglerho. They were undoubtedly the best-dressed party. *How will they mount wearing such stiff and finely embroidered tunics and split leg hose? That's what ye get, choosing Southern fashion over function of the heat-preserving Northern trousers.*

From deep in the mountains and river valleys came three trapper parties, roughly twenty each. They drove oxen-pulled carts laden with massive bundles of furs of all kinds and colors netted down tight.

A party of sixteen shepherds cast sidelong glances and kept a much larger herd corralled on the far side of the arena. They would be in competition at the Capital, but that would be set aside until the end of the journey. At least, she hoped. She wasn't sure they should trust those shepherds, but the veteran traders of her party did, so she kept her qualms to herself.

Most fascinating to her was the party of fifteen Dwarves from the Dwarf Lands in the center of the Cairngrom mountains. They held a vast territory that split the Northern Empire in half. They were not part of the Empire but lived and traded alongside it as allies.

Dwarfish craftmanship was well-renowned. They carted all manner of iron works aboard their massive, horned highland sheep. Big as ponies and much more sure-footed, the great sheep had been tamed and trained by the Dwarves to be ridden and to be pack animals.

It was hard not to stare as she had never seen Dwarves before, but Erika lightly hit her arm and scolded her under her breath. "They'll take offense if you keep gaping. We don't want to alienate the best fighters in the bunch. No doubt, we'll need them before the trip is over."

"Sorry," Asha mumbled back and tried to find other places to look.

The remaining three parties, about ten to twelve each, were various merchants from Inglerho with all manner of clay, wooden, and bejeweled wares packed into carts that were covered with the thick, colorful fabric she had recognized from the market tents.

It wasn't long before Jetti and Jolli returned and informed them that their party was traveling rear left, toward the mountains and at the backside of the caravan, with the Dwarven party covering the seaward flank.

"No doubt, the lowland shepherds are nice and tidy in the center, away from the action," Arne scoffed.

"Wouldn't do us any good to have 'em anywhere else," Jolli said back cheerfully. "Ye know they're useless in a fight."

"Useful enough as a warning for the rest of us," Crispin said disinterestedly.

"At least they had the sense to put the Dwarves at the pirates' most likely point of attack," Alaric pointed out.

"They just want the first casualties to not be human," Arne corrected.

"If pirates attack that flank—" Jetti eyed the grim faces of the heavily armed Dwarves— "I don't think the first casualties will be Dwarves."

No sooner had he made his comment than the other parties began funneling out of the arena and falling into the agreed-upon formation. The goatherds went first. Then the trappers. Next there were the architects and, as predicted, the lowland shepherds. Then each set of merchants. Finally, Asha's party with the Dwarves close behind.

After the caravan left the staging area and the last of the city streets, they turned south, following a well-worn road that skirted between the edge of the Cairngrom Mountains and the rolling sands of the Inlet. They would follow this road for several days; exactly how many, Asha wasn't sure. It seemed to be a point of disagreement among the parties. Those on mounts wanted to push through in two days, while those with carts insisted that they could make it in no less than three. No one wanted to linger on this part of the journey, as this road was the favored raiding stretch along the trade route. Raiders could come down from the mountains and pin travelers against the shore, or pirates could anchor and pin travelers against the foothills with cannon fire.

Once the road widened about a mile from the city, the parties shifted the formation. Instead of riding three people abreast, one party in front of another, with any stock in the center, the parties shifted the stock to the left side of the road toward the mountains and away from the sea. Leading still, the goatherds spread out in a shape that reminded Asha of a spear tip, with a few driving the goats off to the side. The trappers' carts were forced into deep ruts cut into the dirt road by the many carts that had passed before them. Following them, the lowland shepherds tried to rub elbows with the architects but were snubbed and fell into a wide semi-circle behind them, with sheep in front. Next, came the merchants, in the same fashion as the trappers.

Asha's party rode left flank in a rough sort of scalene triangle. Jetti was on point, Jolli not far behind him and slightly toward the sea (and the Dwarves), with Alaric in a similar disposition behind him. Asha rode behind and mountainward of Jetti, with Arne and Bard strung out behind and between her and the mountains. The sheep and mules were in the center of the party, with Erika and Crispin riding rear.

The Dwarves had their pack sheep on stringers, five or six apiece, held by three of them on the left side, toward Asha's party. Twelve were spaced out in diagonal columns of four, with plenty of room to maneuver or close ranks as needed. Asha wondered at their strategy. She thought she identified ranged weapons in the center and with those holding the stringers, and melee weapons on the edges of the formation. Then again, most of the Dwarves seemed to have at least two weapons, so she wasn't confident on that.

Asha was still fascinated by the Dwarves. Her mind ran circles with questions. She wanted to know more about them, their dress, and their weapons. She tried to be more subtle in her observations this time. Tried and failed, as one of the Dwarves in a melee position met her eyes and winked at her. Her face heated to a deep crimson. The horizon suddenly seemed far more interesting.

The day's travel went well. They were moving along steadily, if slower than she had anticipated. She now understood why the trappers and merchants had insisted that this section would take three days to clear. The deeply rutted road was in poor condition. Sometimes she wondered if the merchant's wares wouldn't rattle to pieces, bumping along in the carts.

Every few hours, two of the Dwarves with ranged weapons would break off from their formation and ride away from the caravan, one out toward the sea and the other cutting behind Asha's party toward the mountains. Each would urge their mount to a faster pace and find a hill, dune, or other high point, usually a mile or two ahead of the caravan and scout the countryside, ahead and behind, trying to spot ambushes and watching for tails. They would remain at the observation point until the caravan had passed and then caught back up. On the first day, the scouts saw nothing.

On the second day, the Dwarf who had taken the seaward observation reported back that there was a ship moored in the Inlet, only about four miles from the point where the road turned inland. It seemed to have anchored as close to shore as a hull of its size would allow. Perhaps, it was a fishing or trading ship that had taken damage while traversing the Inlet, sending crew ashore to gather supplies for repairs. Alternatively, it could be a pirate ship, lying in wait. The general consensus of the caravan was that if it was pirates, they had chosen a poor location for an attack as the distance and terrain would inhibit their greatest advantage over the caravan, the cannons. They rode on with cautious eyes scanning and nervous fingers on steel.

The camp that night was tense and watchful. Anticipation hung heavily in the air like a fog. Asha thought the caravan had been careful and on edge before spotting the ship, but that night, there was an entirely new level of dread. Everyone whispered, and the cooking fires inside the circled carts were kept small and easily extinguished. Each party supplied a watch to guard the perimeter, but several more than were needed stayed awake. Whether they were unable to sleep or intentionally supplementing the guards, Asha could not discern.

A watchful night turned into a restless morning, and the caravan started out once more. Jetti told her that they were making good time and they would be able to camp further inland that night, out of range of the ship. The most vulnerable part of the journey was nearly over. *Had he meant dangerous?* Vulnerable seemed an odd choice of words, but she kept that question to herself.

Throughout the morning, she noticed the Dwarven scouts went out in pairs and spent more time in the vantage points. She hoped the goatherds in the front of the caravan had also taken such precautions. Still, the morning turned to afternoon, and the caravan continued without harassment.

Two hours after midday, they came to the great curve in the road, where they would leave the coast behind. The caravan paused for about half an hour while the goatherd scouts scoured both sides of the road for a mile before and after the curve. This was where the pirates (if, in fact, that ship had been pirates) were most likely to strike. The scouts found nothing, so the caravan pushed on.

She should have felt relief. She should have felt safer as the foothills of the Cairngrom range rose on both sides of the road. She should have, but she did not. Worry gripped her harder than at any other point on the road. Was this what the sheep felt like when they were herded into the chutes prior to sheering or slaughter?

She urged her mount closer to Uncle Jolli's. "Are we safe now? Or safer at least?" she asked him, but she saw the answer in his stiff, ready posture. His ever-present smile might've fooled people who didn't know him, but he was waiting for something to happen as well.

Before he verbalized this, a gravelly voice came from one of the Dwarves manning the stringers. "Me and my kin still think an ambush is possible from that ship. Keep yer weapons handy and yer spells handier."

"Aye, but them uppity goatherds don't need no help scoutin'. Oh no," another chimed in. "Took mighty offense to our suggestion and offers of help."

"Well, let us all hope that it is the goatherds that are right, and all our worry is for naught," Jolli answered, but he traded knowing looks with Jetti and Alaric. Then he turned his horse and went around the Dwarves holding the stringers to confer with the Dwarven party's leader. They trudged in silence for two more miles.

Boom. Boom. Boom. Three cannons rang out in perfect succession. Within seconds, there were explosions and screaming from the front of the caravan.

"I hate being right!" the first Dwarf hollered.

Several things happened simultaneously. The Dwarves without stringers peeled off and split into two groups, each turning perpendicular to the road and using the hills to cover their advance. Those with stringers suddenly pulled them into the middle of the small herd of sheep and drove what Asha had thought were handles into the ground. They tossed them like javelins, and in a heartbeat, the massive mountain sheep were tethered in place. Immediately, those free of the stringers moved into defensive positions around the herd.

At the same time, Bard threw a hold spell on the sheep, herding dogs, and mules. He, Erika, and Arne took opposite defensive positions to the Dwarves. Jetti, Jolli, Crispin, Alaric, and Asha followed one of the Dwarven squads into the hills on the left of the road, unsheathing their weapons as they went.

Using the terrain, the two partial parties advanced, keeping the mounts at a trot as they merged into one element. Asha glimpsed the merchants turning their first three wagons broadside (the road was too narrow to truly circle them) and dug in for defense. The lowland shepherds and architects had thrown themselves down to the ground and used the ruts, ditches, and other small topography to provide a little cover and concealment. Crispin nearly lost his seat when his pony was spooked by a sheep running away from the road full tilt. A Dwarf lost his seat when his ram tripped headlong over several others. Luckily, he recovered nearly as fast as it happened.

The trappers had attempted the same maneuver as the merchants, but the foremost wagon had lost its front wheels, and another immediately behind it lost its oxen to the pirates' cannons. Asha hoped she couldn't see the trappers who had been driving them because they were taking cover, not because... She snapped her thoughts away from that. There'd be time for that later; she needed to focus on their counterattack.

Of course, the goatherds had taken the brunt of the ambush. She could not wonder which of them had survived the first volley to take cover. Goats and their herders lay strewn out in silent answer. Not all, though; at least half were returning arrows and fireballs the best they could from behind rocks and out of ditches. Two had piled up goat carcasses to make themselves cover where none could be found.

The pirates fired the cannons a few more times, but they were largely aimed high, attempting to not damage the caravans' goods, but still raining shrapnel down on the pinned goatherds and trappers. Now the attack relied more heavily on archers, attempting to pick off the survivors.

One cannon, however, was different from the others. Asha wasn't sure exactly what, but she could see the red glow of destructive mana from the cannon and on its balls as they flew. These balls did not explode shrapnel but instead turned into fog midair, which choked anyone it descended over. The mixed element pulled up and paused to seek the best way to interfere.

The pirates' focus was on the goatherds and trappers. Perhaps they were confident in their method of isolating the front of the caravan, thinking the others would dig in for defense. They learned their mistake when the other Dwarven sub-party hit them with a ranged attack from their right flank. The first volley of arrows and fire took out at least a dozen, but the others quickly took better cover and shifted one of the cannons to assault the hill the Dwarves used as cover. Dwarven bows had a very impressive range, as they continued to send volley after volley while the hill took the brunt of the cannonballs.

Utilizing their companion's attack as a distraction, the mixed element rounded the left flank and closed in for a melee attack. Both leaders signaled that the priority was to neutralize the cannons. *How had they even gotten the cannons this far inland?* Again, no time to wonder; they were nearing the end of their concealment, and Asha steeled herself for the charge.

She flexed her left hand and formed a fist, sending mana down her arm. Her bracelet glowed, and a red iridescent shield formed on her arm. If it had been made of wood or iron instead of raw magical energy, it might have looked plain, a simple round disc slightly convex blocking her torso without inhibiting her range of motion. Her whip had been ready in her hand since the first cannon fire. But she tested its weight all the same. She was no longer afraid; she simply acted, almost piloting her body from outside herself.

They leaped over the hill that separated them from the pirates around the nearest cannon and charged. The distance couldn't have been more than thirty yards, yet it seemed to take forever to cross.

What didn't take forever was for the twelve pirates in that position to respond. The four manning the cannon tried to turn it to face the charge, but mountain sheep were extremely swift, and Asha's parties' mountain-bred ponies were not even a full yard behind. The eight other pirates with bows raised their weapons to answer the charge. Asha's whip flicked out and struck at the pirates nearest the charging line. One, two, three, four cracks shot out in rapid succession. Dark red mana whizzed out with it, flowing along the runes she had carved into the leather before braiding it, and out past the reach of the physical whip to strike the pirates. One, two, three, then four pirates fell dead, their skulls split in two.

Then the Dwarves and traders were upon them. Swords and war hammers struck and slashed, blood splattered and bone cracked, and in seconds, it was over. The mixed element had taken the first cannon.

"What d'ye say we gives 'em a taste of their own medicine?" the Dwarven leader hollered.

Several Dwarves dismounted and turned the cannon toward its companions and began to fire. They focused their volleys on the cannon assaulting their kin on the other side of the road. This was quite effective as there was a large explosion and lots of screaming from that position. The Dwarves on the right flank were then able to mount their own charge. Asha hoped they had the same success.

Unfortunately, this gave the middle cannon with spell rounds time to shift fire from the caravan to its flank and former companion's position. The first round misted overhead, and the terrible fog dropped. Coughing and choking, they attempted to shift their fire as well, but cannons were hard enough to move when they had all their strength and air available. Without this, it seemed impossible. The Dwarves fared slightly better than the humans; maybe those thick beards were for more than decoration.

A volley of arrows and grapeshot followed the spell ball. Those of the mixed party who remained conscious took cover under shields and mounts.

"Ash—" Jolli wheezed through coughing fits— "Asha, darling."

Endearments at a time like this? She couldn't help but shake her head.

"Asha—" more coughing— "can you—" he hacked— "do something about this damned fog?"

"Not without touching the cannon!" she shouted back only to fall into a coughing fit herself.

"Oh, is that all?" the Dwarven leader said, sarcasm dripping from every word. But he turned and shouted in his native tongue, and within moments, Asha found herself surrounded by four grim-faced Dwarves. One tied a handkerchief around her face, and she started to breathe easier. She thought that surely cloth could not make a difference, but then the delicate breathing spell tickled her throat, and she understood. The same Dwarf gripped her upper arm and drug her with them as they weaved from cover to cover toward the final cannon.

They reached the end of cover, and he winked at her as he released her arm and readied his great war hammer. Unfamiliar runes glowed deep red, reminiscent of the forge coals they were undoubtedly created in.

"Here we go again, love." His voice was a whisper, but if she heard him, it had to have been closer to a shout.

Again, they charged, and again, her whip cracked and split the skulls of the closest pirates before the Dwarves fell upon them with hammer and sword. Asha released her whip, knowing that the tether runes in the handle would return it to her belt. She kept her shield up, pulling the glove off her right hand with her teeth. Running flat out toward the cannon, she silently prayed her Dwarven escort would strike true, as she could not heed anything but the cannon to succeed. As she reached the cannon, one of the pirates manning it pulled out a dagger and lunged at her.

Without a focus this time, she shot the dark red mana straight out of her hand, but there was no missing at such close range. The pirate turned to ash before he reached her. His companions saw him turn from flesh to char, turned tail, and ran. No longer impeded in Voiding the cannon, she gripped the hot metal, blistering her flesh, but her adrenaline was too high to feel it. She let the rest of the world fall away and focused on the mana coursing through the cannon. Then she pulled it out and into herself. She might despise her father, but his blood in her veins was going to save them. Hereditary mana might be a blessing from the Gods, but to her, it was also a slap in the face.

It took only a moment, and the spelled cannon was just a cannon again. She repeated this on the pile of spell balls ready for loading. Although it may not have been fully necessary as the Dwarves finished off the pirates who didn't flee.

Her task accomplished, she looked around, shield still raised, her burnt dominant hand swinging down toward her whip. But there were no more pirates. No more fireballs, arrows, or the ringing of steel striking. Just the stench of powder, cries of the wounded, and her hand throbbing with her rapid pulse. *Did we win? Is it over?*

Chapter 5

Asha

The fighting may have been over, but someone needed to tell Asha's nerves that. The calm clarity that carried her through the skirmishing had fled. She felt jittery and wound tighter than a compressed clock spring, and her hand hurt more with every passing moment.

"Ye alright lass?" She turned to see the Dwarf who had given her the handkerchief approaching her. He paused to look down at the pirate-shaped charcoal and chuckled before stepping over it. "Your work, I'm guessing. Glad you're scrappin' on our side." He smiled awfully broadly considering the circumstances.

The handkerchief! She reached up to untie it and yelped when her burned dominant hand met the cloth knot.

"A no would have sufficed," he teased as he took hold of her wrist and gently inspected her palm.

"It's fine," she said, trying (and failing) to pull her hand away.

"It's not," he said more firmly this time, keeping his grip around her wrist to prevent her from pulling away without hurting. "That'll swell and ye'll not be able to use it for weeks if we don't do something about it now. I'll ask my kin about herbs that might bring it down a bit. Are ye hurt anywhere else?"

"Just the burn from touching the cannon," she said, not meeting his eyes. She was intrigued by the size of the hand encircling her wrist. Her education told her that Dwarves were shorter and stouter than most humans. She hadn't known that they had slightly different proportions as well. His hands seemed far too large and thick for his stature. She glanced down at his boots, and they matched his hands in proportion.

"Do you always have to touch something to break it?" he asked, finally releasing her wrist.

"No, but I didn't break it. It's still in working order, and those runes could be recharged by someone who knew how. I just pulled the mana out," she explained, gesturing to the cannon.

"Oh, we've heard tell of Void Mages but never seen one my own self."

"I'm not a Void," she said in a rush. "I mean, not really. I can do a little Voiding, but it's not my main affinity. I'm a Destructive. My father is a Void, so I..." She trailed off, realizing he probably didn't care, and she should stop talking, but the nervous energy demanded relief, like a tea kettle close to boiling over. Turning away slightly, she tried to undo the handkerchief with her left hand without success.

"No need to explain. Allow me." He reached up to untie it for her.

This gave her a chance to look at him without feeling awkward about it. He was shorter than her, of course, but taller than she had expected for a Dwarf, maybe five feet. A broad, friendly face, with an angular nose and matching cheekbones, protruded from a ginger-red beard that fell to the top of his riveted mail shirt. His beard was decorated with twin braids on either side of his jaw that were fastened with brass beads. Curling up like a bar with two hooks; his mustache gave him a playful look. That merriment echoed in his cerulean eyes with flecks of brown around the iris. The hair peeking out from his felt bush-hat was pale blond in contrast to his beard. As he leaned closer, she focused on the iron hat band. She didn't recognize the runes, but protective mana emanated from it. *Very clever*, she thought.

No sooner had he removed the handkerchief than his three companions joined them and spoke to him in their language. He answered them in kind.

One held a makeshift bandage to his left forearm, keeping pressure on a deep gash from a pirate sword. The others seemed unharmed.

"My cousin, Bard, could help with your arm," Asha offered. "Our family always sends us with healers' kits, and being a natural, he's the best at applying them."

"Oh? Well in that case, lead on, lass," the first Dwarf said.

"I always forget that humans have healer Mages with them fancy mana herbs," the wounded one added.

"Pretty handy," the other agreed.

They began to walk back toward the first cannon where they had left her uncles and mounts.

"I'm Glormhar Tuasg, by the way. That's Dofrik—" he pointed to the wounded one— "and those ugly sum bitches are Krusur and Krinrun."

"Nice to meet you all. I'm Asha."

"We know." He smirked.

She didn't know why, but she blushed again. They must have heard her uncles calling her name.

When they returned to the first cannon, they found their companions and mounts had moved about fifty yards away from it, outside of the slowly dissipating choking fog. Jetti sat groggily, leaning with his back against Crispin's, who looked only slightly more conscious. Alaric attempted to inspect one of his ponies' flanks that was covered in blood. It must have been hit by grapeshot, but his frequent coughing fits kept startling it. Between that and pain, the poor animal wouldn't hold still long enough for him to determine the extent of the damage. Jolli encouraged the seated men to drink from a canteen, his words broken by his own coughing fits. The Dwarves who remained seemed to breathe much easier but were also coughing occasionally. Asha scanned for injuries other than abrasions, minor cuts, and burns. The mixed party seemed to have fared quite well.

She asked one of the uninjured Dwarves to assist Alaric in holding his pony still enough to apply a healer patch from his saddlebags, and she retrieved one for Dofrik. It was a tightly woven, twelve-inch, square-folded linen cloth with a mana-charged poultice on the inner side. Asha silently thanked Estesbryd that her family had so many talented healers.

"This will stop the bleeding and start the healing," she said as she held up the cloth in her left hand.

She attempted to unfold it and found it was impossible with only one hand, for fear of dropping the poultice on the ground. Glormhar saw her struggling and took it from her.

"Probably should be putting one on yer own hand there. Jest tell me what to do, Ash."

"Those aren't much good for a burn. I'll have Bard help me with something else when we get back to the sheep. Just unfold it and place the herbs side down on the wound, covering it as best you can. Then apply some pressure, and the runes will do the rest."

Glormhar did as instructed. As he applied pressure to it, the linen began to radiate green light from the previously invisible runes that were woven into the fabric and filled with healing mana. He then attempted to peel the linen back and found it clung quite tightly.

"No! Leave it there," Asha said quickly. "It will naturally loosen and fall away in a few hours, but you don't want to pull it away before the scab has formed and the mana dissipated."

Only after she finished speaking did she realize that the other Dwarves had gathered around to watch.

"You humans are full of all kinds of surprises," the Dwarven leader remarked. The others muttered their agreement.

Once all the wounds were tended and everyone was breathing well, they mounted and skirted around the edge of the cloud toward the other cannons to reunite with the second Dwarven sub-party. They stopped briefly at the second cannon as the Dwarven leader wanted a look at the previously magic cannon. Alaric also dismounted to look at the now obsolete runes and shot. He frowned, clearly perplexed. Digging into his saddlebags for paper and charcoal, he made a rubbing of several runes he found on the cannon barrel and wheels.

"Never seen anything quite like it," he observed pensively after they remounted. "The runes on that cannon matched the runes on the other."

"But the other only fired regular ball," Jetti added.

"Aye, the choking mist spell was in the shot, not the cannon. I can't be sure, but I think the cannon runes were a movement spell. It includes weather runes."

"That would explain the lack of hauling beasts. No way the pirates moved the artillery so far inland with only their own backs," one of the Dwarves commented.

"Could be for accuracy or better range, though," another contradicted.

They argued back and forth until they reached the third cannon and the other Dwarves. The other sub-party had taken more casualties, and one

Dwarf was laid out with a blanket covering him. Asha quickly looked away from the blood still pooling from under the makeshift shroud and took several deliberate breaths, fighting back the urge to vomit.

She helped Alaric and Crispin the best she could with her good hand as they used all the linen healer patches they had left on the injured Dwarves. Miraculously, they had just enough to bind all the large wounds, and the smaller wounds were wrapped with the Mundane bandages the Dwarves carried. The repetitive nature of the bandaging calmed her nerves some, but her right hand throbbed and swelled far faster than she had expected. Crispin insisted on washing it with what was left in his canteen and wrapped it loosely with a clean bandage. She vomited after he finished, though she wasn't sure if that was from pain or nerves.

One of the Dwarves, Krinrun if she remembered correctly, brought a few necklaces that had been pulled from the pirate corpses. They had smooth driftwood pendants trimmed into ovals with sigils carved into them, each hanging by braided leather straps. Krinrun showed them to Alaric and asked his opinion on whether they were runes or not. Alaric seemed to think they were likely designators or alliance markers of some kind and not spell work. Krinrun passed this to his leader, who was in conference with Jetti, Jolli, and the Dwarf who had commanded the sub-party, discussing whether they should pursue the pirates who had fled. Alaric kept one necklace and placed it with the rubbing he took in his saddlebags.

The decision was made to send a few scouts to follow the pirates and report back. If the pirates returned to the ship, as was most likely, the caravan would simply move on, as there was no point wasting lives assaulting a ship. If they had a camp on land, however, the Dwarves were eager to repay the loss of their fallen brother. Asha looked around at the not-yet-cold pirate bodies and couldn't help thinking that the Dwarves had already repaid the pirates tenfold.

She noticed that Glormhar was one of the four sent to track the fleeing pirates. He smiled intimately at her before turning his mountain ram to follow the trail. She was once again blushing and confused, feeling like he'd silently told a joke she didn't understand, but she had to admit to herself that she didn't hate his attention.

They made their way back to the road and approached the caravan cautiously. Asha swallowed back bile when they reached the remnants of the goatherds; the stench of blood, spilled guts, and burned goat hair was strong. An odd sense of guilt rose in her, as they had no more healer patches to offer the goatherds, though most of them were past saving. Jetti told them he would send some healing supplies forward once he reached their pack animals, and the goatherds mumbled acknowledgment and thanks.

The trappers had fared a bit better. They had less wounded, but her hope that the trappers from the front two carts had been taking cover was dashed. The drivers hadn't survived long enough to do so.

Among the lowland shepherds, architects, and merchants no casualties had been taken, thankfully. Crispin had some choice words about hiding and cowardice, but he kept them low enough to only be heard by his own party.

Erika, Arne, Bard, and the Dwarves who left with the pack animals had also taken no casualties. It seemed the pirates had not made any efforts to flank or surround the caravan, being secure in their superior firepower and assumption that their quarry would not be able to effectively maneuver on that portion of the road.

Bard debrided and washed Asha's hand. It was the worst pain she had ever felt, and she nearly blacked out, even though he worked as quickly as possible. After the debridement, the ointment application felt like a tickle. The thick, pungent ointment began to glow green, and the throbbing pain eased. He wrapped it in a clean linen bandage, and its woven runes lit up.

"Next time ye gotta Void a magic cannon, maybe try grabbing the wheel or the cascabel. Ye know, anything not roughly the temperature of a forge," Jetti teased as he and Bard packed up what healing supplies they could spare, allowing for the estimated maintenance of the Dwarves and Asha's wounds.

"I'll try to remember that next time," she said through steadying breaths.

Bard tended to a few other Dwarves who needed more than the initial patches. Then he and Jetti took the gathered supplies forward to the goatherds. This had given Jolli and the Dwarven leader—Masnachwr, Asha had learned his name finally from one of the other Dwarves—time to assess their situation and confer with the other parties' leaders about the next course of action.

Evening was fast approaching, and they were not going to be able to move far with the damaged trappers' carts and sheer amount of wounded and dead. The goats and lowland sheep were also scattered, and their keepers were loath to leave them behind.

It was decided that they would move the intact carts forward to the location of the pirates' cannons, since it would be the most defensible area to set up camp without moving too far off. There, the carts were circled and guards were set. Then, the wounded were moved and cooking fires lit inside the cart perimeter. Finally, the pack animals that hadn't been lost were also brought into the perimeter.

Camp was solemn and quiet that night. The Dwarven scouts returned a few hours after dark to report that the pirates had indeed fled back to their ship. Curiously, though, the scouts had not found any trace of the cannon's movement to the ambush position. The pirates had run back the same way they had come, but if the caravan did not currently control the cannons, they would not have believed that any artillery had passed overland. Asha was too tired to ponder this for long, however, and promptly passed out from exhaustion.

Naively, Asha had thought that tending to the wounded would be the worst part of the cleanup. She had not considered the dead. The dead goatherds and trappers were still where they had fallen the day before. A single large grave was dug beside the road, and one by one, the bodies were lowered into it. Fallen livestock were piled and burned.

The fallen Dwarf was left on the hill where he had been killed, and the rest of the Dwarves gathered around his body that they laid on top of piled stones and sang mourning songs for hours. Asha could not understand the words, as they sang in their native tongue, but the songs chilled and haunted her all the same. There was grumbling among the other parties that the Dwarves weren't returning to help with the other dead, but no one was brave (or stupid) enough to say anything to them.

This left only wagon repairs and catching the lowland sheep. The architects were surprisingly helpful to the trappers repairing their wagons. Or maybe she shouldn't have been surprised. She didn't know them, and they were an official government delegation. It was their job to help people, on parchment anyway. The first wagon was declared beyond saving, and without enough oxen to pull it, it wouldn't have been worth trying. So, they cannibalized it for treated lumber to repair the second damaged wagon, while drawing up new loading plans to redistribute the salvaged furs from the unsalvageable wagon.

Uncle Jetti had volunteered their party to help with the roundup of the lowland sheep. They split into small groups and began systematically combing the hills beside the road. The first sign they came across was the ewe that had tripped the Dwarven mountain sheep during their maneuvering the day before. She had a broken leg and was quickly put out of her misery. The rest seemed to have scattered in all directions, then grouped up in small, sheltered areas.

To speed the tracking along, whenever they came across a sign, Bard would speak a tracking spell as he dismounted. Then he touched the signs and sent out his mana. The prints would then glow a shimmery blue and were easily followed to the animals. He taught Asha the words and how to hold her hands when she touched it and filled it with mana. Her spell worked, but instead of shimmery blue light glowing from footprints, a line of fire shot out of her fingertips and burned through the vegetation until it reached the frightened sheep.

Erika laughed. "Well, we certainly can't miss that."

"I should rework it. If I can see your spell notes, I could adapt it—"

"No point," Bard cut her off. "It would be a waste of time we don't have, and I learned that so long ago, I don't have the notes anymore." He paused to smile encouragingly. "Besides, Erika is right. Your version works, just differently is all."

"Is that why you haven't been fixing your hair with your spells?" Erika asked, grinning as she gestured to Asha's now loose and messy braid. "Afraid you'll burn off your hair?"

Asha looked down at her boots. "Yeah, a bit." She had washed her hair at The Pretty Pike back in Inglerho. When she re-braided it, she tried multiple times to weave the spell her sisters had used to keep it clean and in place. But every time she started reciting the words, the spell felt hot. Like an ember that was fanned and starting to catch fire again. She had consulted her spell notes, adapted to her destructive mana, but had been too nervous that she would weave fire or something worse into her braid, so she stopped trying. Better to have hair in her face than end up bald or with the braid rotting off her head.

Erika howled and doubled over in the saddle. The others didn't find it quite so funny but chuckled at the thought. Asha didn't know why she was so embarrassed as she remounted her pony. Her version of the tracking spell worked, and it was normal for Mages to have difficulty casting a spell designed by another type. Bard's mana was tied to the natural world and in tune with it in a way she couldn't really be. His spell was easy and light and had no lasting effects. Her mana was rough and destructive, so hers burned fire. She should have been grateful that she had enough power and training to cross-cast such a spell on the first try, even if it came out a little twisted and fiery. Many less powerful Mages couldn't. Maybe that's why her family had called her foolish; she was too easily embarrassed by trivial things.

She straightened her shoulders and raised her chin in a physical effort to be more confident and less self-conscious as they finished gathering the sheep from their assigned area and herded them back to the circled wagons.

When they returned to the camp, the Dwarves were still absent. The singing from the hill had died down, rose every so often, then petered back out. She supposed that they were talking in between but couldn't imagine what about. Funerals she had attended were brief, solemn affairs. Families and friends would gather at the burial site (or memorial site if the body was not present) and everyone would take turns expressing their love for the deceased, then give a brief prayer to Trunii, asking for mercy and kindness to be shown to them. Then, the body was buried, and all who had been present were to keep silent until nightfall as a token to Trunii, the God of Death and the Recorder of Lives.

Her curiosity continued to rise, for as the twilight turned to darkness, there was a flash and explosion from the hill where the Dwarves still sat.

She turned to look and saw a fire burning where the body had been. It glowed red with mana. The Dwarves remained there until the fire burned out, then a few minutes longer. Were they gathering something from the stones where the body had been laid?

She didn't want to be disrespectful, so she kept her questions to herself and tried not to act too interested when the Dwarves returned to the fire. Since they had integrated for the counterattack on the pirates, Asha's party and the Dwarves had not separated. In fact, they all seemed to get along swimmingly and shared a cooking fire and grazing arrangements. Glormhar sat next to her on the log where she rested and tested her injured hand through its range of motion. It was healing well, thanks to the mana-infused ointment that Bard had helped her apply multiple times that day. The swelling and pain were nearly gone, but Bard and Erika had warned her not to use it as much as she could, moving it a few times a day to keep it from getting stiff.

"How's yer hand?" he asked, breaking her reverie.

"Healing well, thanks for asking. How's Dofrik's arm?"

"Good, good. Much better for those fancy cloths and herbs. Human healing is a mighty handy thing. Perhaps we should keep ye around." He smiled playfully for a moment, then fell back into a somber expression.

"I'm no good at healing, but I wouldn't mind sticking around." She returned his smile, then noticed the item in his hands as he passed it between them absentmindedly. It looked like an urn, about eighteen inches tall with an eight-inch circumference, round and bulbous at the base and gently tapering up to the lid. Delicate Dwarven script was chiseled into the sides, with depictions of a bow and short sword, but it was made of stone. *Why would anyone make an urn out of stone? Where had he gotten it? Surely, they didn't carry urns with them in case they died. That would be horribly morbid.*

She glanced back up at his face and realized he had caught her staring. "I'm sorry," she mumbled.

"For what, lass?"

"For staring, being rude."

"Well, I don't suppose ye've ever seen a Dwarven warrior's urn. No need to be sorry fer looking. I didn't take it as rude."

"I haven't seen one." She glanced back at it, then at his face. "I hadn't seen anything Dwarven before this trip. Well, nothing except a dagger and a few forge tools that Uncle Guy has from when he was assigned to train with the Dwarven smiths under the alliance."

The alliance of Dwarves and Greater Anitaris had many facets and effects, most of which were political gobbledygook that had made her eyes glaze over while her aunt had droned on and on in her lectures. One thing that she had understood was known as The Trade. The Empire would supply the Dwarves with a regiment of healers to be distributed among the ranks of the Dwarven army in exchange for the Dwarves taking human Artificers as apprentices. It was a one-for-one deal. A healer would be assigned for the duration of the Artificer's apprenticeship, both to be released and, presumably, replaced at the same time. This was how Aunt Eve had met Uncle Guy. Asha thought it was a very romantic story and had led to a second romance when Guy's partner, Mortimer, visited post-release and met her Aunt Dawn.

Asha realized she had been staring and silent again. She opened her mouth to apologize again, but Glormhar cut her off.

"Would you like me to explain?"

"Yes. But only if you want to," she hurried to add. "Your customs are very different from mine, but that doesn't mean you owe me an explanation."

"No," he said slowly. "I don't owe you anything, but it would be an honor to share." He smiled tightly and went on. "When one of our kin dies, they are buried in a sacred ground, kept and guarded by our people. We have done this as long as our stories record. When our people began to venture outside of our mountain range, this presented a problem, as not all came back, and it was not always possible to bring back the bodies, especially during war." He paused and turned the urn in his hands.

"So, after seeking Feorach's guidance, our priests found a way to ensure our dead warriors and adventurers could return. The funeral is to be held by all Dwarves near enough to attend. While they sing and tell tales to honor the fallen ones, an Artificer among them carves an urn from the stone of the earth where they died." He held up the urn to emphasize his words. "Once the urn is ready and when the moon rises in the sky, rather than burying the body, a destructive is to burn it. Then, they gather the ashes into the urn. Once sealed, the urn is given to the nearest relative and kept safe until it can be returned to the burial ground. There, the seal is broken, and enough ash is kept back to make the Clach Shinnsirel. The rest is buried in the sacred ground."

"What's a Clach Shinnashil?" Asha asked, completely enthralled.

"Clach Shinnsirel," he gently corrected. "It's a gem made from compressed ash. Our jewelers make them so we may embed them into our weapons."

Asha was horrified. "Why would you do that?" She tried to keep her voice even. She meant no offense, but she could not imagine why they would want to carry a literal piece of someone around with them.

He chuckled, luckily, not offended at all. "To give us strength. When we weld a weapon with a Clach Shinnsirel, our ancestors fight with us."

That was less horrifying. No less strange, though.

"I see." She couldn't think of anything else to say. Just then, Erika returned from her post on the perimeter, so she didn't have to.

"I'm sorry, but I have next watch. Thank you for sharing and explaining your customs."

"Anytime, Ash," he replied. "You're not hard to talk to, lass."

Asha stood and gathered her things from where she'd leaned them, a bit awkwardly with her left hand. She started to walk away but paused and gently touched his shoulder, drawing his attention away from the fire where he had been staring mournfully.

"And I'm sorry you lost your nearest relative."

"Tis what it is, lass." His smile was doleful and full of memory. "Tis what it is."

Asha whispered silent, thankful prayers to all seven Gods that she had not lost any of her relatives in the fighting. Then guiltily prayed that Glormhar feel peace and comfort for the loss of his. She spent her watch suppressing thoughts of how many more opportunities she might have to lose someone before the journey ended.

Chapter 6

Asha

Asha was grateful that they moved on the next morning's warm dawn. With the bodies buried or burned, the stench of blood and powder had lifted, but the whole place still felt like death in a way she could not explain. Her mind was weighed down and morose. Not that she would dare complain; she hadn't lost anyone she cared about. Guilt nagged her for feeling sad and she wanted to put this place behind her.

They had a few more days' travel before they reached Carados, where they would take the river barge the rest of the way into the Capital. Thankfully, things went smoothly, with no more attacks or disturbances, though the caravan kept on alert and a steady rotation of guards. This time, when Masnachwr or Jetti or Jolli made a suggestion or observation about security, it was not disregarded.

Caravan order was largely the same as before. The remaining goatherds took second place behind the farmers' wagons but were still acting as the advance scouts, with a few supplements from the Dwarves. Behind them, the merchants, architects, and lowland shepherds had not shifted at all, and the Dwarves and Asha's party still took up the rear. However, since they had integrated, they mingled more than they rode side by side. The great mountain rams, which had been let off the stringer and mixed with the mules and sheep, were ornery and gave the two herding dogs a bit of a challenge. Asha supposed that moving the animals at this pace and in a straight line might have been boring for the dogs. Nipping and dodging the obstinate rams was a nice change of pace for the high-energy dogs.

She also found out how chatty Dwarves could be. They seemed to find excuses to ride close to her and her companions, especially Jetti and Jolli, as they were equally verbose. It didn't escape her notice that the Dwarf who was most often riding within chatting distance of her was Glormhar. Not that she minded at all; she enjoyed his company, and the attention was flattering. She had little experience with male interest, other than from relatives, and that was definitely not the same. She did mind the sly looks Erika kept sending her every time Glormhar drew near, but she simply ignored her cousin's suggestive smirks and eyebrow raises. Nothing could come from flirting with a Dwarf she would never see again, and he was so easy to talk to. She might as well enjoy herself.

Despite being separated by culture and race, she found that they had a lot in common. He was also a destructive Mage, which she had suspected after seeing him fight. It was nice to talk to someone who was comfortable with their destructive mana. Her family had always been kind and supportive, but they were almost all naturals and healers, with some weather Mages and married-in Artificers. Only her Great Uncle Luca had been able to understand her mana and therefore train her.

To her surprise, she learned that they had similar experiences in childhood. His family was not quite so large, but his immediate family bred and raised the great mountain rams the Dwarves used for mounts and pack animals. She was, however, deeply shocked at how long ago his childhood had been. If she had been asked to guess his age before he had told her, she would have said thirty, give or take a couple of years. She would have been incorrect by five decades. He was eighty-three. *Eighty-three years old.* After he finished laughing at her flabbergasted face, he explained that Dwarves aged differently and lived much longer, which she had known, but that wasn't the same as being confronted by a 'young' Dwarf who was older than her grandmother. He had told her that a Dwarf is considered an adult at seventy years and would typically live between two hundred and fifty and three hundred years. A quick calculation made her realize that, adjusted for race, his childhood hadn't been that long ago, and he would be considered a young adult like herself. It didn't fully make sense to her. He had seen so much more, lived so much more than her. How could he be in a similar life stage?

His easy chatter and casual flirtation made the awkwardness flee and the miles seem short as the foothills gave way to flat woodland, the caravan pushed further south toward Carados and the barges.

The second night after they had left the foothills behind, Asha gathered firewood for the cooking fire, with Glormhar's help, of course. Jolli was, by far, the best cook, and the Dwarves had been contributing to the general camp chores but left the cooking to him. Somehow, Jolli could always turn pottage and dried meats into something not just edible but enjoyable. He was quite proud of it, too. She supposed he had every right to be.

Most nights, Glormhar's chores seemed to coincide with Asha's, which couldn't have been coincidence as Asha's party rotated the chores as well as watches so that no one person was stuck with the same job all the time, except the cooking. Asha had also been assigned chores that could be done mostly one-handed up to that point, but that day, her hand felt good. The swelling and blisters were completely gone and the soreness only flared up if she used it too much. So, she had gone back to her regular activities. She was incredibly grateful for the healing ointment her aunts had sent with them. Glormhar had told her of a forge burn that he had received as a young man that had put him on light duty for six weeks before he could tolerate the heat of the forge on the unfortunate finger.

They talked more than they gathered in the waning light of a warm spring evening, when Asha's toe struck a large root. Her foot caught, and then there was a small burst of red light, and the root exploded into splinters. She regained her balance quickly after her steps stuttered.

"Punishing trees now?" Glormhar chided. "'Twas only reaching out to shake yer hand! Though I must say, very impressive to cast without yer hands."

Asha looked down at her arms full of wood and back at the offending root. "I don't think it was so innocent." She chuckled. "The root should have known to avoid runed boots."

"Oh, aye?" Glormhar focused on the boots while somehow successfully avoiding tripping himself. "What sort of runes makes roots into toothpicks?"

She blushed a little. "I mean, it's just a basic protection rune. Ensures good footing."

"Basic, she says. Not what I saw." He chuckled. "Alright, keep your spells secret if ye must. Maybe someone else would spare the poor tree, but ye don't get a twisted ankle either way. Personally—" he drew out the word playfully— "I prefer to avoid the roots myself, but I must admit, smashing 'em ta bits is also effective."

"Well, I imagine it's easier to avoid them when you're that close to the ground," she quipped.

He laughed outright as they turned back toward camp.

The scenery seemed incredibly flat to Asha the further south they traveled. Her whole life had been spent in a glacier valley, surrounded by mountains on three sides, with a view of a distant range across the river on the fourth. She had not realized how empty the landscape would feel without them. Not that the woodland wasn't beautiful. It was just unfamiliar and seemed to roll on forever without breaking. She often found herself turning in her saddle to look at the Cairngrom Mountain Range fading behind her. Jetti had teased her that she would get a permanent twist in her neck from doing it so often.

Unable to recognize about half of the tree species that made the dense forest lining the road, she had asked a few of her companions. None of her party had known more than a couple obvious varieties, and the Dwarves had known even less. It seemed that their knowledge of botany was only related to which trees made good handles and buckets and the like. They did point out a few that were handy for that. But Asha was not much of a crafter and would never be a smith, so she hadn't paid that much attention.

Asha was content to leave the creation of things to Artificers and smiths. She would stick to what she was good at. After all, it had taken her four tries to create the whip she used as a focus. She might have been better served to have one of her family Artificers make one for her, but a focus was better created by the Mage who would wield it. The six other types of Mages couldn't create items that others could fill with mana, nor could they modify Mundane items to be magical, or 'tinker', as her uncles called it.

A highly skilled Artificer could make a focus for someone else, but there was something about creating the item by your own hand, from raw materials, that made it more effective. She remembered a lesson from an aunt that had explained about passive mana infusing in the creation process, sort of personalizing it. She could make items (with proper training that she definitely didn't have now) that she could fill with mana. If she built runes into them, she could even build items that would hold and later discharge her mana, like the magical bandages her family's healers had made. But only Artificers had the 'gift of creation' to make items that anyone could use. That is why, in her opinion, it was better to leave the crafting and all that to them. Why should she spend her time learning something that she would never be good at?

She was roused from her ponderings when the road turned, and the forest suddenly opened into a river delta with a large town right on the riverhead. They were on the outskirts of Carados. She would be very grateful for a roof and a bath.

Carados appeared nearly as large as Inglerho, but it felt different to Asha. Perhaps it was that the buildings were more spread out, meandering along the riverside. Or perhaps it was the close press of the woodland up to the outskirts of the city. Or maybe it was the slower, friendlier demeanor of the local populace; they seemed to wander as much as the river did. Whatever the exact reason, she found it felt more like her local village, and it didn't inspire so much of a panicky feeling in her chest. She was still on edge once they entered the city limits, but she didn't feel like the buildings were caging her, and she could still breathe.

The sprawling nature of the river city allowed the caravan to pen their animals near the local inn without the extra charge that had been necessary in Inglerho. Not immediately visible from the purchased rooms, but the pens were close enough to be heard if there was a commotion or shout from the person left on guard. The trappers and merchants elected to sleep out under their wagons. They deemed this more appealing than sleeping in rooms and posting guards. Then again, maybe it was more appealing than the public rooms. Not all the parties in the caravan were rich enough to pay for private rooms. The inn also didn't provide food. Instead, the patrons had to seek out the tavern across the street.

Asha's hopes for a bath were quickly dashed. The inn didn't have an associated bathhouse. When she inquired about one, she was informed by a serving girl that Carados didn't have true bathhouses at all, only designated eddies along the river for bathing—one for women and one for men. Since darkness had already fallen and she wasn't eager to traipse around in a dark, unfamiliar city, she supposed she would have to settle for a sponge bath with the basin in the room she shared with Erika once again.

She tried not to pout about it; it was a silly, childish disappointment, but she had had just enough ale that she couldn't let it go. The rough, wooden table prickled her elbows where she rested them. She focused on that.

A moment later, Glormhar offered, "I wouldn't mind escorting ye and watching yer back. If'n ye wanted to go fer a dip."

She felt a little guilty then. It wasn't right for him to go out of his way and lose sleep for her creature comforts. She also wasn't so sure that it would be comfortable to bathe in the river this time of year. The days were warming and there was less frost the further south they moved, but she didn't imagine the river water was any less cold.

"No thanks, Glormhar. I appreciate the offer, but a basin bath will be just fine."

"If ye change yer mind, all ye gotta do is ask." He smiled.

"I just don't understand. The whole town bathes in the river? That seems absurd." She huffed.

"I reckon most of them have basin baths except in summer," Masnachwr chimed in. "Goes to show how a bad guild leader can ruin a whole town." He drank half his ale in one swig.

"What do guilds have to do with bathhouses?" Asha asked. "Don't tell me there's a bathhouse guild. Not in a town this size."

"Bathhouses, inns, taverns—the guilds got their fingers in all of 'em," Dofrik interjected. He was much chattier now that his arm had fully healed.

"Oh! Don't get me started on the guilds." The serving girl huffed as she delivered yet another round of ales to the Dwarves.

"No, I think we shall get ye started, lass," Glormhar replied. "Our pretty but naïve companion here doesn't understand why a guild would make a whole city bathe in a river. Care to explain to her?"

The serving girl placed her now free hands on her hips and color rose in her face. "Alright, never deny a customer a reasonable request, me good ole mum always said." She pivoted on her heel and faced Asha directly. "We did have bathhouses once. Proper bathhouses with hot water and tubs so big ye could drown if ye wanted to. Why, you could scrub yourself cleaner than a kettle and never get chilly! But then we got a new master of the innkeeper's guild. Strange fellow, with rotten teeth and a nasty way about him.

"Well, the new guild master convinced the city nobles that it wasn't right to charge for a bath. Bathing is a right, he said. Well, they made it illegal to charge an Imperial citizen for a bath. Then the owners had to find other ways to feed their families, and all the bathhouses shut down. So now we all bathe in the river, cold and miserable all damned year! Or no bath at all, just a basin!"

By the time she had finished her explanation, the Dwarves had finished their ales, and Asha's party had all risen from the adjoining table and began to file out of the tavern. "Don't forget you've got middle watch tonight, Asha," Uncle Jetti called over his shoulder.

"I won't," she assured. The serving girl went back to her duties, and she cleared both rounds of empty ales and went to fetch another at Dofrik's request. Was that their third? Or fourth? Asha couldn't remember, but they drank like fish. She was still nursing her second ale.

"I guess that makes sense. People do have a right to bathe," she said softly.

"Ye can't have a right to another's labor, lass." Masnachwr took on a lecturing tone that was all too familiar from her aunts. "Sure, ye got the right to bathe, and no one should stop ye from doing so, but what about the building ye're bathing in? Do ye have a right to use that? Do ye have a right to the hot water the workers heat and haul? How about the girls who clean the place? Do ye have a right to them?"

"No, I guess not," she answered. "What I don't understand is why the innkeeper's guild master cares about the bathhouses?"

The Dwarves exchanged disdainful glances. "Competition," was all Masnachwr answered.

"I don't—"

"Ye might have noticed," Glormhar interrupted her, "that the inn here is different from in Inglerho."

"Yeah, we stayed at The Pretty Pike. It was much better equipped than this one."

"Aye, we know it. Best human-run inn in Inglerho," he acknowledged. "We usually stay at a Dwarven-run one. But that's the key, huh?"

Asha scowled at him but didn't reply.

"In Inglerho, the guild's gotta compete with Dwarves and in some cases even Elves. They can't just bully everyone into doing what they want on threat of refusing to shut down every inn in the city. So, in Inglerho, the innkeeper's guild allows the keepers to charge extra for additional services, like a bathhouse or hot food. Thank you, lassie, may the sun always shine on your face." He paused his explanations briefly when the serving girl brought the next round of ale and took a long draught. "But the guild master here, well, he comes from the northeastern province and has got funny ideas about rights and fairness. Well, he and his members didn't bother offering extra services. Then one tried to offer more, and what do ye know? He got more customers than the others. Didn't take long before the other members were complaining to the master—"

"Lazy bunch a ..." Krinrun started in Common but devolved into what she could guess was curses in his native tongue. She was glad she couldn't understand it based on his tone.

"Indeed!" Glormhar had finished his ale and raised his hand to summon the serving girl again. "I imagine that had a lot to do with his sudden conviction that bathing was a right."

"But guilds protect their members. Surely, he had a better motivation than to limit competition," Asha objected.

"I disagree, but even if his intentions were pure as fresh snow in the moonlight," Masnachwr grumbled, "it doesn't change the outcome. He hurt those working in the bathhouse, the inns, and the rest of the town. That's why there has to be a framework, to keep bad men from using structures meant to protect against evil."

"But what if the innkeepers elected the bad man, or what if they thought he was a good man? How would more structure fix bad structure?"

"Sure are pretty when you philosophize." Glormhar's eyes twinkled, and the others rolled theirs.

"And you're drunk!" Asha shook her head and tried to stifle a grin. There was nothing she could do about her burning cheeks.

He chuckled. "Not yet, lassie, but I hope to remedy that soon."

The serving girl had returned but refused to fetch more ale. After a bit of cajoling, she said, "I can't. You've all had your limit. Guild says no more than four ales per customer, except on feast days, and today ain't a feast!"

"I've had four. But my brother, Jer, ain't had none!" Glormhar pulled the urn out and placed it on the table. He set a few coins in front of the urn and gestured to the girl.

The poor serving girl stood with her mouth agape. "I can't serve that—him—it..." she stammered.

"Now, now, now, he's a paying customer and deserves his four ales. Surely, the guild wouldn't deny a customer," he added gleefully, and the other Dwarves chuckled. Asha decided it was time for her to go to bed, she had had enough drunken Dwarven shenanigans for one night. There was still plenty of time for her to laugh at their antics before they all reached the Capital.

Chapter 7

Mago

The scent of salt was heavy on the warm, humid air. Waves crashed on the steep, rocky shore, and gulls cried high, piercing calls. Mago opened his eyes and watched the sun begin its descent below the distant edge of the ocean, throwing yellow and orange streaks and purple shadows across both the clouds and the water. He should head back to his camp. Nightfall signaled the end of the day for most legitimate businessmen, but for winehouses and whore masters, it was just beginning.

He remained seated on the stone outcropping, his legs outstretched, his back leaning on the cool stone. It was tall enough to cast him into its shadow, and while he might've appeared relaxed, he had practiced rising quickly from this exact position while drawing a dagger hidden under his robes. He was exceptionally fast at it, even from a dead sleep. His thoughts drifted back to when he had been but a winehouse owner, straining to hear any valuable words each week when he had made deliveries to the Dragon Riders fortress in the western crags. Not that they had been called the Dragon Riders then.

It hadn't been enough. He had been just as shocked as every other tribesman who paid tribute when the Warlord had descended into the village square, seated atop a dragon. So, he had changed professions. Wine sellers might hear the newest gossip, but a whore master had much better access to intimate locations and knowledge. He had found doors previously sealed suddenly thrown open in welcome.

The wind shifted, and he got a whiff of death, ash, and decay. Hadrumentum had been under siege for weeks. It hadn't been that long in terms of a siege, most lasted months, some over a year, but Hadrumentum had been the first real sand in the grindstone of the Dragon Riders' conquest of Lower Anitaris. Dragon fire did have some limitations, he learned. It could not melt stone. Therefore, the walls of the largest port in the southern continent had held.

Hadrumentum's leader, he called himself a king, but could one be a king if he only held a single city? Whatever he was, he was crafty and proud. This was not the first siege he had weathered. He had ensured that his city entrances were easily cut off and defended, that his walls were always being repaired and reenforced, that he had food stored within the city and a fresh water source. As further precaution, he had also ensured to be on friendly terms with the larger factions of local pirates, and that he had large catapults. He even had good trading relations with the Elves and might be able to appeal to them for assistance.

But he had never fought anyone with dragons; catapults fling stone but are not built from it. The Dragon Riders had taken to the air and destroyed all the city's major weapons within an hour of the failed negotiations. They had launched multiple attacks on the gates, but the city had some powerful Mages. They had somehow restored the gates as quickly as they burned. Having no mana himself, Mago couldn't be sure what type of Mage could do that, but warriors closest to the gate had described it as the wood 'regrowing' over the burnt parts. So, perhaps a natural Mage, more likely multiple; it seemed like a task too large for a single Mage.

After that, the Dragon Riders had decided to starve the city out. Or at least Bomilcar had been instructed to do so by the Warlord before he took the larger portion of the army to continue conquering eastward. One city, no matter how important, could not be allowed to hamper their progress to subjugate the entire lower continent. Two dragons with their riders had been left here to continue the siege and general harassment, with about one-third of the warriors. The other five dragons and the rest of the army continued their march.

Mago probably should have gone with the army. It made more business sense. Once the city fell, there would be no shortage of whores, paid or otherwise. But his gut told him he should be here. The Warlord wanted something from the city. Mago had no idea what, but the impression rankled him, like a bit of meat stuck in his teeth. It felt like the answer should be easy to tease out, but no matter how he worried on it, he could not get it free. They wanted something from the city. Something that they needed intact. If they were content with wholesale destruction, why not have all seven dragons fly above the walls and then dive down, landing inside the defenses and decimating the defenders? The city's army might take down a dragon, maybe even two, on the ground. But they surely couldn't take all seven. It didn't make sense to simply use the great beasts to harass the towers and guards on the walls and not be more aggressive. There had to be a piece he was missing.

Even if he was wrong, exactly how the Dragon Riders attacked and eventually took the city would be valuable information to the Empire. Perhaps, it would give them enough strategic information to avoid falling themselves.

The sun was now just a small glowing crescent on the horizon, and nearer above him, stars peeked out of the twilit sky. He rose with a slight groan. *I'm getting too old for this.* He was approaching his fortieth year and could expect to live another twenty to forty, if his misdeeds didn't catch up with him. His own death occupied his mind, as his bodyguard closed the respectful distance and fell into walk about an arm's length from his master. *How will the Recorder judge me?*

"What God do you serve, Gisco?"

The eunuch was used to odd questions from the whore master and seemed neither surprised nor terribly interested. "Dynawach, I suppose. The Seventh gave us life, or so they tell me. Seems right to honor our mother."

"You suppose? They tell you? Have you given no thought as to whom you should honor and in whose house you shall dwell in the next life?"

The big man chuckled and shrugged in the darkness. "This life has always given me enough trouble, master. Too much to worry about the next. I'm not even certain there is a next. No disrespect, but I don't think the Gods care how we spend this life."

"Not even Ciirtas?"

He shrugged again. "If he cares, why doesn't he do something? Why doesn't he stop the Dragon Lords or whatever they call themselves?"

"He sends his servants, I believe, to do his will."

"Well, his servants are doing a piss-poor job so far." The big man stiffened as soon as the words left his mouth, realizing his error. "Apologies, master, I did not mean—"

"Nonsense, don't apologize." Mago waved a hand and stuffed the sting of the words down deep. It wasn't Gisco's fault that he was ignorant of just how much his master was doing to try and stop the Warlords. "I am a piss-poor servant of my God. Just a bit too selfish, I suppose."

"If you don't mind the question, master, why does a whore master worship the God of balance and justice?"

This time, Mago chuckled. "The worship came first, my friend, the whores later."

"Aye." The big man nodded as though he understood the pitiful non-answer. "You are the fairest, most balanced master I have seen. Perhaps you serve your God by treating his whores well."

Imperial priests would likely have an epileptic fit if they heard such words uttered. But Mago didn't want to take this line of thought any further, unsure how to without revealing too much. So, he said, "I hope that Ciirtas and the Recorder agree with you, or I am in for a wretched afterlife."

They walked the rest of the way back to camp in silence.

The whore master's camp was situated a respectable, but easily traversed, distance from the main army camp, away from the city walls and toward the steep cliffs of the sea. Though it would not be completely accurate to call it his camp. He was the largest merchant but was not the only one in the group of camp followers. Armies were full of men, and men had needs. Not all were illegitimate, either. He was the only seller of women, but there was another wine vender. There were cobblers, carpenters, smiths, and various other merchants. He was the richest, most favored of the motley group, and therefore had his much larger tent pitched in the center of the camp.

Most of the fires were banked and the keepers beginning to retire, but his burned a bright welcome. He nodded to the two eunuchs who guarded the entrance as he stepped inside. Sophonisba came to greet him. She was the oldest of his whores, near to his own age. In another life, she might have opened her own brothel when she saved the funds, but he paid her well to manage his. He ran most of the business side, and while she would service clients if they paid a high enough fee, her tasks were mostly related to the whores themselves. Keeping them healthy, working, and from fighting amongst themselves.

"Welcome, master," she said, kissing his cheek. "I have two girls who wish to speak with you," she whispered in his ear.

"This early in the night? Thank you, Sophonisba."

"Indeed, we have already had several customers."

Mago looked around the spacious tent. Most of the women lounged around the common area in various stages of undress, but at least half a dozen and the only male whore he kept were not. Six of the curtains were drawn, and the lewd, wet sounds of customer satisfaction rose beyond them. He was suddenly very grateful for the burning incense that his mistress always lit in the evenings. The sounds of such things didn't bother him, but the smells—especially of unwashed bodies—bothered him a great deal.

"I have papers to go over. Have them meet me in my chamber," he told her, and she walked away.

'His chamber' was an exaggeration. It was simply a second, smaller tent, pitched directly behind the main tent, connected exit to entrance by a covered walkway. But giving it a high-handed name made him seem more affluent than he truly was. Often, obtaining and maintaining people's respect was all about perception. Perception was oddly important in the trade of flesh.

After entering his tent, he hung his yellow and orange outer robe and small, stiff matching hat on hooks next to the entry flap. Adjusting his knee-length green tunic with golden embroidered trim, he sat down on the cushions in front of his low wooden desk. He rifled through papers and receipts, checking figures, expenditures, and income. When he had switched trades, he had been slightly surprised by the similarities of the business side of running a brothel to running a winehouse. Nearly a year in, and he was no longer surprised but annoyed. Not even whore masters could escape accounting.

The entry flap swished, and a woman came to stand before him. She was small and delicate, with rich chocolate skin and black braids that hung past her breasts that were barely covered by a sheer blue linen robe.

"Zamar, what do you have for me tonight?"

"I serviced a cook from the Warlord's own kitchen," she said eagerly.

"And?"

"He said that the lord's sons are fighting. Arguing something terrible every night over the meal."

"What are they arguing about?" he asked, shifting to a better position on the cushion, but did not look up from his expense sheet.

"The younger son took a girl from the baggage train and kept her in his own tent. Says he's going to make her his wife. The older one says that slaves can't be wives, and she is a concubine at best. Threatened to slit the girl's throat if his brother tried to free her."

"I see," he said noncommittally. Bomilcar did have some strange ideas about wives. For a Warlord's son, he was remarkably legalistic. "Anything else?"

"No, master."

"Thank you, Zamar." He reached into his money pouch and gave her a brass coin. The information was completely useless to him, but he didn't want to give his whores enough information to be able to discern what was and wasn't useful. That would have been too dangerous. So, he paid for all the information they could gather and sorted it himself. The coin was about a quarter of what she would have earned from the cook. As master, he received three quarters of the fee and gave the whores one, but if they got information for him, he doubled their earnings. He had also taken the precaution to have his mistress start a rumor that he was seeking information to use as blackmail if he ever felt the need. It kept his whores keen and unsuspicious but often meant that he got trivial gossip like this.

No sooner had the first girl left than another stepped inside. She was taller and nearly a decade older, full-bodied, with slightly lighter skin. Her hair was cut much shorter and fanned out around her face in a round, springy halo. She wore a dark purple linen sash that was tied around her middle so that it just barely covered her breasts, midriff, and hips. It was an improvement from the last time she had reported to him. Last time she hadn't bothered to put on anything.

"Kanmi, what do you have for me?"

"Well, master, a warrior came in, and he was so dirty that Sophonisba made him wash. So, of course, when we get behind the curtain, I asked him why." Mago stifled a groan and set down the papers to look at her. He had forgotten that this one had no ability to separate information from the story of how she came by it. She charged on, taking his action as encouragement. "I be dirty cuz I was in the dirt, says he. Well, that makes no sense, a big, strong man like you. You're obviously a warrior, not a digger, says I. I was a warrior, says he, and when we're done digging, I will be one again. What are you digging for, says I. Well, says he, cuz the dragon masters want to go under the wall. To do that, ye gotta dig. But if ye keep asking questions, I'll find something else for your mouth to—"

"What wall?" Mago asked, trying to get her to focus on the information and not the client. *This might be valuable.*

"That's just what I asked next!" she exclaimed, self-satisfied. "The city wall, he says, down by the western guard tower. That's the best place for digging, he thinks. It's less rocky, good, soft dirt, you know?"

"Kanmi! I don't care about the quality of the dirt," he snapped and regathered himself when she looked sheepish. "For what purpose are they digging in this fine, soft dirt?"

"Well, he wouldn't tell me that at first. But you know me, master, I'm a good little whore and a good listener. So, I waits until I'm riding him, see, got him real close but not too close, ye know?" Mago did not know and didn't care to, but he nodded encouragingly anyway. "Then I slows down, gets a real nice rhythm, one that feels real nice but not nice enough to—"

"Did he tell you why or not?"

She had the audacity to look offended at his brisk question. "Of course, he did. A man who's close will tell a woman anything she wants to hear if she just takes it slow enough! My mama taught me that. Sometimes I do it just to make them tell me how pretty I am, even if they don't got no information for me."

"Kanmi, why are they digging?"

"They're gonna collapse it."

"Collapse what?"

"The wall. I know it sounds like a Gnome scheme, but he swears that's why. They're digging a wide tunnel under the wall, says he, putting up logs to hold the roof up. And when they've dug far enough, they're gonna have a dragon breathe fire and burn all the logs. He says that'll collapse the tunnel, and without that good dirt to hold it up, the wall will go, too."

Mago had never heard of such a thing, but it made a good deal of sense. If the wall collapsed, the Dragon Riders' army could charge through the gap, overwhelming the defenders while the dragons could pick off any pockets of strong defense from the air. No wonder they hadn't been more aggressive; they didn't need to be.

Digging into his coin pouch again, he was tempted to give her two brass coins, but it might be dangerous to indicate that certain types of information were more valuable than others. And besides, being forced to hear a description of how the information was obtained made him want to dock her pay. He had the rationality to do neither. As she left the tent, nearly floating with pride, he pulled out his supply ledger. He had a report to make, and that meant he needed to find a friendly winehouse that dealt in Imperial ale exports.

Chapter 8

Asha

Asha found herself once again surprised by the resilience of Dwarves. After how much ale they consumed the night before, she had expected to see bleary-eyed, ragged Dwarves stumbling their way through morning preparations in the dewy pre-dawn twilight. Instead, she was greeted by a whistling, bright-eyed Glormhar. A quick glance around the stables showed her that his companions were in equally good spirits.

"Good morning to you, too, Glormhar. Though I can't imagine how you're having a good morning after so many drinks," she answered his greeting and elicited hearty laughter from all the Dwarves.

"Oh, sweet summer child." Uncle Jetti clapped her on the shoulder. She frowned, not understanding the joke and not appreciating that it seemed to be at her expense.

"What exactly is so funny?" she asked as she shrugged off his hand.

"Asha, lass, four ales don't count as 'many drinks' to a Dwarf," Glormhar replied.

"Especially not yer weak human ale!" Dofrik shouted from across the pen where he was tightening a pack saddle on a ram.

"I don't know if I could hold enough o' that barley water to get drunk," Krusur added from where he leaned against the feed barrels.

"You come visit us sometime in our home, and I'll show you some real drinking." Glormhar curved an eyebrow and smiled as he handed her the reins of her pony, which she realized he had caught and saddled for her. She stared for a minute at the leather in her hand, then looked back into his eyes. It was too early to appreciate how stunningly blue they were, but they gleamed in the lamplight all the same, causing her to forget exactly why she was so annoyed.

"Th-thanks," was all she managed to stammer out.

"Anytime, lass, anytime." He turned to retrieve his own mount.

It wasn't until he had walked away, and she had led her pony out to where the rest of her party waited while the herding dogs roused the sheep, that she realized she hadn't specified if she was thanking him for his help or his invitation. She was grateful for his assistance, but she had no intention of visiting him.

In fact, she was confident that after this trip, they would never see each other again. Why would they? They were from completely different worlds, and when he returned to his, she would join the Order of Holy Heroes to fight whatever trouble the Empire had gotten into next. They were 'ships passing in the night' as the poems she had read in her grandmother's small collection described. She hoped she wasn't leading him on. He had to know that nothing could come from their time together. She had enjoyed their connection for what it was. He had to be doing the same...hadn't he?

These thoughts weighed her down as they rode the short distance to the dock where they would load the barges. They looked familiar to her but were a good bit larger than anything she had used back home. Each barge was about fifty feet in length, mostly rectangular, nipping into raised points at the bow and stern. It was flat across with a single sail, currently stowed, in the center of the deck and a quarter rudder in the stern. The sides were raised to about waist height, which meant they had to lift the sheep up over them, but it also meant the sheep wouldn't be able to jump and take a swim.

There was a second barge fastened bow to stern that was nearly identical, except that instead of a sail, it had a small cabin in the center of the deck. Most of the animals were loaded onto the first with enough room to walk among them, and the majority of Asha's party and the Dwarves loaded onto the second. The ponies and most docile mules joined them on the second barge, and they would rotate which people managed the animals on the first.

Behind them on another set of barges, the merchants and trappers loaded their goods and furs. They didn't have to worry about managing any animals as they had elected to sell the wagons, carts, and various pulling teams there. They would be able to load goods directly from the barge to the market square, so it made more financial sense to downsize and not pay for the weight or feed. Behind them, the lowland shepherds and goatherds each took up a pair of attached barges. She didn't see the architects. It seemed they had split from the rest of the caravan.

She didn't have long to wonder where they had gone and why they weren't continuing with the rest of the parties, as the bargemen approached and began to untie the rigging. Four bargemen managed each pair of barges: Two in the forward bow with long, thick poles that they used to push away from the dock and direct the barge; one in the forward stern, at the rudder. He seemed to be the captain of the tiny vessel and directed the others. There was also one with a pole in the rear stern, making the final shoves to get them into the pull of the river.

One by one, the barges pushed off the docks, caught the current, and began the float downstream.

Sitting on the barge, she watched the riverside pass by. This method of travel seemed slow, relaxing even. But the current was swift beneath the surface of the water, and the miles were eaten up quicker than they would have been by the sheep's hooves. She chose to enjoy this time, as they were only a couple days from the Capital. The desire to linger in this meandering illusion before she had to face the Order was overwhelming. She still hadn't figured out what she would say to them, how she would convince them to accept her in her sister's place. Anxiety began to rise at the thought, but she pushed it back down and watched the passing trees, listening to the rush of the water and the harmony of birdsongs. What to say was a problem for another day. She would have to face it whether she worried today or not. So, she chose not to.

The day passed and turned to evening. When the sun began to dip in the sky and paint the horizon in pinks and oranges, the bargemen guided the boats out of the current. She had thought that they would use their poles to push the barge to the edge of the river and make camp. To her surprise, they merely found the shallower waters that were several fathoms from the riverbank, but not directly in the powerful main current. Here, they dropped anchors and began evening meal preparation on the barge.

Once a stew was heating in the cabin on the rear barge, one of the bargemen gathered up things from the cook and the passengers: Wedges of cheese, a few hand pies, a loaf of bread, a fishhook, a handful of spare buttons, and a belt buckle. He took all these items, placed them on a small raft made from bundles of twigs, and lowered this off the side of the barge, letting it float from a tether about ten feet off the side of the forward bow.

Glormhar and Masnachwr had joined her and Erika on sheep duty on the forward barge. The fishhook and buckle were their contributions, and she recognized the buttons from among her own party.

"What is he doing?" she asked after watching as long as she could stand in silence.

"Didn't Uncle tell you about the Gnomes?" Erika replied with little interest.

"No. What are Gnomes, and what does that have to do with floating bits and bobs on a tiny raft??" she asked again.

Glormhar opened his mouth to speak, but Masnachwr cut him off. "Better to let her see for herself than try to explain." So, they sat and watched the gift-covered dingy in anticipatory silence.

Fortunately, they didn't have to wait long, maybe a quarter hour, and the water around the raft rippled. Then a little creature shot up from beneath the surface and landed deftly on the raft next to the food. It was about a foot and a half tall, with a humanoid composition. Its face and limbs were thin, and weather worn. She thought it was a male, but that was only based on the fact that it had a dark brown beard and narrow hips, she knew nothing about the species. It was dressed in leaves and moss sewn into a shirt and trousers, with a little brimmed hat that came to a sharp point at the top made from reeds.

The Gnome circled the raft slowly, checking for traps or tricks. As he did so, several more ripples appeared on the other sides of the raft, which were soon followed by three small heads, each with matching beards and pointy reed hats. The one on the raft appeared satisfied with his inspection and knelt down to grab a button. On his cue the other three quickly shot up out of the water and joined him, tucking into the food and squabbling over the remaining buttons and fishhook. They picked up the buckle to play with but quickly dropped it.

Asha was nearly entranced, when another Gnome popped up onto the barge rail beside her. She jumped and gasped. The Gnome laughed and mimicked her. She was too surprised and confused to do anything but stare. The Gnome stared right back, unblinking, its fish-like eyes without any discernable iris. It was incredibly creepy, but she couldn't look away. She jumped again when Glormhar pressed something into her hand. Asha whirled on him.

"For our little friend." He gestured to the Gnome.

She looked down at the small coin he had given her and then back at the Gnome.

"Friend?" the Gnome said, drawing out the word, still not blinking.

"Friend," Asha said a little more forcefully than she had meant to and held out the coin to the Gnome.

In a flash of green leaves and river water, the Gnome jumped off the rail straight at her, grabbing the coin and tweaking her nose before it clutched her braid, hanging loosely over her shoulder. Grasping the end of the braid, it swung around her shoulders and back over the rail, diving beneath the water again.

Glormhar chuckled. "I think he liked ye, lass."

Asha rubbed her nose to be sure it was still fine, even though it had startled more than hurt. "He's got a funny way of showing it."

"That's just how they are. Funny little tykes, but they run these waterways, and it ain't wise to anger 'em."

"What do you mean 'run the waterways?'"

"They got a strange type of magic about them. They can keep disasters away, but only for those they consider friends," he replied.

"Easy to keep disasters away if you're the one causing them in the first place," Erika cut in.

"Oh, they don't cause disaster. Mischief at best," he tossed back.

"So saith the chief cause of mischief in my company." Masnachwr gave Glormhar a hard sideways look.

"Who, me? I am innocent as a lamb." Glormhar feigned an offended expression.

"Don't think I don't know who's been loosening the stirrups from the saddles, so we fall on our asses instead of stepping up onto our rams."

"I can't imagine who would do such a thing, but I assure you that I will keep a sharp watch."

Masnachwr grunted in response. Asha covered a smile and turned back to the sheep. They seemed completely unbothered by the whole affair. She found this odd, considering their general flightiness. But perhaps this was the 'strange type of magic' that the Gnomes had.

There was a soft splash behind her and she turned sharply. There was a small, smooth, red stone sitting on the rail where the Gnome had stood. She picked it up and tucked it into her pocket. Perhaps it had liked her.

The rest of the night passed uneventfully. Asha and Erika were relieved after a few hours and sought their bedrolls. She woke to the straining of anchor ropes and smell of the breakfast fire.

A beautiful dawn broke and painted the world in color once again. As they shoved off, she wondered if they would see their Gnome friends again. The morning passed slowly as they floated ever nearer to their destination.

Several hours later, strange sounds came from further up the river. Something meaty thudded, water churned and splashed, and wood creaked and cracked. The bargemen advised the parties to arms, but there was no need. No one who heard it thought there would be anything but trouble. The sounds grew louder as they floated downstream.

They rounded a bend and saw the wreckage. Asha couldn't be sure what type of boat it had been, as it was only broken pieces of buoyant wood now. Timbers and planks were strewn all about. Thick canvas had caught on a large rock. Barrels and bundles bobbed further from the wreckage as the current caught them.

Part of the hull remained intact, and a huge fish rammed it with its head over and over, determined to change this. The fish was roughly ten feet long, with a large, lithe, round body. It was a swampy, slimy green with pale yellow stripes along its spine and white spots on its sides. The head it used as a battering ram was narrow and sharply pointed, with a lower jaw that curved slightly up.

Off to the side, in the shallower water near the canvas-covered rock, another equally large fish thrashed and used its large, serrated teeth to rip up a human arm that was no longer attached to its body. Nausea choked Asha and made her jaw ache. She glanced down at the silver ring on her finger. As she had suspected, it wasn't glowing. Jessa had good intentions and had made a beautiful ring, but creatures weren't evil; they just were what the Gods made them. As gruesome as the scene she saw before her was, there was no evil here.

They didn't see any survivors, so the barges floated by without stopping. A third large fish surfaced and charged at the passing barge but suddenly veered sharply off and turned in a circle.

Asha reached into her pocket and brushed the river stone with her fingertips.

"Strange type of magic," Glormhar muttered beside her.

"Strange, indeed. Those men paid a steep price for their lack of friendliness," Uncle Jolli said from behind them, his usual smile nowhere to be seen.

"All that happened because the Gnomes didn't like them?" Asha whispered.

"Not exactly," Glormhar replied. She turned away from the wreckage, waiting silently for more explanation.

"This river can be quite dangerous," he continued. "The Gnomes don't cause the dire pikes to attack, or rapids to be swollen, or a log to float just low enough to snag. People float this river without major trouble sometimes and never see hide nor hair of a Gnome. They often lose small valuables or find their food stores raided or ropes unknotted or knotted too tight at the most inopportune moment. Those who make friends experience no such mischief and find the real dangers seem to avoid them."

"Like the charging fish." She thought she understood. "The Gnomes only protect their friends."

"Aye, lass, only their friends."

"If one can avoid certain danger with trinkets and cheese, why wouldn't everyone do that?"

He blew out a long breath. "Not everyone believes that the Gnomes are magic, much less that they use their magic to protect anyone. They think it's all luck. Good or bad."

"There's no such thing as luck," she retorted.

"I don't know about that, lass."

"There isn't. Everything people blame on luck is consequences they don't understand from actions or inactions they aren't connecting but cannot escape," she said more firmly, turning to watch the cargo of the wreck floating away.

"If a tree falls on your house, eh? That a consequence?" he pressed gently.

"Yes, you had a rotting tree that wasn't taken care of. You might not have even known it, but it was a natural consequence. Not luck or supernatural intervention. People are too quick to blame the Gods or bad luck when bad things happen."

"That last bit I agree with, but I still believe in luck. Not a consequence if the tree comes down in a storm, now, is it? People are too quick to blame the Gods, sure. But sometimes it is bad luck, and sometimes it's favor of the Gods."

Asha didn't reply for a while. She didn't want to keep arguing, especially since he had a good point there.

"Maybe you're right, but I don't think so. I don't really want to keep talking about it."

"That's fine. I can convince ye another day." She glanced back at him, and he winked. She smiled and shook her head, turning back to watching the riverbank. He reached out and squeezed her shoulder, then walked away, leaving her to her thoughts.

Asha stayed at the rail, watching the river until night fell. When she returned to her bedroll, Uncle Jetti caught her attention.

"We'll arrive in the Capital tomorrow, likely mid-morning if the current stays this strong. We would appreciate your help getting the stock to the buyers. Then we can escort you to the Order, or you can spend one more night with us at an inn, and we'll drop you off the following morning. Whatever you prefer."

She thought for a moment. Though she didn't want to drag this out, she also didn't want to say farewell. Adding one more night with her family was appealing, but she didn't think she could stand it. That restless energy was building in her chest and fingers again. The next day, she would be practically buzzing. She wasn't looking forward to parting. How could she?

She had never been alone in her whole life. But she wasn't even sure if she would sleep that night, much less if she waited to face the Order by a whole extra day.

"We'll see how the day goes, how long it takes to get there and deliver the sheep, but I think I'd rather face the Order tomorrow. I'll miss you all, but I'd really prefer not to wait."

"Probably better that you don't," Crispin added, slightly muffled by how tight he was wrapped in his bedroll. "Better to surprise the Holy tight asses. If they know that you've come instead of your sister before you show up, it might not go your way."

"We would treasure the extra time." Uncle Jetti glared at the offending roll, despite Crispin's back being turned. "But he's right. It might do ye good to keep them on the back foot."

With that settled, Asha snuggled into her own bedroll. Despite her fears of lost sleep, the gentle lapping of the water against the wooden hull and cool breeze across her face were an excellent cure for nerve-induced insomnia.

Their final travel day began as all the others had: Breakfast and chores in the dim twilight. By the time color painted the large fluffy clouds, the bargemen were already pulling the anchors up and catching the current. Asha was glad for it. Her nerves had turned the gentle sway and bob of the barge into a tempest, and she wasn't sure how long she would keep her morning meal down.

The riverside scene was lovely as ever, but she couldn't enjoy it that morning. Glormhar's chatter was a welcome distraction, even if she had to remind herself to pay attention half the time. The barge rounded a bend, and there it was in the distance: Meditullio, the Capital of Greater Anitaris and seat of the Emperor, and more importantly to her, the Order of Holy Heroes.

They were still an hour, or more's float away, but her throat clenched.

"Take a breath, Ash. The walls don't bite, and there's nothing in the markets nastier than those pirates. Ye handled them just fine." Glormhar's voice broke her nervous reverie.

"The markets aren't my problem, or the walls," she blurted without thinking, suddenly realizing he had no way to know that this was anything more than a simple trading trip for her.

"Then what has got ye in such a tiff?"

She wanted to retort that she was not in a tiff but bit it back. "I'm going to the Order. To answer my sister's summons," she said shortly.

He let it hang in the air a moment. "And what would be the reason that your sister isn't answering her own summons?"

She had not expected that question, though she wasn't sure what exactly she had expected. It jabbed at her like a needle, and she snapped her reply, "Cuz she's five!"

"How in the Recorder's damnation was I supposed to know that?" he bit right back, provoked by her tone.

Asha closed her eyes and took a deep breath. "I'm sorry. I don't want to be short with you. It would be better if we just don't talk about it."

He didn't respond for a long moment, and she thought he might take her advice, not that she was sure at all if she wanted him to. "The Order doubled its orders for weapons these past months. We heard rumors, but I never imagined they'd summon a wee child," he said finally.

"What have you heard?" She snapped her head around to look at him, hoping he knew something useful so she wouldn't go in blind.

"Ah." He hesitated and rubbed the back of his neck. "It's just idle chatter, nothing more."

"Glormhar," she entreated, "I'm going before the Order here. They might just be weapons buyers to you, but to me... Well, they practically are the government to me. And I have to convince them to take a first daughter destructive instead of a seventh daughter." She paused, the impact of her words hitting her even as she said them. "And to convince them not to try and take my sister by force. Anything that I know going in there is useful."

"As I said—" his eyes were full of understanding and compassion—"it's only idle chatter, but the gist of it is that there's trouble on the lower continent. Real trouble. And that trouble is starting to move north."

"What kind of trouble?"

"That I don't know. The rumors aren't what ye would call consistent, but they all say there's one faction that has been rampaging through the whole continent. Their rivals bow or are purged with fire and blood."

She frowned. It wasn't terribly helpful, but it was more than she had known before. The lower continent was always at war within itself, but it had been centuries since that had spilled into the upper continent. From what she understood, pirates and roaming Warlords harassed the fishing and trading villages on the southern coast, especially in the summer after planting was done. But that was a far cry from 'fire and blood moving north'.

Leaning her forearms on the rail, she silently watched the Capital grow slowly larger on the horizon. She started a little when his shoulder leaned against her but didn't move away. His hand covered hers on the railing. She wasn't sure how to prolong this moment, but she didn't want him to leave. The journey was nearly over, and she would soon be alone, striving against the will of the most powerful people in the Empire to protect her family. She interlaced her fingers with his, wishing the current would slow just a bit.

Chapter 9

Asha

The river grew faster and rougher when they drew close to the city. The bargemen unfurled the small sail to catch the wind and slow them, as well as give them more directional control. Asha focused on the countryside and not on her heartbeat in her ears. As the city's walls grew larger on the horizon, they passed fertile farmland and pastures. The population grew denser with every passing mile, with more small stone and thatched homes along the outskirts of the city. There were other barges navigating the current as well. She glanced back at the small trail of barges behind theirs, realizing she had almost forgotten the rest of the caravan, though they had been behind them the entire journey. They had stretched out the interval between the barges to allow for better maneuverability in the busier portion of the river.

Finally, they approached a large dock. It was larger than any she had ever seen, although she hadn't gone to explore the port at Inglerho. She knew from her briefings before the trip that this was only the most northern portion of the massive Capital port. There was so much trade and water traffic that the architects had assigned different craft sections based on size and direction of travel. The smaller barges from the northern continent were to dock at the first available mooring to keep them from interfering with the movements of the larger sea ships coming in from the inlet. This also gave them direct access to the western markets set up outside the city walls. There was also a market on the eastern side of the city, mostly supplied by barges from the third of the three rivers that ran to the inlet. Her party currently rode the second.

The bargemen expertly swung the craft about and nestled it into position along the dock. Then two jumped out. tied the moorings and began the long process of unloading. First the mounts and pack animals, then the packs, lastly the sheep. Before they were halfway done, Asha noticed the other barges settle into place and begin their own unloading.

Once both parties were unloaded and mounted, it was time to part ways. Asha found herself reluctant, though she had thought she was prepared for it. Since they had integrated after the pirate attack, it had been all too easy to forget that they were, in fact, two parties with different goals and missions. She turned to her pony and placed her foot in the stirrup.

"Leaving without saying goodbye? Poor taste, lass." Glormhar's voice behind her made her jump, and her foot slipped back to the ground.

She clicked her tongue and retorted, "I can say goodbye from my saddle. Pretty sure my mouth works while mounted."

"Perhaps, but I suppose I was hopin' that you might not use words to say it." His voice was quiet, just above a whisper as he stepped close to her, tilting his chin up to look into her eyes with a rare serious look.

"I don't know what you mean." She suddenly struggled to take a full breath.

"I think ye do. Though I can't imagine why ye're denying it now. As though there ain't been something between us this whole trip." He took her hand in his own gently. "Don't deny it now at the parting. It'll make the reunion a bit awkward." He smiled and rubbed his thumb over the back of her hand.

"I'm not denying that," she said slowly. "But there isn't going to be a reunion, so I'm not worried about it being awkward."

His head jerked a little, as if her words had stung him. "Of course, there will be. Ash, I know that ye've got an obligation to your Order, but I can wait. I'm in no rush—"

"Waiting on a girl you've known less than a month seems pretty rushed to me," she cut him off sharply, wanting this over, wanting to ride away and not see the hurt in his eyes or admit the ache in her chest.

"We have all the time in the world, lass."

"No, this is the end of our time. Goodbye, Glormhar." She tried to keep her voice firm and told herself to pull her hand away, but she didn't manage the second and barely managed the first. "I enjoyed getting to know you," she said more softly this time. "But there is nothing else for us. I won't prolong the inevitable."

"I hope you change your mind. If you do, I won't be hard to find." He lifted her hand and kissed the back of it, his whiskers tickling her. He turned it over and dropped something into it. Then he was gone, striding off toward his own mount.

She looked down at the item in her palm. It was a small stone pendant, shaped like a shield, with smooth edges and a hole for a chain at the top. On one side was a crest—his family's, she presumed— on the other a mustache that curled upward like his own and some Dwarven script she couldn't read. He really was proud of that mustache. She slipped it into her pocket and mounted her pony.

The others pretended not to watch her, and she pretended not to watch the Dwarves ride toward the city gates as her party moved toward the market. She swallowed against the lump in her throat and blinked rapidly to catch the tears welling in her eyes. *Foolish, foolish, immature girl. Crying over a man-no a Dwarf-you barely know. You just met him and you will never see him again. Get a grip.*

Asha was glad her party skirted the edge of the market; it gave her something else to think about. She didn't understand how people could be that packed together in an open space. But there they were, hundreds of people, nearly shoulder-to-shoulder between the booths, tables, and carts. She had never seen so many people, yet she reminded herself this was only the market. Once they entered the city, it would be so much worse. She focused on her mount's ears for a few minutes until the tight feeling in her throat loosened.

The party navigated around the main market and, to her surprise, kept riding past it and away from the city. They continued for a few miles along a busy road until they reached a small manor. There, they were met by a steward who directed them to the pen for the sheep, while Uncle Jetti and Jolli went to the manor house to greet the lord to whom they were selling the sheep. After the sheep were turned into the pen, Asha noticed the largest mules she had ever seen in a neighboring pen. She went over to take a closer look.

Deep brown bays, the mules stood at least seventeen hands high and were broader than any she had ever seen. She would have doubted they were mules if it hadn't been for the distinctly jack-ish head and ears.

"Ah, your daughter has good taste. She found my new project," an unfamiliar voice sounded behind her.

"My niece has always had an eye for horse flesh," Uncle Jetti politely corrected. "Who couldn't admire such a creature? Asha, this is Antonius Asinus, lord of this manor, breeder of mammoth mules and soon of our sheep."

Asha exchanged pleasantries with the lord, then endured an extraordinarily detailed explanation of how to breed a 'siege mule' as he had called it. Somehow, he was able to kill any curiosity she had previously possessed. How he managed to say 'I bred the largest donkeys possible, then had them cover my hardiest cart mares' in such a number of words was truly astonishing.

"And just wait and see. Once I show the quartermasters how much these fine specimens can pull, why, they'll be begging me to breed until you won't be able to throw a stick without hitting two. I tell you, there won't be a siege engine in all of Anitaris that won't be pulled by a mule from Antonius Asinus in a decade, that is certain."

"We wish the best of luck in that endeavor." Even Uncle Jolli's smile was fading as he tried to steer the older man toward a more productive conversation. "However, our endeavor is to sell you some sheep."

"Ah, yes, yes, of course. I have many plans for sheep as well. I have found the stock around here to be inferior in both health and wool production. I have it on good authority that your family's suffer neither such afflictions."

Asha quietly excused herself, though the elderly lord didn't stop speaking long enough to acknowledge her excuse. She took the opportunity to duck into the stable and make her way to where Erika and Alaric waited, avoiding the predicament she had just escaped. If he kept talking like that, she might not have any choice in waiting to report to the Order until tomorrow. After no less than two hours, the bargain was finally settled, and the party left the manor and went back to the Capital.

She had been right in the market. Once they entered the city gates, it was much, much worse. The press of people milling around, the stench, the stale air, and, of course, the walls made her feel trapped and suffocated. She was determined to master it, though. After all, she would live there, at least for a time. She didn't pull out the sachet Bard had given her back in Inglerho. Instead, she practiced her deep breathing that Great Uncle Luca had taught her to calm her heartbeat and center herself. Then she focused on the rooftops and counted windows. She was surprised at how many buildings had multiple windows, but she supposed glass would be much easier to access here. So, perhaps here, windows weren't a luxury.

Asha was so focused on her breathing and counting windows, she didn't realize how close they were to the garrison until they pulled their mounts to a halt in front of it. *Really should have paid more attention to navigating the city. You have to live here...* She surveyed the garrison in front of her. Despite being inside the Capital, it had its own thick, high stone walls, with a tower in each corner. There were archer slits spaced just enough to provide overlapping fields of fire all along, but unlike the surrounding buildings, they had no glass windows. Its great wooden doors with deeply carved protection runes stood open at the moment, but she had no doubt they could be slammed shut in an instant.

Dismounting, she removed her small pack. She had been told that the Order would outfit her appropriately, and she would have no need for pony or saddle. The others stepped down to exchange farewells. Uncle Jetti and Jolli hugged her tightly and gave her encouraging words that warmed her heart but swirled up and out of her racing thoughts. Crispin and Erika grasped her forearm and clapped her shoulder with a smile and a wink, leaving her with silly words about letters to Dwarves and other nonsense. Bard hugged her without a word. Alaric handed her the rubbing he took from the pirate cannon runes, the medallion, and some handwritten notes.

"I have puzzled over these the entire trip and can't make up nor down of it. Perhaps the scholars of the Order can do more with it," he said, and she looked down at the items dumbly.

"Of course, I'll pass them off," she acknowledged, shoving them unceremoniously into one of the pouches of her pack with other spell notes and such.

"If you find yourself in need or trouble," Uncle Jetti said as he mounted, and Crispin took her reins to lead her mount away, "we will be in the city for a few days selling our wool goods."

"Of course," Asha replied. She didn't want them to leave but also couldn't stand dragging this conversation out anymore.

"We'll be at the western market and not hard to find." He smiled once more, but no cheer was in his eyes.

"Take care of yourself, Asha, darling." Uncle Jolli had the exact same sad smile plastered across his face.

"The same to all of you. I won't be there to Void cannons for you on the way home," she joked, hoping that breaking the tension in the air would break it inside her head as well.

"Ain't even taken her oaths yet, and she's already acting like a high and mighty Holy Hero. Like we ain't never made a trip without her," Crispin joked back dryly. The others chuckled.

"I'll write when I have the time," Asha said and turned on her heel, stepping out confidently toward the garrison.

"Ye better, or your mother will have yer head!" Uncle Jetti shouted behind her, and then their ponies' hooves thumped as they trotted away.

Head up, shoulders back, she strode inside the garrison with confidence she didn't feel. She was stopped by a guard.

"Business?"

"Asha Pacatus. I have a summons."

The grizzled man sighed and raised his eyes to the heavens in a silent prayer for patience. "Summons for what. Are you a courtier? Messenger? New recruit? Be specific, girl."

"Oh, uh, new recruit," she stammered. She had no idea there was more than one type of summons.

"New recruits report to the sergeant at arms." He raised a gloved hand and pointed to the base of one of the towers. "Over there. Go on, off with you."

Asha turned and walked briskly toward the tower. There were two doors. One had a line of other people, mostly her age, in plain clothes. The other was closed but occasionally opened, and armored guards passed in and out. Standing in line was the obvious choice.

She chose well. Once she got to the front of the line, she again gave her name to the man behind the large desk.

"Summons." The gray-haired man clad in mail seemed as annoyed and unimpressed as the entry guard.

"Yes, I was summoned."

He didn't make a plea for patience; he just stared at her, waiting, though she didn't know for what. "Show. Me. Your summons," he grit out between clenched teeth after a few long moments.

"Oh, yes." She scrambled to dig it out of her pack and handed it to him, a little crumpled, trying not to wince as he took it. He was silent for a few minutes while he examined it, cross-referencing it with several books in front of him. "Age and main affinity?"

"Twenty-two years, destructive."

He blew air out of his nose and crossed something out of one of the books, then wrote a correction.

Then he gathered several tokens from stacks on the desk.

"This—" he held up a bronze disc with a breastplate impression in it—"is your draper token. You will present it to the quartermaster's corps to receive your gear and armor. If you lose it, you will go to battle naked for all I care." He handed it to her.

"This—" he held up another bronze token, this one with a loaf and fish impression—"is your entry to the provisional hall. If you lose it, you will find your own food." He handed it to her.

"This—" he held up another token, this one wooden, with a flame carved into it—"is your entry to your trials. The trials will determine what training you lack and your placement in the garrison. The trials start at sunrise every morning in the western training grounds. If you are late—" he paused and somehow his glare hardened—"you will wish you weren't." He smiled a very unfriendly smile that sent a chill down her spine.

"This—" he held up another bronze token, a key impression that had a faint protective aura on it—"is your entry to the female barracks. Males are not permitted into the female recruit barracks; neither are females permitted into the male recruit barracks. Violators will enjoy a stay in the stocks." Again, he paused to glare, then handed it to her.

"That is a map of the grounds." He gestured behind him to a large vellum map stretched across the stone wall. "Look at it, memorize it. Grab your bed supplies, and get out of my sight," he said, waving to a stack of bedrolls along the adjoining wall and turning his glare to the young man behind her.

"Next!"

Hurrying to step away from the desk and scanning the vellum map, she tried to calm her racing heart. This wasn't how it was supposed to go at all. She did her best to memorize the layout. Once she was confident she knew where the female barracks, provision hall, and western training grounds were, she turned and grabbed a bedroll, then left the tower.

She made her way across the garrison and into the barracks. There was another desk with two large wooden doors on either side and another guard. This one was much younger and lacked the impatient glare of the previous two. She wasn't sure what to do but assumed she needed to sign in here, too. He added her name to a roster and gestured to the closed wooden door on his left.

"That's the female side. Other side is male. You're not permitted in there. Don't get caught using your token to let males into your side either. Pick an empty pallet and chest once you're inside. Doesn't matter where."

"I understand," she mumbled and turned to the door. She tried and failed to open it.

"Hold your barracks token in the hand you use to open it," the guard said from behind her.

"Oh." She did as he said, and the door swung open easily. "Thanks," she called over her shoulder as she went inside.

Down a short hallway, she found a large room lined with pallets and barely enough space to walk between them. Each had a chest at its foot. Most of them had bedrolls on them. She scanned for an empty one.

"There's two more levels," a girl about her age offered as she walked past and toward her own pallet. "Most people don't realize that and just drop their gear here."

"Thanks," Asha said as she made her way toward an empty pallet in the far corner. It was against the back wall and next to the hallway. A peek showed a set of stairs. "But I prefer ground level."

"Suit yourself. More room up there."

And yet, this girl hadn't relocated. Asha didn't consider herself paranoid, but she would rather be in a corner than the second story if a fire broke out. She unrolled the bedding and prepared to sleep. Surely there had to have been a mistake. Taking her sister's place couldn't be this easy? Would she not need to plead her case to the counsel of the Order? Her mother and grandmother and great aunts had been sure that it would take a great deal of convincing for her to be an acceptable substitute. After all, they sent for a seventh daughter, a Seer. Asha was a first daughter, and they had no shortage of destructive Mages in the Order of Holy Heroes. Perhaps they had misunderstood the summons. Maybe the Order just wanted a member of the Pacatus family? That would make more sense than summoning a five-year-old.

She laid down on the pallet. That had to be it. There was a misunderstanding. They were clearly summoning many recruits from many families and had just gotten the name wrong. Besides, had they planned to send a five-year-old to the barracks by herself? Or to whatever the trials would be in the morning? That was more ridiculous than summoning a child who didn't even have access to her mana yet.

With that thought, Asha settled into sleep, tomorrow promised to be a difficult day. She grinned as her eyes drifted closed, remembering fondly her last training exercise with her great uncle. *Did Mother ever find out about the mule chips?* Her grin faded as she remembered what he had said about far worse training methods under the Order. *What nasty surprises will my trials hold?*

Chapter 10

Asha

The entire female barracks stirred long before the sun. Asha dressed and used the latrine. She made sure she had all the tokens given to her and went to find the western training grounds. It was a bit harder to find in the lamplight, but she made it by the time first light peeked across the cloudy night sky.

She and the other recruits milled about and separated into groups and singles. After a while, several men and a woman in armor approached the training field. Their cuirasses were covered in rich maroon fabric, the Order's color, with a seven-pointed star in deep Imperial blue on the upper-right chest. The opulent colors hid the rectangular metal plates beneath, evidenced only by the strategically placed polished steel studs. Pauldrons and bracers added additional protection. All wore bright yellow sashes just above their sword belts. They walked purposefully toward the head of the field where there was a desk with three chairs behind it, in front of a large storage shed.

"Good morning, recruits!" one of the men boomed as he stood in front of the desk. "You will form into lines to be sorted and tested according to affinity." He paused while the group inched hesitantly closer. "Listen well, for I will not repeat myself. Destructive Mages will form a line at the farthest end of the desk in front of Brother Gerard. Artificers will form a line in the middle of the desk in front of Sister Cecilia. Everyone else will form a line at the nearest end of the desk in front of Brother Arthur."

Asha had no idea how he yelled that long without taking a breath. He had time for several as no one had begun to move toward the desk. She took a step forward and then he yelled again, and she realized why he was able to yell so long. That had not been the loudest volume he had been capable of.

"What are you waiting for? You have your instructions. Move! Move!"

Everyone swarmed forward in a nearly frantic mass. It was embarrassingly chaotic for people whose instructions had been quite simple. In spite of this, three distinct lines formed in front of the desk. Caught in the swarm, but not frantic herself, Asha had ended up in the middle of the destructive line. The three named instructors (or was tester more appropriate?) were seated at the desk taking tokens and issuing something rectangular and brown that Asha couldn't make out. The one who had shouted the instructions and the remaining instructor stood cross-armed and menacing, overseeing the unloading of training equipment from the shed.

When she got to the front of the line, she looked dumbly at Brother Gerard. He was a short, broad man, with dark brown hair and a matching eye. She was sure that both had been matching at one time before a blade had slashed across his face, relieving him of the right eye and leaving a deep jagged scar in its wake. His square face and prominent jaw were set in a hard, neutral expression.

"Name?"

"Asha Pacatus"

"Token."

She handed over the wooden token with the flame carving. When he took it, a finger brushed hers, and though she couldn't see the shadow in the pale gray light of dawn, the cold dead feeling was unmistakable. Like a breath being sucked out of her lungs. But it wasn't her breath that he took. It was a tiny bit of mana. He was a Void, like her father. Her father, however, usually had to try to take mana from a person. Magic objects, he had told her, were easier for him to Void, to the point that he only needed to make direct contact. When she had first shown her secondary affinity, he had shown her how to use it, and she had found some trouble even with objects. It took practice, and she had to make direct contact, focus, and try to take the mana. She had never tried to take it from a person. This Void, it would seem, was even more powerful than her father as he could take mana from a tiny touch without trying.

He either didn't notice or acted like he didn't as he grabbed an eight-by-ten-inch clay tablet and used a stylus to press her name into the top line. There were symbols she didn't recognize in neat rows, separated by lines. Each had a blank space next to it. After her name was on it, he slid it to Sister Cecilia to his right. She used her finger and a single word to fire the top line and solidify Asha's name into the tablet, all while still speaking to the Artificer recruit in front of her. Then she handed it back without turning her head.

"Don't lose this, and don't smudge the wet clay. We won't issue another. So, if we can't read it—" he gave a spiteful grin that squished the scar upward and made it redden slightly—"we will just assume you failed all tasks. Over to the shed where Brothers Richard and Philip will give you further instructions."

She wasn't sure which was Brother Richard and which was Brother Philip, but the one who had shouted instructed her to take several wooden swords from another recruit inside the shed and carry them to the far end of the training ground where there was a pit dug into the earth. The pit was only about a foot and a half deep, but the perimeter was lined with iron with runes pounded into it. There were wooden swords, axes, war hammers, and spears laid out on the ground in lines beside it. She grouped the swords she carried by type and laid them down as well.

Looking around the field, there were four stations being set up by the recruits. Each looked different, and she could guess that there were several different trials. There were several more armored men and women with the same yellow sashes leading horses to one of the stations where a quintain was being set up by recruits. Another had various-sized bows, and recruits counted paces to place targets under the supervision of an instructor. The final station was at the far end of the training ground, with the most open space and only a few wooden targets.

Each line had been sent to a different station, leaving the cavalry station without recruits as the instructors began putting the horses through warmup drills. Presently, Brother Gerard and the one who hadn't yelled made their way over to the pit and the destructive recruits standing around it. He introduced himself as Brother Richard and began to explain how the trial would work, while Brother Gerard took a small dagger and pierced a vein on the back of his left hand. He dripped blood along the runes in the iron circle surrounding the pit and murmured an incantation. A shadow settled over the pit and sank down into the sand, giving it a dark, grimy look.

"As you can see," Brother Richard continued. She should have paid more attention to his words and not Brother Gerard's actions. Hopefully, she didn't have to go first and could figure it out from other recruits. "There will be no mana enhancing your skills for this trial. You will pass or fail based on your own merit."

"What happens if we fail?" a small woman who looked younger and skinnier than Asha asked. Clearly, she worried about her chances with weapons without the edge only mana can provide.

"Our fell beasts are always in need of fodder," Brother Gerard answered flatly, wrapping a binding around his hand, then pulling on leather gauntlets.

Brother Richard shot him a sideways glance. "Failure can be corrected by proper training. If you fail any trial, it will lengthen your individual training regimen before you move to the core formations training."

Many shoulders went slack in relief at this revelation. Asha, however, was even more motivated to succeed. She didn't want to spend a day more there that she didn't have to.

Brother Gerard picked up a wooden sword and shield and stepped down into the pit. All the other recruits rushed to grab one as well. There weren't enough for everyone, but before Asha could grab a wooden battle axe, the woman who had spoken up earlier whispered for her to leave it. They were all going to cycle through with the one-handed sword first.

One by one, each recruit stepped into the circle and faced Brother Gerard. He would give them a few moments to attack first, but most did not, and he tested their parries and guards with a flurry of attacks. Then he would order or goad them to attack him, blocking and parrying with ease. When Asha's turn came, she decided to spare them both the trouble. Her access to mana cut off the moment she stepped into the pit, and it made her a bit queasy. The faster she could pass, the faster she could step back out and wait for the next set of weapons.

She took several steps forward and swung low at his legs. He parried. Perhaps it was her imagination, but she thought she saw a hint of respect in his eye at that. She didn't let up and was the first recruit to force him to give ground and circle around to avoid stumbling backward into the pit edge. Her strategy came at a cost, though. He quickly turned his circle into an attack of his own, and she was the one on her back foot, seeking better ground. She had also been wrong about ending it quicker. The more skill she showed, the more he pressed her, checking her strikes and testing her blocks and binds for strength and structure. It felt like an hour before he finally dropped his stance and nodded to Brother Richard, who pressed something into her clay tablet with a stylus. She handed the training weapons to the next recruit in line and retrieved her tablet. Looking down at what he had pressed into it, the symbols were just as foreign to her as before.

The other weapons went roughly the same. Each recruit took turns fighting with shields and one-handed swords, axes, war hammers, spears, maces, and clubs, then two-handed swords, two-handed spears, two-handed war hammers, and finally, two-handed axes. The Brothers swapped back and forth between grader and tester at every weapon change, but even so, Asha was impressed with their endurance and stamina. *I suppose that's what a lifetime of pledged service will create*, she thought to herself.

Asha had no idea what the grader had put on her tablet, but she was confident with both types of swords. She was moderately confident she had done well with the one-handed hammer and axe, and bludgeoning weapons. Her two-handed weapon skills definitely needed improvement. Great Uncle Luca had strong opinions about shields. So, while she was familiar with them, two-handed weapons were not something she had trained with frequently.

After every recruit's last weapon test, Brother Richard had used the same incantation Sister Cecilia did to fire the results into their tablet. It took up nearly half the tablet. After all the destructive recruits had gone through the weapons trial, they took a short break to funnel through the provision hall for midday meal. Asha wasn't sure she would be able to eat as the nausea lasted after her access to mana returned. However, as soon as she took the first bite, her stomach righted itself enough to remind her that she had performed weapon-based exercise most of the morning and had not eaten since midday yesterday.

Once midday meals had been completed, the groups changed stations. The destructive recruits were sent to the mounted trials, and the Artificers were sent to the weapons trials.

This trial was overseen by Brother Arthur, with several unnamed assistants who had brought out and warmed up the horses. Each recruit was tested on riding ability, which almost all seemed to do quite well at. Then came the mounted weapons tests. Very few did well at this. Again, Asha was confident with her prowess with a sword, slashing the target accurately at a canter. The spear throws gave her more trouble. She had trained to throw accurately since she was a small girl. Later in her teen years, she had done a fair amount of training with javelins. Doing so while riding and guiding the enormous war horse was quite a different matter. Her accuracy left much to be desired. She knew she failed the lance test—miserably failed it. Only two other recruits did passably well at it, but that was small solace. Nobles' sons by the quality of their dress and boots. No doubt they had been groomed for knighthood from a young age and therefore would have lance training and possibly even joust experience.

While she waited for the rest of her group to finish and be moved to another trial, a massive thunderclap grabbed her attention. She and pretty much every other recruit turned their attention to the fourth trial station, the one with the targets and empty space. That empty space was currently filled with a whirlwind. Spinning targets, clouds, and dust rose up high above the walls of the garrison, occasionally spitting streaks of lightning. It was guided by a very tall woman with a spear. The other line had at least one powerful weather Mage.

Presently, the destructive group was moved to the archery trials. A quick glance showed that the Artificers were still at the weapons trial. It made sense that it was the longest of the trials. The archery trial was undoubtedly the most straightforward. Each recruit was given a quiver of arrows. Then they shot for accuracy, starting at target weight bows. With every three successful shots, they were moved to the next bow and target. She couldn't know for sure, but she thought they were increasing by twenty pounds on each bow. After annotating the highest strength achieved, they were again given the target weight bow and a new quiver and tested for speed. Finally, they were instructed to show all the types of draws they knew how to fire with. Most only knew the two- or three-fingered draw. A few, like Asha, also knew the pinch draw. A couple knew a draw she had never seen before that used the thumb to draw and release. It looked strange but she could see the security of the arrow as it was stabilized by the primary fingers.

She was afraid that she may have failed this trial. Though she did well with the target weight bows, she had only been able to draw back two of the increasing weights. She had never pulled back a bow greater than one hundred pounds, and even that she couldn't have fired more than a few arrows. War bows were often much heavier than that. Did the order expect every member to be able to fire a war bow? Or to use all types of weapons for that matter? It didn't seem likely, but she had no idea what to expect.

Finally, they were moved to the last station on the far side of the training field. This was where the fun would begin. Sister Cecelia stood waiting for them.

"Recruits, for your final trial, you will show us your best offensive and defensive spells." Her voice was loud and matter of fact. It lacked the menace that most of the brothers had shown. In fact, she seemed bored and disappointed in the recruits. Asha couldn't help but wonder if that was intentional as this, in theory, should have been the most exciting station. "I don't care what spells you use. The type matters much less than the power of them, so put all your mana into them. The only other thing I care about is that you do not injure your fellow recruits. Keep all mana directed down-range toward the open field. Don't make me hit you with my own defensive spell. I haven't had a good knockout in three cycles." She smiled, and there was the menace Asha had thought she lacked.

"So, who will go first?" she invited. Again, the crowd of recruits hesitated without clear direction. It was as though all of the confidence in each individual had been sapped when they were shuffled into a group. Asha stepped forward and held her tablet out to Sister Cecelia.

"I will."

"Excellent. Start with your best offensive spell."

Asha stepped a few paces away and faced the open field. She took up her ready stance, feet shoulder width apart, right foot slightly set back, knees with a slight bend. Rolling her shoulders back, she closed her eyes for a moment, feeling her well of mana.

When she felt centered, she took a deep breath and opened her eyes, drawing mana as she did so. Then she stomped her right foot. The earth shook and cracked. A small gorge opened in the field in front of her, five feet wide and running the entire length of the section set aside for casting, about one hundred fifty to two hundred yards. She realized she could have made it wider, but she didn't want to damage the integrity of the garrison walls with the earthquake that would follow such a displacement of dirt. Raising her hands from where they hung loosely at her sides, she bent her elbows, palms up, with her fingers spread up and slightly out, as though she was holding a ball just a little too big for her hands inside each palm. Fire rose from inside the gorge, hot and deep orange red, she raised it until the wall of fire was even with the height of the garrison wall. Then she turned her wrists and swung her hands quickly, clapping them together. The gorge snapped shut and the fire disappeared.

She turned back to Sister Cecelia, who was recovering her footing after stumbling when the ground shook for the second time in less than a minute. Once she was stable again, she nodded at Asha. "Now, your best defensive spell." Asha had hoped for a better reaction than that, but the good sister was holding onto her contrived boredom. The other recruits were not, jaws hanging and eyes wide, while they too regained their feet. Asha couldn't help but give a tiny smirk.

Again, she took a moment to center. Then she took another deep breath, gathering mana, but this time, she kept her eyes closed in concentration. She rolled her shoulders back and spread her arms as wide as she could, swinging them forward like she was gathering a bundle of wool. Then she made tight fists and crossed her forearms in front of her face. She held her arms there and opened her eyes. Seeing the dark red mana shimmering around her and the entire group of destructive recruits, she smiled. It was the largest shield she had cast. She held it for a few more moments, then dropped it, releasing her hands to hang down at her sides again, chest heaving and heart pounding rapidly. She turned back to Sister Cecelia.

"Very good. Move over to the side and have a seat to rest if you need to," Sister Cecelia said as she pressed a stylus into Asha's clay tablet.

Asha nodded and moved off to the left of the instructor, out of the way of the other recruits. She didn't think she needed to sit, but she was going to get water from the barrel. After she used the large ladle to fill a cup and refresh herself, eyes still burned into her. She turned her head and made eye contact with Sister Cecelia, who was still holding her tablet. Asha thought the sister must have been glaring at her because she hadn't retrieved it, so she quickly went back for it.

She held out her hand, but Sister Cecelia didn't move to give it to her.

"If you don't need to sit, you didn't put all of your mana into that spell." One of the other recruits gasped and Sister Cecelia paused. "As I instructed."

"I didn't think I could keep it from hurting others or damaging the walls if I made it bigger," Asha explained and dropped her hand.

"Have you ever used all of your mana? Ever trained at the fullest reaches of your capacity?" Sister Cecelia's face was hard and unreadable.

"I did once, but no, I've never trained that way." Asha's shoulders dropped, and her confidence evaporated. Surely, she hadn't failed this trial, too.

Sister Cecelia didn't respond to that. Instead, she made another mark on Asha's tablet and fired the entire clay, locking in all the day's marks.

"You won't be needing this back. Go wait over by the water barrel for the others to be done."

"Yes, ma'am," Asha said instinctively and did as she was told. Her heartrate had slowed, but as dread settled into the pit of her stomach, it hitched back up for another reason entirely. She had used a good amount of mana; she felt weary and sat down to watch the others.

The other destructive recruits cycled through casting offensive and defensive spells. Targets splintered and burned, what little grass was left also turned to ash, and smoke hung in the air, following lots of fireballs and explosive blasts of various sizes. One decaying spell looked gruesomely fascinating, like watching a lifetime of rot hit the target in less than a minute. Another recruit seemed to compress the earth downward in a circle with a twenty-foot diameter. But the ground didn't shake or split again, nor were there any high walls of blaze. The recruit who cast the compression ring also cast a ring of fire around himself as his defensive spell. Asha thought that was a very interesting spell and wondered if he might teach it to her. It was also about twenty feet in diameter and chest height. Perhaps not as useful as a traditional shield, but she was sure there could be some situation in which it would be beneficial. Most of the other recruits used a similar shield spell to hers, but only around themselves or possibly up to a ten-foot diameter.

All of the remaining recruits did have to sit down afterward. The one who cast the fire ring stumbled when he released it and nearly fell down. He sat down hard and made no effort to get to the water barrel. Asha poured him a cup and offered it to him. He took it, and she had an excuse to look him over. He was just over her height, thin, with simple, squarish features, walnut brown hair and greenish-brown eyes. Asha couldn't decide if she thought he was handsome or not. Not that it mattered.

"Thank you." He promptly drained the cup.

"No need to thank me. Do you want another?" Asha responded.

"Please." He was still breathing heavily.

She went for another. When she came back, she said, "I'm Asha. I liked your ring of fire."

"Wilford Artifex, but please call me Will. I thought your fire gorge was terrifying. Glad we're on the same side."

Asha chuckled. "People keep saying that."

"Can you blame them? " He scoffed as he got up and returned the cup himself.

"Alright, recruits!" Sister Cecelia raised her voice above the murmuring. "Tomorrow you will report to the archives to be tested on your reading and writing. After that, they will issue you study material for your required histories and such. That evening, you will be assigned to your pseudo ballasts and positions under a pair of instructors who will oversee all further training. Until then, rest up, and for the sake of the Gods, hit the bathhouse! You all stink!"

The recruits sheepishly filed off the training field to do just that, grateful for the rest and refresh before new trials.

Chapter 11

Asha and Bernard

The next morning, the female barracks was up before the sun, and Asha was up with them. She was used to early rising, though she was not used to sharing a living space with so many people. It was going to take some time to get used to the noises of fifty or more women coming and going and making latrine trips at all hours.

On the eastern side of the garrison, the archives were tucked directly against the wall. From the outside, it appeared to be just another storage space added onto the twenty-foot-thick stone, made of similar materials. Inside was a long, narrow room filled with closely packed desks in front of narrow benches. Every wall had shelves cut into the rock from floor to ceiling, which were nearly bursting, they were packed so tight with bound books, loose manuscripts, rolled parchment, and vellum. Asha pitied whoever had the unfortunate task of dusting and cleaning the place. There were doors on either side of the room that were halfway ajar, revealing more of the same.

A thin, tall woman, with salt and pepper hair pulled back into a severe bun, sharp brown eyes, and round glasses atop a crooked nose stepped into the room from the door on the left side. She wore a linen tunic bearing the Order's sigil and had a dagger in her belt but no other visible weapons. This was the first sister (or brother for that matter) who Asha had seen in the garrison without armor and with only one weapon. Though she did notice the padded appearance and additional stitching indicating many layers of fabric, it was likely gambeson and therefore not a fair judgement to say she wasn't wearing any armor. It would save her from a small amount of slashing damage and would fit easily under more substantial armor. Carrying a stack of thin, worn books and loose papers, she stepped to the center of the back wall and faced the recruits.

"Good morning, recruits," she said in a nasally voice with a faint accent Asha didn't recognize. "Here you will be conducting your literary trials. File through one at a time and collect your primers and work papers, then find a seat at a desk. You will find the assignments in the primer, but do not write in my primers. That is why you have the paper. Once you have completed all of the assignments, you will return the primer and finished papers to me."

When she finished these instructions, the recruits did as they were told. Asha estimated there were about twenty of them in the small room, only half the number at the training ground yesterday. Even so, they filled the room, which was probably why they were split up. She wondered how the other half knew not to be there that morning. Had they already done this trial? Then she realized that all the recruits present were from the destructive group, so the others had likely received different instructions after the trials ended yesterday.

After a few minutes, all of the recruits had collected a primer and handful of paper and found a desk. They sat quietly for a few moments, and then a younger man, dressed exactly the same as the woman even down to the dagger, came in from the opposite door, carrying a large tray full of inkwells and pens. Without a word, he distributed them. Each recruit was issued their own pen but shared an inkwell between two of them. The man with the tray left as silently as he had come.

"Now that you have all of your supplies, you may begin. You have two hours," the woman said and sat down in a wooden chair in the corner, facing the desks. She picked up a book and opened it to read. Then she spoke again, as if she'd forgotten something. "Oh, and no talking amongst yourselves. Despite what you may think, cheating will not actually assist your brethren. And it will result in your expulsion."

This seemed a bit extreme to Asha but didn't truly affect her. She didn't know anyone there, and therefore had no one to talk amongst, much less cheat with. Opening the primer, she read the first assignment. It was written in the common language of Anitaris, Antitase. All citizens of the Empire were required to speak and write it fluently, so this was unsurprising. Asha's education may have been home-spun, but she slipped in and out of common as easily as her native northern Labhairt. It instructed her to label her papers with her name and number them in order, front and back, in the upper-left corner.

The other assignments seemed to focus on reading comprehension and vocabulary, with each one getting progressively more difficult and requiring a longer answer. Then it abruptly switched to easier questions but required the answer to be written in her local dialect. These followed suit by progressing in difficulty for a while. Then it switched to Gallico, the high tongue of the nobility and religious. Asha understood it spoken very well and could speak it decently, but she struggled to read and write it. The conjugation and sentence structure had never made sense to her. She did her best, but it took her a long time, and she wasn't sure about half of her answers. Sighing, she wished then that Jenna, her fourteen-year-old middle sister, was there. Jenna liked languages, calligraphy, and other boring academic pursuits. She was exceptional at them as well.

After the Gallico assignments, there were assignments in two other languages she didn't know, so she skipped them. Staring at each one, she tried to guess what language it was. She had no idea, and looking at the words wasn't going to make the answer suddenly reveal itself. Raising her head, she saw that about a third of the other recruits had already finished and left the room. So, she got up and delivered her papers and primer to the sister who still sat in the chair, facing them. She didn't look like she had moved at all, except to turn her page, but based on the stack of primers and papers on the table next to her, that couldn't have been true.

"You are dismissed for now. Be back here for your training assignment at the ringing of the third bell. The provision hall will open soon for the midday meal if you are hungry," she told her after she took and briefly scanned Asha's papers. The provision hall sounded like a great idea, so that is where she headed.

As Asha walked to the provision hall, she passed between the great garrison wall and a large but unremarkable stone building. It was the administrative building for the Order of Holy Heroes. Inside it on the eastern lower level, seated inside a small office, leaning with his elbows on his desk, was Bernard Paynes, the Commandant of the training regimen of the Order.

Bernard squinted at the correspondence in his hands. He had to hold it rather close to his face to read the small handwriting, and this made him wonder if he should seek evaluation for spectacles. Could the healers fix his eyes? He didn't want to wear spectacles. They aged the face, and he had enough items to keep track of on a daily basis.

His thoughts were interrupted by a knock on the mostly open door to his office. He looked away from the letter to acknowledge his assistant, Rupert.

"Everyone is here and ready for the meeting if you are, sir."

"Yes, thank you. I will be right there." Bernard stood and straightened his arming doublet from where it bunched while seated under his brigandine cuirass. Then he stepped out into the meeting hall just outside his office. His subordinates all stood around the large table. He sat at the head of the table and instructed them to sit as well. Rupert took the seat on his left-hand side. His three top training officers, Brothers Gerard and Arthur, and Sister Ceceila, were next to Rupert. Across from them were their sergeant counterparts, two sisters and a brother who were well-experienced but didn't have the noble blood to be officers. And on his right-hand side was his secretary, Joan.

"We are here to discuss the placement of our latest batch of recruits by their affinities and skills. Let us begin."

Bernard struggled to pay attention to the lesser Mages' placement suggestions from his team. He trusted their judgement in most things, and he was distracted by the letter he had read before the meeting began. It foretold of another meeting he would have to attend tomorrow evening, with the Order's Master and the rest of the High Council.

A report had reached the Master that the traders from the Pacatus family had finished their sales and were preparing to leave the Capital and return northward. This wouldn't have been of any note, except that, although they had traveled all that way, they had not answered the Order's summons. No messenger, pigeon, letter, or what the Order had truly hoped for, a young Seer, had been delivered to them. In that meeting, they would have to decide what they were going to do about it. They could not allow their summons to be ignored without consequence, but were they prepared to take these children by force? Perhaps they should have sent agents, not letters, to the families of young, powerful children in the Empire. A letter could be ignored or 'lost', but an agent was much more convincing and could impress the importance of a matter, assuage fears, and, if necessary, enforce the summons.

"With your approval, sir." Brother Arthur's voice cut into his thoughts. "That settles all the low to medium mana recruits' placements." Brother Arthur paused and waited for Bernard's nod before continuing. "And brings us to the high mana recruits." His distraction had made him miss the boring placements. Maybe he should have been regretful and more diligent, but he wasn't. He was stretched thin these past few weeks and decided he could apply his diligence where it really mattered.

Sister Cecelia passed three clay tablets to him. "We have several suggestions for the interracial ballast that is being formed."

Bernard sat up a bit more and took the tablets. "Truly? If we wish to add new talent to it, we must be very certain. The High Council and the Master will have their eyes on this new type of ballast. If we want it to work long-term or be permitted in the future, this first trial must function well."

"Of course, sir," Cecelia's sergeant added. "We desire to test them further and trial the ballast as a whole before making our final placement."

Bernard nodded and began reading the trial marks on the first tablet.

"As you can see," Cecelia continued, "the she-Elf performed very well. She exceeded our expectations for a non-human Mage."

Very well, indeed. She received top marks in all two-handed weapons, one-handed swords and axes, and showed great levels of mana in her spells. Then again, he wasn't terribly surprised by her mana level. She had been selected by her people to represent them in this new trial of intermingling the races. He didn't imagine the Council of Queens would send a weak Mage. He quickly calculated how many Iulru would be in three hundred and seven years. Forty-three? After adulthood, mana grew slowly with age, showing an observable increase every seven years. That could make even a tiny bit of mana into a massive power bank. Her archery and riding were passable, but that had been expected for one of the sea-faring Elves. The riding in particular would not be hard to improve with some training.

"Yes, I think she will be an excellent candidate for the interracial ballast. Next?"

He picked up the next tablet. Surprise hit him as he read the name, then frustration.

"Next is a destructive woman from the north. She showed—"

Bernard held up his hand and cut Cecelia off. "The Pacatus girl is here? In our barracks? She was to be brought to me as soon as she arrived. Why is there a child in my barracks?" His tone was hard and flat.

Confused silence answered him for a few moments before Cecelia spoke again. "There isn't, sir."

"Pacatus isn't in the barracks? Where is she?"

"She is in the barracks, but she isn't a child. She's twenty-two years. Fully an adult, sir."

The frustration eased. There was not a five-year-old unattended in the barracks, or worse, near the armory. It was replaced by confusion equal to that of his subordinates.

"She volunteered for service?" he asked. Why would the Pacatus family send an older girl? The summons was clear whom the order sought.

"Uh, I don't..." Sister Cecelia stuttered. Not her area. Bernard turned to look at Joan, who was hurriedly flipping through papers, trying to find the Pacatus girl's intake record. The group sat in a pregnant hush until she did.

"Here it is." She chuckled nervously. This situation had everyone worked up, it seemed. Rightly so, the High Council was preparing to deliberate on the use of force against Imperial citizens, and the girl had already arrived. The consequences for this error could have been (and may still be) great.

"No, she presented a summons, sir." Joan handed him the summons that had been included in her record. He scanned it, then looked at the trial tablet in front of him. The first names didn't match. Had the Pacatus family sent a substitute? A headache grew behind his eyes.

"Rupert."

"Yes, sir?"

"Go and find her. Bring her to my office. I want this directly from the Kelpie's mouth. Now."

"Yes, sir." Rupert stood rapidly and strode out of the meeting hall.

Bernard set the tablet and summons down. He picked up the third and final tablet the trainers had selected.

"I will review her tablet and the possibility of her placement after this error is sorted. Tell me about the final candidate."

"Yes, sir. Another destructive Mage," Brother Arthur answered. "Wilford Artifex, twenty-one years, high marks in two-handed weapons, archery, and riding. His mana levels meet the minimum requirement you set for the interracial ballast, and he has a unique take on defensive spells."

"Unique how?" Bernard asked, confirming Brother Arthur's summary as he scanned the tablet.

"A ring of fire, sir."

Bernard harumphed approvingly.

"His footwork needs improvement," Brother Gerard cut in.

"Two-handed weapons are not preferred for casters, but this is not disqualifying. Does his footwork require more improvement than can be accomplished before the date of march?" He looked pointedly at Brother Gerard.

"I don't think so." Gerard swallowed. "But that will depend on how well he responds to instruction and if the underlying issue is poor prior training or lack of strength."

"I understand. This is what you meant by further testing them?" he asked and set the tablet aside.

"One of them, yes sir."

"Very well. The she-Elf will be moved to the new ballast along with the two Dwarven Artificers. Tentatively adding Artifex as the first destructive Mage, Pacatus as an even more tentative second. I have put out inquiries regarding a healer. That leaves one more position. It should be filled with an experienced Infinitus brother or sister. This group will need a strong, binding hand to guide them. Elves, Dwarves, and powerful youngsters. Goddess help the one who must lead this ballast..." he trailed off at the end of his statement and slumped as much as the cuirass would allow into his chair. The overwhelming weight of this project struck him and chased away any hint of excitement he'd had when he pitched the task to the High Council.

Cecelia finally spoke again. "We did have a suggestion for that too, sir."

"Hmmm?"

"Brother Odo Bleolydd, sir."

Bernard straightened and fully faced her. "Odo? Is he ready?" He paused then added, "Is he willing?"

"He is recovered from his broken bond," she answered.

"That's not what I asked," he chided, then added, "But then I should be asking him those questions. I can't expect you to know them. Joan, when Rupert returns, have him arrange a meeting with Odo as early as is convenient, please."

"Yes, sir," she replied, jotting down a quick note.

"Very well. That concludes the meeting for today. I would also like to see the sentry sergeant that checked in the Pacatus girl. Send him or her to me immediately."

A chorus of 'yes, sirs answered him as he stood and returned to his office to await the arrival of the Pacatus girl. He needed to straighten this mess out and have it done before the High Council meeting the next evening.

Asha had just entered the archives with about half an hour to spare before the instructed time and was taking a seat when a harried-looking young man burst in. He appeared to only be a few years older than her, average height, with light brown hair atop a round face that was currently lined with worry. This brother wore the more familiar brigantine armor that she had seen most of the Order in, and an arming sword on his belt. She imagined there must be a reason for the difference in armament and wondered if the Order saved funds by only outfitting their members for the minimum danger they could reasonably expect to encounter. This made her wonder what greater danger this man could reasonably expect to require both heavier armor and a sword in the garrison, and why the people working the archives wouldn't expect it.

She was jarred from her musing by the sound of her name, not directed at her, though. The newcomer had spoken it to the woman who had administered the written trial and was now presiding over the next assignments that would be handed out.

"I don't know the new recruits by sight," the woman snapped at him. "How would I know if she has returned yet?"

"I have," Asha replied. The pair were startled by the interjection and turned to face her.

"Impertinent thing, aren't you?" The woman said flatly. "Even northern girls should know not to interrupt their superiors."

"In the north, we don't consider someone speaking about us our superior," Asha snapped back.

The woman's face flushed, and she took a step forward, opening her mouth to reply, but the man cut her off.

"You're Asha Pacatus?" he asked.

"I am."

"Not Dendra?"

"No, not Dendra," she replied, not liking where this line of questioning was heading.

"You will come with me. The Commandant wants to speak with you."

That can't be good, Asha thought. That was definitely worse than whatever trouble she was about to get into with the woman in charge of the Academic trial. Not that she had any choice. She stood up.

"You can't take her now," the woman protested. "I am preparing to give out assignments. She can't leave without an assignment!"

"You don't have her assignment," he replied flatly.

She sputtered and started flipping through the papers on the small desk.

He sighed and said, "You don't have her assignment because the Commandant has not yet issued it. He is waiting to speak to her. Do you want to continue keeping him waiting, looking for something that does not yet exist, or can I continue with *my* assignment?"

The woman huffed and stopped turning papers. "Which is?"

"To bring her to the Commandant." He drew out the words, his patience for this jurisdiction match clearly wearing thin. The woman turned away and began muttering about uppity recruits, and belligerent assistants, and all the extra paperwork she would have to do.

"Follow me," he said, leading Asha out of the building. They walked for a few minutes in silence, and she thought this would continue, but then he spoke.

"Word of caution, Asha: I don't know how it is in the north, but in the Capital, the young and non-initiated don't speak back to the instructors. Even if they insult you. Next time, there might not be urgent business to save you from the consequences."

Asha tried to think of something to say to that but couldn't. Especially because his words did feel like a warning, not a scolding. As they walked the rest of the way in silence, she felt very small and out of place. She was very, very far from home and needed to remember that, if she was to do anything worthwhile here.

Fear reared its ugly head in her mind. She had been so caught up in the tension with the instructor that she had missed the context of it. What had the assistant said? *"You don't have her assignment because the Commandant has not yet issued it. He is waiting to speak to her."* That did not bode well for her. Perhaps it hadn't been a mistake that Dendra's name was listed and not hers.

Chapter 12

Mago

The cries of gulls and smell of saltwater were beginning to feel like old companions to Mago, despite only being in, or more accurately near, Hadrumentum for a little over a month. This was only his second visit inside the city. Bomilcar's improvised sappers had completed their tunnel under the city's wall a few days ago. That same night, after sunset, the Warlord's son had used his dragon's breath to burn the wooden supports, and that section of stone had collapsed with the tunnel. Warriors had waited in ranks just outside of arrow range and expected to take the city by dawn. The king of Hadrumentum must have had some idea of their plan, perhaps a spy, but more likely people inside had heard or seen the exhaustive work of tunneling. He had placed a company or so of defenders nearby, and they reached the newly made gap first. The defenders were able to hold back the tide of attackers for a while but took heavy losses doing so. After an hour or so, their semi-circle of shields buckled, then broke. The Dragon Riders' infantryman poured through like a dam breaking. A few pockets of resistance held on for another day or two in towers and well-built nobles' houses.

Now Mago stood on the wall, overlooking the harbor and the boatyard. On the horizon, white sails grew slowly larger where the deep blue of the ocean met the pale blue of the sky. He wasn't sure if there was much point trying to count them now; it couldn't be accurate until they were much closer, or if one had a distance-looking glass. Poor bastards had no idea that they were already too late to provide any relief to the besieged city.

Heavy footsteps struck the stone, accompanied by the distinctive creak and clink of plate armor. He turned his head slightly but was pretty sure of who would appear in his periphery.

"Bomilcar, my friend." He spoke first when the younger man came to stand beside him. "What brings you here?"

"What brings *you* here?" the Dragon Rider asked without malice. "Seems like you're always wandering around staring at things."

Mago forced himself to chuckle warmly. "The smell, my dear man. I'm sure it's too much to ask that your warriors conquer in a less gruesome manner, but I find that up here, the scent of bodies left to rot in the street is blown away by the sea breeze."

"Ah." Bomilcar nodded. "That makes sense. I suppose I have gotten used to it by now, but one cannot expect a whore master to have the same stomach as a dragon knight. You will have to forgive me then, as I must ask you to step away from your relief and join me in walking back into the gruesome streets."

"No need for forgiveness." Mago didn't think that forgiveness for a man like Bomilcar was possible. At least, he hoped it wasn't. "What is it that you need from me?"

"Nothing." Now Bomilcar chuckled. "I am trying to give you a gift."

"A gift?"

Bomilcar nodded and gestured for Mago to follow him as he returned the way he had come.

Walking in silence, the two men descended the wall. Gisco and several of Bomilcar's warriors in mail fell in behind them. Mago let the silence stretch as his companion didn't seem inclined to break it. He desperately hoped that the gift wasn't more female captives.

As they walked through the winding streets, the signs of war were everywhere. Splintered doors and window shutters, burnt hulls of shops, signs and cloth shades dangling smashed and torn, dark brown stains of blood pooling here and splattered there along the cobblestone streets and mud-plaster walls, and, of course, the bodies of the dead, bloating and discolored in the hot sun of the early dry season.

Mago pulled a finely embroidered linen handkerchief from a leather pouch hanging from his woven belt. He held it over his nose and mouth.

It did little to dull the scent, but it was better than nothing. Bomilcar must have seen his action from the corner of his eye and turned to say, "I do apologize, friend. I will speak to my brother about having the slaves or remaining residents remove the bodies, but at the moment, I'm not sure we can spare them."

"I will manage until it can be done," Mago replied. "Though you do make me quite curious about what it is you cannot spare them from? If you permit me to ask, that is?"

"Of course, I permit it." Bomilcar waved his hand dismissively. "Who are you going to tell? Your whores?" He smiled broadly at his own joke, having no idea how wrong he was. Mago smiled back, knowing full well whom he intended to tell. "The slaves are repairing the wall. And the residents, well, that's a project Father wouldn't even want whores to gossip about."

There it was; confirmation of his suspicion. The Dragon Riders did want something from this city!

Something they needed intact and required the assistance of the resident tradesmen and secrecy. He affected a nonchalant air, stuffing his excited interest down deep.

"Repairing the wall? After all the trouble you went through to damage it. May I infer that you intend to remain here a good while then?"

The Warlord's son almost looked sheepish but seemed to cover it quickly. "You may infer that. In fact, that has something to do with your gift, but don't ask now! We're nearly there. Leave it a surprise for a few more moments."

Mago discreetly observed that they were now entering the wider, more ornate streets of the upper-class district. The houses were finer made and not nearly so close together, though they were just as worse for wear as the lower streets. Worse, in fact, as they had undoubtedly been the larger focus of the looting.

"Very well, I won't spoil your fun," he said. "Hopefully, the wall will be easier to rebuild than it was to destroy?" He knew it wouldn't be. Craftsmanship was never easier to repair than it was to destroy. But he wanted to dig deeper without being obvious, so he feigned ignorance instead of interest.

Bomilcar scoffed. "Don't be foolish, my friend. I just hope we can get it done before Father returns from his march eastward. He didn't want me to damage the wall but starving them out like he said was taking ages. And I don't think he can be too angry if the wall is serviceable again before he arrives."

"Your plan was certainly quick," Mago replied, skirting a pair of bodies in fine silks and the wide stain of their lifeblood. "Are you expecting to put the wall to service again? Should I be prepared to move my whores further away from the city?"

"No," Bomilcar said sharply. Then in a gentler tone, "Just wait until you see your gift. No more questions until then."

"As you wish." Mago wasn't sure why that question had struck a nerve, especially considering the approaching fleet. It was unlikely to be a trade fleet, and the Siegers, it seemed, would soon find themselves sieged since they were not moving on.

The street took on a moderate incline as they moved deeper into the richer area of the city. Clay-brick houses grew larger and smoother, with better ventilation and more ornate decoration. Fenced courtyards turned into walled courtyards, and there was an increased amount of shaded outdoor seating areas within them. Mago could see the King's palace at the top of the hill, an impressive sight of carved marble columns and double storied walls that must have taken years of taxes to import and build with.

Bomilcar, however, stopped in front of a mansion that was perhaps two furloughs away from the palace, though they shared a wall along their grounds. It would have been an impressive house if it had been further away from a palace. The gate hung splintered and limp on its hinges, but the chest-height stone wall was intact. Previously well-manicured grounds had been trampled. There were drag marks across the pathways and bloodstains among the decorative shrubs. The front door was in similar condition to the gate, but Mago saw no evidence of fire or damage on the smooth clay walls or window holes.

"Do you like it?" Bomilcar asked him after he had looked at the mansion for a few moments. "Do you think it will be large enough?"

"It is a very fine house. Large enough for what, my friend?" Mago asked.

"Large enough for your retinue. I can't give you the palace, you understand, and this is the next-largest house in the district."

"This is the gift you spoke of. This mansion?"

Bomilcar chuckled. "Of course. Why do you think I dragged you up here? I wish to give you a palace within the city."

Mago smiled back at him. "Our current camp would be an inconvenient walk if you move your own retinue into that palace."

"Indeed." Bomilcar's smile widened. "And so, I can reward my friends and give myself greater ease."

"You are clever, indeed. Such a grand gift calls for grander words than 'thank you', but I find myself at quite a loss for them just now. Perhaps I shall write you a poem later."

"Ha!" Bomilcar laughed. "I think I would prefer a few nights of free services over a poem."

"Then that is what you shall have, my friend."

Tearing down and moving his camp had not taken long; they were quite used to that as followers of the army. Indeed, his retinue of servants, whores, and eunuchs had practiced the process so frequently, they were usually ready to march before the army. Cleaning and settling into the mansion inside Hadrumentum's upper-class district took much longer. Three days had passed, and Mago could no longer smell the death of the former residents. It was nice to be surrounded by real walls and a roof. Walls that actually dampened the sounds of his whores at work, and a roof that kept the sun off as the days grew hotter.

Sophonisba came to stand in the open doorway of his room on the second story of the house but didn't speak until he looked up.

"Lord Bomilcar is here, master. He is not dressed to see the girls."

"I see, Sophonisba. Thank you." He rose and descended the stairs ahead of her quickly without giving the appearance of rushing.

"My friend! How can I help you this day? My debt to you for this lovely house is not yet repaid," Mago said, though he saw that his mistress was correct. Bomilcar usually came in only his tunic and sword belt if he sought companionship. This day, he was dressed in newly acquired full plate with his visored helm held under his arm. Several of the pieces were much less worn and better polished than the rest. It seemed his plunder of the city had included the armories.

Bomilcar smiled at him conspiratorially. "That, it is not, but your debt will have to wait until this eve, I think. In the meantime, I wish to invite you to a spectacle."

"At your wish, sir. What sort of spectacle do you have in mind?"

"We're going to put an end to that fleet that is approaching. My scouts report that they are armed and bearing the old king's colors beside the colors of the pirate confederation of the Trebri. It should be a good show."

"The pirates have confederations now. What next, kelpies will have a king? The Gnomes unite into an Empire? Gisco! Bring my robes. I'm going out."

He pulled on his outer robes, a deep red with stripes of rich blue, discreetly checking the hidden inner lining for his dagger, then stepped out the door with Gisco close behind. Bomilcar turned back toward the palace.

"Forgive me if I don't walk you there myself, but I think the wall overlooking the harbor where I found you before will give you the best view of the action. I, myself, have a dragon to get aloft."

"Fret not, my friend. I remember the way. I wouldn't want to miss the action." Mago hurried through the streets, bodyguard trailing him like a menacing shadow. It was a good thing, too, as he was not watching his way and nearly got himself turned around before Gisco placed a large hand on his shoulder and pointed the correct route to the harbor outlook.

He needed to get a grip on himself. How could he pass along any information of use if he couldn't ground himself enough to pay attention. Not that he had any idea just yet how he would pass this information along anyway; he had not established a contact. First things first, get to the outlook, then he needed to note every detail of stratagem he could squeeze out that might help the Imperial Navy in dealing with the Dragon Riders at sea.

His feet stuttered, and he nearly fell as the realization hit him. He steadied himself and kept walking briskly, shaking off Gisco's concern. One of the Dragon Riders' marshals had complained to Kanmi that his talents were being wasted herding shipwrights and dock workers. He had found the answer to his question. The Dragon Riders needed Hadrumentum mostly intact because they were building a fleet of their own. How hadn't he seen it sooner?

He had felt an urgency to notify the Empire of all the intelligence he could gather because deep in his subconscious, he had known that they would face invasion next. Well, not truly next; next would be the Trebri island chain that lay between the two continents.

Those islands were not truly united, though. At any given moment, this warlord or that pirate captain held any given island. They constantly changed hands, and governors would retreat and return as often as the tides. And how convenient that likely the largest organized force they could muster was sailing within range of dragon flight right now?

He reached the top of the wall in time to hear the beat of leathery wings and the distinctive rumble of the dragons overhead. A bone-chilling sound that never failed to make his heart jump in his throat and his eyes instinctively search for cover. Half hiss, half roar, like the wheezes of a dying lion projected through a hollow ram's horn. The two dragons passed over him, higher than three of the city's walls stacked on top of each other. He could barely make out the saddle girths wrapped behind their forelimbs, which they tucked up underneath them as they flew.

The dragons flew out toward the fleet that bobbed on the surf, still at least a dozen or more leagues away from the harbor. Flying parallel, the dragons slowly gained altitude until they were within two leagues of the first ships. Then they both veered sharply away from one another, turning perpendicular to their previous flight. Mago counted his heartbeats as he watched them bank. Eleven passed before the fell beasts straightened out and continued the new trajectory. How did that compare to whales? Surely, a whaling harpoon would be the only thing tough enough to pierce a dragon hide. That, or a ballista bolt. Maybe a cannon ball? But could any of those be turned toward the heavens? For the sailors' sake, he hoped so.

Banking again, the dragons turned inward once more after reaching some unknown distance from each other. This time, the maneuver appeared slower, but perhaps that was a trick of the distance. He counted his heartbeats again all the same. Seventeen heartbeats, and the right-hand dragon suddenly tucked its wings tight to its body and dove down at the nearest ship. Moments before it would have impacted the mainsail, the dragon flared its wings out and curtailed its downward momentum. In the same motion, its chest glowed a mere two heartbeats before fire spewed from its gaping mouth and engulfed the ship's rigging. Puffs of powder evidenced the firing of cannons. But all the explosions fell dreadfully short of the dragon. The angle was wrong; the cannon balls' trajectory never stood a chance of impact.

The left-hand dragon decreased its altitude at a much more leisurely pace, making wide circles around its chosen ship. It descended in smaller and smaller rings until the dragon could have alighted on the crow's nest. Then the dragon breathed flame onto the deck as the crew abandoned the cannons and dove overboard.

Over and over, this process repeated until Mago could almost predict the moment when the fire would fall on the helpless ships. Only one of the ships showed any real resistance. A ship with three triangular sails and a narrow bow fired a harpoon up at the left-hand dragon, disrupting its slow circles. The harpoon shot up, right at the dragon's belly. But the dragon tucked its left wing and rolled sharply away. Six heartbeats on that one, Mago counted. The harpoon missed, but if a wise operator could estimate the dragon's dodge...

Mago committed all his concentration to memorizing the scene before him. If the Imperial Navy stood any chance at all, they must be able to anticipate the dragon's flight and maneuvers. Perhaps he would send a sketch along with his next report, detailing the dragons themselves as well as the battle.

He pondered how he would send out his next report as the final ship in the fleet caught fire and listed in the waters below the darkening sky. Had evening already fallen? Mago had been entranced by the tragedy before him, hoping against his better judgment that even one ship might survive. Nausea built in his stomach and rose behind his jaw as he realized how unlikely it would be that the Imperial Navy could slow the Dragon Riders. He closed his eyes and whispered a desperate prayer to all seven of the Gods to preserve his beloved Empire. Based on what he had seen this day, only divinity could save it.

Chapter 13

Bernard and Asha

Bernard sat in his office waiting for Rupert to return. He instinctively reached for the brass pendant hanging by a slender chain around his neck. Pulling it out from under his arming doublet, he thumbed it absentmindedly. It bore his family crest. He descended from one of the founding members of the Order, who descended from a wealthy family that fell into hard times and bad trade deals. His ancestor had joined the mercenary band that later became the Order of Holy Heroes with a good horse, better weapons, no money, and a thimble-full of noble blood. After the king had used the band as the tip of his spear to make himself into an Emperor, Bernard's ancestor had much opportunity to make himself into a great man as one of the founding members of a new and powerful order. Unfortunately for Bernard, he had managed his opportunity just as poorly as his predecessors had managed their wealth. He was determined to manage his fortune better than any of them. Nearly thirty years ago, Bernard had entered the Order with nothing but a name and a finely made hand-me-down sword. He worked hard and found that he had a natural skill for dealing with people. Now in a position on the High Council that should have been his by right, he intended to hold it and pass more than just a name on to his own children. He wondered if his ancestors were proud.

Dropping the pendant, he turned his attention to the tablet he had not read during the meeting. He stared at the name for a moment. It was still the wrong one, yet she had answered the summons. Why? Type:

Destructive. She was not trying to pretend to be Dendra, either. Not that she could have fooled the Order.

He let his gaze move lower and read her results. What was it that made his instructors think she should be on the new interracial ballast? Perhaps he should have let them explain. Excellent swordsman. Proficient with all one-handed weapons and shield. Proficient with two-handed weapons. Excellent rider. Failed mounted spear, but the notes indicated that she showed evidence of training with thrown weapons and suggested testing of spears and javelins on foot. Failed lance, but that was expected. Not many recruits came to the Order with that training. She was a fast and accurate archer, topping out at the hundred-pound bow. Impressive for a woman her age; even men her age struggled with higher draw weights than that without substantial training. She must have trained with that, too. In fact, he could tell someone had invested an awful lot of time and resources into training her. Her family wasn't noble, but they had become quite wealthy in the past few decades. Undoubtedly, they poured at least some of that money into trainers for their next generation.

The next line held the answer to his question. She was incredibly powerful, especially for a woman just past the cusp of adulthood. She had received top marks for her offensive and defensive spells, with a note that she admitted to holding back on the offensive for fear of damaging surrounding structures.

Further testing was recommended miles outside the city walls. Her shield spell was basic, but she held it around twenty-three people without straining.

If this wasn't the girl they had summoned, how powerful would Dendra be? How many more top-marked, highly trained young people did the Pacatus family have tucked away in those hills? He sat back in his chair as he realized they might very well have an army holed up in the northern mountain range guided by not one, but two Seers. It would take an even larger army with many Voids to get that girl if they didn't comply. He shook his head and chuckled without humor. They couldn't even siege them and hope to starve them out. The family was primarily natural Mage sheep farmers. No doubt they could produce all the food they would ever need.

Indeed, if they didn't already; they traded often, but surely that was only the excess.

A knock startled him. Joan stepped in. "A message came for you, sir. From Inglerho."

"Thank you, Joan, I have been expecting it."

She handed it to him and stepped back, waiting in case he wished to dictate a reply. He scanned it and looked up at her.

"That is all, Joan. I will need to meet with some others before I reply. Thank you."

She nodded and stepped out.

Well, they had their healer. Almost. Enya was willing to return to the Order and swear a second septum oath on the condition that the Crown give her a proper surname and legitimize her.

The Empire had standardized the method of passing along surnames long ago. There had been confusion in the decades after the unification when the province's nobles had begun to intermarry, and which name the children carried was disputed. The Emperor had decreed that the succession (as well as other inheritance matters) would be written into the marriage contract. Within a few years, this also filtered down to the lower classes. But neither he nor any of the following Emperors or Empresses ever cared to issue an edict on bastards. No marriage contract, no inheritance, and no surname.

Therefore, every province in the Empire had its own way of naming bastards. Berseau in the southeast gave them Waves as a surname. The central farmlands of Colchester gave them Curtassien, which meant cut stalk in the local tongue. Cunabula on the southwest coast allowed them to use the mother's surname. Here in the Capital, they were not called by any surname, and 'Illegitimate' would follow their given name on any legal documents. In the northern provinces, they were called 'Nameless' and were not permitted to use anything but their given name on legal documents.

Enya Nameless wanted a name in exchange for a second term of service. It would be unusual to swear a short-term oath a second time, but there was no rule against it. He would need to seek further counsel on the legal method to give her a name, but he was sure that no one on the High Council would object.

A second knock sounded, louder and faster. Rupert stepped inside with a young woman beside him. She had reddish-brown hair plaited plainly but neatly, sharp and intelligent gray eyes, and a cool, composed expression on her fairly handsome face. Moderately tall for a woman, she was dressed in a simple but finely made woolen tunic and breaches in the northern style. She wore an arming belt, but it held a leather whip rather than a sword. That needed to change. Sturdy boots covered her feet and a bracelet sat snugly on her left wrist. The only other jewelry she wore was a ring on the second finger of the same hand. Different types of runes were etched into the whip, boots, and bracelet. So, the family was rich in Artificers as well.

"Commandant Bernard Paynes, I have found Asha Pacatus," Rupert introduced formally.

The woman brought her right hand up in front of her face in a fist with the clenched fingers facing him, elbow and shoulders at right angles in a Northern salute. Or northwest anyway. The northern province east of the Dwarf lands, Bahay, never had a standardized salute before the Empire conquered them and therefore easily adopted the Imperial salute. It was supposed to be done holding a sword, simultaneously showing no intent to harm with the sword pointed down and no intent to block with the wrist turned in a disadvantageous position. Like all but the most cultured northerners, the only concession to the Imperial sense of propriety she gave was to do it with an empty fist. In her home province of Dihain, she would have been expected to draw her weapon to render proper respect.

He rose and placed his open left palm on his chest, leaning forward at the hips slightly, returning her salute with the Imperial one. His rank did not require him to do so, but an equal to him in the north would have, and she would be less likely to give him the information he sought if he offended her. She returned her arm to her side in response to his salute.

"Thank you, Rupert, that is all for now. Please take a chair...Asha, is it?"

Rupert stepped out, and the young woman grabbed the wooden chair from along the wall and placed it squarely in front of his desk. Then she sat in it, back straight, chest out, shoulders back, hands resting on her thighs, face calm, boots firmly planted on the floor. He was sure she didn't realize that twisting her ring with her thumb broke the bravado she attempted to project. Not that he had any intention of pointing this out, as he reclaimed his own seat.

"Yes," she answered after he had done so. "My name is Asha Pacatus. Your assistant called this 'urgent business'. I don't understand what business with me you could have that is so urgent?"

Bernard had practiced keeping a neutral face for years, decades even, and he still struggled to keep from grinning at her gall. She was technically within the bounds of politeness with that statement but only technically. Wisdom would have called to listen and wait for him to tell her, no matter how badly she wanted to know. Instead, she chose audacity. Blunt honesty would be his best tool to get her to be candid in return.

He placed the summons and the tablet facing her on the lower edge of his desk. "It is urgent because the penalties for ignoring an Imperial summons are quite severe. Why don't you try to explain to me why your family thinks they can substitute whomever they please without the Order's approval?" He paused to let the weight of his words settle. "Unless my administrators are incorrect, and you did volunteer?"

Her expression was anything but neutral. He watched concern, anticipation, and frustration all dance across her face in rapid succession.

"No," she said frowning. "I did not volunteer. What do you mean by approval?"

He kept annoyance from clouding his expression. "You can't really believe the Order of Holy Heroes, His Majesty's Enforcement, and Weapon of the Gods would simply allow their will to be subverted by a family of sheep farmers from the north?"

Anger overtook the other emotions on her face, and she spat out, "I can't believe the prestigious Order would stoop to kidnapping."

"An Imperial summons is hardly kidnapping."

"Having the Emperor in your pocket doesn't make it right!" Those gray eyes blazed, and she lifted off her chair a bit as her voice rose above polite volumes.

He indulged himself in leaning forward and pinching the bridge of his nose. "Belligerence doesn't either. An Imperial summons cannot be ignored, especially not in these treacherous times."

"It wasn't ignored. I am here. I am the eldest and the only of my sisters to be a full Mage! Dendra—" she grabbed the summons off his desk and held it up as she said her sister's name—"is five! She can't even use her mana yet! So, unfortunately, she will have to be excused from 'these treacherous times,'" she sneered his words back at him. "Better luck next calamity."

The Commandant snorted at that and regained his composure. He really needed to get a better hold on himself, but it had been a long day, and for all her piss and vinegar, he liked the young woman. 'Eldest' she had said. That meant she was the least powerful of her sisters; at least she would be when they all grew up and turned twenty-one. Sweet Goddess, when that happened, not even an army would pry them out of that glacier valley. He needed to cut through the bluster and hot air. He returned to blunt honesty.

"For the daughter and granddaughter of a Seer, you surely are blind to the danger your sister is in," he stated flatly. It had the desired effect. She fell silent, shoulders slackening a little, and she sat back in the chair. He rifled through the papers on his desk until he found the report he was looking for, then he handed it to her.

"Wh–what danger?" she asked as he started digging through the many stacks of paper on the right side of his desk. He didn't answer; he just handed her the report. The one detailing the atrocities in the southlands.

He watched her face blanche a little. Saw the horror and confusion in her eyes. He knew what she read. Knew it by heart now. He didn't enjoy forcing people to accept these Warlords were not only doing something previously believed impossible, but also gathering and murdering the most powerful children they came across.

"Dragons can't be ridden. They're wild animals. Wild fell beasts," she said when she looked up.

"We thought so, too, but this band of Warlords has found a way, and they are using them to great effect," he replied grimly. "We are not trying to kidnap your sister, but we have reason to believe the Dragon Riders are killing anyone who might be able to stop them. Now or in the future."

She stared at him for a few moments, searching his face for something. Whatever she was looking for, it seemed she found it. She deflated a bit and said, "But she's safe. My family can protect her! Surely, they won't make it that far north..." she trailed off, running out of belief in her own words.

"Is anyone safe from warmongers who can ride dragons?" he asked, balancing firmness and gentleness. "The Empire and the Order are preparing to do all we can to stop them at the coast, but we need to also prepare for the possibility that they will push inland. We are gathering the children we believe to be the most at risk and moving them to more protected places. Is that kidnapping, Asha?"

"Moving them and training them?" she countered.

"Receiving an education would be in their best interest," he replied slowly. For one so young, she was very prejudiced against the Order. Perhaps her expensive trainer was a deserter or other complainant.

"And it would be in the best interest of the Order if all the most powerful Mages of the next generation were indoctrinated before they have access to mana and ready to swear oaths as soon as they do. Still sounds like kidnapping."

Dynawach, give me strength. "Do you discount the possibility that something can be in the best interest of multiple people or entities?"

"People, sure." She regained her confidence once more. "Not entities, not Orders who demand people give up their impressionable children for their safety without even telling them the children are in danger. If this is about protecting children and not indoctrinating them for early induction, why not warn their parents and let them bring the children willingly? Why the secrecy?" She picked up the summons again and held it up over his desk. "Why threaten severe penalties?"

He sighed. She couldn't know he had actually suggested that, and he could not explain himself without giving her another reason to fight him on this. "The Emperor and the High Council of the Order do not think it wise to tell people of the dangers yet. It might cause panic. I think early training will save these children's lives, but you have a very cynical view of our Order for someone who willingly took her sister's place in it." It wasn't quite a question, but he had phrased it in a way that he knew would elicit an answer.

"I am not a child."

"And these children will be required to serve, as all Mages are. We are simply summoning them early, hoping that we can ensure their survival until the time for their service."

"They aren't required to serve in the Order."

"No, but the Order is the only entity capable of taking on such a task."

She had no answer to that. He let the silence stretch for a few moments, then said, "Regardless of what you think of our intentions, your sister was summoned, not you. You cannot simply take her place."

"Why not?" she challenged quietly. "You said we couldn't substitute without approval. How do I get approval?"

"Tell me why you're so certain your sister is safe, even from dragon fire?"

She paused, clearly weighing how much to tell him. "If the Order is successful and stops them at the coast, then she will never be in danger. If they aren't—" she paused—"then she would be dead long before they reach the northern provinces. She has a much better chance staying where she is, with a powerful family led by Seers and dug into a glacier valley."

"Dug in? Has your family built fortifications? Are they manned by trained soldiers like the Order has?"

The frustration of revealing more than she intended flashed in her eyes. "All the Mages in our family have met our Imperial obligations of service, and they have built our home in a way that can be defended."

"Perhaps you are right about your sister." She was a tough nut to crack. He would need to compromise with her. "I think she can be excused, but you have to cooperate with me. I like your passion and your audacity. I will speak to the High Council on your behalf, but you are going to do something for me."

"What do you want from me?" she said, eyes wary.

"I want you to dedicate yourself to the Order." She opened her mouth to object, but he raised a hand to stop her and continued, "I don't mean swearing an Infinitus oath, unless you wish to. I mean that while you are part of the Order, you dedicate yourself to it fully. You put aside your cynicism and prejudice and give the Order the chance to prove you wrong. I want you to give all that you have, for however long you choose to be our sister."

She leaned back against the chair as she mulled over his words. It was clear she didn't like them. *Good. If you wish to play at politics, young one, here is your first lesson: Real compromise displeases both parties.*

"I will give the Order my all," she said finally. "I can't promise to stop being cynical. I don't trust the Order. But I can promise to keep my prejudices to myself. If the Order is going to prove me wrong, it can whether I am cynical or not."

He chuckled, despite himself. A tough nut, indeed. If she put aside her distaste for the Order, she would be an exceptional asset to them, with a little training and mentorship. "I accept your counteroffer. You are dismissed. I will send for you again when I have an answer from the High Council."

"Good evening, Commandant." She saluted him and left his office.

Asha slowed her steps after she left the Commandant's office. She returned to the archives in time to receive a large stack of required reading. Falling in with the mass of recruits, she dropped the loaned books in assigned chests, then milled back out to the provisional hall. Surrounded by other recruits, she felt incredibly alone with the knowledge she carried. She needed to eat, but her stomach was tied in an anxious knot.

Warlords conquering the southern continent, *riding dragons*? How was that even possible? Could the Empire stop dragon fire? Could her family? They had a wall, a good armory, many Mages, and supplies enough for a siege. Excellent dragon fire fodder, no doubt. Did her mother and grandmother know about this? Surely their Spirit Sight had told them something. Why hadn't they warned her?

Asha couldn't think of a time before that she had ever wished someone was lying to her. And yet, he hadn't. Not once in the entire conversation. She always knew when people lied, a gift from her mother's blood. Her Spirit Sight was limited, minor affinities always were, but hers especially since it was a second minor. Most human Mages only had one, but being the oldest of a seventh daughter of a seventh daughter, by a seventh son had blessed her with two. She didn't know what the truth was, but she always knew when someone lied, no matter how small. From 'Oh, I'm doing just fine' to 'Thanks, I'll consider that', and even, 'Your mother and I think this is best for everyone' or 'I'm proud of you'. She always knew.

Sitting down at the bench, she went through the motions of eating.

You can't really believe that the Order of Holy Heroes, His Majesty's Enforcement, and Weapon of the Gods would simply allow their will to be subverted by a family of sheep farmers from the north?

Her fingers tightened on the spoon as his words echoed in her head. She wanted to drive it into his cool, brown eyes. He had kept his face a perfect mask of politeness. It almost hadn't felt like she spoke to a human until the very end.

The calm mask had slipped a little, or perhaps he lowered it intentionally.

I think she will have to be excused, but you have to cooperate with me. I like your passion and your audacity. I will speak to the High Council on your behalf, but you are going to do something for me.

She resumed eating, his words weighing heavy in her mind. It was quite unexpected. She had not planned to sandbag her duty to the Order. Keeping dishonor from her family was more important than her feelings. But giving the Order a chance? A chance to do what? Use her as kindling in a war of fire and blood?

And yet, someone had to stop the dragons and the people riding them. Stop them from taking slaves, burning homes, and murdering children.

Anyone who might be able to stop them. Now or in the future.

That could be any or all of her family. Certainly, all of her sisters. Her thoughts turned to their last morning meal together. The smiles, the banter, the ever-increasing volume of conversation. Her eyes watered a bit when she remembered each hug at her farewell.

She would do it. She would face the dragons and give the Order a chance so none of them would have to. She would find a way to get the approval for her substitution. Whatever it took.

Chapter 14

Bernard

The following evening, Bernard, along with his assistant Rupert and secretary Joan, entered the auberge for the High Council meeting regarding the Pacatus family and their apparent defiance of an Imperial summons. It was a large stone building, conveniently positioned next to the provision hall. He was not the first Council member to arrive this time. Other than the Master, he was the last. Six men and two women sat around a large rectangular table that ran down the center of the room. Behind each of them in chairs along the wall with small tables beside them for documents and notetaking were their assistants and secretaries. All of them wore armor and weaponry, as this was a formal meeting, not an evening tea. He surveyed the grim clean-shaven faces, and close-cropped hair or tight buns, most of them graying or showing signs of balding, for not a single member was under fifty. Bernard took his place among them along the inner side of the heavy oak table.

The Master, Louis Fulk, entered from a side door a few minutes later, and all of the low chatter ceased. All who were present rose and saluted him in the Imperial manner. He took his chair at the head of the table and said, "Good Evening, gentlemen and ladies, please return to your seats." When they had done so, he continued, "I assume everyone is aware of the purpose of this meeting. Since this is not part of our usual business, I assume no one will object to forgoing the reading of last meeting's minutes?" No one did, so again he continued, "Well, the traders from the Pacatus family in the north have begun their return home, and they did not acknowledge our summons, much less deliver the child Seer. What is to be done?"

Several of the other Council members shifted or opened their mouths to answer, but Bernard needed a little control to execute his plan and beat them all in answering the Master. "That is not fully true, pardon my frankness, Master."

"What do you mean? Do you have knowledge that the rest of us lack?" All eyes settled on him. Grand Commander Alonso Fernandez seemed the most piqued by the second question.

"Indeed, Master. The Pacatus traders dropped off one of their daughters as a recruit, just not the one we summoned." His declaration was met with silence, so he continued, "They present her as a substitute."

Grumbling and angry murmurs came from all sides of the table, but the Master cut in. "They sent a different Seer. Not the child?"

"No, Master. They sent a destructive. Asha Pacatus, eldest of seven daughters of the Seer, Ava Pacatus by Thomas Iurgium. She is of age for service, and they are—" he paused—"reluctant to send a child of five."

"I don't very well God damned care what they are bloody reluctant to do. They received a summons, and they are to fucking obey it or face the consequences!" Marshall Ramon Despuig burst out.

"Considering the unprecedented nature of the summons and that they have not been briefed on the imminent danger, I don't think it is entirely unreasonable to send a service-aged woman in the stead of a child, Ramon," chided the hospitaller, Isabella Navarre. Navarre had been the only other Council member who objected to hiding the danger to powerful children that the southern Warlords posed.

"That don't f—" Despuig started, but the Master cut him off.

"They sent a substitute? That would require approval and would still leave the child vulnerable if the Dragon Riders invade the continent. Did they consider this in their reluctance?"

"They petitioned me for approval and insist that this child, at least, is much less vulnerable than we may think."

"You," Hadrian West, the Order's High Priest, sneered, "are not empowered with such authority."

Bernard turned a hard stare at him and replied, "Which is why I bring the request before the High Council now."

"A substitution matters little," the Master cut in again. "The child has a service obligation to the Empire in time anyway. But accepting her older sister does nothing to protect her or educate her. What do you mean by less vulnerable, Bernard?"

"I mean that after talking with the older sister, I don't think she is at any higher risk where she is than she would be here, and—" he turned his gaze to Despuig—"that any consequences would be nearly impossible to mete out. Not without serious losses if the family should resist."

"Meaning?" the Master asked curtly.

Instead of answering directly, Bernard turned to Fernandez and asked, "What intelligence do we have of the Pacatus family and their capabilities? They are quite a large family, correct? Located inside advantageous terrain, with plenty of food, weapons, and Mages?"

All eyes shifted to the Master's second-in-command. He beckoned for his secretary, and the young man rushed forward with a few selected papers. "Indeed, Commandant. The Pacatus family has recorded approximately three hundred and fifty persons, more than two-thirds of which are Mages or will be when they reach adulthood. They are extremely affluent, owning nearly the entire western side of a large glacier valley. Locals report that their grazing lands are bordered to the west by mountains, to the east by a silt river, to the north by the glacier that feeds the river, and that they have established a fortified wall along the only passable route to the south. The family mana runs primarily to naturals, weathers, and healers, but in the last two generations, they have married in more than a few Artificers. The girl who reported was the first destructive born into the family; however, she will have several cousins of that type that are not yet mature. Locals also report that while the family's primary exports are agricultural, the married-in Artificers are Dwarf-trained and excellent weapon makers when commissioned. The fact that they are led by two living Seers and nearly all Mages born in the family are above average mana level, of course, goes without saying." He finished his monologue with a sardonic smile.

"Above average training, too," Bernard added, producing Asha's trial tablet and passing it around the table to be examined.

The Master held out his hand for it first, and after reading the summary, his eyebrows rose. "They sent the eldest, you say? Sweet Dynawach, what blessings you have given this rebellious family. Alonso, do we know who is training these young people?"

"I do not know precisely, Master. My intelligence is limited as I have no direct reporters in that region and can only rely on what the local Prior and governor gather. However, all of Ava Pacatus' generation and their spouses have fulfilled their service obligations, several of them in our Order. The girl's own father, Thomas Iurgium, is an Infinitus brother. They are certainly not incapable of homegrown training."

"I fail to see why that matters," Despuig cut in again. "Unless, Commandant, you are suggesting that the Order of Holy Heros cannot handle one rich, upstart family from the north? "

"I am suggesting nothing." Bernard kept his tone flat, even as Despuig's face reddened. As much as he might enjoy seeing the Marshal blow his top, he would get nowhere by antagonizing him.

"It is a fair point," Emery Ponte, the Order's Harbinger, added, "that the Commandant is not suggesting." His grin was somewhere between sarcasm and feline joy. "The resources alone required to fetch a child from such a location would be immense."

"Such an expense would only be compounded by valuable lives." The Treasurer, Martin Redin, now spoke. "Lives that will not be easily replaced with a threat nearly at our doorstep."

"Let's not be dramatic, Sir Treasurer," Admiral Matilda Tewkes chided. "They are not at our doorstep. We don't even know if they are eying the northern continent yet. And they would still have all the Trebri Isles to cross. If they manage to subjugate the islands that no one has held in written memory, well then, they have my Navy lads to deal with. Dragons or not, we'll give 'em a fight to be sure. There might as likely never be a doorstep disturbed."

"Be that as it may," The High Priest said with his usual cool derision, "whether or not it is expensive in resources and lives is secondary to the fact that leaving her where she is does nothing for the Order. Even if she is safe. The Dragon Riders are killing powerful children, and I do not accept that it is only a long-term strategy. After all, when has anyone from the lower continent thought about the future?"

Bernard looked hard at him, trying and failing to deflate the man's condescension. "What do you mean? Have you some insight into their reasons for such heinous slaughter?"

"I have no insight. What I mean is that it makes no sense to kill the next generation. Indoctrinate or subjugate, yes. I think that these Dragon Riders see a threat to their advance now. There is something about these powerful children we are missing. Something we can use against them."

"That is a thin thread to justify a raid of a powerful northern family. One that has served the Empire faithfully for generations," Navarre refuted.

Turmoil was stealing away all the threads of control he had tried to weave. He took a mental inventory. The Treasurer, Harbinger, and Hospitaller seemed firmly on his side. The Marshal and High Priest firmly against. The Master, his Second, and the Admiral were all judiciously listening and had not indicated either way. Robert Beaumont, the Order's Draper, was the only one who had yet to speak. He rarely did, and, as such, was very difficult to read. Bernard needed to make sure this didn't devolve into an ego-fueled pissing match that would result in a detachment going to take the girl by force.

"What I am suggesting—" he raised his voice a decibel or two then paused for effect and brought it back down—"is that we accept the substitution for now. The girl is safe and likely to receive excellent training in the meantime. As the Admiral suggested, we do not yet know the extent of the threat." He kept his face neutral, despite not believing those last words. Why on earth should the Dragon Riders stop at conquering the southern continent? They had met no real resistance and had no reason not to try and conquer the entirety of the known world. Besides, the Elves and Dwarves were worried enough about the looming threat to agree to battle treaties never previously made, including his interracial ballast. That alone should scare the Council members. "Therefore, I think it is imprudent to spend the money to send a small army north to pry a child from a powerful, citizen family. Not when we can summon her again." He emphasized 'citizen family', trying to play to conscience and rights rather than adding fuel to Despuig's accusations of defiance.

Several angry replies were readied then cut to pieces by his last sentence.

"What in Ciirtas's name do you mean, summon her again?" Despuig asked incredulously. "You can't be suggesting a false acceptance."

"No, I am not," Bernard said, turning his head to make eye contact with as many of the Council members as possible as he spoke. "But a substitute to a summons is dependent on circumstance. Should the circumstances change, and there is a threat on our doorstep, not on the far side of the Trebri Isles and the world's best Navy—" the Admiral chuffed at that, and Bernard hoped he had won her vote—"and we know the strategy behind the murders and whether or not the children can be used against our enemy—" the High Priest harrumphed under his breath—"then we can send a new summons and be confident that the cost is worth it to deal with these northern upstarts." Despuig murmured a curse-laden agreement.

"We could certainly justify it if we got to the point of raising an official army and service compulsion," The Master agreed, and Bernard knew he had triumphed. "All in favor of the substitution, say aye." A chorus met his command. "All opposed, say nay." Only the High Priest said nay, glaring at Bernard all the while. He was always a sore loser, and tonight would be no exception. Bernard had found himself increasingly at odds with the man lately. He needed to think of a way to smooth things over before spats and opposing votes became an enemy. That was a problem for later as the Master declared, "That settles it. Asha Pacatus is accepted. Be sure to extend my welcome to her in the Order, Bernard."

"With pleasure, Master."

"Now, tell us how you plan to use the girl, Bernard. Alonso, have you examined the tablet? Most impressive, most impressive." He handed the tablet to his Second, who almost kept the eagerness off his face as he took it.

"I plan to assign her as a caster on my interracial ballast," Bernard answered. "I think she will be a great asset to the Order and want to be careful not to waste her talents."

"I cannot think of greater waste than to be bound to an Elf and two Dwarves." The High Priest's voice was high-pitched with poorly controlled anger. Bernard was unsure if his anger was from losing the vote or if he really hated the idea of binding the races so much.

"Indeed. I'm sure we can find other uses for her talents," Despuig chimed in, taking the tablet from Fernandez. He did not keep his face from showing his admiration as he read it.

"I see no issue with assigning her to that new type of ballast. We shall have her for seven years, regardless," The Master said. Bernard disliked how flippantly the Council discussed the young woman's life. It was their prerogative, but that didn't make it twist his guts any less. "How is that going by the way? Have you chosen your seven? Or, I suppose, four, as the Dwarves and she-Elf make three."

"I have chosen three, in addition to the Elf and Dwarves. The Pacatus girl, a second destructive, and a healer. But I will need approval to legitimize the healer. Fernandez, were you able to find an answer to my inquiry on the legality and method?"

"I was. Since she is not the bastard but rather her father, in order to give her a surname as she requested, we would have to legitimize him." Ferandez ignored the incredulous and disapproving looks that came in response to this revelation. "It should be easy enough to give him his mother's surname and therefore pass it to her. Though it will scandalize the northern nobles."

"Let them be scandalized. Who gives a Gnome's hat what they think? But why are we going to all that trouble for a healer? The Order is not short of them," Despuig interjected.

"She is the best shielder the Order has ever trained, and we were unable to convince her to take an Infinitus oath the first time. Legitimacy is her price for a second Septus oath," Bernard replied.

"Wars are good at encouraging Infinitus oaths." Redin chuckled.

"Do what you must to get her to join," the Master said decisively. "If we have to face dragon fire, we shall need all the shields we can find. Have you appointed an Infinitus brother or sister to the ballast? A shepherd to guide our lambs and foreigners?"

"I have one in mind, but I have not yet spoken to him to see if he is willing, Master."

The Master made a dismissive sound. "If he is an Infinitus brother, he will obey your will. Make it so."

"Yes, Master." Bernard would not, could not, bring himself to force Odo into this, but since he had not given a name, it mattered little. He could always choose and present someone else.

"Well, then, if there is nothing else, I think this meeting is concluded," the Master said, striking the table with his open palm.

"I have one more item pertaining to this matter," Fernandez interjected before the meeting could be officially ended.

"Go on, then Alonso." The Master made a permissive gesture.

"I would like to not have to rely on the Northern Prior and Governor's discretion for intelligence on the Pacatus family. I think it would be in all parties' best interests if we placed a reporter within the locale. This could give us a better understanding of the capabilities, loyalties, and limitations of the family should the need for a new summons be determined. He or she can also act as protector, if the danger to the girl becomes suddenly greater. Of course, I will need your approval to fund and place such an agent."

"Excellent forethought. Discuss the revenue with Martin and have the formal requisition on my desk as soon as possible. Instruct the reporter to get as close to the family as possible."

"It will be done, Master."

"Now, anything else?" He paused and looked each member in the face before nodding. "Very well. Meeting adjourned. You are all dismissed back to your duties. Enjoy the evening."

He rose, and all the members and their staff did the same. They all saluted as he left the room. The High Priest swept out next, petulantly avoiding any further discussion or conversation. Bernard instructed Rupert to leave a message at the female barracks for Asha to report to her trainers at first light. Then he joined the remaining Council members on the short trip to the provision hall for the evening meal.

The food was as blandly nourishing as ever; the conversation was more engaging. Though Bernard observed that none of the Council members alluded to the problems discussed in the meeting, obviously they could not speak of it openly. Perhaps that was the only reason, perhaps not. He hoped they were not waiting for him to leave to gossip about his conflict with Hadrian, but his mind was soon overtaken by other issues: the substitution, his inter-racial ballast, who would lead it, and the very reason it was needed at all. He ate quickly and excused himself, wishing for nothing more than to distract himself for a while with his lovely wife and cheerful children.

Chapter 15

Asha and Bernard

Asha read the small missive again.

> *Substitution accepted with conditions. Report to western training grounds at first light to begin integration into interracial ballast.*

The message was simple, but it left her with more questions. What conditions? When did the Commandant plan to tell her what she needed to agree to? What on earth was an interracial ballast? To her admittedly limited knowledge, there was no such thing. When the races occasionally fought together, they maintained their own unitary structures. The real question crossed her mind and brought all the others swirling around screeching to a halt: Did any of those questions really matter? There were very few conditions that she would have refused to keep her baby sister from being pulled into this garrison. So, when they decided to inform her what she had agreed to, the unusual nature of her assignment would mean very little. She was in this for at least the next seven years, and it seemed likely the Empire would face war within that time.

Rising, she dressed with all the other female recruits, making her way to the training ground before the sun crested the horizon. All the other recruits from the trials were there. She had no idea where and exactly with whom she was supposed to integrate. Luckily, the trainers appeared shortly after she did and began giving instructions. Some she recognized from the first day and others she didn't.

The morning started with physical exercise. She knew how intensely the Order valued physical conditioning and endurance from her family members who had served. This at least she agreed with the Order on. Regardless of mana level, a Mage could only expect to cast as long as their body could endure. Unlike mana level, physical endurance could be trained and strengthened. When she had been a tiny, angry girl of seven with new access to a mana none of her other family understood, Great Uncle Luca had started her training with physical exercises, much like the Order was doing with the recruits now, she realized. Perhaps the Order had influenced her childhood more than she had realized back then.

Trainers spread them out and took them through a brief warm-up. Then they gave commands for simple body weight exercises, interspersed with sprints. It felt good to Asha. She had always enjoyed physical exercise, to feel her body work and move, to feel her heart pounding and her lungs stretching to draw in enough air. The journey down to the Capital had been physically taxing but not in the same way. That was a long, drudging use of the body day after day. This was short bursts of force from the body. She had missed the feeling.

Exercise as a group was new and different to her. She had exercised with her aunts, uncles, cousins, and siblings, but due to the variance of age, strength, and daily responsibilities, she had rarely done so with more than a few others and never in a group of about fifty.

A sprint iteration brought her close to the tallest woman in the group. Asha was slightly tall for a woman, standing at 5'8", but this woman was nearly an entire foot taller than her. When they both descended into a round of push-ups, Asha realized she was not a woman but an Elf. If her height hadn't given her away, the slightly inhuman proportion of her long limbs and barrel chest might have. Had that been written off, no other explanation would have suited for her ears and fingers. Her ears were large and flared to three cartilage points that looked remarkably like a fish's fin, and her fingers were webbed to the first knuckle. She wore boots, but if she had been barefoot, fully webbed toes would have been visible.

Her skin was a dark caramel brown covering lean, muscled limbs and neck. Rich, black hair was pulled back into intricate braids that were woven into a thick knot at the nape of her neck. Her eyes were almond-shaped and so dark brown that in the early morning light, they looked as black as her hair. She had strong, thick eyebrows set over a wide nose and high-rounded cheekbones. Her wide mouth stretched into a grin, and white teeth contrasted her otherwise dark appearance as she spoke, startling Asha. "Enjoying the view?"

Asha instantly felt guilty. She really needed to figure out how to observe discreetly. "I'm sorry," she said. No use trying to deny it.

"Don't be," the Elf grunted on her next repetition. "I'm growing accustomed to being the first Elf people have set eyes on. It can be flattering."

Asha chuckled but had no time to reply because it was the Elf's turn to sprint. She was unable to conceal her surprise at the Elf's sheer speed as her long legs carried her across the group faster than seemed possible. Asha supposed for a human, it wasn't possible to move that fast, even if they had matching height, which no one here did.

As she completed another round of push-ups, Asha kicked herself for not paying attention to the group she was in. She hadn't realized that one of the group members was an Elf for Goddess's sake! Her uncles, especially Great Uncle Luca, had drilled into her the importance of awareness of her environment. Tried to, at least. Discreetly, she began scanning the group as they continued exercising.

She recognized Will and a few other destructives whose names she did not know. Then she felt foolish and blind all over again when she noticed there were two Dwarves in the group. They were off to her right side with several Mages she didn't recognize in between them, so she couldn't get a good look without being obvious, but they were definitely Dwarves.

Seeing them made her think of another Dwarf. How long had it been since she had parted ways with Glormhar? A few days? Had it been a whole week? Regret nagged her again. She hadn't wanted to be cold or push him away. But she didn't know how else to go about saying farewell forever. Especially since he had been intent on saying farewell for now. She liked the idea that they might cross paths again, but it was foolish. They had met by chance, and chance wasn't likely to bring them together again. Holding on to the spark that they had and trying to force it to burn while apart would have only ended in resentment and heartache. Even still, part of her wished that it could have gone better, and another part of her, the part she stuffed down and silenced, hoped that he was right. If her assignment kept her here in this garrison, and if he guarded another trading caravan, could he be right?

The exercise ended, and the instructors divvied up the group into smaller sections to give more detailed instructions. Asha found herself standing next to the Dwarves, the Elf, and Will. But before any introductions could be made, they were told to clean up and meet back at the draper's to be fitted for their kits. Suddenly, she stood alone, staring at the instructor. She turned and scurried off to the barracks.

A basin bath and change of clothes later, Asha trotted to the drapers. She had needed to return to the guard tower to peek at the map on the wall to find it and was cutting the allotted time close. The others were already there. Her group, the interracial ballast, she corrected herself—was not the only one there. In fact, they were third in line.

She joined her ballast, or part of it; they still needed two more people. But that was the Order's problem, not hers.

"Good morning." She tried to sound cheerful, but it felt hollow to her ears. "Seems we are to be a ballast in the future. Shall we introduce ourselves?"

Will smiled, and the Dwarves looked a touch sheepish. The Elf gave no expression at all, only turned to look at her.

"The rest of us have already met," Will said. Of course, they had. Asha flushed. The rest of them hadn't been held back dealing with that nonsense about summoning and substitution.

Cheeks still hot, she raised her chin and said, "Well, you all haven't been introduced to me. I am Asha Pacatus."

Will bowed his head slightly in acquiescence. "You have already heard my name." He then turned to the Elf.

"Mayumi Mandirigma." She gave an Imperial salute.

"Thrarber Tuasg, at your service, miss," the first Dwarf said. He was a full foot shorter than her, perhaps an inch or two more, and nearly as broad in the shoulders as he was tall. His hair and beard were a rich cinnamon brown. Both fell just below his shoulders with a few artfully placed braids keeping it out of his dark blue eyes and decorating the beard. He had bushy eyebrows and a bulbous nose, balancing the beard on his oval face. A war hammer hung in his sword belt that seemed a bit larger than it ought to be, but she was pretty sure it was similarly sized to the hammers carried by the only other Dwarves she had met.

"Throil Tuasg, at your service," the second Dwarf chimed in, grabbing her attention. He was equal in height and breadth to the first, but his hair was a few shades lighter, more like bronze. His eyes and nose were identical, as were his braids. The rest of his face seemed a bit thinner, though. They had to be related; both had the same surname, after all, and the resemblance was striking. It was a familiar surname, but they gave her no time to ponder that.

"What type are ye if ye don't mind my asking?" Thrarber asked.

"I'm a destructive. I would ask you the same. Except Will, of course." Will smiled again. She was slightly annoyed by it, not that she had any reason to be.

"My brother and I are battle craftsman. I believe your lot would call us Artificers." He smiled broadly and gestured to his Warhammer.

"My affinity is with weather mana," Mayumi answered.

"Two destructive, two crafters, and a weather. Mighty fine group, I'd say," Thrarber said decidedly. "I suppose they'll add a healer. Wanna bet on the seventh?" He nudged his brother with an elbow.

No bet was made. It was their turn to enter the drapers, and Brother Gerard was waiting for them at the door.

The building was made of the same thick stone as all the other garrison buildings. Along the wall were thick wooden shelves holding fabrics, thread, and various types of raw metals. The other wall was lined with work benches, high-backed chairs, large trundle sewing machines, and a raised platform with a small desk beside it. Along the back wall was a small forge in which a smith churned out small steel plates. There was a worker at each trundle and several others fastening links with rivets faster than Asha would have thought possible.

Brother Gerard addressed the woman leaning on the desk with a measuring tape in her hand. "We are ready. Casters all, so be sure not to weigh them down too much."

"Ah, casters are vulnerable, too, dear Brother Gerard," she drawled in an accent Asha didn't recognize, placing extra emphasis on her 's's. "They'll get used to the weight if you drill them enough." She wagged a thin finger at him.

"You leave the drilling to me. Just do what you do best."

She huffed, then spoke. "Give me the humans first. The others will have special dimensions."

Brother Gerard looked pointedly at Will and gestured with a jerk of his head that he was to go first. Will stepped up onto the platform and held out his draper token. The draper sister looked him over a moment, then handed him a gambeson shirt that had been sitting on the desk.

"Put this on," she said. "Save the token for when you pick up the final kit."

Will did, and the gambeson fit him well. She took the tape and measured his legs and the circumference of his wrists.

"Go ahead and take it off," she said, annotating her measurements. "Pretty standard size, this one. Easy. We'll just need a few hours to join the mail links to size on his wrists." She took two worn wooden planks out and turned back to Will. "Put your dominate hand here, aligning the palm with the bottom of the outlines." Will placed his right hand inside the concentric outlined hands, and the woman annotated which his hand matched the best. "Now, take one foot out of your boots and do the same," she said, tossing the second plank down next to his feet. Will did, and she again annotated. Then she handed the quill to Will. "Place your name at the top and then move out of the way for the next recruit."

Asha was next. The woman pulled out a different gambeson for her to try on. It fit, but not quite as well, a little tight around the chest. "Lift your arms up and around in a circle," the woman told her. When Asha did, the fabric restrained her movement a bit. The woman stepped close and measured her waist, bust, under bust, and shoulder width in rapid succession, annotating in between.

"Simple alterations to the padding, but this will require additional time to adjust the cuirass," she said over her shoulder to Brother Gerard as she knelt to get the leg and wrist measurements.

"I expected so for a female," he replied.

The woman huffed again. "I have standard sets for females, Brother Gerard. Don't act daft. This one just is in between them in height and breadth."

"I did not mean to imply that you are unprepared."

She made a noncommittal sound as she presented Asha with the same two planks and continued her task. Then she looked at Asha's waist. "Is the whip to stay where it is? Instead of a sword?" she asked.

"No. She will carry a sword," Brother Gerard answered.

"It is my focus," Asha cut in, not liking the feeling of being talked about and not to.

Brother Gerard opened his mouth to say something, probably to correct or scold her, but the draper sister spoke first. "In addition, then, not instead. I'll have the sheath put on the left side for a cross draw. Standard for a caster. Is the whip's fastener removable to put on our belt?"

"Yes, ma'am," Asha answered. The woman scribbled another note and passed the quill to Asha to label the paper.

Next were the Dwarves. Thrarber went first, and the woman did not have him try any shirts. She just began measuring him, tutting all the while. "Odd dimensions indeed," she kept muttering under her breath. She attempted to use the planks, but to her surprise, his hand was larger than any of the outlines. Returning to the desk, she pulled out a scrap of cloth and some chalk. She traced both of his hands and repeated this for his feet.

"This will take much time, Brother," she said to Gerard more gravely than Asha thought necessary.

"Take all the time you need to do it well, Sister. The Dwarves and Elf have kits from their own people. We simply wish to integrate them fully into the uniform of the Order."

The woman nodded. "Good. Having this now will make repairs or re-issue much easier in the future."

Throil and Mayumi's measurements went similarly, except Mayumi's hands and feet fit on the largest outline of the planks. The draper expressed uncertainty, however, regarding gloves and her partially webbed fingers. Mayumi pulled a pair out of a pouch on her belt and offered them to the draper to examine. She turned them in and out, examining the seams, scribbling notes, and finally traced them as she had the Dwarves' hands and feet.

"The humans can return for their kit after the evening meal. The others will take a few days. I will send you notice when they are ready," the woman said to Gerard when all were finished.

He turned to the group. "You heard her. Artifex, Pacatus, return here for pickup this evening. All of you are dismissed to your studies for the day. Meet at the training field at sunrise. Once your kit is issued, you will be required to wear it from daybreak until after the evening meal each day."

They all acknowledged him and left the drapers.

"To the provisional hall before we part ways?" Will suggested.

"Aye, I could eat," Thrarber answered him, and they all turned in that direction.

"It's good of the Order to outfit all their soldiers. I've never seen it so," Throil mused as they walked.

"What do you mean?" Asha asked.

"Well, where we come from, each must provide his own kit and weapons. If'n ye can't make it, ye must buy it. The Order is making and giving it to us. Do you suppose they will charge us?"

"It is the same for most others. If one joins a noble's army, you only have what you can afford," Will interjected. "But the Order is very rich and very determined to have uniformity. To my knowledge they only charge the recruits if no oath is sworn."

Throil nodded.

"Well, there's no chance of that for us." Thrarber chuckled as they entered the provisional hall.

Bernard thrummed his fingers on his desk.

"Are you in need of anything else, sir?" Rupert held the letter to Enya Nameless, informing her of the High Council's acceptance of her terms and instructing her to take the fastest ship she could find to the Capital. Her father—and, by extension, she—would be given a legal surname upon the renewal of her oaths to the Order.

Bernard sat back in his chair, contemplatively. "More exercise, Rupert. Could any of my meeting slots be exchanged for that?"

"They could, if you wish," Rupert said slowly. Bernard understood the implication. Anything could be done, but it may be incredibly inconvenient, not just to his assistant, but to the others attending said meetings.

"Your morning exercise is not enough, sir?" Rupert asked.

"It is enough for a few hours. Then I sit through meetings. Sit through paperwork. Sit through evaluations. Sit through planning. By the evening meal, I feel soft in the middle and like my blood is clotted in my veins." The sedentary nature of administration had been eating at him lately.

"Your performance in drilling is not lacking, sir. Have you consulted your wife on this matter?"

Bernard stifled the grin, but not the wicked gleam that came to his eyes. "I have. She was...exuberant in her assurances of my conditioning."

Rupert looked down and his lips twitched. "I see. We can expect a sixth child soon then?"

"No, I doubt the Gods will so bless us yet. Little Jobert is only a few months past a year and still on the breast." He paused. "It was her opinion it is my mind that is atrophying and not my body. I still think additional exercise will benefit if she is correct."

"Well, sir, the provision hall offers hand pies or stew and bread for the midday meal. Like the kind in the market that you can take and eat while you walk. You could drill during that meal, and I could fetch that for you. You could eat here before your first afternoon meeting."

"An excellent suggestion, Rupert. It would break up the day."

Joan knocked on the open door. "Brother Odo is here as requested, sir."

"Excellent, thank you, Joan. Rupert, send that letter with utmost haste, and direct him in."

A tall, dark-haired man with more weapons than was strictly necessary bent his head to clear the door frame and stepped inside to give a salute. "Commandant," he said respectfully.

Bernard rose and returned the salute. "Odo, good to see you. I find myself quite stifled in this office. Would you mind having our meeting on horseback?"

Odo smirked slightly, making the barely visible scar from his left eyebrow to his hair line turn white. It drew Bernard's mind to the day he had gotten it. Odo had grappled a particularly nasty weather Mage who nearly killed their whole platoon with lightning. That had been Bernard's first broken ballast; it had not been Odo's.

"Growing fat and comfortable as an Administrator? I thought you wanted to slow down, brother."

"I did, but now I'm starting to wish it would speed back up." Bernard smiled as he motioned Odo out and pulled the door shut behind him. They walked past the captain of the guard, who rose in salute, but Bernard ignored her. Calling the captain and then making her wait was quite rude. But the offense would be passed down to whichever sergeant had failed to properly check in the Pacatus daughter and notify the Commandant. Bernard preferred the cold impropriety to a shouted redressing, and he needed to ensure that this would never happen again.

They walked briskly to the stables, where the stable hands caught and saddled their mounts. Not more than half an hour later, they cleared the garrison gate at a trot. They could have raised their voices to be heard above the street noise, but Bernard had no intention of including outsiders in their conversation, even if only for a moment before they rode past. He led them through the hustle and bustle along side streets and alleys, weaving westward until they came to the small western gate out of the Capital proper. It let them out onto a small bridge, which they crossed and cleared the watchtower on the far side. They were in open country now and rode southwest along the road as it wove in and around farmer's fields.

"You're probably wondering why I summoned you," Bernard started to say.

"No," Odo cut him off dryly. "I'm pretty sure I know. It's about that fancy new mixed species ballast you're putting together, isn't it?"

Bernard was a bit stunned. He supposed it wasn't a secret, but he hadn't expected Odo to be familiar with it. He had only just returned from convalescence leave.

"Yes, my interracial ballast."

"They want someone with more experience to lead it?"

"Yes."

"And if that someone happens to be a seventh son of a seventh son, all the better?"

"It's not like that, Odo." Bernard shifted in his saddle and continued looking straight ahead.

"But it is. You're gathering a bunch of high-powered foreigners and adding them to a couple higher powered kids." He chuckled mirthlessly. "You'd be a Gnome mad fool to not put a very strong Void in charge of them."

Bernard turned his head and saw Odo leaning comfortably back in his saddle, those sharp blue eyes drilling into him.

"You are the best man for the job."

"But...?"

"But it would mean binding again, taking a new blood oath to a ballast that is going to be in the thick of whatever mess comes our way. If this works, the generals aren't going to have this ballast performing palace tricks or even off the front lines. They will be in the thick of it."

"In the thick of dragons?"

"Yes."

"Some folks think that those Warlords will never leave the southern continent. Others think they might try, but the islands and the Navy will stop them."

"They're wrong," Bernard spat out with more venom than he intended. "All of them. There will be an army on our shores within the year. I can feel it in my bones."

"Seems like the thick of it is right where I should be then," Odo said without hesitation.

Bernard had thought he would say so, but once he said it, he found himself wishing that he had not, that Odo was a little less brave. A little less dedicated. "How can you be so certain? Have you not given enough? Many will die. Likely within this ballast."

Odo shrugged easily, as though they were discussing meal arrangements or hilt decorations. "Is this not what Ciirtas put me here to do? Is this not what the Order requires of me?"

"You are not required. I can find another. Do not be so careless with your life, or your soul."

Odo's face did not change, but a hard glint entered his eyes. "You of all people know that I am not careless."

Bernard looked away first and focused on the horizon. "What number would it be? Do you even have any soul left to bind to the others? It is unbalanced, brother, to ask so much of one man."

"I still breathe; my story has not yet been told to the Recorder. That means I must have some soul left."

Bernard glanced back at Odo, and he looked at the horizon as well, or at least in the direction of the horizon. He didn't know if what he looked at was present or phantom.

"You are the best man for the job, but I fear it is too great of an ask."

"Then don't ask. I am offering. Ease your conscience."

"That does nothing for my conscience."

"Then save the tears and moaning for my funeral."

Bernard chuckled despite himself. "Very well, then. Meet with Brother Gerard and Sister Cecilia to integrate into their training."

"Are they all new and young?"

"No, not even close. The She-Elf is over three hundred and the veteran of many naval battles and several amphibious assaults. The Dwarves are about a hundred, I believe, and have seen many border skirmishes. The healer is on her way or will be soon from the north. This will be her second Septus oath."

"That's unusual," Odo cut in.

"Took some convincing, but she will be well worth it, I believe. The only youths are the two destructive recruits."

Odo harrumphed approvingly. "With that lot, we may be able to take a dragon."

"With that lot, I fear you will have to."

They fell silent for a few paces.

"Are you sure you are ready? Are you healed, I mean?"

Odo sighed. "You fuss like a mother hen. I'm back, aren't I? What isn't healed never will be."

"At least talk it over with your wife. Make sure she agrees."

"Outsourcing your heavy conscience?"

That stung, but Bernard pushed on. "She deserves to know the risks. You've been in more ballasts than anyone in the Order ever has. Many have lost their sanity long before this."

"Who said I've kept my sanity?" Odo chuckled. "I will ask her, but not even she may persuade me from my destiny."

"Perhaps ask the priests, then. Be sure that this is your destiny."

"The priests want me to repudiate my wife because she is barren," Odo spat the words like they tasted rotten. "I don't give a bat's whisker what they say of my destiny."

"But she is pregnant now. Surely, they will have to take that back."

"She isn't pregnant anymore." The words were flat and hollow. Bernard knew that Odo and his wife had been trying to conceive for the better part of twenty years. He had lost track of the number of miscarriages and still births in that time.

"I am so sorry, brother."

"I never know what to say to that." Odo's voice caught just slightly. "It isn't fine, so I can't say that. But your sorrow does no good, so I can't thank you for it."

"Well, if there is anything that would do you or her good, you have only to send word."

"Thank you, but I don't know if she would want me to speak of it."

"Then we won't speak of it, but when you go to the temple this week, I shall send our servant girl to clean your house and leave a fruit basket."

Odo nodded. "That would do her good." He turned his horse, and they rode back toward the Capital in silence.

When they were a few miles from the guard tower before the bridge, Odo spoke again. "If the Gods will not permit me a child, much less seven, to replace myself in the divine duty of justice, how can we question that it is my destiny to continue to serve as long as I am able? Whatever the cost."

Bernard sighed deeply. "That is a question for a man far wiser than I."

"I knew I shouldn't bother asking a bureaucrat." Odo smirked.

"I am not a bureaucrat. I am the Commandant of the Order's training academy."

"Whatever you are, you have lost your seat in the saddle. I never saw such a curved back."

Bernard shook his head. Perhaps it was a good thing that Odo would be too busy training youngsters and foreigners to bother him. He had no time for such banter, though he missed it dearly. Perhaps his pursuit of position was a fruitless one. No, not entirely fruitless, but it was increasing his distance from his old friends. Not that that would matter if dragons invaded the skies, then he would be distanced from some friends until they reunited in the houses of the Gods.

Chapter 16

Mago

Mago smudged the charcoal, dragging it across the parchment. If he was honest with himself, the shading on his naval battle sketch was unnecessary. He told himself that it was a rare opportunity for him to practice his childhood hobby. Drawing was an old love of his, but it rarely came in handy anymore. It was just too obvious, too easily understood for reports like his that required secrecy, cyphers, and misdirection. He was not honest enough with himself to admit that he hoped that putting the image on paper might erase it from his nightmares.

The sketches were a risk he felt he must take. The Imperial Navy needed every detail he could give them. As he added the line of the harpoon rising up from the three-sailed galley, he wondered what type of ship his mother had rode on when she crossed the sea as a refugee from the very city he now sat in. It was unlikely to be anything like the one he had just rendered in charcoal. That was a warship. Fast and maneuverable, not well-suited to carrying hundreds of starving, desperate souls from a war-torn continent, many nautical miles to the shores of the peaceful, orderly Empire. What would she think if she knew that her son had returned to the place she fled in service of the Empire that had saved her?

Finishing the final touches on the battle scene, he set it onto his best version of a biographical sketch of a dragon wearing its saddle and rider. He was drawn to that galley, the only of its fleet to make the dragons flinch. What type of ships would the Dragon Riders force the shipwrights of Hadrumentum to build? More fast galleys? Or larger, deeper cargo ships, like a cog or the newer and larger carrack? He didn't know many types of ships or their uses. Hearing soft footfalls on the stairs, he buried his sketches inside a pile of tedious expenditure reports. Hidden in plain sight might be an old wives' adage, but it was occasionally useful.

Sophonisba rapped her knuckles on the frame of his open door.

"Am I needed, my dear?" he asked her.

"Not particularly, but I wanted to tell you that we are low on wine for this coming evening."

"How low?"

"Not enough for the number of customers we typically serve in the first three hours."

Mago sighed. "How could we have depleted our stock so quickly?"

"We haven't depleted it quickly. At least not any quicker than usual. What is unusual is how slow our master has been to find us a new supplier." She smirked.

"I haven't found one that is up to my standards," he retorted.

"You haven't found one that can supply both local grapes and Imperial ale. Not that most of our customers drink that."

"It is important to me that we offer it, Sophi."

"I know." She dropped the smirk, and her voice softened. "What I do not know is why. You rarely drink either."

Mago kept his face still despite the chill that gripped his chest. He was letting her get too close. She was noticing inconsistencies in his carefully curated story. Served him right for picking a competent mistress. Also served him right for limiting his consumption of ale. Should he throw her off the scent or simply remind her of her place and offend her? Before he decided, she spoke again.

"That is why I found one for you."

"How?" He spoke sharper than he'd intended.

She smiled again. "I have my ways. I once worked this city before, many years ago. Luckily for you, one of my old companions and his winehouse survived the sacking. Mostly survived, at least."

He shouldn't take her up on this. It was sloppy. He should do his own search and find a contact. Would her former companion tell her what else he asked for? But he needed a supplier, badly by the sounds of it. He could change tactics and maintain a supply of wine separate from his contact with the Empire. It was risky, but he had repeated the same pattern many times while following the army. The nomadic nature had minimized the risk, but remaining here in the city for Gods only knew how long would change that equation.

"Have your ways arranged a meeting with this companion?"

"Of course," she quipped in her native tongue and winked at him before turning to leave. "Gisco has the address. You should dress yourself to leave. You don't have much time before your appointment," she said over her shoulder in the common tongue.

"Sophi."

She turned back to him.

"It ensures a certain standard of service—" she raised an eyebrow but didn't reply; he went all in on misdirection—"that a winehouse can maintain trading relations with the upper continent. Anyone can ferment grapes. But the business is more than fermentation."

"And a businessman who can maintain his own supply and negotiate for others demonstrates a shrewdness and stability that makes it unlikely you will be dissatisfied. Yes, I see." She smiled warmly this time, understanding and affection blooming on her face. Damn, he almost wished it were true. It was actually a valid test of dependability. He would have to remember that.

"Especially if he also has survived a siege and sack." He returned her smile and rose to grab his robes.

Gisco led him through the streets to the eastern trading district of the port city. The wall rebuilding must have been progressing well; the bodies had been cleared from the street as Bomilcar had promised he would do when manpower could be spared. When Gisco led him outside of the city gates, he realized why this winehouse had survived the sack.

He observed the low walls surrounding the rolling vineyard, the small building housing the press, and the generous outdoor seating area. This had been a luxury winehouse. The kind that sold an 'experience' as much as a beverage. It was certainly worse for wear now, but it had survived. That was what counted.

Sophonisba's former companion, a small old man with a boyish smile and an arthritic limp, was eager for a new customer. Mago was certain by his mannerisms that he had not seen coin since the siege started, and his survival had been quite costly. With fresh ink on contracts, Mago rode in the wagon with his wine and ale back to his mansion.

He returned just before sunset and found the mansion's torches lit, with incense burning and music lilting in the garden. Several of his whores danced in loosely wrapped silk and jewelry for a few men seated in chairs next to the incense. He was going to pass them when he saw that one of the men was Bomilcar. A greeting was required to avoid offense. He approached the men.

"My friend, welcome. I trust you are well cared for in my absence?"

"Mago, my friend. Yes, yes. As always. Though I was not expecting your absence this evening. What were you up to?" Bomilcar asked. The other two men, commanders whom Bomilcar also counted as friends, grunted or spoke a single word of greeting but ignored Mago in favor of the dancing women.

"Business." Mago forced a chuckle. "Keeping my customers well cared for requires wine and food. Among other things. I needed to acquire more wine."

"Wine is good," one of the commanders said as he reached out his hand and seized the nearest whore playfully, dragging her onto his lap with a smile on his wide, dark face. "But I think I prefer the 'other things.'" The woman giggled and batted her lashes in a show of false shyness. She was good. Mago would have been convinced she was shy and found the commander intriguing if he didn't know that she had been selling her body for seven years and that she told Sophonisba that she wouldn't serve these men unless asked for by name.

"Always the business, my friend." Bomilcar scoffed. "You work too much. Do you ever partake in the 'other things'?"

Mago feigned indifference as the other commander scooped up two of the whores, tossing one over each shoulder and carrying them laughing and squealing into the mansion. "I don't. I don't think it's good for business." He smiled in a manner that he hoped was playful as well. "If my girls are serving me, they aren't serving you."

The first commander slid the whore off his lap and encouraged her to her knees to provide him services that Mago did not want to watch out in the garden. He quickly cast about for an excuse to return to his office, where he would be surrounded by papers and figures and estimates, not his women at work.

"Your girls are very talented. Perhaps she can serve us both," Bomilcar said as he gestured to the last woman who had remained dancing but slowly discarded her silk wrap. He rose and gripped her hand, angling himself to take her inside as well, but looked at Mago expectantly.

"Her talents would be wasted on me. You ought to keep her to yourself," he said hastily. He did not like where this was going, but he smiled anyway.

Bomilcar shrugged and turned away. "Suit yourself, businessman."

Mago waited a few moments to give him plenty of space to ensure the offer was not repeated, then hurried across the garden and through the main house, up the stairs into his office. He hung up his robe absentmindedly, struggling to name why he was so unsettled by the request. Plenty of customers wanted to share women. Some with other women, some with a friend, and some with the one male whore he employed. But he had never been asked to before. Perhaps this was a natural expansion of his friendship with Bomilcar. But something felt different. He tried to think back and couldn't remember any instances of Bomilcar wishing to share a whore before. With anyone. That didn't mean it hadn't happened, he supposed, as he left the particulars of customer satisfaction to Sophonisba.

A short while later, Sophonisba brought him a tray with roast goat that had been curried, rice, candied currants, and a large tankard of Imperial ale.

"Thank you, Sophi," he said before he heard movement in the doorway. Bomilcar leaned on the door frame, wearing only his cotton braies.

"Ah, I see your real reason now, my friend." Bomilcar grinned wickedly, then stepped forward, eyeing Sophonisba like a hunter.

"Pardon? My reason for what?"

Bomilcar crossed his arms and stood inches away from Sophonisba. If he meant to cow her, he failed. She stood before him with perfectly curated poise and feigned diffidence. "It has nothing to do with business, and everything to do with your lovely mistress." He turned his sharp, dark eyes back to Mago.

When he didn't want to explain himself, Mago found it useful to allow people to form their own opinions about his motives and actions. They often created much more convincing stories than he could. "It seems I am caught." He smiled ruefully. Bomilcar laughed heartily.

"Sophi, would you bring a tray for my friend as well?" Mago asked, hoping to give the poor woman an exit.

"Thank you, but no." It shouldn't have irritated him that Bomilcar addressed himself instead of Sophi. Why should the Warlord's son show her any respect? "I cannot stay. I needed some amusement, but I have large preparations to see to."

"Preparations? Anything I can help with?" Mago asked as Sophi bowed and stepped out.

"No. No. A messenger reached me this morning. Father has completed his run across the continent and will be returning in three days. I am preparing a victory feast."

Mago nodded, but before he could speak, Bomilcar added, "I'm just glad the wall repairs are completed. I had the slaves working under torchlight, but it is repaired. Perhaps there is something you can help with. Can all of your girls dance like that in the garden?"

"Not all, but most can."

"Excellent. You can be our entertainment for the feast then. Well paid, of course." He smiled and turned to go. "And bring your mistress with you. I would love to see her by your side at the feasting table."

That doesn't bode well. Entertainment means everyone will be watching us, even the Blind Seer.

Chapter 17

Asha and Bernard

Asha once again was up before the dawn, doing her best to don her new kit in the dimly lit female barracks. She started with one of the two sets of linen tunics and split-leg hose cut in the Imperial style that had been issued to her. There were also two sets made of wool, but it was far too warm for that in the southern climate this time of year. Then she added the arming doublet. It was gambeson from the collar down to the lower hem that fell a few inches above her knees, with riveted mail sleeves that were well-fitting at the wrists and loosened slightly up the arm into the armpit and overlapped her shoulders where it connected. Next was the brigandine cuirass. It was somehow heavier than it looked but lighter than she had imagined it should be. Tempered steel plates were shaped and riveted to a vest of cloth in the Order's colors, nipping in slightly at her natural waist. The curve was not as great as most plate metal cuirasses but would still help deflect the force of blows.

She reached for her boots and realized she had erred. Sighing, she undid the front fastening buckles and removed the cuirass. The boots from the Order were not as comfortable as her own, and they weren't runed. She had a fleeting hope that once she broke them in, it would improve. Undoubtedly, they would but would still be less comfortable and definitely wouldn't save her from tripping on roots or rocks.

That made her think of the night she had been gathering firewood with Glormhar. It felt like a completely different time, but she wasn't that far removed, a few weeks at most. She glanced at the pendant that he had given her. It still sat on top of her pack, where she had left it after examining it the night before. The crest matched the one she had seen hung around Thrarber and Throil's necks. Tuasg. Glormhar had known that he had family working with the Order. Had he guessed that they would end up in the same ballast? She hadn't known about the interracial ballast. Had he? Even if he had, he couldn't have known she would also be added to it. That knowledge certainly explained why he had been so disappointed by her rejection, but he might have explained why he was so sure they would meet again. She was embarrassed but also slightly hopeful. An awkward reunion might just be possible.

Grabbing the round, open-faced helm, she trotted out of the barracks toward the training field, buckling it as she walked briskly. She felt like she was always short of time these days, rushing.

When she got to the training field, she took her place next to Wilford and Mayumi, Throil and Thrarber nearby. The instructors shuffled all the recruits into a square formation, then just before they called out the commands to move out at a double-time march, a man fell in on the outside of Wilford. As they jogged, Asha practiced discreet observation.

He was tall, a good bit taller than Wilford but still a few inches shy of Mayumi, so Asha guessed six foot three or four inches. His thick black hair was cut close by his ears, and his broad, handsome face was clean shaven. As his face reddened slightly with exercise, she saw two scars become visible: One over the left eye and one along the jawbone on the same side. His face was weathered and leathery, with prominent crow's feet by the eyes, but with the angle, she couldn't see the color of his eyes. She would guess his age to be near forty.

He carried the weight of his brigandine and fully mail shirt well across his extremely broad shoulders, like it was as much a part of him as the scars. His age, practiced ease, and amount of weaponry on his person made her quite confident that he wasn't a recruit, but a full-fledged member of the Order.

Although, he didn't wear the yellow sash of an instructor either.

The recruits had not been issued weapons yet. Her non-human companions carried their own, and no one had mentioned her whip, other than the sister at the draper. This man carried several. On his back was a heavy, wooden composite war bow, currently unstrung, with about two dozen arrows in a leather quiver. At his side was a hand-and-a-half sword that his hand rested on to steady it as he jogged in the formation. Opposite that was a rondel dagger, with a silver inlay in the blackened steel discs of the guard and pommel. Next to it was a smaller knife, only a few inches long in the blade and an equal amount in the wooden handle. The guard on it had been carved into an odd double bulbous shape. She briefly wondered about the function of it. If it was an archer's pick as she suspected, there was no need for a guard at all, and certainly not in that suggestive shape. Next to that was a steel buckler covered in cloth heralding that she couldn't place but was vaguely familiar.

The formation had traveled to the other side of the garrison by that point, and the instructors called a halt. They were in another training field in front of a large obstacle course. The instructors called them by columns to run it one at a time. Asha was sure she would have done well if she had not been in brand-new boots and unfamiliar armor. But then, that was the point of being mandated to wear it for such activities. Armor did one little good if they could not perform in it.

She navigated most of the obstacles slower than she would have liked, but without trouble. Several times, she had to wait for the recruit in front of her or the recruit in front of them while they waited. While she did, she looked around to see if her ballast members had fared better. They did, but Will struggled on the horizontal rope climb, and that made her feel a bit better. There were a few that she failed and fell off of, namely the vertical rope and the climbing wall without the ropes. As she did the remedial exercises to move on, she noticed that Mayumi was the only female who successfully crossed those. She was going to change that. She would not be embarrassed like this again.

By the end, she was red-faced, panting, and feeling elated. She hoped that the obstacle course would be a frequent part of their morning exercises. Making her way back to her ballast members, she found the tall man with them, as well as Brother Gerard.

"There she is. The last one, except for the healer, but you'll need to seek information on her from the Commandant," Brother Gerard said to the tall man when she approached.

"Excellent. We are nearly complete and can begin drilling then as soon as weapons are issued," was his reply. Then he turned to face her fully, where she saw his eyes were a deep shade of blue. "I am Brother Odo Bleolydd. I am going to be leading this ballast. You are...?"

"Asha Pacatus." She gave him a salute.

He nodded, and his eyes crinkled like he might smile, but it didn't make it to his lips. "You should practice the Imperial salute. It is better accepted from a member of our Order."

She wanted to retort that she wasn't a member of the Order. But just as quickly as the urge rose, so did the reminder that she soon would be. It felt like a foul taste in her mouth that she couldn't spit out. She was going to join the Order she so despised. She had even promised Commandant Payne to give the Order a chance while she was in it. Maybe this was the first step.

"I will try to remember that," she said. He nodded again in acknowledgement.

Then Brother Gerard addressed the group. "Speaking of weapons. After you get the stink off, report to the armory for weapons issue. Pacatus, you will report to the Commandant and meet us at the armory whenever he releases you. He has unfinished business with you."

Everyone acknowledged the orders and hurried off.

Bernard Paynes arrived at his office that morning to find the Pacatus girl already waiting. His secretary had directed her to a seat along the outer wall of the larger meeting room.

"Pacatus. Excellent. Come in. I have very little time this morning," he said, walking briskly past her, waving as he did so to encourage her to follow him. She followed him into his office and stood in front of his desk. Now in her issued armor and uniform, she looked like a proper recruit. Once she had been issued proper weapons, she would fit right into the Order. Or at least, she would appear to. He didn't know where her animosity toward the Order came from, but hopefully it was the result of rumor and ignorance and therefore would be easy enough to dispel in time. She still wore the leather whip in the place of a sword.

"Why the whip?" he asked. The focused calm on her face broke into surprise. He would have to teach her to control her expressions better, everything in her mind paraded across her face. That would be a detriment to her. He shook off the thought. He was not her instructor, nor relation. Why was he thinking of teaching her anything? Certainly, she was his responsibility as a commandant, but not directly. He plowed on. "It makes a poor weapon."

"By itself, it would," she answered. "It is my focus. Channeling destructive mana improves even the poorest of weapons." She smiled slightly.

"That is true enough. Do you rely upon it? Do you struggle with channeling?"

"No, but I find it makes targeting easier," was her simple reply.

"Hmmm." He supposed targeting such large amounts of mana as she carried would require much practice—practice that a twenty-two-year-old simply had not had enough time for merely one year past becoming a full Mage. His mind flashed brief but amusing projections of what havoc she must have wreaked in her mountain home before they decided that it would be better to give her a focus.

"I will confer with Brother Odo to teach you some drills to assist with your targeting. A focus is fine, but one should not rely too heavily upon it."

A frustrated shadow dampened her features, but she nodded. He definitely needed to teach her to temper her expressions.

"Your message said that my substitution was accepted. What conditions were on it?" she asked.

"Yes," he said, realizing he was still standing behind his desk and sat down. "Grab a chair if you like, but it will be brief. The terms are simple."

"I will stand. Thank you, sir." She seemed to want it over with. Fair enough, toss the chamber pot quickly then.

"You are accepted in your sister's place, for the time being. Should the situation change to outright war requiring military service compulsion or something unexpected happens in the north and we no longer believe she is safe, the Order will reevaluate. The High Council reserves the right to revoke the substitution if the situation dictates."

"Meaning that you can just change your minds whenever for whatever reason." Her voice was hard and flat. "Not me, though. I'll be locked into a service oath."

"Meaning exactly what I said, Pacatus." He kept his voice even. Meeting her jaded words with his own would do no good. How had a girl so young gotten such a rotten taste for the Order? He found it hard to imagine she had much, if any, direct experience with them.

"Yes. I heard you. Those qualifiers could be twisted to fit just about any situation."

"I cannot account for situations that have yet to happen. We are not trying to bend you over a barrel, Pacatus."

"No, you're just trying to do what is best for the Order. Regardless of what that does for me and my sisters."

That statement had threads that would unravel the deeper reasons she had such a poor view of the Order. He couldn't pull on them today; he hadn't been lying about being short of time, but he tucked that knowledge in the back of his mind.

"I cannot put the offer into any defined legal terms that would satisfy you. I can only offer you my word that I will ensure neither you nor Dendra are merely cogs in the Order's wheels."

"All due respect, Commandant, but I don't know you. Your word means very little to me."

He permitted himself a soft chuckle. All due respect, she had said, then said something so disrespectful he could have put her in the stocks for it. Questioning a superior's word was grounds for such punishment, or worse. Questioning a nobleman's word was grounds for a duel. Questioning a senior member of the Order's word was borderline mutinous. Here she was doing all three. Did she even know?

"Alright. Let's change that."

Her brow furrowed. "Change what?"

"My word means nothing to you, you say, because you do not know me. Let's change that."

"Why do you care to change that? Regardless of how lecherous your terms are, I am not in a position to refuse them. So, what do you care what I think of your word? Why are you offering me your word at all?"

"Because I think that you could do great things, but I think that you have no idea yet how to do them. I enjoy your cutting wit, but many others, especially in the nobility, will not. If you are to do anything of consequence, you will need a guide in such things."

"That doesn't answer why you care to be that person." She shifted her feet slightly and twisted her ring with her thumb again.

"Not myself, but you will have met your preceptor today, Brother Odo?" He asked it for politeness, but he knew the answer. Odo was not one for delay.

"Yes," she cautiously agreed.

"He is a very good friend of mine and a former ballast mate. Learn to trust him, and you can feel confident trusting me. He will vouch for my word."

"That—" she sighed—"is an incredibly unsatisfying answer."

"I'm sure." He smiled gently. "But it is the truth."

"I know," she answered softly, leaving him to wonder how she was so sure.

"Whatever you think of our Order, we are trying to do the best for everyone. Someday, I hope you understand that. That is all I have for you, Pacatus. You may take your leave if you have no further questions."

"I don't. Good day, sir." She was already turning away. He decided not to make an issue of the fact she'd failed to salute. That would be for another day.

"Good day."

Asha only got turned around once between the Commandant's office and the armory. She was getting a better idea of the layout of the garrison. Her ballast stood outside of the wide, squatting stone building, just off the side of the door. She hoped that they had not been waiting long.

As she approached, she noted that Brother Gerard was absent, and in his place was his second. She was a lean, middle-aged woman of average height, with a long nose and pale blond hair pulled back into a tight bun. Unlike most of the instructors, she wore only a mail shirt rather than a brigandine cuirass. Brigandine couldn't stretch to accommodate her swollen abdomen. Asha wondered if she would be expected to wear armor and weapons throughout her entire pregnancy. She wasn't sure how far along the sister was, but other than directly bending over, the woman seemed to be completely unencumbered by it. There was an odd comfort in knowing that the Order didn't sequester all their pregnant members away, but then she wondered if perhaps the Order fell into the opposite camp, asking its female members to continue their lives as if they didn't bear the cost of childrearing. It was a good thing she would only be in the Order for seven years.

"Excellent," the sister said at Asha's approach. What was her name again? Mary? Marian? Margaret? It started with an M, but Asha couldn't remember. "Now that we are complete, or as complete as we can be, let us enter."

Inside was lined floor-to-ceiling with weapons racks. The sheer amount of metal would have probably paid for the Empire's budget for months. Asha was amazed. Axes, hammers, spears, maces, and swords were everywhere, packed in tightly and hung with care. One wall was dedicated to shields of various sizes, lain on their faces and stacked from the canvas on the floor to the rafters. There were half a dozen young men and women scattered through the armory, polishing, oiling, and replacing weapons on the racks.

The room was distinctly warmer than outside, and from beneath the floorboards, at least ten or more hammers rang against metal. Unlike the drapers with a small forge in the back of the building, it seemed that the armory was built on top of a forge of equal size to itself. There was a large opening that descended into a staircase at the very back of the room, leading to the forge.

Clever, digging the forge down into the cool earth and letting it heat the building.

A tall, wiry man with flaming red hair and freckles stood at a merchant's counter in the center of the room.

"Brother Darshen. Where's Sister Alice?" the instructor sister asked him.

"Had her baby, Sister Marie. She won't be back for a while."

"Had her baby? When? I thought she had a few more weeks?"

"I guess not." He shrugged. "She delivered just a few days ago. Another boy."

"The Gods are smiling on her." Sister Marie smiled and rubbed her hand absentmindedly on her own protruding stomach, making the mail tinkle a bit. "Well, I have two recruits that are in need of weapons. Casters both."

"Only two?" The temporary armorer skeptically glanced at the ballast, perhaps counting.

"Aye, the foreigners have their own, and well you know Brother Odo. The seventh has not yet joined us."

"I see. What were you thinking? Casters ought to have swords, but do you or Brother Odo have any particular interests for them?"

"Just a simple arming sword for the female. But the male had better have a two-handed sword."

"That's not ideal for a caster." The man scratched his neck awkwardly.

"You got any more of these?" Odo pulled his hand-and-a-half sword partly out of the scabbard as he spoke. "Would play to his strength with a two-handed but be easy enough to switch to single and cast with the offhand."

"They aren't standard," the armorer agreed. "They have increased in popularity of late, but I can check with the sword master downstairs. He has a younger brother working on one as we speak. I do not know if it is already claimed. If so, it may take a few days to add one to the forging load."

"That'll be just fine," Sister Marie answered.

Thrarber coughed and spoke as the armorer began to turn toward the back.

"If'n it wouldn't be no trouble, my brother and I would be most interested in seeing the Order's forge setup?"

"No trouble," the armorer tossed over his shoulder. "Just keep close to stay out of the apprentices' way."

The Dwarves shared a smile and trotted off behind him. Mayumi sauntered over to a rack of spears and bent a little to examine them.

"Is this standard size for your Order's spears?" she asked no one in particular.

"It's standard for humans, if that's what you mean," Odo replied quickly. "We can't all have the wingspan of an albatross like you wave riders."

"Indeed. No wonder the Seventh gave you sand crawlers more mana. Needed to make up for the lack of reach," Mayumi quipped.

The instructor looked a bit offended, but Brother Odo chuckled and replied, "Must be. Must be."

The armorer and the Dwarves reemerged at that moment. A sizable sword was in the armorer's hand, with a length of cloth wrapped around it to protect him from the still warm metal.

"You're in luck." He smiled and raised it a little. "Fresh off the grindstones. Hasn't been oiled, though."

Brother Odo nodded appreciatively. "You know how to care for a new blade, Artifex?"

"I know how to keep the rust from forming, sir," Wilford answered quietly.

"Good. And don't call me sir. I earn my wage."

Sister Marie rolled her eyes. "You'll need to return to the drapers to have it measured for a scabbard," she added.

"Yes, my la—Sister?" Wilford stuttered.

She didn't acknowledge him as the armorer passed the sword to him and began to annotate something in a large tome on the desk. Asha stepped closer to Wilford to examine his new blade. It was a fairly basic sword without any decoration or ornament. It was a long, straight, double-edged blade with substantial fullers to reduce weight. It had straight steel cross guards with rounded ends, a wrapped leather handle, and a thick, round pommel that matched the cross guard.

The armorer then swiveled the tome around and pushed it slightly toward Sister Marie. "I'll need your glyph," he said, then stepped away from the desk and grabbed a smaller sword from a nearby rack. He twisted it around and held it out, handle-first, to Asha. Once she took it from him, he returned his attention to the instructor. "As always, you'll have one week to return them in good order without charge, if the recruits need an exchange. After that, it'll come out of their wages for a new one."

Asha tested the balance of the sword. It was essentially a smaller version of the one issued to Will, with considerably less length and breadth, and shallower fullers. The balance was nice, and it felt good in her hand.

"We can rewrap the handle if it is uncomfortable," Brother Odo said to her. He had approached her and watched her giving it slow swings.

"It doesn't feel uncomfortable now, but I should probably wait to decide that until I've drilled with it a bit."

He nodded then turned back to the armorer. "What about daggers?"

"New guidance. Daggers are only to be issued to members with two years of service under the belt. Recruits must fund their own," the armorer replied.

Odo snorted. "And how are they to do that when they don't draw wages yet?"

The other man shrugged and leaned on the counter. "I don't make policy, Brother. I only follow orders. I think they're saving the steel for larger weapons."

Odo only grunted, but Sister Marie spoke next. "They must be worried of something big to save steel."

"I know not," the armorer said. "Perhaps it is only politics, but perhaps they expect to outfit a larger force soon."

Asha thought about the report the Commandant had given her to read the first time they had spoken. If the Order expected an invasion, they would be wise to save steel. Not that she had any idea where else to procure a proper dagger.

"Shall I go to the draper to get a scabbard as well?" she asked.

"Yes. They ought to have a stock one to fit your sword, though. Then report to the archives for a lesson in basic offensive casting as a unit," Sister Marie answered, then turned to Mayumi and the Dwarves. "You lot can meet us there as you won't need to see the draper." Everyone acknowledged her instructions and headed off in two groups, the armorer's words and implications heavy on their minds.

Chapter 18

Asha

Now that the recruits had been organized into ballasts and issued all the necessary kits, the structure shifted around them. Asha found the days to be an odd mixture of exciting training set inside a routine that quickly became familiar, predictably unpredictable in a way. She found herself adapting and even enjoying it. Perhaps her promise to Bernard wouldn't be as hard to keep as she had expected. She was, if she dared to admit it, enjoying being a part of something bigger than herself, and looked forward to the day that their healer would arrive so her ballast would be complete. Then again, she had always been a part of something bigger; her family was fairly large, and she had always been a part of that. This felt different in a way she couldn't quite explain, yet still familiar, a different type of family perhaps. Maybe the Order wasn't as bad as she had thought it would be.

Most days fell into a pattern, starting with some form of physical exercise at dawn. The obstacle course was still her favorite, and she only had to do remedial exercises for failing obstacles occasionally now, but most days were calisthenics or some variation of running. The Order really liked to make them sprint. That was followed by drilling. Odo and the instructors drilled them extensively in their issued weapons, teaching or improving techniques, flows, and footwork. The recruits were also drilled in organized movements, shield walls, and various flanking maneuvers. They practiced these individually, as a ballast, and as a larger group with all of the recruits. Then after the midday meal, they attended classes at the archives until the evening meal. They learned all of the offensive and defensive spells the Order considered essential and standard. Once they learned them, these were incorporated into the drilling. They also received instruction from the list of required reading and were then tested on each book. Asha's tall pile was dwindling as she returned books after each assignment.

Sometimes, specialists taught the classes. Today was a combination. They were going to receive instruction from one of the Order's priests, then would have to write an essay explaining which God they had chosen as their patron and why. Asha was not sad to turn in the extensive copy of the High Priest's treatises on the matter; it had been the driest read so far.

All of the recruits had been seated at desks in the small room for a while now. The sister who oversaw their classes (the same one who had thought Asha impertinent before) seemed to be the only one unbothered by the apparent delay. Odo leaned on a wall in the back next to Brother Gerard and a few other instructors.

"Timeliness isn't a holy virtue it seems," he remarked quietly. Brother Gerard chuckled. His second, Sister Marie, glared, and the archive sister pretended not to notice his words. He was opposite the room from her chair at the front, but it wasn't a large room, and Asha was pretty sure she would have heard.

The room was silent for a few more moments, then Odo spoke again, louder, and addressed the archive sister. "How long are we going to wait for them? There are other things the recruits could be working on if the priests need to reschedule."

She finally looked up from her papers but let a few heartbeats pass before she answered him. "The priests have many duties, Brother. They have graciously worked this into those duties. I think the least we can do is wait for them."

"And here I thought that instructing young minds in the ways of the Gods *was* their duty."

Her face tightened around the eyes and mouth. It seemed she disliked sass from anyone, not just recruits. Asha should have been ashamed of how much the woman's annoyance delighted her, but she couldn't bring herself to be.

"Perhaps, you could do that in their stead, Brother. As you know so much of the duties of priests," she said slowly, putting unnecessary emphasis on the you and brother.

"What an excellent idea, Sister," Odo replied with mock enthusiasm. Brother Gerard muttered something to him that Asha couldn't catch as he pushed off the stone wall and strode forward.

"Eyes up, recruits, all of ye," he said a little louder than necessary. When he was confident that everyone was paying attention to him, he continued in his normal volume. "It is official edict from the Emperor that citizens worship all of the Gods and do not neglect any. This will be echoed in the vows you will take when you become a member of the Order. Being a brother or sister of our Order is as much about being holy as it is about being a hero." He paused and smiled to himself. "Yes, that is why it's in the name, and yes, it will get tedious hearing that saying during your life with us. That being said, no one outside of the priesthood or perhaps the higher levels of nobility can actually do that."

The archive sister scoffed and said, "I retract my statement. You certainly do not know enough to—"

"Untwist yer braies. I'm not finished. As I was trying to say..." She outright glared at him now, but he pressed on. "No one who has other responsibilities can dedicate equal time and worship to all seven of the Gods. There is also the small matter of in whose house you'll spend eternity after you die. So, you must choose a patron God or Goddess."

He leaned his hip on the archive sister's desk, increasing her visible annoyance. "Now, as our good sister wished to point out, this doesn't mean one ignores or disrespects the other six. One must still observe the feasts and festivals of all the Gods and give them proper prayers when you pass their temples.

"For some of us, the choice is easy. Voids are the creation of Ciirtas, so it makes the best sense for us to choose him. I imagine similar logic follows for the Dwarves and Feorach." He nodded to Thrarber and Throil, who were seated next to Asha, and they nodded acknowledgement back. "But your mana affinity doesn't have to determine your patron. We are all given spirits by Dynawach, so she is also a wise and quite common choice of patron. I have known destructives to worship Iilusen as they feel a deep desire to balance their nature with her growth and kindness. I chose Ciirtas, not only because he blessed my family with a seventh son of a seventh son, but also because I believe in his divine mandate to his Voids to mete out justice and balance the world that it may be good."

The door at the front left of the archive room creaked open, and a man in long brown robes tied with a rope instead of a belt, bare feet, and a shaved head and face stepped inside. A priest of Dynawach, no doubt. The Goddess of perseverance did not demand that her followers give up items like boots, hair oils, and leather belts. But there was a significant faction of devotees, particularly among the priesthood, that did so to prove their devotion to her. He did not appear to be much older than herself, and Asha was surprised by this, although she wasn't sure why. All the priests in her village temple had been old, but it followed that to be an old priest, one must at some point be a young one.

"An excellent testimony, Brother," he said to Odo. "Thank you for sharing that, and I apologize for my lateness."

The archive sister rose and gave him an Imperial salute. "No need to apologize. I'm sure you had excellent reasons," she said, cutting her eyes at Odo.

"My reasons, be they excellent or wanting, are of no use to you and your recruits. I am only grateful that there are worthy and able brothers among the instructors to step in when needed." The archive sister looked like she was about to say something else, probably a snip about Odo not truly being an instructor, but the priest gave her no time. "I would, however, like to add a caution to the words of our good brother."

The priest looked at Odo as though he were expecting a reply, but Odo only gestured acquiescence and walked back to the rear of the room. So, the priest turned to the recruits and continued, "While I do think one should take the Divine mandate of their patron into consideration before selection, it cannot be overlooked that there may be consequences if you choose a God opposite your affinity." The priest smiled pleasantly. "A destructive who worships the Goddess of Growth and Kindness, Iilusen, may balance out the harm that they innately cause, but a healer who worships Niiwyd, the Goddess of Sea and Sky, may find themselves without divine assistance when they must use their mana. We must balance the weight of our affinities and gifts with our own desires and practicality. Whereas a weather Mage will find the Niiwyd a ready and practical patron, less so the God of Smithing and Craftmanship..."

No amount of pleasant smiles would make this lecture more interesting to Asha. Her mind drifted, and she focused on a scroll in the upper-right corner of the room that looked a bit dustier than the rest. It was seated precariously on top of several leather-bound tomes on a high inset shelf. The young priest still talked, and she should have tried harder to listen, but she wasn't sure he could tell her anything she didn't already know. Everyone knew there were advantages a patron could provide, and she knew that if one didn't choose wisely, those advantages could be less advantageous. A good harvest wasn't very helpful when staring down a fell beast or a bandit. But Odo had a point about believing in a patron's mandate. *Brother Odo*, she corrected herself. He was her superior, and she had only known him a short time. Too short a time to be on a first-name basis. She must remember to include his title, even internally.

Brother Odo had made a good point. Choosing a God based on what that God could provide felt wrong and hollow. She mulled that over for a few minutes, trying to put words to her discomfort with the idea until the priest said something that cut through her thoughts and recaptured her attention.

"So lastly, recruits, whom I hope to very soon call brothers and sisters—" there was that smile again; it was disarming and warm, but she didn't like it—"I will add that although you do have a written assignment today, including your choice, I would like to reassure you that the Gods wish for no unwilling devotees. Despite what you write today, you can change your mind up until you swear your vows. Even after that, though it is not encouraged—" he paused, and his smile dropped to a soft expression—"changing devotion is not forbidden." Again, the archive sister opened her mouth to speak, and again the young priest charged on before she could. "That doesn't give you leave to shirk the essay but rather use it as a tool to strengthen your understanding of your faith and make that decision before your vows firmer."

He turned and saluted the archive sister. "I will take up no more of your time; however, I will linger in the next room if any recruits have questions they would like to ask."

She rose and returned the salute. "Thank you, brother." Then as the priest stepped back toward the door he had entered, she turned to the recruits and said, "You all heard him. You may seek guidance, one at a time, but if you have no need, begin your essays."

Asha reached for the quill in the shared inkwell and gently tapped her offhand thumb on the parchment in front of her. She was distracted by a whispered conference between Mayumi, Thrarber, and Throil off to her right-hand side. After a few words, the three stood and approached Brother Odo and Gerard at the back. The instructors were intent on integrating the Elf and Dwarves, but there were some things they were exempt from. It seemed this essay was one of them, as they filed out the rear entrance with the instructors.

She turned her mind back to her assignment. The truth was she wasn't at all sure who her patron God should be. She wasn't normally indecisive so perhaps it was best to consider each God in order.

The first Goddess, Estesbryd, was the Goddess of Hope, Rest, and Rejuvenation, one of the Twins. Typically, the patron of healers, she was also the creator of the sun, stars, and (with the help of Feorach) the moon. She blessed her devotees with stronger mana under the light of the stars. Her divine mandate to her devotees was to provide places of rest and hope for others. Probably a bad choice for herself, Asha decided. Not only was healing directly opposite her mana affinity, but her mandate was not something Asha felt she could dedicate herself to.

Next was the other Twin, the second God, Trunii, the Recorder, the God of Death, Darkness, and Pity. Asha wasn't sure what advantages he might give his devotees, but his mandate to them was to do in life what he himself would do in death: Record the lives of others and mourn their sorrows with them. Of course, after death, the Recorder would also judge people based on their lives, but Asha was pretty sure his devotees had nothing to do with that. She remembered a husband and wife who followed Trunii had come to the village when she was about twelve. The husband had taken down any story anyone would tell him, while the wife had held the person's hand and silently cried, as though she felt every sorrow expressed. Definitely not the way Asha wished to worship.

Next, the third Goddess, Iilusen, Goddess of Growth, Fertility, and Kindness. Her mandate was that her devotees must protect and steward her creations: Plants and animals. She did not forbid killing, only cruel or unnecessary slaughter. Odo's suggestion that a destructive worship her to balance themselves was not the first time she'd heard this suggestion. Her mother and aunts had strongly encouraged her similarly. Iilusen blessed her devotees with better harvests, healthier animals, and often larger families. Perhaps she was just being obstinate, but she really had no interest in the third Goddess.

Next, the fourth Goddess, Niiwyd, Goddess of Sea, Sky, and Passion. She had also assisted Iilusen in the creation of the Elves before Dynawach gave them spirits. Her mandate was to protect and appreciate the wild and untamable things in this world. Asha wasn't entirely sure what that meant and was definitely not sure how to practice it. Her blessings to her devotees were equally obscure: In the scriptures, Niiwyd promised that if one truly followed her, she would be a rock to them in gale or wave. What good was a rock in hard times? Asha also didn't like directives in the form of riddles. Niiwyd was not the patron for her.

Next, the fifth God, Feorach, God of Craftmanship, Smithing, and Curiosity. He was the creator of the Dwarves before Dynawach gave them spirits and assisted Estesbryd in the creation of the moon. His mandate was to shape the world with care and to continually feed a sense of curiosity. He blessed his devotees' creations and gave them divine assistance while crafting. Asha was not particularly good at creating anything; her talents lay in destruction. Similarly, with Iilusen and Estesbryd, Asha didn't think she could dedicate herself to something so opposite her affinity.

That left only two: The sixth God, Ciirtas, and the seventh Goddess, Dynawach. Ciirtas was the God of Balance, Justice, and Rationality. He gave seventh sons their Void mana and mandated them to enforce justice and protect the world. "Nothing unbalanced can be good," his scriptures said. That was a mandate she could believe in.

Finally, Dynawach, the strongest of the Gods, the Goddess of Spirits, Life, and Perseverance. She breathed mana into the world and created humankind. Her mandate was to be good and accomplish hard things. That seemed incredibly broad to Asha. She was undoubtedly the most common choice of patron, but commonality alone shouldn't make it less desirable, Asha reminded herself. It was a bit funny; again, she found herself rebelling internally. She would be expected to choose Dynawach. After all, she was the daughter of a seventh daughter of a seventh daughter; some would say she owed Dynawach her fealty for such a blessing to her family. Destructive Mages also didn't have a patron that perfectly corresponded to their affinity like Naturals, Voids, Weathers, Artificers, or Healers. So, in several ways, the Seventh Goddess felt like a default patron. Asha didn't want to choose a God just because it was expected of her, but she also felt incredibly childish choosing a different patron only because it was counter to expectation.

Asha was also the daughter of a seventh son, and surely enforcing justice would require some good old-fashioned destruction. She recalled Odo's words about the mandate being the most important factor to him. Looking down at her parchment, she realized she had absentmindedly written down all seven of the mandates. She read them over a few more times, trying to see which resonated most in her heart. Her eyes and heart kept returning to Ciirtas's mandate. Warmth and determination settled in her chest when she focused on it. She could make the world a more balanced and just place, with or without the Order. Nothing unbalanced could be good, and Asha wanted the world to be good. She didn't believe it was, not yet, but perhaps, just perhaps, she could change that. Re-inking her quill, she began to write her essay.

Chapter 19

Mago

Mago's eyes watered a bit at the intensity of the incense and burning herbs in the torches of the palace.

"Have I ever mentioned that I appreciate how well you use incense?" He leaned down slightly to whisper the words to Sophonisba. Her perfect, neutral smile didn't change, but she squeezed the inside of his arm where her hand rested as they walked across the marble floor toward the large dining chamber.

"You mean that I cover the smell of lovemaking without making one feel that they have entered a pungent fog?" she whispered back.

"Can you call it lovemaking if it's paid for?"

He couldn't identify what on her face changed, but sadness flit across her expression.

"No, I suppose not," she said.

He had the urge to comfort her somehow. But he wasn't exactly sure what had saddened her, let alone what to say to cheer her. He decided to ignore it for now; there were other things to worry about.

Even in the relative coolness of the evening, the tightly woven silk robes felt oppressive on his skin. He much preferred his lighter linen, but Sophonisba had insisted that it was insufficient for a victory feast. She was right, of course. It wouldn't have been wise to be seen as disrespecting the conquerors of the entire lower continent by dressing lowly. So, he had donned the imported silks dyed with vibrant purple and red patterns, and all the gold jewelry he owned, which was admittedly not that much. Not even half the weight that adorned his mistress next to him.

He scanned the opulent room as they entered the feasting hall. More marble, and more incense and torches. An ache pulsed behind his eyes. It would be a long night. Large, low wooden tables were arranged around the perimeter of the room with feather-filled cushions that many guests had already reclined upon around them. The head table, separated from the rest by a small stone platform, was mostly empty. He had expected this but was still slightly unsettled. It was natural that the hosts and conquerors would arrive last, but it was not helpful in pursuit of his goal to avoid the Blind Seer.

As it turned out, his goal was of no consequence. The door servant led him and Sophonisba to cushions at a table in the back of the room to the left of the head table. The seating was arranged then. He was slightly surprised but hopeful that this was because Bomilcar wanted to keep him close by. Bomilcar didn't like his prophetic half-sister and would likely seat her on the opposite side of the head table from himself.

He found himself unable to release the tension in his shoulders as he accepted a gold-plated goblet of wine from a serving girl. Sophonisba artfully arranged her matching purple and red silks around her legs after reclining. She made an incredibly alluring picture on the cushions of the royal feasting hall. He had always seen her beauty, composure, and poise as assets to himself, but tonight, he found himself worried that she would attract attention. She noticed him watching and shifted her legs to flash a bit more flesh above her knee. He looked away and knew that behind her small, seemingly open smile, she was laughing at him. She found his modesty amusing. If he put himself in her point of view, it was. A whore master discomforted by his whores' bodies? It was preposterous and therefore comical.

Not that he could blame her, she had no idea that he was worried about drawing the Seer's attention. She played the part of head mistress of a whore house at a feast perfectly. It wasn't as if he could explain the fear he repressed. Bomilcar might doubt his half-sister's proclaimed ability to see when individuals were dangerous to the Dragon Riders, but Mago couldn't take the chance that he was wrong. For Mago intended to be very dangerous to them, and he didn't desire to meet the dragon fire that was reserved for those Dido impugned.

Avoiding her had been easier than he had expected while trailing the Dragon Riders' army, up to this point. He allied himself with her competitive, hateful half-brother. So, Mago had never aroused suspicion by keeping a wide distance from her. He wasn't sure if he could continue that now that they were all in the port city, and he was living in his gifted mansion, right down the street from the palace, not to mention attending feasts.

Mago sipped his wine and affected a bored look as he continued to observe the room around him. He still hadn't found a contact in Hadrumentum to get his reports to the Empire. If he died tonight, the Imperial Navy wouldn't have any warning of what was coming. Sophonisba shifted her body and leaned toward him. She whispered, "Smile. You're going to start tongues wagging that you aren't happy about the victory."

He kicked himself internally and closed his eyes. Sophi was playing her part well, and he was about to throw the whole game away by failing to play his. He imagined grabbing the image of himself standing before Bostar's dragon, its scaley breastplate glowing before the fiery breath erupted. He shoved the image inside a wooden chest, locked it, and slid it under his bed. His fear would not control him. It was unhelpful and therefore unimportant now. He fixed his face with a calm smile and opened his eyes.

"Much better, master." Her eyes crinkled a little, highlighting the crow's feet. She was so beautiful and had so many perfectly curated smiles that she wore like masks, but he liked this one best because it wasn't perfect. The wrinkles told of her experience and belied her true emotions. Sloppy. He was becoming sloppy, sedentary, and wistful. If his fear didn't get him caught, his heart might. These feelings, too, he stuffed into a chest and shoved under the proverbial bed.

"How long do you think we will have to wait for our hosts?" he asked her, sipping the wine and realizing he had drained the goblet.

"Not long." She pulled her eyes from his and scanned the room. "The servants are growing restless. That likely means they expect their masters to appear soon."

As usual, she was correct. Only about a quarter of an hour passed before the massive double doors were thrown open and Bostar, Warlord of the Western Craigs, Master of the Dragon Riders, and Conqueror of the South was announced. His six living children followed shortly behind him. Predictably, Bomilcar, eldest son by his named wife, and conqueror of Hadrumentum was first. He came and stood behind the cushions nearest Mago at the head table, while his siblings and half-siblings were announced.

Had Bomilcar meant offense by having Dido, the Blind Seer and seventh daughter of her mother, announced last? If he had, Mago wasn't sure that it had worked. First was an honor, yes, but so was the seventh. Counting their father, she was still honored. Mago breathed a sigh of relief as she was indeed seated on the far side of the head table, and he was spared her intense, glassy stare.

Bomilcar also watched her, disdain clear on his face. But he cleared it before Bostar glanced at him, then the Warlord addressed the standing guests.

"Thank you for joining us in our victory feast that was prepared by my eldest son. The Gods smile on us this day. I know it is common to ply guests with speeches. But since taking the fealty of the entire southern continent with dragon fire is not common, I see no reason to make you listen to common, useless words." His voice was exactly as Mago could imagine a villain in a story meant to frighten children into behaving. Grizzled, harsh, and with no small amount of pride and malice. But those villains would never pass the opportunity to monologue before a captive audience. Bostar continued, lifting his goblet. "To victory!"

"To victory!" the guests roared back, raising their goblets.

"To Dragon Fire!"

"To Dragon Fire!"

"To the Gods!"

"To the Gods!"

"To Lord Bostar, and the strength of his army!" Bomilcar added his own shout at the end of his father's last.

"To Lord Bostar!" the guests roared obediently, and Bomilcar smirked at his siblings who barely covered their glares. Mago wasn't sure exactly what that meant, but he knew that Bomilcar had scored a small victory. Was there unrest among the children of the Warlord? Was this normal political play for favor, or something deeper?

Bostar basked in the shouts of praise, then drained his goblet. His children and the guests followed suit. Then he took a seat on his cushions amid the cheers. All the guests remained standing until everyone at the head table reclined comfortably.

Immediately, Mago found his goblet refilled and a platter of soft, white bread with herbed oil and sheep's cheese ground with garlic and pepper was placed before him and Sophi. As the feast began, so did the tributes. One by one, the surviving nobles of the port city rose from their tables and brought gifts to the Warlord, then knelt and swore undying fealty to him and his heirs.

If the seating arrangement was a true guide, then further away from the head table, the lower the nobles were considered. It struck Mago then that by this logic, he, a mere whore master, was elevated above almost all of the nobles. Surely, that had to be a mistake, but Bomilcar did hold tightly to such ceremonies. He wouldn't have overlooked such a thing. Perhaps he had meant to offend more than just Dido tonight.

With this on his mind, he turned toward Bomilcar and unexpectedly met his eyes. Bomilcar's lips turned up into a full smile, and he leaned over close enough to be heard without shouting over the nobleman currently offering allegiance.

"Are you and your woman enjoying the feast?" he said.

It was a silly question. Did he expect Mago to say no?

"Very much. You have outdone yourself," Mago answered cheerfully.

Bomilcar's smile widened at the praise. "You always know what to say to me, my friend."

"Would I be your friend if I didn't?" Mago quipped as the previous platter was replaced by another with flatbread, smoked hard cheeses, and diced olives dressed with fresh herbs, vinegar, and oil.

Bomilcar chuckled, then his eyes became serious. "I suppose not, and what a shame that would be."

Mago covered his confusion by sipping the wine. He should slow down on it; he could feel it going to his head. "A shame, indeed. For both of us."

He filled a flatbread with the cheese and olives and ate it hungrily. Something in his stomach would help. He couldn't afford to make any mistakes tonight. A servant came to pour him more wine, and Sophi whispered something to her. The servant didn't fill the goblet but returned with a different pitcher, then topped his goblet off. He raised an eyebrow at Sophi, but she smirked at him and returned to her conversation with the nobleman on the other side of them. He raised the goblet and found the wine was significantly watered down. Sophi thought of everything.

Mago listened briefly to the next nobleman professing his compelled fealty. This nobleman had slaves present a large timber, with promises of many more to be collected at the Warlord's leisure. A valuable resource for shipbuilding. This brought his mind back to his dilemma; he desperately needed a suitable contact to warn the Empire that ships were being built.

He turned his attention back to Bomilcar. If he sought praise, Mago would give it to him, and hopefully get information in return. A fresh platter was set before him, filled with sliced peaches and apples, candied walnuts, and a paste of beans ground with eggs, wine, honey, and ginger. Mago continued to feign enthusiasm.

"Your skill in planning such a feast cannot be overstated. Forgive me if I was brisk earlier. I am merely in awe," he said. Others might have found such unctuous flattery obvious and therefore repulsive. Mago felt like a bootlicking sycophant saying them, but Bomilcar loved it. He preened under the praise as he always did.

"You are forgiven. I only hope that Father agrees with you. I need him to see that I am capable of managing such political endeavors." Bomilcar held his goblet aloft to be refreshed, and no less than three servants nearly tripped over each other to assist him. One was a delicate girl of no more than twenty, with ebony skin and jet-black hair in tiny braids with wooden beads at the ends. She was unfortunately pretty, and even more unfortunately, Bomilcar noticed. He seized her by the arm and forced her to join him on the cushion, tossing aside the pitcher she carried and pulling her to recline back against him.

Mago could play the bootlicker if it meant that no Imperial women found themselves on such a cushion with this man. "Anyone can see that you are competent in such matters. Surely your father is no exception?" He softened the second statement into a question, just in case they were overheard by someone who might take offense. Like the father in question, who was receiving another nobleman's gifts and oaths as a new platter replaced the last. This one had mussels stewed with leeks, cumin, and wine from white grapes, alongside seared sea bass seasoned with lemon, dill, and pepper.

"My father is questioning my political prowess after he heard my method of conquering this salt-soaked city!" Bomilcar seemed unbothered by the rigid posture and trembling of the serving girl. *Keep talking, friend. Tell me more that I can use to unravel you.*

"Your method was quick and tactically sound, was it not? Forgive me, I don't understand such matters."

"Tactically, it was sound, but he wanted something more diplomatic. I don't know what he expected me to do, but he just went on about judicious withholding of strength and alliances."

The Warlord was concerning himself with alliances and diplomacy. That meant he was trying to create a stable foundation with which to cement his rule of the newly conquered territories. He intended to turn the territories into a kingdom of his own, then—a dynasty. Mago had suspected as much, but it was a shame to see that Bostar was so good at it.

"I see," Mago said as he thoughtfully sipped his diluted wine. "Are the promises of fealty and lavish gifts we endure now not evidence that your method achieved the desired results?" If only the father could be pushed to the impulsiveness of his son, it might open avenues of weakness for the Empire to exploit.

"They are, my friend." Bomilcar grinned wickedly, meeting Mago's eye for a moment before attempting to feed a bite of fish to the trembling serving girl. She opened her mouth obediently but gagged instead of swallowing. Fish and bile were regurgitated onto the Dragon Rider. He threw her forcibly off of him in disgust, and she scampered away. Mago noticed that the servants who came to clean his silks and clear away the contaminated platters were male. Bomilcar met his eyes again. "By the end of the night, Father will have to admit that fear and pain are tools of diplomacy as well."

Mago didn't think the Warlord disagreed with that sentiment, just with his son's application of them.

"No doubt you are right, my friend. You always are." He lifted his goblet slightly in a mock toast.

Bomilcar plastered on a triumphant grin. "So well put. Mark this word of mine, as well: Withhold all doubt. If all goes well tonight, Father will choose me to fly ahead of the ships when they sail under the next full moon."

Fly ahead? Before the next full moon? Would the Warlord push north so soon? It could not be. Mago couldn't keep the surprise from springing up on his face. Bomilcar's eyes narrowed and knew he had erred. He quickly neutralized it but scrambled to think of a way out.

"So, you're telling me that if tonight goes well, I shall lose my most frequent customer? Should I wish for the night to go poorly?" He pasted on what should pass for a wry grin.

"Not if you know what is good for you, you won't." Bomilcar's expression was hard to read at first but relaxed a bit after he took a few moments to ponder the humorous tone. "Always the businessman. You call me friend often, but not when I speak of leaving." The platters were changed again. This one carried pork stewed with apples, leeks, and garum, topped with an herbaceous sauce.

"Forgive me," Mago said, "I meant only to make light of such heavy news."

Bomilcar waved dismissively as he chewed his pork. "I'm sure you did. Perhaps I am too sensitive to such suggestions after having my capabilities undermined all day."

"An understandable reaction, my lord. Surely, such disrespect will be silenced when you lead a party eastward." It was a petty tactic, but Bomilcar could never resist correcting him.

"We aren't going east. We are going north. And it isn't certain that I will be leading them. Haven't you paid attention to anything I've said?"

Oh, I am paying attention. "Poorly, it seems. As you know, I am a businessman. I know nothing of campaigns and conquering."

Bomilcar glanced at his father and siblings, but they were all paying attention to the noblewoman pledging fealty and canvas for sails. He leaned a little closer, remaining discreet, and spoke quieter so Mago had to strain to hear. "We're pushing north to teach those pirate isles a lesson they'll not soon forget. Then after that, on to the northern continent. See if the mighty Empire has an answer to dragon fire. We don't have enough ships for all of the army; not yet. Father wants to send an advance party. Scout the coasts, soften up the Navy, and find a port to land the rest of the army. We will conquer the whole world, and I intend to be the first to fly my dragon over foreign shores."

There it was, plain as day, everything he had suspected. The pork sank in his gut like stones, but he forced a calm expression and took a few more bites before answering. "Well, favorite customer or not, I cannot help but wish tonight goes well for you, my friend. I could not deny you the glory such an endeavor would bring." Bomilcar did not answer him, staring off into the distance.

He needed the timeline and scope. How long between the advance party and the rest of the army? How many ships in each? He bit the questions back. They were too obvious, and he could not allow himself to press. He couldn't afford to ruin this now. Not when Bomilcar had only trusted enough to give him this much.

Another platter, likely the last, was placed before him, filled with bowls of pulse mixed with raisins and currants, smelling of honey and cinnamon. Sophonisba caught his eye and gave him a nod. He would not get to enjoy this platter, even if the rolling in his stomach had allowed. It was his turn to make pledges and gifts.

He rose from the cushions and walked before the head table, conscious to carry himself with a dignity he didn't feel. There was no hiding from Dido now. At what distance was her gift useful? How far away from the head table could he stand before it was obvious he was avoiding something? He stepped as far away as he dared, then knelt.

"Most prestigious Lord of Dragons and the Southern Continent." He had given much thought about what to say during this encounter, particularly about how to survive it without actually swearing loyalty. He thought his solution was quite clever. "I cannot express adequate gratitude that a lowly merchant such as myself would be permitted to not only attend but also to address your eminence.

"I have followed you from your fortress in the western craigs, across the plains and plateaus, past the foothills, here to the coast. I have witnessed your power and majesty. I beg leave of you to permit me to continue to follow you, wherever you go."

Mago kept his head bowed in reverent display. Flattery and reference to past loyalty, implying more of the same in the future. It should work, especially as he intended to continue just as he always had. And if it wasn't a truly proper pledge of allegiance? He was but a lowly whore master, a camp follower. He couldn't be expected to understand the proper etiquette.

"I grant you leave, whore master," Bostar said finally.

"Thank you, most gracious lord." Mago lifted his head and stood. As he did so, he made a mistake. He glanced to the far side of the head table. His heart stuttered in his chest. How could eyes so dull and glassy pierce so deeply? *She can't see you*, he told himself. *She's blind.*

She can see your soul, and all its treachery, his fear whispered back. *She can see through your clever words and hollow praise.*

He jerked his eyes back to the Warlord's face and covered his fear with a broad smile. "I have no timber or canvas or even much gold to give you. Please accept this offering. It is the best of my wealth."

As he finished speaking, all but a handful of his whores entered the hall from servants' entrances, filing into the center of the reception. They were all dressed identically, tiny red silk wraps woven finely to be nearly sheer, wrapped around their breasts and hips, just barely covering each, exposing the midsection and legs. Golden bangles around their wrists and ankles, and delicate golden chains around their necks and bellies caught the torchlight. They began to dance as he returned to his cushions.

His heart still raced as he reclaimed his seat. He took note of each part of his body, checking for tension, forcing each muscle to obey, relaxing and showing all the world a carefree posture. Sophonisba eyed him. She leaned close and kissed his cheek. "Unlock your jaw. You look like a puppet with a painted face." She breathed against his skin.

"Only capable of singular expression?" he whispered back.

"Body limp but face rigid and unnatural." She pulled back but still spoke quietly enough that her voice was unlikely to be heard by others.

The chuckle that escaped him did more to relieve tension and slow his heart than all his best efforts had. He shook his head slightly and picked up his wine, scanning the room. Most of the nobility were enthralled by the dancing women, a few stared blankly elsewhere, some glared with open hostility. Bomilcar was enraptured, no doubt deciding which he would bed that night. Bostar looked bored. Mago did not look at the others at the head table. He did not want to catch *her* eyes again.

The song came to an end, and the dancers stilled but prepared to begin again. But the opening notes didn't come. Someone had silenced the harpists. A servant led Dido out in front of her father. Mago's heart pounded again, and it was so quiet in the hall, he would have sworn all the nobility could hear it. His whores exchanged discreet glances and made themselves scarce. She waited to speak until the servant had also made herself scarce.

"I know it is not customary, as my fealty was pledged long ago, but I also have a gift for you, Father." Her voice was clear and light, like the tolling of a bell.

"My children are not bound by such customs. Proceed, daughter."

The chatter in the hall did not return. Everyone listened intently. Mago glanced at Bomilcar. He was seething, gripping his jeweled ceremonial sword. Knowing the Warlord's son, ceremonial or not, the sword had a good edge too.

"My gift is a prophecy."

She paused for effect. It worked, too. If anyone hadn't been watching or listening, they did now. Bostar leaned forward. Bomilcar snorted derisively, and his hand left his sword for his goblet.

"Tell me," Bostar said low and eagerly.

"I have been having dreams. Under the night skies, I fly northward upon the back of a dragon made of wind. Across the seas, past the coast of Anitaris, through the fertile fields. Up the rivers to the mountains from which they spring. Past the brown heights to mountains of gray and white. I fly over a valley fed by a river that births from a plateau of ice.

"As I fly, I see all the north men and women bow the knee to the Dragon Riders and their Lord." Mago didn't think she could have said more terrifying words.

"Until I reach the valley of ice. There, I see a woman, now but a girl. No one else can see me in my dreams." What did a blind woman see in her dreams? Perhaps she was not always blind.

"But this girl sees me, as she is also a daughter of seven. She sees me and she catches the wind beneath me. She unmakes the dragon and reforms it by her will into a mighty sword. With this sword, she leads the people against us. With the sword of wind, she strikes our dragons from the sky. These also she remakes into swords. Not to wield herself but to be wielded by others. Those she called kin. When our dragons are gone, she takes the sword of wind and strikes you down. Your blood flows upon the earth, and every soul you have taken cries out in victory and revenge."

The hall collectively gasped and quietly began to whisper. Sophi caught his eye, dread overwhelming her countenance. He gripped her hand in comfort. It was possible then. The Empire could win. They just needed this young woman from the north.

Bostar had slumped back against his cushions. This was not the prophecy he had wanted at a victory feast. Not when he was preparing his advance party for invasion. Bomilcar was the first to speak.

"She's a liar," he nearly shouted, rising slightly off his seat. "Father, pay her no mind. She doesn't have the Sight. She lies and chooses children to die at random. She cannot see their futures nor yours. She jockeys for your favor and now intends to undermine my position before I prepare to sail."

Bostar turned a wrathful gaze from his son back to his daughter. "How do you answer this charge, seventh daughter?"

The words hung in the air for an entire minute. Then she said, "If my brother doubts my Spirit Sight, I will prove myself. I do not choose at random. I can see whose souls will be dangerous to our family."

"You can't prove that!" Bomilcar retorted. "That's exactly my point, Father. She demands that we take her at her word while forcing you to rely on her for the safety of our future. It is nonsense created to solidify her position in your court."

Bostar took a noisy sip of wine. "How will you prove yourself?"

Dido turned, and those dead eyes pierced Mago once more. "The whore master."

Fear choked him. He should run. He should fight. No. No. He had to think of something!

"What?" Bomilcar screamed, and Bostar spoke in unison.

"The whore master is a traitor to us. I saw it when he made his pledge. His soul is dangerous to us. He must burn, or he will strike us a mortal wound."

Triumph edged into fear. *A mortal wound? Ciirtas, preserve me. I must strike that wound. Even if I die tonight and face the Recorder before the morn. Let me strike them. Strike them deep and true. Let me be your instrument of justice against these monsters.*

Chapter 20

Asha

Asha stepped forward and to the right swiftly, a small buckler clasped tightly in her outstretched hand. Her sword was resting with the blade on her right shoulder as she held it with her elbow bent. The casual nature of the stance had fooled Will before, costing him several of these sparring matches. That morning, he was prepared when she swung the blade with incredible swiftness from its resting position into a high cut toward his neck that was covered with an ill-fitting gorget. He caught her blade with his in a cross guard, reinforcing his larger hand-and-a-half sword with his own borrowed buckler. He then attempted to shield knock her and open her up for a thrust to her closed-helm-covered head.

The barrel-shaped great helm was the practical option for sparring as it provided excellent protection while being easy enough to pass from recruit to recruit with simple adjustments to padding. Still, she hated the closed-off, caged feeling she got as soon as she slipped it on. She much preferred her issued open-faced helm to the two narrow eye slits and dozen or so small air holes. Drawing in a deep breath of hot, recycled air, she evaded Will's shield knock and deflected his thrust with her buckler. She stepped back and to the left, disengaging but hoping Will would attack her right side with the newly opened space.

He did, thrusting low toward her brigantine-covered side with his buckler covering his hand from above. It was getting harder to beat him; his footwork was improving rapidly, and he was beginning to learn her fighting style and tells. She caught his thrust with a hanging guard, similarly, covering her hand with her buckler. In a single fluid motion, she pressed her buckler forward against his, binding both it and his sword as she rotated her arm to bring the tip of her sword around the bind she had just created, and counter thrust him, sliding her blade along his into his armored middle. She couldn't see the surprise on his face, but it was in the set of his shoulders when Brother Gerard barked out the word that signaled the end of a match.

Stepping back, she gave him a quick salute with her sword before ripping the wretched great helm from her face. He did the same but with much less urgency.

"Just when I think I'm doing well, you go and do something sneaky like that," he said with a false moroseness belied by a grin.

"You were doing well. Better than you have since we started, but not good enough." She grinned back.

"Enough chatter. Clear out of the pit and go practice some guard to casting drills on the field. There are others that need to spar," Brother Gerard said with irritation, but then again, it seemed like he said almost everything with irritation, so it was hard to tell.

Will shrugged at her, and they both handed off their helms, padded gorgets, and bucklers to the next recruits waiting. They retrieved their issued helms and jogged over to the far side of the training field where a dozen or so recruits were already engaged in such drills. They both fell into the line, standing even at the shoulder but with a good double-arm distance between them. The sun was getting close to its zenith, and the midday meal couldn't be far off. Asha was grateful as her stomach rumbled, and she began to sweat. It was as warm now in the late spring morning as it would be at the height of summer back home in her northern glacier valley. She had known that the weather would be warmer further south, but she dreaded just how much warmer.

Setting her feet in a ready stance, she raised her left arm and filled her shield bracelet with mana. She began familiar drills with her sword in her right, listening for the command from the instructor.

When he yelled at irregular intervals, she shifted her grip on her sword, gripping it with only her palm and thumb, splaying her fingers out and shooting a bolt of raw destructive mana from them into the open field in front of her. She didn't like this drill at all. It was a terrible way to hold a sword, very insecure. But it ensured she shot the mana out past her sword, not down along the length of it. She was already on her third sword, the first two having melted right in her hand. The armory had already thrown a fit about reissuing it. Odo had intervened, but she wasn't sure if he could do anything if she turned in another misshapen lump of steel.

She watched Will in the corner of her eye and wondered if perhaps she should speak with Odo about changing to a sword like his. Will held his sword in both hands while he practiced his drills. When the instructor shouted the command, he switched his grip, so the sword was only in his right hand and shot a bolt of fire from his left. It seemed a wiser choice, but she was awfully fond of her shield. If she didn't get better at her current method and melted another sword, she would pose it to Odo as a solution. She had only been shooting out raw mana, but after a few iterations, she began to try simple spells: First fire, then rot, alternating them back and forth. Her success brought her a small degree of pride, and when the instructor called the end of the drilling, she still had an intact blade. So, she must've been improving, even if it still felt wrong.

After the end of that drill, her ballast fell into a small semi-circle around Brother Gerard and his second, Sister Marie, for instruction on where to report after the midday meal.

"No training this afternoon. You're dismissed for the day. Don't get into any trouble, or I'll make sure you're not dismissed again until your vows. You know where to be next daybreak," Brother Gerard said curtly.

Asha and Will glanced at each other in surprise but didn't want to ruin it by questioning anything. The entire group turned toward the provision hall; they could discuss what to do with their unexpected freedom while they ate, away from meddling instructors.

"Find something of use to do with yourselves! Don't while away this time," Sister Marie half-shouted, half-panted at their backs. The panting was no doubt the result of her preborn infant stretching its legs up into her ribs. Asha had never felt it appropriate to ask how far along she was but was fairly sure that Sister Marie would be delivered from such discomfort within a few weeks. Her stomach was so large now, she couldn't even wear her mail shirt over it, and recently, her stomach sat lower, and she waddled more than walked across the training field. She still wore her sword belt and other equipment, though, modifying the instructor uniform as little as necessary. And she seemed to gain some degree of catharsis taking out her frustrations in the final period of pregnancy on the recruits. Perhaps that was why the Order seemed to pack its archives and academy with its pregnant and freshly delivered members; they had no patience for recruits' nonsense. Asha respected that choice.

The provision hall was packed as it always was at midday, and the ballast had trouble finding a bench. They were about to take their trenchers outside and sit in the grass when Mayumi spotted a freshly vacated bench along the back wall. Asha tucked into her black cod that had been baked with fresh herbs and salad of spring peas, leeks, and ramps. The food from the provision hall was simple and repetitive, but it was good, or at least as good as one could expect from food production on such a large scale. She was glad that cod was in season; it was a nice break from salted beef and pork.

"Well, what shall we do with our spare afternoon, men?" Thrarber asked after shoveling his food faster than was safe. Then again, he rarely waited to start eating until they had found ample seating. "Uh, and lasses," he added quickly. Asha had the distinct impression that he was unaccustomed to working with women. Not that he seemed to be discomforted by her or Mayumi; more like he forgot sometimes that either of them were not men. Perhaps it was a racial difference? Asha had never seen a Dwarven woman firsthand. Perhaps Thrarber forgot he wasn't surrounded by males because none of the females around him looked female in his mind.

"It must be 'of use', whatever it is," Wilford replied, rolling his eyes.

Both he and Asha glanced at Odo after he said that. He wasn't an instructor, but he also wasn't their equal. His odd role as member but superior meant that they often looked to him for such decisions. Odo, however, grunted noncommittally as he often did.

"My mother would like to meet the ones I will be binding myself to," Mayumi answered. "She has been asking this of me for a while now, but it has not been convenient to do so. I would be honored if you would all come to eat in my home. My husband will only need an hour or so to prepare the house."

Asha didn't know why she was surprised that Mayumi had a house nearby. Mayumi wasn't in the barracks with the other female recruits, so she had to have rented accommodations somewhere. Asha had assumed that was a room in an inn, and also that Mayumi was without a husband or close family. She shouldn't have assumed things about the people that would soon be bound to her in a blood oath.

"That sounds lovely," she said. "It would be nice to get to know each other outside of the garrison."

"Your husband will prepare the house?" Throil asked, his brow furrowed. Thrarber seemed equally confused but didn't echo the question.

"Of course. He is very skilled in such things. He has been an ambassador to the Empire for, oh, nearly a hundred years. I only need to go ahead and warn him to prepare," Mayumi answered, not seeming to understand what the Dwarves were confused by. Asha knew that Mayumi was hundreds of years old, but she didn't look over thirty-five, and it was still shocking to hear small reminders of her true age.

"While you do that, the rest of us can seek daggers for Wilford and Asha," Odo cut in. "Steel rationing or not, I want all our members to have a reserve weapon, even if I must pay for it myself."

"I can pay for my own," Asha said. "My family sent me with a little money, and I have yet to use any of it."

Odo nodded.

Will hesitated, then said, "I cannot, but I would be grateful for your assistance and will pay you back for it once we begin receiving wages from the Order."

"I'm not worried about it," Odo replied. "I could always take the dagger from you if you don't. I know where you sleep." Odo smiled wickedly. He was joking, but it was still slightly unsettling because it was also true. Will, however, seemed to find the jesting threat reassuring, and his shoulders relaxed.

"An excellent idea," Thrarber added. "I am quite curious about human smithies and what passes as quality metal wares in your Capital."

"We have our plan then," Odo said, then resumed eating.

After they ate, the ballast made a quick stop at the barracks so Asha could retrieve her coin purse from her lockbox. Then they made their way out of the garrison. Mayumi broke off from the group and headed south, while Odo led them east, deeper into the city.

Asha felt like she was struck with a hammer right in the center of her chest as soon as they stepped into the streets beyond the garrison gate—a hammer made of the noise of people shouting and milling past, the heavy scent of manure from cart animals and residents, and the acute awareness of being surrounded on all sides by strangers. Perhaps a hammer was a poor comparison for the tightness in her chest and throat. The door of a cage slamming shut would have been a better one.

Inside, the garrison had felt isolated, familiar, and certainly better sanitized. She had almost forgotten that it was a compound inside the largest city in the Empire, but the press of people in the streets was a vivid reminder. Asha took deep, slow breaths through her nose, steeling herself against the panic that tried to break free and swallow her. She walked close enough to Odo that she almost stepped on his shadow.

Asha started counting windows again, and though it was calming, she wouldn't be able to navigate the city via its window number or composition. So, she switched to counting turns and crossings. Rudimentary, but it worked reasonably well if she wanted to be able to get within sight of the garrison.

Three turns and nine cross streets later, the smell of manure was overcome by the scent of smoke and metal. The noise dulled as many people raised collars or hood tassels over their mouths and noses, and the crowd thinned a little. Asha found it a slight improvement. She didn't know if it was possible, but the air seemed hotter from the forges. Perhaps it was only the time of day but sweat beaded down her legs and face now.

She had never seen so many smith shops in her life, and so close together, too. They all looked roughly the same. A large, covered stone forge, with the smith, one or two journeymen, and a varying number of apprentices at work, work benches and racks of metalwork along one side. Past that, between the forge and the street, was a stall, mostly run by women who were the wives of the smith or perhaps his journeymen. At the very top of the stall, carved or burned into the wood, was a large symbol, all the same, with a smaller differing symbol next to it, though some of the smaller symbols repeated, but never immediately next to one another. The large symbol must have represented the smith's guild membership. Asha didn't know what the smaller symbols meant, but Odo clearly did as he scanned them, looking for something.

He must have seen her observing him. It would have been hard for him to miss, as close as she kept to his side. He turned and explained, "All smiths fall under the metalworkers' guild, but the metalworkers' guild in Meditullio has grown so large that they agreed to split into smaller guilds within the metalworkers. Wheelmakers' guild, toolmakers' guild, sword-makers' guild, etcetera. Help me look for a dagger overlaid on the rune representing 'K' in the old tongue, with an anvil beneath. That'll be the knife-makers' guild. They can sell us daggers."

"The sword-makers can't sell us a dagger?" Asha asked.

"Didn't you hear what I said?" Odo retorted. "If a sword-maker made a blade that was small enough to be a dagger, he would be ejected from his guild, and no one in the Capital would ever buy from him again. He would have to leave in disgrace and, depending how far word spreads, perhaps find a new profession."

"All that just for making a short blade?"

Odo nodded. "The guild issues dimensions and such. I don't know them. But the smiths do. Sometimes you have to find a knife-maker for a custom short sword, depending on how short it is. And may Estesbryd light your path if you want to add gold plating or jewels to the handle. The same piece of metal might have to go through three or more master craftsmen's hands."

"Did your dagger have to go through three sets of hands for the silver inlay?" Asha asked, grateful for the distraction. It helped keep the anxiety tamped down.

"It was a gift, so I don't know, but likely it went from the knife-maker to the silver smiths. So, only two sets of hands. Ah! There is one!" He pointed at a stand on the far side of the street and hurried toward it. It had the symbol he'd described burned beneath the larger metalworkers' symbol.

The five of them packed into the open stall behind a few other customers. They only waited for a few minutes before the woman manning the stall smiled at them and asked how she could help. She was short and plump, with dark hair streaked with gray and prominent crow's feet by her warm brown eyes. Odo stepped forward to do the talking.

"Two of my friends here need daggers." He pulled his own from its sheath and held it out to her, handle-first. "Like this one, but without the silver or carvings on the handle."

She turned it over, examining it and testing its weight. "So, by 'like this one', you mean the size and shape of the blade?"

"And in the style of guard and pommel."

"I understand." She handed it back in the same manner and turned to the back of the stall. Lifting the lid of a large trunk along the back wall, she retrieved a few daggers from it and brought them to the counter, laying them in front of Odo. "We have several sizes of ready-made rondel daggers, as you can see. If none of these meet your needs, I can take dimensions for special order. It will take a few days to work into the schedule, though."

Asha stepped closer to the counter and looked at the four daggers. All had a thin, double-edged, triangular blade, tapering from a few fingers' width down to a needle point, as well as a round disc guard, with a through tang. Two had octagonal pommels, and two had round. The main difference was the length of the blades; the smallest was about twelve inches long, and the longest was nearly twenty. Odo picked up the second-to-largest dagger and tested its weight and balance.

"This will do. We will take two of these."

"An excellent choice, sir," the woman said and took the other three to exchange for a matching rondel. "Will you be needing scabbards for them, sir?"

"Aye. Do you have a recommendation for a scabbard-maker nearby?" Odo asked her.

She smiled slyly and said, "I recommend that you purchase them here. We have a contract with a scabbard-maker for all our ready-made daggers. You need not search elsewhere. All guild-approved, mind you. We pay him, and you pay us."

Odo smiled back at her. "Very convenient, ma'am. We will take two scabbards as well."

"Very good, sir. That'll be ten silver imperia, and that's with a discount for being a part of the Order, so don't try to haggle me."

Odo smiled again and waved Asha's hand away from her money pouch. "I wouldn't dream of it, ma'am. Thank you." He pulled the amount from his own pouch.

"Not that I'm complaining about business, mind you," she said as she took the coins. "But I thought the Order forged their own swords and such."

"Swords, they do, but not daggers," Odo replied. "At least not anymore."

"I see, sir. Well, if these please you, would you be so kind as to tell any other members which smith made them?"

"I would be glad to."

Her smile brightened, and the lines on her face deepened. "Thank you very much, sir! It has been a pleasure. May Dynawach smile on you."

"And on you, ma'am." Odo saluted the woman, causing her to blush, and left the stall. Asha was right on his heels again. Will and the Dwarves, who had been examining the wares and smith's work at the forge and conversing quietly in their own tongue, trotted to catch up.

Asha reached into her pouch and retrieved half of the amount the smith's wife had charged Odo.

She passed him the coins. He took them, then said sharply, "We are well-armed and marked by the Order's colors, but you should not make a habit of handling coin in the streets. You're practically inviting robbery."

Asha blushed deeply. "Sorry," she mumbled. "I didn't think of that."

"Likely nothing will come of it today, as I said. But this isn't your mountain village. You need to remember that," he replied more gently.

"Yes, sir," she replied quietly. She felt very foolish. Here she was, anxious and uncomfortable because she wasn't in her mountain village. But she was making silly mistakes, acting as she would there.

Perhaps she could channel her anxiety into something useful, or she could just tamp it down, and ignore it. Either way, she needed to adapt to life in the Capital. How would she face a war if she couldn't even handle business without making a fool of herself and endangering her ballast? *I will do better. I must.*

Chapter 21

Asha

Asha still felt the anxiety tight in her chest, but it had loosened enough that she didn't have to consciously breathe now. She still felt trapped, surrounded on all sides, but perhaps the cage had expanded a touch. Backing off of Odo's heels, she still stayed close enough to touch him if they both had stretched out their arms. She went back to counting turns and cross streets.

Two cross streets and one left-hand turn later, she realized that the heat of the forges had been filling the street. It was cooler there, but she still would have traded the stench of manure and poorly washed bodies for the scent of smoke and iron. The next cross street brought heat back, but the stink of feces was overpowered by the aroma of bread, meat pies, and other baked goods. Two more cross streets and a right-hand turn later, the air cooled again, the sweet scent of fruit, especially citrus, broke through the foul stench but didn't overpower it. Asha wasn't sure if it was better or worse.

She struggled to keep her count running. Six cross streets and three turns from the smith's street, the air was pleasantly filled with various spices. She made the mistake of inhaling too deeply and coughed as her lungs protested taking in powdered ginger. Eight cross streets and three turns, more floral scents than she had names for tickled her nose. Color swam in her vision on all sides, blending into a brilliant kaleidoscope. Nine cross streets and four turns, the colors remained but in larger swaths; the florals were replaced by the acrid scent of wool and linen dyes. Thirteen cross streets and four turns, Asha swallowed back bile at the heavy scent of fish and blood. The gray and pale pink of the fish market was a poor replacement for the bright colors of the weavers, dyers, and tailors.

Fifteen cross streets and six turns, the air turned cooler, and a salt breeze swept away most other scents. She scanned her surroundings as Odo slowed, and the crowd thinned. The shops and carts had turned into houses. Large, ornate houses with windows facing the harbor and modest courtyards with outdoor seating. This must have been the district in which Mayumi rented a house. Houses like this would not be cheap to let out, but then again, an ambassador from a foreign nation would have no small amount of money.

Back home, Asha's family was generous but reticent. Rich enough in resources and coin to be tolerated as eccentric, but poor enough in influence and power to be avoided as aberrant. As she tried to assess the value of the houses and the clothes of the few visible occupants, she concluded that Mayumi's family must have been moderately well off in both wealth and influence. Not 'money is no object' rich or royalty-level power, but also not more than a few steps down from either.

Oddly, here, in one of the higher-class residential districts, is where the tension in Asha's shoulders loosened. Will moved in closer to her and Odo. He still held his shoulders high and head forward, but his steps were a touch less confident, and his eyes shifted more. Like he didn't belong. Thrarber and Throil seemed unaffected.

"Here we are," Odo said to no one in particular as he veered toward a large stone house with a male Elf standing outside the gate. The Elf was taller than the gate; Asha estimated that he was in excess of seven feet tall. He wore the plain brown servant's habit cut in the Imperial style but had a vibrant red sash with black geometric patterns tied over his left shoulder and polished brass earrings, tattoos peeked out of his sleeves.

"Welcome, honored guests of Mayumi, to the house of Mandirigma," he said when they approached, then opened the gate for them, taking care not to fully turn his back to them as he did so. Once they had entered the courtyard, he gestured to a male human servant dressed similarly standing near the door of the house, then fell in to the right and slightly behind them. "I am empowered to provide exposition of the grounds and answer any questions until my esteemed matrons arrive to greet you themselves. Have you any needs I can address at this time?"

The ballast all mumbled polite refusals to the servant. Asha looked around the courtyard in quiet, unabashed awe. The landscape burst with colors. Red brick pathways, as were favored by the upper classes of this region, but the flat uniform green grass with artfully trimmed shrubbery that flaunted the owner's ability to have non-productive land was missing. The paths were lined with flowers of every color: Roses, irises, tulips, germaniums, lilies, and at least half a dozen more that Asha didn't know the names of. Beyond the flowers was the bushy growth of various kinds of tubers, squashes, and flowering shrubs that would soon boast berries. These surrounded fruit trees, most of which were also currently in bloom. Asha recognized cherry trees, pear trees, and several varieties of apples. One section had the tallest, thickest sunflower stalks she had ever seen. Vines climbed the stone of the walls and house. She closed her eyes and inhaled the fragrant blend of florals, and mana hummed along with the buzzing of honeybees. This was a natural Mage's masterpiece.

Thrarber swatted at a bee near his face.

"Don't hurt the pollinators," Asha scolded.

"It's trying to hurt me, lass," he retorted.

"No, it isn't." She smirked. "Just ignore it, and it will ignore you."

He grumbled something she couldn't understand in his native language, but she thought it sounded good-natured, so she ignored him.

"What is that?" Will drew the servant's attention to a structure separated from the house by a gazebo. "Is it made of glass?"

"Yes, sir. The esteemed matron of this house misses the tastes of our islands. So, her son-in-law commissioned a garden to be built and covered in glass so the climate may be adjusted to better suit the needs of our tropical plants. Would you like a tour of it?" he answered.

Before Will could speak, Mayumi and an older female Elf stepped out of the house. Mayumi wore the same garb she always did, though Asha thought she looked slightly strange without her large spear in her hand.

The Elf beside Mayumi could only be her mother. They shared nearly every facial feature. Her mother's cheeks were a bit fuller, the lines by the corners of her eyes deeper, and her thick, black hair had streaks of gray woven into the braids. She wore a long dress, draped and folded artfully in the same vibrant red and black geometric pattern as the servant's sash. Asha thought it was likely the house colors of Mandirigma. She also had the impression that Mayumi's mother had once been much more muscular than she was now. Not that she could put a finger on exactly why. She held herself with strength and dignity only a few inches shorter than her daughter. Frail, she most certainly was not. Still, the impression that she was also not as physically capable as she had once been lingered on the edges of Asha's mind.

"Welcome to our home," Mayumi said. "Allow me to introduce my mother, Genoveva Mandirigma. Mother, this is Brother Odo, Sister Asha, and little brothers, Thrarber, Throil, and Wilford." Throil's face tightened at the distinction of 'Brother' and 'little brothers'. Thrarber openly frowned. Asha thought it odd but didn't know what to make of it.

"I thank all of you for coming to meet me today. My daughter is her own woman, but I am grateful to meet those to whom she will bind herself," Genoveva said. "Come, Sister Asha, walk with me." She offered Asha her arm, and Asha took it, allowing her to lead them toward the gazebo. Mayumi and the rest of the ballast followed, shadowed by the servant.

The gazebo was large and furnished with wicker chairs, which were heavily cushioned with pillows of red and orange, all with the same geometric patterns as Genoveva's dress and the servant's sashes.

There was a low wooden table in the center, but it was bare. Mayumi's mother led Asha to a chair near the head of the table. She took the head seat, and Mayumi took the seat directly opposite Asha. The servants seated Odo and the others further down the table, leaving an open seat beside Mayumi and Asha. The servants brought all of them watered-down sweet wine in large crystal goblets.

"My husband has made the dinner arrangements, but he had a meeting this afternoon that I was unaware of when I extended the invitation. He should be returning shortly. Please forgive me if we do not serve the food until he does," Mayumi said.

No one replied for a few moments, and both Mayumi and her mother looked expectantly at Asha, so she supplied, "No forgiveness is required. We are happy to wait for him."

"You are most kind," Genoveva replied. "My daughter should have expected such things when she married an ambassador. Her son used to assist in such matters before he was married off. Ah, the troubles of a political husband." Mayumi's expression didn't change, but her fingers tightened on her goblet until her knuckles and the webbed skin between them turned white before she took another sip. Was that a jab? Asha would have thought a husband with such an important vocation would not be reason for scorn. "Have you a husband or children, Asha?" Genoveva continued.

"No, neither," Asha replied.

"Hmmm...odd, but then I am terrible with judging human ages. How old are you, dear?"

"That is a rude question to humans, Mother," Mayumi cut in.

"I don't mind." Asha smiled at Mayumi before turning back to her mother. "I am twenty-two. So, I think it is hardly odd for one just past legal age to be unmarried. Not that it would be odd to be married either."

"Ah, so young. No matter how often I am reminded, human youth astounds me. Perhaps that is why it is so rude to ask in your culture," Genoveva said, then finally turned her attention to the men at the other end of the table. "What of the rest of you? Wives and children?"

"I have a wife. No children," Odo answered.

"Neither, ma'am," Will said. Thrarber and Throil echoed him.

"So many men out in the world without wives to guide them." Genoveva scoffed.

"It is not their way, Mother," Mayumi said tensely as Thrarber and Throil shifted in their chairs.

"Can I not comment on it at all then?" she said to her daughter. "You have already forbidden me from voicing my concern that your group is led by a man. Must you always police my speech?"

"When your speech is rude to our guests, yes," Mayumi snapped.

"Brother Odo is very experienced and quite capable of leading our ballast. We are grateful to have him," Asha cut in, hoping to smooth over the concerns, although she was unsure what exactly the concern was. Was Genoveva unhappy that her daughter was not the leader?

"He is incapable of creating life and therefore unqualified to take it," Genoveva said in a tone that attempted to hide condescension with false compassion. "A rather disqualifying trait for the leader of a military ballast, regardless of experience."

Odo's face grew hard, but Mayumi spoke again. "Mother, humans do not share our customs regarding the guiding and taking of life. You knew that before I agreed to this position. I knew that. It doesn't require further discussion."

Genoveva opened her mouth to speak, and Asha was certain her reply would have been nasty from the look on her face. Luckily, an Elf man wearing formal Imperial clothes with the same red and black patterned sash around his waist entered the gazebo at that moment, drawing everyone's attention. He was tall, likely seven-and-a-half feet, with a square, tanned face, wide nose, and impossibly dark eyes that glittered in the evening light. His black hair was cut short, and tattoos peeked out of his sleeves and collar. There were gold earrings between the three flared cartilage points on both of his ears. He also wore a large, curved sword in a sheath on a belt hidden by the sash.

Following him closely was a short, stocky human woman, standing just over five feet tall, wearing a wool traveling habit in the northern style. Her round, soft face looked quite young, but the crow's feet by her eyes indicated she was older than she first appeared. She had deeply intelligent dark blue eyes, a button nose, and curly straw-colored hair that was barely contained in a thick twisted bun. Her sword looked remarkably similar to the one Asha had been issued by the Order.

"Welcome, guests. Please excuse my late arrival," the Elf said as he stepped up to the open chair beside Mayumi, smiling broadly.

Mayumi smiled back, and her shoulders relaxed a touch, then she stood to introduce him. "This is my husband, Alden Mandirigma, Ambassador of the Queen to the Empire. Alden, this is Sister Asha, Brother Odo, and Wilford, Thrarber, and Throil."

Alden saluted each in turn. Then he turned to his companion. "You'll never guess who arrived just as my meeting ended, dear wife. This is your final member, Enya. I insisted she join us for dinner."

Enya saluted the table, then said, "I have traveled hard from the north, so very little insistence was required." She flashed a smile. "Though please excuse my appearance, on account of aforementioned travel."

Mayumi saluted her. "A pleasure. Please meet my mother, Genoveva Mandirigma."

Enya saluted her as well, then moved to take the chair beside Asha without waiting for direction from the servants. Alden gave a quiet command to the Elf servant who had received them at the gate. *He must be the head servant*, Asha deduced.

"I hope you have not been waiting for me long." Alden's smile was easy and carefree as he made sure to split his eye contact evenly with all of his guests.

"No, not long at all." Asha kept her voice light and easy.

"Longer than we would have, if your duties did not so often take you away from the home," Genoveva said with narrowed eyes. That was definitely a jab, though Asha still struggled to understand the social convention that was apparently being trod on.

"Then it is good that I have such a reliable staff, an amenable wife, and patient guests." Alden didn't waver.

"How was your trip down?" Asha turned to address Enya, annoyed by whatever power struggle was going on within this family. "By what route did you travel?"

"It was fine." Enya picked up on Asha's bid to change the subject and jumped on the opportunity. "I took the first ship out of Inglerho which had a direct route to the Capital. I am not overly fond of sea travel, but we had good winds and outran the only pirates we saw."

At that moment, servants bearing large trays laden with food began streaming out of the house and into the gazebo. The servants formed a line. First, they laid polished stone trenchers and silver dining forks in front of each person, starting with Genoveva, Mayumi, Asha, and Enya, then the men and Dwarves, lastly Alden. Then, all following the same order, each servant offered the food on their tray and, if accepted, served a portion. Asha found her trencher piled with chicken that had been grilled and spiced with ginger and black pepper, raw white fish marinated with lime and coconut milk, seared salmon tossed into a salad with tomatoes, onion and salt, yams that were stuffed with butter and vanilla and steamed, as well as a dull purple paste that had a faint sweet flavor. There were also bananas, pineapples, and other fruits that Asha didn't know the names of.

The conversation lulled as everyone dug into the meal. Another two servants began to play soft music on a goat's skin drum and a small flute.

Thrarber finally broke the silence with, "'Twas a spread well worth the wait, sir. I couldn'ta named most of the foods, but all fine eating. Fine eating, indeed!"

Alden's eyes lit up. "Thank you, Brother Thrarber. I only wish my dear wife had given me more notice of her intentions. I would have had the chef prepare a pig in the imu. It is one of my favorites of our foods to share with guests."

Genoveva briefly scowled when Alden called Thrarber 'brother', but she didn't comment.

"Prepare a pig in a what?" Thrarber replied, apparently not noticing.

"An imu. We dig down into the earth and light a fire, place the pig on top, wrapped in banana leaves or cloth, then bury it all. It cooks the pig to perfection, but it takes at least half a day, if not more," Alden said. "We shall have to have another dinner. The next one better planned."

"Ballasts usually feast together after they have sworn their oaths," Odo interjected. "As the leader—" he looked Genoveva right in the eye as he said that part, then back at Alden—"I was planning to host, but if you wished to, I am sure my wife would not object. She will, of course, want to assist you wherever possible."

Genoveva did not attempt to hide her displeasure and tried to speak, but Mayumi cut her off. "That would be wonderful. I'm not sure how much assistance my husband will need, but we are glad to host."

"Pardon my ignorance," Throil spoke for only the second time that night. "But is it customary for Elvish husbands to keep the home and arrange such things? Or is this a necessity of our sister Mayumi's vocation?"

Genoveva sighed, but Alden answered. "It is customary. I understand that your people have different views of this, but my people find that the greater strength and stature of males suit them better for the labor inherent in agriculture, building, and maintaining a home. The Goddesses gave females the power over life, speed, and higher intuition required to lead, judge, and rule. All of our culture reflects this."

"We do have different views," Throil said, giving a small gesture to silence his scowling brother. "But it is interesting to learn about other cultures. We have not had much opportunity before being assigned to this new ballast."

"Speaking of," Alden said, looking around the table, "if everyone is finished, I would like to entertain you with some of our culture before we serve dessert."

Everyone mumbled thanks and consent. The servants quickly cleared the remnants of the meal and the table itself. In its place, they piled wood and rocks, then lit a fire with the rocks scattered among the wood. In front of Alden, they placed a large basket of coconuts, a stone basin, and wooden tongs. Alden drew his sword and picked up a coconut. "Have any of you seen coconut milk prepared?" he asked, flourishing the blade, eyes twinkling playfully.

Mayumi looked proud as the group murmured no. Genoveva looked distant. Alden swung the blade swiftly and stripped the coconut of the furry fibers on the outside, then struck it with a loud crack, splitting it in two and pouring it into the basin, scraping the interior meat into it as well. He did this several more times, impossibly fast. Asha was sure he would cut right through the shells and into his palm, but he never did. He passed the last few halves around, encouraging the guests to drink the coconut water. While they did, he used the fibers from the husks to squeeze and strain the solids from the basin.

"Now, we have our milk." He gestured to the head servant again, and a bowl of rich, brown sugar was produced. Using the wooden tongs, he fished a rock from the fire that was starting to die down. "Time to make the milk into a sauce for our dessert." He placed the heated rock into the stone basin with the fresh coconut milk, and it steamed and bubbled slightly. Then he sprinkled the sugar on the rock, letting it caramelize before scrapping it off and stirring it into the milk. He repeated this step several times and then discarded the rock.

The servants appeared again with bowls filled with buns still steaming from the oven. Alden used a coconut shell to ladle the sauce over the buns, and everyone was served in the same order they had been at dinner. It was seamless and perfectly coordinated. Despite Genoveva's jabs, Alden was an excellent host. The guests ate with enthusiasm. The buns had a simple flavor and light texture, enriched by the simple sweet sauce.

"Fine show, lad! Fine show, indeed." Thrarber emphasized his words with a slap on the table, all previous offense forgotten.

"Thank you, Brother Thrarber. I never tire of performing it. Had I been more lowly born, perhaps I would have been a street performer," Alden said. Mayumi tutted and gripped his hand affectionately. "But then I suppose I wouldn't have such a fine, noble wife. I shall content myself with dinner parties and feasts." He winked at her. She rolled her eyes playfully. Whatever the conflict or displeasure from the mother, the couple seemed happy with their arrangement.

Soon after, goodbyes were said, and the ballast took their leave. The night streets were not nearly so crowded, and Asha found she didn't need to focus on breathing or counting to keep herself grounded.

Instead, she pondered what the Mandirigmas had said regarding the place of women and men. Particularly regarding the power to give and take life. It was an interesting prospect, but she found it didn't sit right for a reason she couldn't quite express. Women bore children, true, but not without contribution from a man. Raising a child required input from both parents. Asha hated her own father for being so absent from her life. She hated herself for missing the man she hated. That hatred burned hotter watching him be so present and involved with her half-brothers. She couldn't help but wonder sometimes if he would have stayed with her had she been born a boy. And she was one of the lucky ones. She had many uncles, a grandfather, and Great Uncle Luca to love and nurture her in the way only a man could.

Still, she couldn't argue that men and women contributed differently, and each had areas of strength and weakness. Elevating women above men felt wrong. Asha felt guilty for not speaking up against it when her brothers were seated lower at the table. But what good would it have done? Would she undo an entire lifetime's worth of social convention by making a scene at a dinner? Was she a poor sister to her ballast for simply letting it happen?

Only Dynawach could create life. Women only carried it into this world. That's what she would say to Genoveva if the older Elf repeated the same nonsense at the feast after they took their oaths. If she got the chance to speak against such imbalanced perceptions again. If. That word had been in her mind much of late. If her substitution was accepted, if war would come, if she and her ballast would be strong enough, if her family would be alright, if, if, if.

Chapter 22

Mago

The hammered gold bracelet chafed where he had been turning it over and over on his wrist. Mago supposed it could be worse. It could be iron shackles that chafed him. Or he could feel nothing, burnt to char by dragon fire. That was still a possibility. Bomilcar had disputed Dido's claim that he would cause the Dragon Riders harm. That was the only reason he remained alive to worry his bracelet on his wrist. *How will you get out of this one, whore master?*

Out the window, the dark sky was turning purple, and light edged the horizon. Had it only been a few hours, not even a full night since the Blind Seer's accusation? A mortal wound, she had said. He must burn or he would strike the Dragon Riders a mortal wound. *Would* strike them. So, he had not yet. All his spying, all his cyphered reports, all his black deeds in the name of gathering them had not mattered. He could change that. But how?

He paced the small room, stepping over the unrolled bed mat and few belongings. Was it Sophi's? No, not hers. She would have a cot or bedding platform. Maybe it was Gisco's. He needed to get out of there, and he needed to find a way to sail north. The Empire must have warning of the coming invasion. That was the mortal wound; it had to be.

The guards at the door of the room might have been bored, but they tensed a little whenever he got close to them. It would do him no good to try and bull past them and run away. The other soldiers had searched his house, starting with the whores and their belongings. Based on the amount of time they had taken, Mago was fairly certain the soldiers had done more than search them. They were in his room now, he thought. They would find nothing there, but when they got to his office... How could he have been so foolish?

He almost wished he had drunk more ale so he could at least have something to blame his stupidity on. All the way across the continent, he had been careful. Never writing his reports down until the last moments. Seeking and vetting his contacts first. Now he would be caught with battle sketches among his expenditures. *What I wouldn't give for a good Gnome prank right now...*

His toe caught on the floor, and his steps stuttered. There it was. His solution to evidence and escape. A fire. Burn the house down and all the evidence with it. Escape into the darkness while the soldiers tried to keep the fire from spreading to other houses. Would burning down the palace around the Dragon Riders count as a mortal wound?

Mago looked around for anything he could find to create a spark. There had to be something here.

"Don't get antsy," one guard growled. "We haven't tied ye up outta respect, but we will if ye give us trouble."

"Yeah, I'm not being held responsible if ye do something foolish," the other echoed.

That stilled him. He needed to work carefully.

"I apologize for worrying you, sirs." He turned to face them with all the friendliness he could muster. "I am but a nervous lamb, wandering my new cage. Confused and alone."

The first guard looked unconvinced, but the second relaxed. Both startled to attention a moment later when Bomilcar approached. He strode in quickly, his red cape flicking and slapping against the guards in the close space.

"I don't have to tell you this is outrageous, my friend." He stood in the doorway with his arms crossed, a deep frown on his face. "I'm afraid you will have to endure the indignity. Once your home is searched and nothing found, that vile bitch will have to eat her accusation. And you and I will feast again until it is forgotten."

Mago affected a sad, vulnerable look. "I do not doubt your word, friend. But I do doubt that."

"What do you mean?" Bomilcar snapped.

Mago looked pointedly at the guards and said nothing. Bomilcar turned to them and said, "Find somewhere else to be until I call you back." They bowed and nearly tripped as they fled.

"I doubt your half-sister will eat her accusation, and even if she does, it will not be forgotten," he said, stepping closer. Maybe he could use Bomilcar. Or maybe he could kill him. Was that the mortal wound? "Think, Bomilcar. She made this accusation at your victory feast, just before you sail. This was no coincidence. She has looked upon me before." A lie, but if he could turn the Warlord's children even more against each other... "Why did she say I was dangerous now? She did it to hurt you. To make you look foolish."

"She wished to take my place in the advance party." Bomilcar struck the doorframe with an open palm.

"Perhaps. Or perhaps she just wishes to undermine you more generally. But rest upon my word. They will find something in my home."

Bomilcar whirled on him. "What? What will they find?"

Mago saw his error. He had aroused Bomilcar's suspicion, but he needed to redirect it. He gestured weakly. "I don't know, but they have to. Do you know which soldiers were sent here to search? Are they loyal to you? Or to her?"

"She will plant the evidence. Then you are dead. I am a fool, and her false prophecies will never be questioned again." He clenched his fists as he spoke, and Mago was glad he was out of arm's reach.

Before Mago could ask for help escaping, Bomilcar spoke again. "I have to get you out of here. I cannot let her win. She will not take you from me."

"Perhaps you should." A new idea was forming.

"You wish to die in dragon fire? That is what will happen if she wins."

"No." Mago didn't have to force the shudder or the waver in his voice. "But perhaps it would be best if she and your father thought I did."

Bomilcar went utterly still.

"You can take back the initiative from her. Tell the guards to stop searching. That you've found all you need to. Burn the house, maybe all the soldiers don't get out. I can escape, and you are no longer a fool."

The thoughts flitting across Bomilcar's face. "You can't just hide in the city or swim away. We need a better plan. And surely, they will search the rubble for bones. Besides, then her prophecy is still confirmed. I will not bow to her false wisdom."

So Bomilcar would help but not in a way that spurned his pride. It might have been easier to convince him to help in the first place than to solve the riddle of an escape without pursuit or embarrassment to himself. "You are correct. We do need a better plan. One that will save us both."

Bomilcar cocked his head to the side. "I wasn't aware I needed saving."

"Metaphorically." Mago shrugged playfully. "Your reputation does. You said last night that your father is questioning your wisdom and diplomacy." The Dragon Rider's face hardened at the reminder, but when one bets against death and fire, only bold hands have a prayer at winning. "Wise men admit when they have erred. And a diplomat can turn any error into an opportunity."

The irony that this was likely the only time he had given Bomilcar good advice did not escape Mago. "She thinks that she is striking you when you are weak. She expects you to fight. To dig in your heels, cling to your pride, and expose your folly. So, don't.

"Admit your error. Punish me yourself. Show your father that you have grown, that you can listen to advisors and change course. She will think she has won, but you will have regained your father's trust."

Bomilcar rubbed his chin, then cracked a small smile. "A feint. Let her think she has won... Until the time is ripe to return her favor. Meanwhile, I grow in power, but she cannot use you to harm me again. But I can't command them to stop searching. It's too obvious. I still need to get you out of here."

"That's where the fire comes in, my friend." An inkling of relief tickled his mind. He felt close, but that was foolish. They had not even begun to implement such an escape.

"You have wine and ale suppliers here. Can any of them get you a boat?" Bomilcar asked.

"I don't know. But Sophi might."

"I'll send her to you. I will take over the search myself and allow some time, but if I wish to remain in control of what happens to you, we must move quickly." Bomilcar called the guards back and began walking the halls, shouting orders.

Moments later, Sophonisba appeared in the doorway. One guard glared, the other reached out a hand with a leering look, but she deftly avoided both.

"I don't fully understand what is happening, but I—" she glanced at the guards—"need to speak with our wine vender? At a time like this?"

"See what your former friend can tell us about a small order of exports. For his lordship, Bomilcar. As quick as you can. Our time for smoothing over this misunderstanding draws short."

Understanding dawned on her face, along with surprise, but she quickly flattened them into her typical composure. "Of course, master. Whatever his lordship requires. How many barrels shall I inquire about?"

"I am not certain how much our line of credit will allow. You will likely only be able to deal with what coin you can safely carry. Spare no expense, though. Any stock that remains here—" he paused—"will likely be scattered to the winds."

She nodded sharply. "As my master commands." She turned with grace and ever-present poise, but when she was out of sight, her footsteps quickened.

Bomilcar had made a good show of upending his room and office. Nothing was left unturned, unopened, or unscattered. He'd even 'questioned' him a second time, without guards, of course. They spoke quietly about nothing in particular. Bomilcar occasionally struck or kicked the firm mattress, and Mago dutifully groaned or shouted with the impact. It had almost become a sick game when Sophi returned.

Blank-faced and stiff-backed, she entered the room, eyes flitting from one man to the other. Her shoulders lowered nearly imperceptibly when she saw that Mago was not, in fact, a bruised, bloody mess.

"Our wine vender can export several barrels for you, my lord." She bowed her head to Bomilcar. "We are in great luck that he has a shipment set to leave the harbor at dawn tomorrow."

It was mid-morning now. "I don't think we can keep up this ruse that long, my friend," Mago said.

"No, we cannot. My father will want a report. We may have already drawn this out too much. If I am to be the one meting out the punishment, we must act swiftly."

"We will have to risk our escape in daylight. Perhaps we can sneak aboard during the lunch hour."

"Daylight complicates things," Bomilcar mused. "You will be seen if you flee."

"Disguise then," Sophi said. "Perhaps one of the girls has a dress you can wear."

Bomilcar scoffed. "A man in a dress will be more obvious than just a man."

Sophi turned a disbelieving eye to Mago but said nothing. "What about a uniform?" he asked. "You said it is likely that the rubble will be searched. They should find bodies. It is unlikely that anyone will look too closely at soldiers while dragon fire flies."

"Their companions will," Bomilcar rebutted, then reached out and pinched the back of Sophi's arm. He smiled when she shrieked in surprise, then shrugged. "This is still an interrogation. Besides, dragons have a way of making weak, frightened people look anywhere but at them. And if I return to the palace to fetch my dragon, I will have to give a report first. That will likely end with Father returning with me. There will be no escape then."

"No dragon then." Mago would rather avoid that anyway. "Just regular fire. If you let the whores leave first, perhaps they have an escort? Then the others are called to keep the fire from spreading. Gisco and I can avoid their notice until we can turn toward the harbor."

"Can't let everyone leave." Bomilcar kicked the mattress again, and Mago yelled sharply. "No one will believe you didn't have help."

But I didn't. Is that why I got caught? "Surely, no one would suspect my whores. They are soiled, yes, but not malicious."

"Perhaps not, but your eunuchs will have to die. The whores can flee and melt into the city, but I can't let everyone live."

Nausea twisted Mago's belly, and his jaw clenched until it ached. He couldn't let innocent men burn to death.

Bomilcar didn't notice; he held Sophi's chin in his fingers. "Scream for me, beautiful. Like you do for my friend in the nights he doesn't focus on business."

She obliged him. Mago wanted to scream, too. He wanted to pull out his dagger and cut off Bomilcar's fingers, so he never touched another cornered woman. Stifling the urge, he reminded himself why he couldn't do that. Bomilcar was more essential than ever. He needed to escape and warn the Empire. That meant that he needed to go along with this plan. If he didn't, far more than a dozen eunuchs would burn.

Bomilcar released Sophi. "Go find this Gisco, and two soldiers that match sizes of him and your master. Bring them here to me."

She turned and swiftly obeyed.

"This part will have to be done quickly, friend, so there is no time for anyone to notice you." Bomilcar paused and, for the first time Mago remembered, looked genuinely sad. "I suppose this is farewell. I didn't consider that we would part so soon."

"I don't think either of us was prepared for this possibility."

"That is our mistake. I will not underestimate the conniving whore-spawn again."

Mago didn't doubt that.

"If you can, wait for me on the Isles. I can find a way to hide you among the advance party."

Not if the Gods themselves commanded it of him. "I will see what way the wind offers."

Bomilcar shuffled and looked away, then he pulled off his signet ring. He offered it to Mago. "To remember me by." Then he pulled out his coin purse; this, too, he offered. "For the journey."

Mago accepted both with mumbled thanks. This felt strange, but he only needed to keep up the ruse a little longer, and he could shed this monster's friendship forever. He removed his gold bracelet from his chafed wrist and offered it without a word.

No sooner had Bomilcar placed the bracelet on his own wrist than Gisco, Sophi, and two soldiers returned.

"Excellent." Bomilcar smiled wickedly. Then he stretched a hand toward the open window. Mago couldn't believe his eyes as the tree branches grew and bent into the window. They wrapped around the soldiers' necks in an instant and lifted them up off the floor. The two men choked, kicked, and flailed, but Bomilcar simply squeezed his fist tighter. Their faces turned red, then purple, and the gurgles stopped, and they fell limp.

Bomilcar released his fist, then flicked his wrist dismissively. Just as quickly, the branches withdrew out the window. "Take their uniforms. Quickly," he snapped.

Mago stripped the mail shirt, leather belt, sandals, and linen tunic. He picked up the dropped spear but retained his own dagger. Lastly, he retrieved the helm the soldier had been carrying rather than wearing. He put it on, hoping the cheek guards would cover his features, if only a little. He saw that Gisco had done the same.

"Let us begin, beautiful." Bomilcar gripped Sophi's elbow and pulled her with him. "Stay in the back and keep your faces down as much as you can."

Mago and Gisco stayed several strides behind him as he went down the steps into the main room of the house where the whores and eunuchs were gathered in a large circle surrounded by guards.

"I have learned all I need to," Bomilcar shouted. "You three and you two—" he gestured at the impersonators behind him—"take the whores somewhere they can be useful. The rest of you, make sure no one leaves this house."

"Go! Get up and follow these men. Do not test the Warlord's mercy!" Mago had never heard Sophi shout. It seemed his whores hadn't either, as they stood and rushed toward the door like frightened deer. The three soldiers grabbed and shoved the running women and successfully slowed and herded them out the door, through the garden, and toward the palace. Gisco and Mago fell into the rear. Mago grabbed a whore by the arm, using her tall body to block the eunuchs or soldiers from seeing his face. As they exited the courtyard, Mago turned to look back.

The mansion glowed red. Bitter wood smoke was softened by incense. He must have overturned the torches and incense pots. Windows and doors were guarded. Screams and cries for mercy arose from the trapped men. One broke out and was promptly gored by a soldier's spear. Mago looked away, swallowing bile, thankful he had nothing else in his belly.

He kept his grip on the whore's arm, though he didn't know why. Suddenly, Sophi veered off toward an alley, as the three real soldiers shuffled the first few whores into the servant's entrance to the palace. Gisco made a show of chasing after her. Two other whores followed, and Mago joined them, shouting something he forgot as soon as it left his lips, but he hoped he put on a show of a chase, dragging the tall, light-skinned whore with him.

The group broke into a run for a few blocks. Then Sophi signaled them to slow. She fixed her dress and gestured for the other women to do the same. The last one ripped her arm out of Mago's grip, glaring.

"Where we headed now?" Gisco asked.

"To the docks," Sophi said, stepping out like she might for a stroll. The other three whores linked arms and joined her, even as Mago heard the bells ringing the alarm for the bucket brigade. "We have exports to tend to, my dear," she spoke so conversationally, as though they truly were only seeing to wine barrels.

Chapter 23

Asha

Asha fiddled with her sword belt, shifting it slightly, absentmindedly trying to find if it needed to be adjusted or if she needed to grow accustomed to the new weight. It was growing a bit crowded now. Or at least, it felt that way. It had her sword, of course, on the left, contrary to the Order's standard right-sided quick draw.

This had gotten her stopped and scolded multiple times by various instructors and senior members until she had explained that yes, she knew the standards. Yes, she had special exception. No, she did not have her exception in writing. Yes, she would ensure that she asked her instructors to issue a writ. Her lead instructor's name was Brother Gerard. Yes, she knew that if she was lying, she would do a day in the stocks or be expelled and that they would be checking with her instructors.

On the right side, where her sword should have been, was her whip focus. Behind that was her new dagger. On the left, behind her sword, was her utilitarian knife for eating, carving, and such. It could absolutely be a weapon. Asha imagined unarmored humans carve up just as easily as a leg of lamb or a stick for kindling. But slashing and piercing was not its primary purpose.

"Did a Gnome putting an itching spell in your braies? Why ye squirming, lass?"

Asha turned a glare to Thrarber. He winked a blue eye, and his bushy brows wiggled. She rolled her eyes away, unable to keep the image of the last Dwarf to wink at her from her mind.

Where was Glormhar now? No doubt back in his mountain home. Would he be preparing to accompany another trading party? She needed to stop thinking about him. Even if he was, and even if he returned to the Capital, there was no reason to think he would want to see her. And that was all for the best. It was a foolish, girlish flirtation. Nothing serious.

"Don't need a Gnome spell to itch. This heat is doing plenty," she said, and she was indeed already beginning to sweat, despite the fact that it was barely sunrise.

"No tall tales there, lass." Thrarber chuckled.

"Aye, going to be hotter than Feorach's forge before the sun sets," Throil added.

"The heat gets more tolerable with time," Odo said quietly. "Soon enough, you'll be shivering like a babe when you visit home."

"Or maybe we'll be lucky enough to be assigned to a northern post," Enya chimed in as she approached the ballast and fell in. Asha's heart squeezed at the thought of being home again, surrounded by her family. She needed to focus on something less sentimental, so she practiced discreet observation again.

Enya looked different somehow in her uniform; older perhaps, wiser, and more serious in an intangible way. The colors were faded a bit, closer to the shade of Odo's. But her armor and weapons were in excellent condition. She had the same brigantine and mail as the rest of them. Her sword was identical to Asha's but worn on the standard right side. Opposite it was her utility knife and dagger, side by side. Her dagger had the same strange double bulbous shaped guard as Odo's archer pick. Strange. Was it in fashion? Not that either member seemed particularly fashionable. Her helm had her healers' sigil, the moon cupped in two hands. Aside from that, the largest difference was she carried a canvas pack.

"I'll need someone with proper rank," Eyna continued, unaware of Asha's observation, "to tell the dispensary that I am, in fact, authorized to draw herbs, salves, and runed bandages."

"They gave you trouble?" Odo asked sharply.

"They didn't give me shit!" She jabbed a thumb at the pack. "All that's in here is what I already had on me from the trip. Nobody will bleed to death or fall into fever sleep, but past that, I make no promises."

"I'll take care of it." Odo said, clearly angered.

"Thank you much, Brother."

The ballast moved forward at the instructor's command in front of the dwindling rock pile. All the nicely shaped rocks were taken already. Asha grabbed one that was a bit too square for comfort but a good weight to challenge her without embarrassment.

"Who took my rock? My lovely sandstone!" Thrarber moaned, looking with dissatisfaction at the remaining pile.

"Just pick a different one." Mayumi sounded bored. "Unless they're all too heavy for you?" she said as she hefted a stone one and a half times the size that Asha had chosen.

"Too heavy? Too heavy!" He sputtered. "I'll show you too heavy ye splay-eared ocean bobber. Even if I have to settle for granite to do so!" His tone was entirely too jovial for the slurs he uttered, and Mayumi didn't seem offended.

"Whatever you say, tunnel tracer," she tossed back casually while Thrarber picked up the largest rock from the scattered pile.

Throil shook his head and said nothing but picked up the next largest rock. Odo selected one about the same size as Mayumi. Wilford and Enya each grabbed rocks between that and Asha's. She nearly put her rock down in favor of a larger one but reminded herself that dropping a larger rock on her face would be much more embarrassing than having the smallest one.

With rocks held before them in both hands, the group began walking in large circles around the training field. Conversation dwindled as breath came faster and harder, and muscles flexed. Thrarber, however, didn't let it die. He and his brother seemed nearly unencumbered by the large stones, and he decided now was the best time to educate the others on types of rock.

"You see this here hunk—" he bent his elbows and lifted the rock slightly to add emphasis—"does perfectly well for construction. Very solid. Bit difficult to split, but once properly shaped, she'd make a fine wall. Fine wall stone. Don't suck up a bit of water. Granite don't. Don't give me those eyes, Asha, lass. Granite is resistant to all types of weather. But it's hard on the hands! That's why I prefer my lovely sandstone. She is still solid, excellent for indoor construction. Makes very fine fireplaces, stairs, and the like. But she has much finer pores, ye see. Don't cut into your fingers when we go a'walking."

"What type. Of. Stone. Is best." Enya panted. "For cutting. Out tongues?"

"Oh, for that—well, any cutting really—ye want a good obsidian or basalt." Thrarber was undeterred. "Very hard to find in this region, though. And lapping it into an edge takes practice."

After their third circuit, the group stopped and set the rock down for a few moments until their heartbeats slowed again. Thrarber continued, "Sandstone works for outer construction, but it is not the best. The pores take on too much weathering, ye see. It only lasts a few decades without repairs. But for our purposes, that means she'll hold a bit of water weight if it has rained." He said this last bit with a huge grin.

Will stood up from where he had flopped after dropping his rock unceremoniously. "You want the rock to be heavier?" he asked as he and the others retrieved the rocks again.

"Aye, then this might actually be a challenge." Thrarber laughed. He and Throil hadn't dropped their stones to rest.

"I'll be sure to place a requisition for larger exercise stones," Odo chimed in, grunting as he lifted his stone over his head, releasing it with his left hand and holding it straight-armed with only the right.

All the others did the same. Now the real contest began. Throil and Thrarber faced off directly, staring into each other's faces, Mayumi just off to the side, towering over both, forming a competitive triangle.

The other four formed a loose half-crescent around them, all allowing plenty of room in case anyone had to bail their stone.

"Would you? Very kind of you, Brother Odo," Thrarber said.

"I'd like one as well, if ye please," Throil added. "What of you, She-Elf?"

"This one is sufficient. But I would like to request that we make our circuit at a faster pace once these new rocks are acquired," she answered. Thrarber's arm wavered a moment, then steadied.

"Faster? What do you mean faster?"

"Oh, just an easy lope." Mayumi grinned. Asha's arm burned, but she would not allow herself to lower her rock first. "Nothing too quick for those as close to the earth as yourselves."

Both Dwarves grumbled but neither had a ready retort.

Enya was the first to lower her rock; Will and Asha followed immediately, both hiding slightly trembling hands. Odo followed suit a minute or two later, leaving Mayumi in her contest with the Dwarves. They would not lower theirs until she did. She managed another minute longer, then lowered hers. The Dwarves' lips twitched in matching half-grins, but they did not flaunt their victory.

Instead, they lowered their stones and immediately switched arms, raising them again. Everyone else followed suit. The same jabs and useless chatter continued until the left arm was sufficiently exercised.

Asha deliberately drew long slow breaths in through her nose and out her mouth, willing her heartbeat to slow as the group reformed into a line, facing the same direction as all the other ballasts, so there would be no cross-strikes. Her hands trembled as they all raised the rocks to their shoulders and threw them as far as they could. The rock landed even with Will's but closer than all the others. She didn't care about Thrarber and Throil's. She doubted any human could match their throws.

After confirming all the stones were discharged, they retrieved them and threw from the left shoulder. Asha's stone fell barely two arms' lengths away. Her face flushed with embarrassment, luckily exertion would cover it. Her throws became increasingly shallow in repetition. She told herself that it was expected for being the youngest and a woman, but she couldn't force her frustration down, nor stop her hands from trembling.

On the third left-hand throw, she heaved the stone with all the strength she had left, and it exploded to dust midair. Everyone else ducked down and tucked their chins, no doubt grateful for the helms. Asha stood there staring blankly. She hadn't felt herself drawing the mana, much less pushing it into the stone.

"You'll need to add a new stone for Asha, as well." Thrarber broke the stunned silence. "A nice sandstone."

Everyone broke into surprised, cathartic laughter. *The ballast that laughs together* as they say. Asha just wished it wasn't at her expense. It had been a while since her last unintended destruction. At least it was only a stone this time.

Chapter 24

Asha

Asha breathed in and out slowly through her nose, count of four inhale, count of three hold, and count of four exhale. It was helpful, except for the ever-present smell of mud and manure. She had thought the heat might dry out the streets and reduce the stench, but she had vastly underestimated the humidity in the Capital. The air was not just hot, but sticky. She thought she might just be breathing in someone else's breath, or perhaps thousands of someone's. At least the sweat running down her neck and thighs was a slight distraction from the tightness in her chest.

She forced herself to keep a proper distance from Odo as he led the ballast through the streets. Trailing him like a lost puppy was unbecoming a military ballast member. They had returned to the merchant district, specifically the merchants who dealt in steel and iron. The sheriff had left notice that they were to meet him at the home of the Grand Master of the Wheelwrights Guild.

This gave Asha hope that her ballast's rotation with the city watch would involve more than just hours of patrolling. Now that the ballast had all of its members, they were permitted to attend the most intense training exercise. The Order tested each of its potential ballasts before joining them together in a blood oath. In recent years, the Order had come to an arrangement with the Sheriff to integrate the training ballasts with the city's watchmen. This intersection of live training and supplementary manpower-preserving resources for both parties was a rare bureaucratic accomplishment.

The ballasts needed to face some form of combat together before they were permitted to swear oaths. Great Uncle Luca had told her stories of his training, of chasing fell beasts and subduing rogue mercenaries. Now a training ballast was much more likely to spend many shifts patrolling the Capital's streets until they caught a petty thief or arrested a fraudulent merchant.

Asha was a bit surprised, though, as she had thought that being 'merchants of steel and iron' meant the wheelwrights would have been close to the sword and dagger smiths they had sought out only a few days ago. She didn't recognize the streets they traversed. Perhaps Odo had taken them a different, more circuitous route, or more likely, 'close' meant something entirely different in the Capital.

Panic gripped her throat as the expanse of the seat of the greatest Empire in the known world was impressed upon her. *I am just one person in a sea of people. Like a minnow struggling against the current, surrounded on all sides by hundreds of thousands of others, hoping to stay near enough the edge of the formation to eat, but near enough the center to avoid being eaten. What do I matter in the grand scheme of Empires, Holy Orders, and Dragons?*

She closed her eyes and imagined her home. The safety of the walled compound. Crisp, mountain air, filled with the scents of trees, rain, and the occasional wildflower. The deafening roar of her family chattering around dinner. Her mother's soft head shakes when she said something foolish or comical. Great Uncle Luca's war stories after a few tankards of ale. Her sisters' sweet faces.

Asha tripped and barely caught herself before she smacked her chin into the rutted street. *That's what I get for closing my eyes while walking.* The others looked at her with concern, but she waved them off, blushing. Thankfully, they were nearly there as she saw the sheriff and a few watchmen, clad in rich Imperial blue, outside a large, ornate house. Asha hoped that despite the fact that she could see him, he hadn't seen her fall.

The sheriff, a lean, wire-haired man of about fifty, with a deeply lined face, turned as they approached and greeted Odo. After salutes had been exchanged, the sheriff said, "I know this is a highly unusual assignment for a greenwood ballast. But I am criminally undermanned at the moment. A feverous contagion has half my watchmen in the healing houses. And I saw that you were part of this ballast, so..."

Odo nodded, understanding what the Sheriff wasn't saying. Asha knew that Odo was highly respected inside the Order, but it seemed he was also respected outside it. "Well," the sheriff continued, "there is not much I can tell you. We have reports of a break-in last night. The Guild Master's son opened his own shop a year or so ago. Thieves sacked the place and beat the son and his Dwarven shop assistant. The shop assistant died in the wee hours. Anything beyond that, you'll have to find for yourselves. The son is here, laid up under the Guild Master's roof until he recovers."

"We'll start by interviewing him, then. If he's capable of talking, that is. Will you be coming with me to make your reports?" Odo asked.

"No, I have many other reports to make. This one I leave fully in your capable hands." The sheriff made a halfhearted attempt at a smile.

"Highly unusual, indeed." Odo did not return the smile. The words hung there for a few moments. Then Odo added, "But having only half a regimen to guard the Capital is also highly unusual. I suppose I can take a single report off your hands."

The sheriff's lean shoulders lowered about an inch. "Thank you, Brother Odo. I would not delegate so without great necessity. I look forward to seeing the thieves in the gaol and reading your report."

Odo saluted him, and he returned it. Then he turned and departed in a brisk, long stride, his watchmen trotting a bit to keep up.

Glancing down at Asha, Odo said, "Don't get a reputation. Causes all kinds of problems. If you do get a reputation, make sure it's not for being good at anything. Government officials have a tendency to reward hard work with more work."

Enya chuckled. "Ain't that the truth."

"In this way," Mayumi said with a small grin, "I think our cultures are the same."

With that, the ballast entered the large house. They were met by a maid who escorted them up a set of stairs into the living quarters of the family.

"Must be excellent wheelwrights," Thrarber commented, "to be able to afford a second story in their quarters."

"Me master is the finest wheelwright in the whole Empire. That's how come he's the Guild Master, you see, sir," the maid responded with an upturned nose before she knocked on a closed door. Once leave was given from inside the room, she opened the door and stepped to the side to let them in.

It was a small room, with a good-sized bed in the center, a fireplace along the wall, a few hard-backed chairs next to the bed, but little other furniture. The walls and floor were covered in overlapping woolen carpets. A badly bruised young man lay in the bed, reclining on overstuffed pillows. One chair, the one closest to the head of the bed, was occupied by a small, plump, gray-haired woman who was trying to convince the reclining young man to eat something from an alabaster bowl that smelled offensively herbaceous. The other chair stood empty, but a tall, broad-shouldered and round-middled older man paced behind it.

The ballast filed into the room, and Will, Thrarber, Throil, and Enya had to press up along the far side of the bed for them all to fit. Immediately, the air felt closer and, though she wasn't sure it had been possible, hotter.

"Well, I sent for the sheriff, but I am quite happy to see the Order has answered. This must be taken with the seriousness it deserves," the Guild Master said. "Though I must say that this is the strangest ballast I have seen from the Order."

"Quite a day for strange things I am told," Odo replied evenly, then turned to the man in the bed. "Tell us what happened as best you can remember it."

The young man squirmed a bit, perhaps trying to sit up a bit further, but if so, he made no progress. He licked his split and bruised lips, then spoke. "We had closed up long before. Taken our supper and all. Flinok was taking longer than usual to sweep up and arrange the shop for the morrow so I—"

Odo raised his hand and interrupted. "Who's Flinok?"

"He's my—" the man swallowed hard—"he *was* my shop assistant. He's not anything to anyone now."

"He was unjustly killed, and that makes him something to us," Odo replied. "Continue, please."

"When I came in the side door to check and see what was keeping him, I saw him standing off six men in hoods with his forge hammer. I don't know how they got in or anything. When I entered, two of them looked at me and moved to attack me. I suppose he thought that was his chance to get an edge. Flinok struck out and hit the one closest to him. But four to one, they still took him down. I didn't see how that happened. I had my own problems with the two coming at me.

"I had no chance of fighting them off unarmed. So, I tried to run back through the door, but they struck me in the hip and knocked me against the doorframe. Then they drug me back inside and bolted that door. One was kicking me anywhere he could hit, and the other took swings with his hammer, though not as many as the one kicking me."

"The attackers had hammers also. What kind of hammers?"

"I didn't see them very well. I was mostly trying to avoid them, but I think they were smithing hammers just like Flinok's—I mean, *my* hammer that Flinok was holding."

Odo nodded and gestured for him to continue.

"As I said, I didn't see how Flinok fared, but I heard him scuffling and the blows landing." He paused and shuddered at the memory, grimacing and lifting a hand to his ribcage. "I think he kept his feet longer than I did, but they got him on the ground, too. I saw them striking him with the hammers, and I think—" He cut off again and looked away.

"Go on, lad, tell them what ye told me," the Guild Master said. When his son still hesitated, he supplied, "They held out his hands and struck them repeatedly with the hammers. Even if the poor Dwarf had lived, he never would have held so much as a broom again from the state of his hands when we found him."

"After that, one hit him on the back of the head, and he went limp," the young man added. "They kicked me again, aiming at my head. I took most of it on my forearm, but I played dead while they smashed up the shop and took whatever they were after. I might not have been fully playing because I don't remember them leaving, but I remember the shop being cold and darker and empty before I was able to crawl into the street and get someone's attention." He almost looked sheepish about that, which was quite silly from Asha's view.

"What all did they take?" Odo asked.

"We have been a mite busy to take inventory." The Guild Master bristled.

"Did you recognize any of them?"

"What are you implying?" The Guild Master raised his voice.

"They were wearing hoods," the young man answered with shifting eyes.

"You might be surprised how often people are attacked by others that they thought were friends or at least friendly. And hoods aren't always effective at hiding identities." Odo did not rise to the Guild Master's anger. "The sheriff mentioned that your shop was fairly new. That might be a motivation for the attack."

"It was all legal!" The Guild Master was no longer shouting, but he was still scowling. "He has been my apprentice for years and passed the trials to open his own shop under our guild."

"That doesn't mean that everyone is happy he did. Some might feel he is taking their customers. There is much competition in this city," Odo said quietly. He turned back to the young man. "Is there anything else you can think of that might explain this? Have you angered anyone? Stolen from anyone? Kissed anyone's wife? Sent any employees away on bad terms?"

"My son is not a thief nor a philanderer!" The Guild Master clenched his fists, and his face turned an unnatural shade of red. Odo ignored him and maintained eye contact with the young man.

"No," he said.

“Has your shop assistant?” Odo asked.

“I don’t know.”

“How did you come to have a Dwarf as a shop assistant? It’s hardly common, and there must be plenty of young boys who would like to assist the Guild Master's son in the hopes of an apprenticeship someday."

"It just happened that way. I don't know what you are asking for. You should be looking for his killers!" The young man sat forward and raised his voice, then collapsed back on the bed.

"We are," Odo said and crossed his arms. Then he turned to the Guild Master and said, "I assume there will be no objections to examining the shop and the deceased?"

The Guild Master squared his shoulders but answered evenly. "No objections. I will send the maid to guide you."

The shop was only one street away. Once they arrived, Odo stopped the maid from departing. He turned to Thrarber and Throil. "I think that one of you should examine the body. There might be clues that you notice that one of us might miss." They both nodded.

"I'll go. Anything in particular that you wish me to look for?" Throil asked quietly.

"No, but keep in mind the questions I asked his master. There has to be a reason the thieves crushed his hands. Run-of-the-mill robbers would have only beat him until subdued. It is rare to see an act of such malice without cause."

"Speaking of such," Enya said, "I think I should examine the body as well. I got a better understanding of injuries and such than the rest of ye."

Odo nodded and commanded the maid to take those two to the deceased. She rolled her eyes but complied wordlessly.

The lock on the shop door had been forced, but in a way that wasn't obvious until one's hand was almost on it.

"What does that tell us?" Odo addressed the remaining group before entering.

After a few quiet moments, Will answered. "Not professionals, but well-prepared."

"What makes you so sure?" Asha asked. "Just from the lock?"

Will glanced at Odo, and he just nodded for him to explain. "Well, professionals would have picked the lock. Not broken it. But they were prepared because to break it like that requires a pry bar and mallet. They didn't just smash it or unhinge the door, likely to escape notice."

"Now, Wilford, lad," Thrarber said with false seriousness, "how do you know such things?"

"I learned it in Nunya."

The brushy brown brows furrowed. "Where's Nunya? Is that on the coast?"

"None o' your business," Will quipped.

Thrarber roared in laughter. Odo smiled but then hushed them as he opened the damaged door. Mayumi grinned, too.

The thieves had taken no such precautions with the interior. Splintered wood was scattered everywhere, the remains of stools, racks, and what she thought had been a desk. Metal bands and rods were bent and driven into the walls. A large and small anvil, along with the forge hammers, tongs, and other various metalworking tools were dropped in the center of the forge and covered in a pile of mostly dried concrete. The bellows had jagged slices revealing a crushed interior mechanism, and the stone flutes of the forge had been broken as well. Dark brown blood was splattered and pooled across the sand of the floor, next to deep scuffs.

"Did they bring a hurricane with them? Or an earthquake?" Asha asked in a whisper.

"A force of nature, even a targeted one, would likely been reported by neighbors. The Sheriff is busy, but I don't think he would have failed to inform us of that. The door has tool marks. Why use tools on the door if one can wield a spell?" Odo replied.

Asha paused and looked around again. "This is a great deal of destruction to be done without mana. And the breaking and banging was not reported either."

"Perhaps the neighbors do not find a ruckus in the evening unusual. Or they simply do not care," Odo said. "I have seen no evidence that the Guild Master's son was well-loved."

"Strong box is intact," Will called out. He crouched off to one side of the room, next to the worst shattered display racks. "I don't think they even looked for it. It's not well-hidden. And the lock isn't touched."

"Not a robbery then," Odo acknowledged.

"Definitely not," Thrarber chimed in. He stood over the damaged forge. "Come look at this. Bet my own hammer those are chisel cuts. They meant to ensure this forge never held heat again."

Odo walked over and examined the cuts. "Certainly, looks like it. It also explains taking the time to drive the metal into the walls. They could have offloaded the rods at least. How much for forged iron rods, Wilford?"

"Not much, but enough coin to make carrying it off worth doing," Will answered, then caught himself and looked away. "I mean; I have no way of knowing that for sure."

Thrarber and Odo exchanged amused looks. "Of course not, lad. No way of knowing."

Mayumi held up a large, wooden bucket with a rope handle. "This has concrete residue in it. They carried it wet. Should we go question the son again? Ask him why someone would go to so much trouble to sabotage his shop?"

"I think I would prefer to ask the saboteurs," Odo replied. "Look for boot prints. Cloth threads. Dropped belongings. Anything to help us trace the murderers."

The group spent about an hour meticulously sifting through the shop before Enya and Throil returned.

"What did you find?" Odo asked as they entered.

"He's a fucking fighter, that's for sure. He went down hard," Enya said. "I think it's damned likely he got a few good blows in himself, but it's hard to be certain. Guild Master was right about his hands. He couldn't have held a fucking feather if he'd lived. A good healer might have been able to mend him some, but he likely would have been crippled for the rest of his miserable life. Crushed small bones are a sight hard to heal.

"It was the final blow to the head that killed him, I think. Got him right at the base of the skull. I've never heard anyone surviving that kind of strike. What I don't understand is why they did both? Makes no fucking sense to cripple him just to kill him?"

"Abject cruelty. Or they didn't mean to kill him," Odo answered.

"I don't know that leaving a Dwarf to live without his hands is any less cruel," Throil said in a low voice. "But I have an idea as to why."

"Go on," Odo prompted.

"He had a healed burn on his right shoulder," Throil said, and Thrarber shook his head. When no one else seemed to understand, Throil wadded up his right mail sleeve, exposing a tattoo. It had Dwarfish letters in a circle around a crossed hammer and sword. "When a Dwarf joins a guild, the masters tattoo him with their guild symbol. If he is expelled—" he paused and drew his sleeve back into place—"the masters remove it with fire."

"So, the son of the Wheelwrights Guild, who just opened his own shop, happened to have a disgraced Dwarf as his shop assistant?" Odo smiled humorlessly. "I'd place good odds he wasn't helping a destitute foreigner out of the goodness of his heart."

The Dwarves both grunted in agreement.

"You think he was doing something untoward?" Asha asked. "And someone tried to stop him?"

"I think he described the forge hammer as 'Flinok's', not as his own. Maybe a slip of the tongue. Or maybe he was outcompeting his fellow wheelwrights because he was selling Dwarven craftsmanship as his own."

"Which might make other guild members angry enough that they decide to destroy his shop and maim his assistant," Wilford said softly.

Odo nodded. "It might. Or the son of a master of a guild does help a foreigner with a disgraced past, and the other guild members can't fathom that someone so young could churn out better products than them and decide he must be doing something 'untoward' and assume exactly what we are."

"Passing off a non-guild member's work as your own is a crime," Asha said. "Why wouldn't they take their suspicions to the Guild or the sheriff?"

"The same reason anyone else takes justice into their own hands. Jealousy, indignation, rage, and lack of trust in the system foment together in their hearts until it turns them black and foul as any fell beast. Then they commit cruelties with the permission of their own conscience."

Asha looked around the small shop, recalling the state of the young wheelwright, and her mind's eye painted a picture of the Dwarf pinned to the floor, being maimed. She remembered a passage from the Creation scriptures. The passage where Ciirtas warned Dynawach that humans were the most dangerous creatures the Gods created, for only they were capable of cruelty. She hadn't believed it then, but she did now.

"We will need to survey the neighbors," Odo continued. "Find out who saw what. Who heard what. Then we get a tally of the guild members and their apprentices. Find out who isn't around who should be. Try and trace them."

"We could just follow them," Asha suggested, pointing at a boot print smudged in blood. Was that the Dwarf's blood, or the wheelwrights'?

Odo looked at her for several long moments. "Have you ever tried to follow prints in a city?"

Asha flushed. "No, but I have a spell that might make it easier."

Everyone looked at her like she had lost a riddle to a Yaoguai. "Go on, then. Show us," Odo said blankly.

Asha closed her eyes, breathed in deeply, then spoke the words Bard had taught her. Then she touched the print. The blood smear turned to fire, sparking up and darting out of the shop into the street, leaving a charred line behind it.

Condescension turned to disbelief or astonishment. Odo grunted approvingly.

"Well, that's right handy, lass," Thrarber said.

Odo stuck his head out the door and looked at the burnt trail. "Looks like they headed toward the east gate. I'll go get mounts and meet the rest of you there. Follow it, and if it turns a different way, send someone to meet me there anyway, and we will catch up to the rest of you."

Everyone acknowledged, and they started out. Asha still felt fidgety back on the street, but the charred trail gave her something to focus on.

The burnt line was broken in a few places, particularly where the traffic was heavy and already beginning to trample the ash back into the dirt. She was able to find the trail again easily enough on the other side of the street or intersection. Asha understood Odo and the others' hesitation at her suggestion. There was no chance they could have followed plain prints here.

Sure enough, the trail led out of the eastern gate. The ballast waited for Odo to arrive, then mounted and followed the trail at a brisk trot for about a mile and a half before it petered out in the farmland surrounding the Capital.

"It has a max range it seems," Asha said and prepared to dismount. "If we can find another print, I can cast it again."

"No," Odo said. "We can track it without spells out here, and I don't want to alert them before we are ready for them to know we are on their tails."

The tracks were fairly plain now. Asha doubted the men had taken much effort to disguise their passage at all. They kept off the actual roads but paralleled them through fields and vineyards. The ballast followed it at a walk. Asha thought they could have gone faster, but Odo had spent about half a mile pointing out the sign to Will, and now they went at the pace Will could read it.

Even so, they made good time. After another ten winding miles, they came to a large ridge leading into a set of cavernous, rocky hills, surrounded by a walled orchard. The sign pointed into the orchard; the ballast split and circled about halfway around. There was no sign leading out.

"Do you think they passed through it?" Wilford asked Odo.

"Either that, or they are still in it," Odo said. "Riding around would take a few hours, and the sun will set before that. Very hard to track in the dark."

"This would be a good place to lay low for a while," Enya said. "Outside the city. Walled with elevation. Orchards don't need as much tending as crops, so less likely to be found."

Mayumi dismounted and handed off her reins. She stood with both hands on her spear, the butt of it on the ground. She closed her eyes and murmured words in Elvish, then inhaled deeply through her nose, which took on a faint purple glow.

She coughed and snorted, then rubbed her nose. "Seven men. All human. They have a cooking fire going, roasting mutton and potatoes."

"What?" Will, Odo, and Asha all said at once.

"Don't tell me you can smell the bastards. I have heard many rumors about Elves' physical feats, but I fucking refuse to believe that," Enya said.

Mayumi turned a dour eye to the healer, then regained her reins and remounted. "It is not a physical feat. It is a small spell on the wind. But yes, I can smell them, and there are seven men in this orchard."

"We're only tracking six," Odo said. "So, it may not be our quarry, or they met up with another man here. Either way, we wait until dark. If it isn't our men, we can shelter here and pick up the trail in the morning. If it is—"

"Then that's where the fun begins," Thrarber supplemented, twisting his war hammer in his hand.

Indeed, what fun to fetch murders out of an orchard in the dark. Asha wasn't sure what she was hoping for as anxiety twisted her gut. *At least the pirates we fought in the daylight.*

Chapter 25

Asha

The ballast secured their mounts inside the low stone wall of the orchard, near the exit but out of view from the road. Asha wished for one of her family's tethering spells, but they had no natural Mage to cast it. She didn't want to know how her destructive mana might twist the spell. Melt the horses to the ground? Sink them knee-deep into the earth? Best not to try it. They would have to trust the shadows and reins knotted around stakes. At least the horses could graze and rest.

Odo walked in front, acting as point man, with the others in the loose, staggered triangles of the Order's basic ballast formation behind him. He walked slowly and silently, his bow and three arrows held in his left hand, his right outstretched, projecting a Void shield a few feet in front of him. It was doubtful the murderers had placed any magical traps, but it cost the ballast little to let Odo lead and negate them if they had. In the darkness, it was difficult to see the Void shield. It looked like Odo was pushing the darkness itself; she was unable to tell where his shield ended and the shadows of the fruit trees overhead began.

The others stayed far enough back to not feel the nauseating, nullifying effect of his Void mana, but close enough to react and reinforce. They matched his speed and silence. Asha and Enya walked behind him, each covering one of his flanks. They had their swords sheathed so as not to catch light and expose their positions. Asha kept her right hand on her sword hilt, and Enya had her hands in the shape for a shield spell, though they hung loose at her sides.

Past Enya, Thrarber and Throil flanked Will in a similar manner, forming their own small triangle off of the one Enya and Asha formed. Will held his sword in his right hand; his left held the scabbard, still encasing the blade but detached from his belt. He thought it would be faster to remove than drawing the blade from his belt, and Odo consented to letting him try it. The Dwarves' war hammers were held easily in their hands, having no scabbards to conceal them, though their construction made them unlikely to reflect light.

Several yards off to Asha's right, Mayumi ducked under branches with her spear held low and ready in both hands. She also had no scabbard and was chosen to cover that flank in case she was seen so as not to give the others' positions away.

Any other night, Asha might have taken comfort in the crickets chirping, frogs croaking, and night birds' occasional calls. She might have realized that she missed the sounds of nature or the cool, dewy scent of the night air that she had not heard or felt since entering the Capital. But as they silently stalked closer to the keeper's hut, past the trees, before the slope of the hills, only anticipation raced through her. Her heartbeat pounded in her ears, loud as all the murmurs of the night. She forced herself to breathe slowly and deeply. Her fingers twitched with every step forward, every rustling branch, every dancing shadow.

She strained every sense, trying to predict where a man might be hiding, crouching to fire an arrow, concealed behind a tree trunk to swing a sword. The tree cover lessened, and the keeper's hut came into view. Light danced out from the cooking fire and conversation echoed, but she could not quite make out the words. Odo dropped his shield and signaled a halt about fifty yards before the clearing.

He used the hand signals the Order had taught them to command Will, Thrarber, and Throil to move around the left side and fall into an encircling position back behind the hut. While those three maneuvered around quietly, he identified where the murderers had posted a watch on the nearest hill overlooking the hut and the path approaching it.

Then Will called out an impressive imitation of a barn owl, signaling his squad was in position. Odo's next signal brought the three women into a loose line beside him. Enya drew her sword, and Asha quietly followed suit. Mayumi's teeth flashed white in the shadows; she grinned from ear to ear.

"On my mark," Odo whispered. He replaced his bodkin-tipped arrows into his quiver, then drew an arrow with a bulbous wooden head. It was modeled after the kind hunters used to stun small game or birds without fear of losing the arrow in a tree or long grass. Although, it was thicker than any hunting arrow she had seen. Fired from the heavy, recurved, composite war bow, it knocked the man on watch flat on his ass. It must have made quite a thud when it hit, but neither Asha nor the men serving themselves roast meat heard it. She hadn't seen where the arrow caught the watcher, but he didn't cry out the alarm as Odo and the women advanced in a swift, sure-footed jog toward the four men seated around the cooking fire and the hut.

Asha's attention was on the men and the fire, so she didn't see Odo fix the bow to his back and draw his large sword, but she saw it in his hands as they broke out into the clearing. It must have been a frightening sight, three members of the Order with swords drawn and an Elf with a naked spear appearing out of the trees as if out of thin air.

One man screamed out in surprise and stumbled backward, also falling flat on his ass. The second turned and ran toward the hut. Two others jumped up from the log they had been seated on and grabbed at their hammers resting along the same log. Odo was on them in a flash, sword swinging and clanging against the hastily raised hammers. Flesh squelched, men cried out in pain, and the forge hammers thudded to the ground.

Mayumi moved so quickly, Asha almost thought she flew. Elves truly were freakishly fast. She caught the fleeing man before he made it three steps and struck him a solid, overhand blow across his shoulders with the shaft of her spear. He collapsed, gasping and moaning. She stepped over him and toward the two men that rushed out of the hut, meeting the swings of another hammer. The second tried to circle her with a dagger.

Enya leaped forward, sword in her right hand and left outstretched, a green shield shimmering before her. She leaped onto the man who tumbled backward as he tried to rise with her sword at his throat, dropping the shield to place pressure on his opposite arm. "Show me your hands or die, motherfucker," she roared at him, and he whimpered as he complied.

Asha ran forward; sword held in both hands and cut off the man trying to circle Mayumi as hammer rang against spear. He hesitated, computing his chances of overtaking her sword with his dagger. Decision made, he threw an obvious feint, and Asha blocked, then shifted her grip and sent a fist-sized fireball into his chest from her outstretched fingertips. He screamed in panic and tried to beat out the flames with his off hand. The burst of flames she had thrown was easy to brush off his felted wool tunic. She hadn't intended it to stick, just distract. Asha rushed into him, knocking aside his dagger and sweeping his leg, pinning him to the ground the same way Enya had his companion.

"Hands! Stop moving!" Asha's voice broke as she yelled at him. Her words may not have formed a cohesive thought, but he stopped moving and kept his hands in view. She stood over him, unsure what to do next. Luckily, Will appeared next to her, kicking away his dagger, then bound the man's hands together with cordage.

Asha stepped away and looked around. The man Enya had subdued was sat up and bound as well as the two Odo had wounded and disarmed. Odo was now flipping over the one Mayumi had collapsed as he begged pitifully. Mayumi had already tied up the one who had confronted her and was dragging him bound toward the fire.

Odo looked around, silently counting. Enya slipped her pack off and retrieved bandages and a jar of ointment. Then she knelt to examine the two bleeding men.

"Where's the man on watch?" Odo asked sharply.

"Thrarber and Throil went to fetch him," Will said.

Odo nodded, but before he could speak, the ground shifted and shook. Mayumi cocked her head and said, "I thought there were no quakes in this part of your continent?"

"There hasn't been in a hundred years," Odo said, his eyes shifting toward the hills. "No natural quakes anyway."

"What do you—" Asha abruptly cut off. She gasped and drew in a full breath, the air felt thin, like it was suddenly sucked away. Hairs on the back of her neck stood up, every nerve raw and sharp. A foul scent assaulted her. It reminded her of when she had helped bury the blood-soaked dirt in the fall slaughter pits. Old blood and soil, fear and stone.

A rumbling and scraping echoed out, like a rockslide in the passes. Asha instinctively turned her eyes upward, attempting to scan mountain peaks that weren't within a hundred miles of her. Then came the thrum of two sets of heavy running feet. The bound men struggled in vain, and the ballast turned with raised weapons toward the sound.

Thrarber and Throil broke out of the darkness at a run.

"The crazy fucker woke it!" Throil shouted. Asha had never seen fear on his face before.

"The watchman? Woke what?" Odo asked.

"A troll," Thrarber huffed out, hands on his knees, breathing deliberately to regulate himself. He broke into a string of Dwarfish that sounded profane. "Smashed the cairn to bits—" more Dwarfish—"arrogant, ground tiller. Supercilious son of an uninspired, skilless woman!"

"Not so high and mighty now, *Holy Heroes*," sneered one of the bound men. "When Adrian brings that troll down here, you'll get what's coming to you."

"One does not bring a troll anywhere," Odo snapped. "Enya leave that bandage! We'll need your shield. All of you, take up defensive positions."

They all moved to comply as two large glowing eyes appeared high in the trees. Branches cracked and snapped, and the sounds of rock scraping against rock echoed as the hate-filled eyes came closer.

"Who else spilled blood to bind the fell beast?" Odo grabbed the man who had spoken by the collar, lifting him off the ground a bit. "Where is the cairn?"

"Just Adrian. It's his family's orchard." The man smiled viciously, then coughed against the pressure on his throat. "But he's the only one left, and he won't shed willing blood to help you, bureaucrat."

"Not even clumsy-fingered farmers ought to be foolish enough to bind a troll with only one bloodline!" Thrarber exclaimed.

Indeed, Adrian would never spill willing blood again, for a bureaucrat or anyone else. When the troll entered the clearing, it dragged a body whose head was crushed beyond recognition. Throil, Thrarber, and Odo all began cursing in different languages when they saw him.

The creature was nearly two-thirds as tall as the mature fruit trees. It was broader than two oxen, shoulder to shoulder. It lumbered, body shifting and feet sliding along the ground, giving Asha an impression of a mountain remembering how to move. Skin gray and hard, it looked like stone. No, it *was* stone. Eyes as big as fists, glowing red with viciousness and malice, were set in its enormous head. Long arms hung from its massive shoulders down to its knees, terminating in huge, bear-like paws where the jagged rock thinned into pointed claws.

"How do we defend against a creature of stone?" Will asked, the tremble in his voice matching the one in Asha's hands.

"We have to rebind it," Odo said, and the troll dropped the mangled body it carried and continued advancing toward the firelight.

"No," Throil countered. "If it killed the only one who spilled blood in the binding, we must complete an entirely new ritual. Can't refresh what is shattered."

Odo cursed again, firing a ball of shadow from his fingertips at the fell beast's head. It paused but shook its massive stone head and kept coming.

"I don't know the ritual," he said to the Dwarves. "Do you?"

The troll was nearly within melee range. They began moving forward to meet it.

"Aye, all Dwarven children learn it," Thrarber said. "We'll need cover, though. The beasts aren't fond of being bound."

Enya pinched both of her middle fingers to her thumbs and drew the shield sign in a wide doublehanded circle. Her hands ended the gesture, crossed across her chest. Green mana shimmered in front of the ballast.

Mayumi moved to the right, trying to flank the stone beast. Will followed her. Odo moved in the opposite direction. "Asha! With me. Enya! Let's see that famous shield prowess."

"Would be a sight easier if you dolts would keep closer together." She sounded irritable, which puzzled Asha. Not that she had time to wonder about it.

"Make do," was all Odo replied. Enya mumbled something that was no doubt even more vulgar and irritated.

At that moment, the creature seemed to realize it was being maneuvered. It swung a massive paw at Mayumi's head. Its feet slid and dragged slowly to turn and add momentum without exposing its back to

Odo and Asha. The arm, however, swung with a speed that was jarring compared to the lumbering lower half.

Mayumi was faster. She ducked and jumped to the side, shouting a word in her native tongue and lightning shot out of her spear tip, catching the beast in the chest. The stone skin crackled and melted where the lightning impacted. The fell beast roared in pain, a harrowing, rumbling cry that shook Asha to the core. But the beast didn't stop its advance.

The troll swung its other arm, this time at Will. He was not as quick as Mayumi, and though he ducked, the stone claws struck and scraped along the green mana in front of Will's belly. The shimmering changed, and it seemed to solidify at the impact. Enya grunted, even as Will flung a ring of fire around the beast and danced back.

Asha drew in a large breath. The anxiety and tremors were gone. She felt numb, like she was watching this happen to someone else. For three heartbeats, she drew in as much mana as she could, then threw it at the creature's center. She shaped the mana into a fire spell, envisioning the hottest forge fire she had ever seen as she did so.

A column of fire hit the beast, exactly where Mayumi had struck it. Rock-like skin began to glow red, cracking and melting. The beast slid back a step, then turned and shifted its advance on Asha, no longer concerned about showing its back to Will and Mayumi. Asha drew deeper into herself and continued to feed the column. Her heartbeat raced, and salt stung her eyes.

The troll's chest was fully glowing now, and a hole melted into the center. Asha's chest heaved, but she still poured mana into the column.

Odo moved further around the beast. He shouted and stamped his feet, swinging his sword and trying to draw the creature's attention away from Asha. It didn't work. He stepped within a foot of Will's fire ring, and the flames flickered, then extinguished.

Asha wasn't sure if Odo Voided it or if Will dropped the spell. But then, Will threw an explosive blast at the troll's outstretched arm. It shattered and flew in all directions. Will fell to his knees. Mayumi jumped to him, blocking him from the troll in a crouched, ready stance.

"Toss me that arm!" Thrarber yelled over the rushing of Asha's flames. "We need a piece of the beast for the ritual!"

Odo ran forward and dove toward a large chunk of rock. He rolled up and over, and continued back into a run, the rock in his offhand as the troll swatted at him. A jagged paw came within inches of his back, but ultimately only struck air. The green shield flexed, then shimmered, then turned to mist around Odo.

At the same time, Mayumi summoned a great gust of wind that picked up several small pieces and blew them toward where the Dwarves were arranging a tiny altar next to the keeper's hut. The altar fell in the gust.

"Oi! Easy there!" Throil called out, jumping to right it.

"Almost lost yer head there, Void! Ye know damned well ye can't use my shield, but the least ye can do is not fuck it up!" Enya roared.

"Don't whine," Odo quipped, eerily nonchalant. He tossed the rock and caught it again as he walked past her and delivered it to the Dwarves. "It's unbecoming."

"When she melts this blasted child of Ciirtas, I'll show you unbecoming," she gritted out.

Asha heard them through a haze. Her breath came in great, ragged gasps. She spared all the focus she could to try and breathe in slowly. Her arms started to burn, and her fingers trembled. But the troll still inched toward her.

She didn't think she had ever summoned so much mana in her life, but she reached down deeper and pulled up more. Tilting her head to her chest, she visualized connecting to her spirit center. Then she drew in a belly full of air, pulling mana with it. She held the breath and continued pulling mana until her lungs burned, and she felt so full of raw power she thought she might burst.

The troll's arm struck the green mana shield in front of her. Once, twice, three times, the stone paw slugged the protective barrier. Enya grunted, then gasped, then yelled something guttural. Will and Mayumi yelled, too, probably telling her to move.

Thunder rumbled, or was that the troll? Asha wasn't sure. But then lightning struck the beast. Once, twice, and Asha stopped counting, but the strikes continued coming while she continued to draw. The troll writhed and swatted at the air above it but still moved forward.

Instead, she released the mana and her breath with a deep-throated scream. Extending her burning, aching arms out farther, she intensified the spell. One of her aunts had told her about the volcanoes out past the coastline. Great mountains that spew fire so hot that it melts rocks into rivers. She shaped the mana into that fire, that heat, commanding the mana to turn the beast into a river of melted stone.

Before her eyes, the troll melted like candle wax. Starting in the center where her fire column had burned a hole, the stone body began to drip downward, then gush. The legs went next, then the arms, then only the head remained in a pool of liquid rock. It, too, slowly melted. The eyes were the last thing that disappeared into the hot glow of the lava.

Asha's knees buckled, and she couldn't catch her breath. She forced her steps backward, away from the puddle of molten stone, in a stumble. The ground became disconcertingly close before she realized she was falling. Then strong, mailed arms caught her. Embarrassment crept up in her, but she couldn't pull herself off of Odo's armored chest.

"Take a minute, Ash," he said gently as she tried and failed to regain her feet. "That was quite a feat. Even for a first of a seventh of a seventh." He lowered her to a seated position and knelt behind her to support her back.

"Two." Asha gasped. "Two arms."

"Most trolls do have two arms." She felt as much as heard his chuckle.

"Will blasted one." She forced her breath in her nose and out her mouth as Will and Mayumi circled the widening pool of lava toward her. "But there were two. When it melted. Should have. Been one."

"Trolls heal themselves."

"What?" Asha and Will exclaimed at once.

"They're made of stone, lassie." Thrarber raised his voice and a beckoning hand. "You would have to melt the whole formation it is born out of to truly kill it."

Odo helped her stand and stayed close as she took slow steps toward the hastily made altar. Her legs burned, too. She hadn't felt this bone-deep exhaustion in quite a while.

"My sword!" She looked around the ground and tried to turn back. Mayumi flipped something lumpy, misshapen, and metallic over with the balance point on her spear.

"Not much left of it, I fear," the Elf said.

"The armory won't issue me another." Asha hated how whiny the words sounded coming out of her mouth, but she couldn't temper them right now.

Throil looked up and made eye contact with Odo. "I remember what you said about not modifying anything for the ballast until after we were full members and out of training. But surely this qualifies for an exception."

"I would say so." Odo nodded.

"Bring it here," Throil said. "And the rest of ye, help Thrarber. We will add many more than one bloodline to our binding."

Mayumi reached toward the metal but quickly pulled her hand back from the heat. She murmured quietly, and a small spring bubbled up under what was left of the sword, lifting and carrying it to the Dwarf's feet.

She changed the course of the stream suddenly and swirled it around one of the bound men who had regained his feet. He slipped on the suddenly wet surface and fell back to the ground. Mayumi bounded over on light, wide strides, catching another who had been sawing at his ropes with a rock with a swinging kick, sending him sprawling. She began checking bindings and repositioning the struggling captives. Odo assisted her.

"Best leave the sword for later," Enya said. She was also trying to catch her breath as she once again reached for the bandages from her dropped pack. Another quake punctuated her words. "Asha gave us a wonderful break to complete the ritual. Shouldn't waste it."

Enya knelt next to one of the still bleeding murderers. This one was pale as clean wool and barely conscious. She forewent the ointment and wrapped the bandage tightly around his slashed arms, murmuring clotting spells as she did so. The wounds beneath the bandage glowed faintly green.

Asha glanced to the small altar surrounded by Ciirtas's runes carved into the rich earth. It was a pitiful attempt at sanctified ground, but she supposed it would have to do for a ritual binding. She looked back to the melted troll. Was it growing? It was cooling far faster than it should've been. And the surface was shifting and hardening.

"I can heat it again," she offered. "What did you mean about the whole formation?"

"Trolls are made of stone you see." Thrarber smiled patiently at her as he withdrew a small chisel from a pouch on his belt. "This one, particularly, is made of shale. Very poor rock, if you ask me. It flakes and is not good for building." He placed the chisel into the altar and started to delicately tap it with his war hammer. Orange tendrils of mana floated off of it as he worked, and the altar rapidly began to change shape. "But it is plentiful. Likely to run all throughout these hills and caves. We call that a formation. All the rock that was formed at the same time. A troll is part of a formation, so it can pull more and more rock to heal itself. Only way to kill it is to destroy every last bit of rock in the formation."

Asha always enjoyed watching Artificers create things. She found herself calmed by it now, despite the circumstances. "So, we would have to level all of these hills? How would we even know if we had destroyed all of the rock in the formation?"

Thrarber returned the chisel to his pouch. The altar now looked like an offering stone in a proper temple. It was still small, but it was perfectly flat, perfectly rectangular, with the words 'Balance' and 'Justice' imprinted on the sides six times.

"When the troll stops healing itself," Throil said, pointing at the pool that was now fully returned to stone.

"But with a bit of divine assistance—" Thrarber winked at her—"we can bind it into the ground where it cannot wake as long as willing blood fills the runes on some of the troll stone. A cairn is most common, but with a—" he hesitated, searching for a word—"a, shall we say, easily smashed stone like shale, I think some extra precautions should be taken. Aye, brother?"

"Aye," Throil replied as he gathered charred logs from the dying cooking fire.

"Now!" Thrarber said with a smile as the ground shook again. "All willing, please line up to shed blood."

"It's moving!" Will said urgently.

Asha turned, and sure enough, the rock pool was reforming and shifting upward. As she watched, the head took shape, great glowing eyes flickering back to life.

"Asha, lass." Thrarber regained her attention. He had the shale chunk of the troll's arm on the altar and a dagger in his hand. He reached for her left hand with a questioning look.

"I don't know what to do," she said, realizing she still felt bone tired, but she had finally caught her breath. She extended her hand to him.

"Call on Ciirtas in whatever way feels natural to you. Ask for his divine help and blessing in protecting these lands from the fell beasts created by his hands."

Asha closed her eyes and said a silent prayer to her patron. She asked him for help and renewed her promise to bring justice and balance to this world. Then she asked that he bind this creature as it didn't seem just to her to level an entire orchard.

When she opened her eyes, Thrarber nodded at her. He asked, "Asha Pacatus, do you willingly shed sacrificial blood to bind this fell beast back to the earth from whence it came? Will you agree to let your precious lifeblood be used in this ritual in the name of Ciirtas, God of Balance and Justice?"

"Yes," Asha said softly as the ground shook again. Thrarber swiftly cut her palm and let the blood pool in it. Then he dipped his finger in her blood and used it to draw runes on the troll rock. Asha felt a power she couldn't explain, something deep and ancient. She found herself breathless for an entirely different reason.

Thrarber shooed her off and gestured Odo forward next. Asha turned and looked at the pool of rock. It was no longer a pool but a massive boulder with the head, arms, and chest of the troll formed at the top. The hate-filled eyes dimmed, even as it roared in protest and swung its arms toward them.

Thrarber repeated the same questions to Odo, then drew fresh blood runes over Asha's. The troll flailed and moaned, then went still.

Thrarber repeated this with Enya, Will, Mayumi, and Throil. Then Throil took his place behind the altar and performed the ritual with Thrarber's blood. The Dwarves took the charcoal from the fire and beat it with their hammers, one striking after the other, chanting in their own language, orange mana glowing from the charcoal. Quickly, it turned into clear gemstone, and then they shaped the gem into an urn.

Thrarber carefully placed the still wet shale into the urn while Throil beat out a lid. They slid the blood-runed rock into the gemstone vessel and sealed it tightly.

"Pure diamond!" Thrarber exclaimed. "No half-wit orchard tender will be smashing this cairn to bits. I tell ye that." He grinned.

"Still want to take the prisoners back tonight?" Mayumi asked Odo, now that the binding was finished.

Enya picked up Asha's hand and pressed green mana into the shallow cut. It stung, but soon the blood dried, and the flesh reknit itself. Enya repeated this for everyone but Odo. To him, she merely offered a bandage, which he wrapped and tied himself, thinking.

"No. We'll rest here until morning. But we'll have to set watches. I don't want any escapees."

Relief coursed through Asha, after all that, a long ride guiding uncooperative prisoners was the last thing she wanted to do. Especially without a sword, she didn't know if her trembling, aching body could draw more mana right now.

Chapter 26

Asha

Asha looked at the ring on her finger as she sat next to the fire. It wasn't glowing. She thought hard, trying to remember if it had been while they fought the troll. The troll certainly felt evil. But feelings weren't a trustworthy guide to reality. Like a compass in iron-rich mountains, sometimes feelings led one astray.

She wanted to stand by her words that creatures and even fell beasts weren't evil, despite the name. They simply were what they were. Evil, true evil, required the ability to be better, the option to do good, the capacity to reject kindness, truth, and balance. Did a troll have the ability to be anything other than a monster? Did a troll have the capacity to not attack? Could it choose to accept a binding? She shuddered at the image of the troll's great, glowing eyes as it moved toward her, the angry embers burning into her as she burned it.

Turning, she observed the great stone beast, now frozen still and lifeless, bound but not dead. It was half-formed, head, shoulders, and arms sticking out of the boulder. It was an eerie sight, looking as though it might begin reforming or moving at any moment.

"Don't fret, lass," Throil said gently as he dropped wood between the fire and the anvil that they had found behind the orchard keeper's hut. "The binding is solid. By the mercy and power of Ciirtas, the beast will not move again this night."

"How long will it hold?" she asked quietly. "Will someone else have to..." She trailed off, unsure what she was even asking.

"The binding holds as long as the blood does. On a traditional cairn, ye must refresh it every season or so, depending on the weather. But in a sealed gem urn, the blood will last as long as we who gave it do. Unless someone meddles of course." He shrugged, entirely too nonchalant in her opinion. Perhaps because she was tired. Or more likely because he reminded her of another Dwarf.

"Of course," Asha whispered. Her thoughts turned from the troll and her silver ring to a sapphire-eyed Dwarf. She didn't like admitting that she missed him, but tonight, she didn't have the energy to lie, even to herself. Or perhaps it was because he was a far more pleasant memory.

Throil set about silently banking the fire with rocks as reflectors, stacking the bed of coals to concentrate the deepest heat on the metal lump that had been Asha's sword.

"Add a bit o' heat to this if ye don't mind." Throil indicated his makeshift forge.

Asha pushed aside the debilitating fatigue and summoned more mana. She brought her hand close to the coals before she released it. Not trusting herself to aim right now, she wouldn't forgive herself if she burned her ballast mate while he was trying to fix her latest spell damage.

"So, when we all die...it will be released?" she asked him. "Perhaps we should try to destroy the formation. I don't know if I can tonight, but I can't just leave it to be someone else's problem."

"Well, I plan to live for a few hundred more years." Thrarber dropped his armful of wood unceremoniously next to the fire. "I imagine our She-Elf plans the same. And you youngsters surely got six to ten more decades, now, don't ye? That's plenty of time to find more responsible keepers to add willing blood in their own binding."

"One decade or a thousand, aren't we just delaying the problem? Like placing a bucket under a leaking roof, then another bucket on top of the first. We're not fixing anything."

"That's what the orchard is doing." Asha hadn't heard Odo approach. Her awareness was slipping the more tired she felt. *No excuse*, the scolding voice in her head sounded an awful lot like Great Uncle Luca's. *Those who mean you harm will not be so kind as to strike when you are well-rested.*

"I don't understand. How is the orchard doing anything? It's just a bunch of trees." Even as she said it, she knew that wasn't true. She had grown up with far too many natural Mages to believe that. But she didn't see what an orchard had to do with binding a troll.

"By growing. Year after year, plants and trees grow. They sink roots down deep, breaking the soil and splitting rocks. Call it magic or divinity or just the way of things, but the earth is reshaped by living things. I'm sure this troll formation had very little growth before it was bound the first time. You could exhaust yourself, pouring mana into turning every speck of rock under this soil to lava. Or you can be patient and let the roots slowly turn the shale to soil. There have been several generations of orchard keepers here who dedicated themselves to fostering that growth and turning rock to something fertile."

"It just feels as though we're doing nothing. Leaving it half-finished."

He turned his head to look at the stone creature. "It isn't. Do you understand what it would mean to destroy the whole formation? We would reshape this entire glen. Not just the orchard either. If we are lucky, and the formation only runs under these hills and not the surrounding fields, what about the water? Will it flow the same? What of the heat caused by turning stone to liquid? How will that affect the other crops? Letting the change happen over hundreds of years isn't leaving it half-done. It's giving the earth the proper time to adjust, to shift without catastrophe."

Asha didn't like it, but he was more than likely right. It still felt half-assed, but again, she reminded herself that feelings weren't always true. She should probably just go lie down. But her mind felt cluttered. Despite being tired, she didn't think she could actually sleep.

Odo clapped her on the shoulder, then went and checked the ropes on the bound men again. He had first watch. Asha turned her limited attention to the Dwarves' actions.

Throil had removed the metal from the fire and set it on the anvil. He held it with tongs and struck it with his war hammer. Sparks and mana flew. Against the deep dark of the night, with the fire between them, Asha had trouble discerning one from the other. Then Thrarber struck the metal with his hammer. Neither spoke, but their blows were perfectly timed, one after another. It sounded like a harmony of metal on metal. She hadn't spent much time in her family's forge, but it reminded her of the times she had.

Asha knew that most war hammers were designed only to strike people and inflict blunt-force damage. But her uncles had told her that it was a hallmark of Dwarven engineering to make a hammer that was both deadly and practical. Some humans thought it was a secret, but Uncle Guy had told her that the only secret was how Feorach formed the Dwarves. They might be shorter, but they were far, far stronger.

A human couldn't wield a forge hammer with the speed required to make it deadly. Similarly, a light and deadly war hammer was not at all efficient at shaping metal. Dwarves had no such limitation. It was still incredible to see it in action.

The cadence of the blows changed, then stopped. Throil placed the sword—as it was now a sword again and not a metal lump—back into the makeshift forge for a while, letting it reheat until it glowed. Then Throil walked the sword over to the rain barrel outside the hut and plunged it under the water.

"Shouldn't it be oil?" Asha asked them.

"Ye got a barrel of oil under yer shirt?" Thrarber retorted.

She shrugged with a half-smile as Mayumi and Will entered the clearing, leading the ballast's mounts to be retied further from the road and within view of the watch.

Throil laid it next to Asha on a scrap of cloth. "Don't touch it yet. Needs a good half hour I think to cool."

She nodded and refrained from touching it, looking it over. The blade shape and edge geometry looked identical to what it had been before. But there was now a deep fuller running along the blade. The fuller was woven with intricate destructive runes that were familiar. She pulled her whip off her belt and compared them.

"Didn't think we got a peek, did ye? Well, them runes are just the same. So, ye'll be able to cast without melting it again." Thrarber chuckled.

"But I made this myself. How did you... Some of these runes are mine."

"I hate to break it to ye, pebble, but those runes aren't anything special," Thrarber said.

"I could have made the fire hotter myself," Throil supplied. "Using your mana in the heating helped us feel out your particular—" he waved his hand back and forth—"I don't know the word in the common tongue. But it helped us know what runes to use."

"Oh," was all Asha could think to say. Her mind felt fuzzy and slow. She needed to go to sleep.

"Thank you. Both of you."

"Get some shuteye. You can sing our praises in the morning." Thrarber smiled at her.

"Yeah, I'll do that," she said, taking the sword, wrapping it in the cloth to protect her hand. She didn't notice the runes of Estesbryd that Enya had drawn along the threshold, but her mind eased as she entered the hut. The full weight of her exhaustion hit her then, and she lay down next to where Enya had been softly snoring for at least an hour. It seemed she wasn't the only one who exhausted herself by casting. Asha fell asleep without unrolling her sleeping mat. She didn't stir until Will woke her for the last watch.

Breakfast had been a cold, meager affair, a stark contrast from the warm, beautiful morning that dawned as though nothing bad had happened the previous night. The ballast could have stoked the fire, but neither the rations they packed nor the sparce pantry of the hut contained anything that would have been vastly improved by heating.

The distance was not great back to the Capital, but the going was slow. They had tied the murderers together like a string of mules, but they walked far slower than even the most stubborn, eager-to-graze equine Asha had ever dealt with.

They were also far louder. It was probably cruel, so Asha wouldn't say it out loud, but she sorely wished they had an excuse to gag the men.

"You can't treat us like this! We are Imperial citizens!"

"We ain't done nothing!"

"Not our fault that orchard keeper turned the troll on ye!"

"Yeah!" several of them chorused that excuse.

"We was just as surprised as you when the fell beast came 'rounding out the trees."

"You attacked us anyway! How were we supposed to know you were anyone official? Sneaking through the woods after dark and surprising us like that. And for what?" One of them in particular continued this line of thought, addressed squarely at Odo's broad, unflinching shoulders. The others egged him on with affirmative exclamations. "A piss-poor showing from the Order of Holy Heroes if ye ask me! Piss-poor showing." Was he the one who had condescended them about the orchard keeper being the only one involved in the binding? She couldn't be sure. "Nothing heroic or holy about sneak attacks, no sir! Nothing at all. Downright ungentlemanly and dishonorable! Wait until the Guild Master hears about this. See how far the Order goes without wheels! You won't do much of your fancy swordsmanship and spells without your supply wagons rolling behind you. And for what? 'Cause we bruised a high and mighty youngster and his pet Dwarf?" He cut off abruptly when the man behind him, one of the wounded ones, kicked him in the back of the knee. Falling from the force, he brought the entire line to a halt while he regained his feet.

Odo finally turned to look at the speaker. "We both know you did far more than bruise the lad and his shop assistant. Don't think you can whine your way into mercy from me. I am not a merciful man, and I despise men who whine instead of bear the consequences of their own actions."

"Even if we did—" He cut off as he received another kick and turned to try and shove the other man. The action had little effect other than to tangle himself more in the ropes. Was that the point? Getting the ballast's guard down by in-fighting?

Asha moved to intervene, but Mayumi held up a hand to stop her and whispered, "Won't work if we don't take the bait."

Of course, she was not the only one to think of that. Just the only one silly enough to fall for it. Maybe her mother and grandmother were right. Maybe she was a young fool.

"Even if we did what you accused us of—" the belligerent man had righted and unwound himself—"that's no cause to attack us and tie us up like common bandits!"

"Murder is far worse than banditry. As is destruction of a man's livelihood." Odo's face remained impassive, but he didn't turn his mount to resume the journey. "I had cause to kill every one of you, but as I said—" Odo smiled then, not his normal, nice smile—"I am not a merciful man."

"He's not a man. He's a foreigner! He wasn't even created by the great Goddess. He's a lesser creature, allowed to exist by our leave." Throil stiffened and Thrarber's face turn down in an angry, hard look, but neither spoke.

The man who had been kicking the speaker interjected. "We aren't murderers! And this one is just angry at being treated worse than any citizen deserves. His words aren't worth the time it takes to hear 'em."

"Oh, I think the jailer and the sheriff will find his words quite worth the time." Odo's smile started to make Asha squirm in her saddle. She didn't like the side of him that seemed to enjoy the cruel flavor of justice that these men would face.

"We aren't murderers!" the second man insisted, and several others murmured agreement.

"Yeah, we just roughed 'em up a bit. No need to throw out words like 'murder' or 'stolen livelihood!'" another man shouted, and the second one gritted his teeth in frustration. He couldn't keep them all quiet.

"Flinok is dead. And the forge is so badly damaged, I'm not certain if even a guild master's money can repair it." Odo's voice dropped to a deep, menacing timbre. "So, I'll use whatever words I please to describe the scum I see before me."

"Who the fuck is Flinok?" the first man yelled.

"The Dwarf," Odo hissed. "The Dwarf you attacked, overwhelmed, then held out his hands and crushed with your hammers. The Dwarf you killed after you tortured him. His name was Flinok, and you will remember it well as you languish in the gaol. If I have to carve it into your flesh, you will remember his name."

The state of the forge upon their examination flashed before Asha's mind at Odo's words. The state of the Guild Master's son, laid up in bed, struggling against pain to even breathe. She hadn't seen Flinok's body, but he was beaten far worse than the man she had seen. That was true cruelty. Was that why Odo could smile at the idea of what these men would face?

Was cruelty repaid for cruelty justice? It was balance, that she had to concede.

She realized that while she had pondered, the accused men stood slack-jawed and, for the first time that morning, quiet.

"We didn't kill him," the first man finally said hesitantly. "He'll live. We didn't—"

"Yeah, just a tap on the skull we gave him," a man who had not yet spoken interjected a touch more confidently. "Just to put him to sleep. You can't convict us of murder for a guild internal brawl now!"

"People don't just wake up from taps on the skull!" Enya sneered at them. "Fucking empty-headed blight-worms. You shouldn't listen to so many old hero stories. If a person passes out from a blow to the head, they are unlikely to wake again. And even if they do, they are rarely ever the same." She continued to mutter profanities under her breath as she spurned her mount forward. The rest of the ballast and the column of bound men followed her.

"We didn't mean to kill the foreign bloke. We didn't mean to..." the first man muttered incredulously.

"What about the wrong done to us?" The second man seemed to give up on all pretense of keeping his and his companion's mouths shut. "We didn't just go out and start a fight! We were driven to it! The Guild Master wouldn't take care of the problem, nor the sheriff! Why, we had to!"

"You were driven to beat a man and a Dwarf with hammers, and torture and kill one of them?" Odo's smile and malice were gone, replaced with an inhuman indifference.

"We were!" he answered, and several others assented. "Do you know what they were doing? Did you even bother to investigate them?"

"Nothing to deserve maiming or death. Of that, I am certain." Odo didn't even look at the speaker.

"You accuse us of stealing a livelihood, but what about our own? What about a rich man's son who had everything handed to him since the day he was born, coming into our guild territory, given the best location. And then he wasn't even good enough at the craft to compete, so he hires a Dwarf, who was cast out by his own people. Likely some type of swindler or criminal himself, mind you. And he passes the Dwarven craftsmanship as his own! Stealing our customers out from our noses."

"Aye! I got a house full of babes and another on the way! That skilless, wealthy, green-wood brat was taking food out of my babes' mouths. He deserved what we gave him," another chimed in.

"And when we complained to the guild, well the masters, they did an investigation, or so they said. Of course, the investigation found no wrongdoing. So, I ask you, son of Ciirtas, what else were we to do but take justice into our own hands?"

Odo turned a terrifying look upon the speaker. "Do not dare blaspheme the name of Ciirtas by dressing up your petty jealousy and insufficiencies as justice, or I will defend the honor of my patron and ensure that you never speak such disrespect again." Asha wasn't sure if he meant he would kill them or something else, but luckily, none of the men seemed eager to find out. Odo continued after a long moment, "If the masters found no wrongdoing, you could have appealed for an Imperial review. If your charge was found correct, not only the man swindling but also any involved in covering for him would have been stripped of their guild protections and possibly even citizenship. But then, you know that. Don't you? You didn't care. You wished for punishment. Not justice. You couldn't tolerate the thought that perhaps you were wrong. Perhaps the boy is just that good. Perhaps you are a weak, pathetic excuse for a man who cannot provide for his babes."

Again, Odo let the words hang heavy and threatening, staring each of the men down until they looked away in shame or fear. "The next man who speaks will lose his tongue." With that, Odo turned back in his saddle and did not look at them again the entire silent ride back to the Capital's gaol.

Once they entered the city walls, the cage constricted her chest again. But she found that she was still too tired to care if she was trapped. Could there be anything inside these walls more frightening than a troll? She forced herself to sit up straight in her saddle and scan the streets, doorways, and windows all the same. Even exhausted, she would be better at this.

She offered to stay with the mounts outside of the gaol. It smelled of death, rot, and misery. The air itself felt like anguish. And, quite frankly, she didn't want to know what those men would face inside. She knew they couldn't be allowed to remain out in the city. They had brutalized two people, killed one, and they weren't even remorseful. That didn't mean she felt good about what would happen to them in there.

Officially, torture and cruelty were banned in any Imperial gaol. Officially, every crime had a price. A debt to be paid, even murder. Wergild, it was called. Every man, woman, and child in the Empire had a price assigned to their head. From the lowest chambermaid to the Emperor himself. It was supposed to limit revenge, to sanitize justice.

Unfortunately, no one but the wealthiest merchants or nobility would be likely to afford wergild for an Imperial citizen outright. If one couldn't pay for their crime, they worked in the gaol until the jailer determined their debt was paid. There were official calculations, assigned wages for the type of labor, with room and board deducted, of course. But, in practice, the calculations varied greatly based on the crime and how well one pleased the jailer. Asha had heard rumors that no one ever actually paid their wergild and left the gaol.

What was the wergild for a Dwarf? Would his expulsion from his guild factor in? He was technically a skilled laborer but not allowed to work as one. What was her wergild? Would it be higher once she was a sworn member of the Order?

When the others finally came back out, Odo turned his mount away from the garrison.

"Are we going to make our report to the sheriff now?" Asha asked. She had been hoping for a bath and a hot meal, even if it was just from the provision hall.

"No, I'll write it up tonight. We're going to talk to the Guild Master and his son again."

No one else said anything until they were back inside the same cramped room with the same furniture in the same configuration. Asha noticed there was another quilt across the young man. The older woman, his mother, paced nervously, and her wrinkles deepened.

Enya pulled off her pack and began to rifle through it.

"Thank you," the Guild Master addressed her, "but we have a healer coming."

Enya nodded and pulled the pack back on but didn't reply.

"Well?" he addressed Odo this time. "Have you come to waste more time asking my son inappropriate questions while those ruffians are still—"

"They are secured in the gaol," Odo cut him off and turned to the young man. "However, it seems that they are having trouble with the wergild. Did Flinok have any family here?"

Relief washed over the young man's face, and he slumped deeper into the pillows propping up his back. "Not that I know of. He never mentioned anyone."

"Then as his employer, you will need to consult with the sheriff and the jailer to approve the assigned wergild. I told them to set it as a skilled laborer under the employ of an Imperial citizen."

"I don't think a shop assistant fits the definition of skilled labor," the Guild Master cut in, but Odo kept looking at the young wheelwright.

He squirmed and looked away, but Odo didn't. After a moment, he licked his lips and met Odo's gaze. "Look, I know what people think, but it isn't like that. I know I'm young, but I never falsified my work."

"You called the forge hammer Flinok's".

"He missed it, you know? Crafting. So, I let him craft sometimes. He wasn't a bad Dwarf. He just made a mistake. A big one, but he didn't deserve to be cast out. But I never sold his work. And I never let him work the forge during the day. Only after hours, and anything he made was just for our use or donated to the widow and orphan house."

Odo looked back at the Guild Master. "So, when the afterhours work was noticed and complained about...?"

"I had my masters investigate it. I removed myself completely so no one could claim bias. But we didn't feel the need to air the Dwarf's past to the whole city!" He was still scowling, but he seemed a touch less guarded.

"If you had, perhaps he wouldn't be dead. But perhaps not. Only the Gods could know that." Genuine sadness came over Odo's face.

"I married a sixth daughter, not a seventh." The Guild Master's scowl was completely gone now. "It is a shame, though. He was a good lad. No offense—" now he addressed Thrarber and Throil—"but we'll not be hiring anymore Dwarves, at least not until my son is old enough that his skill is believable to such despicable rabble."

For once, Thrarber was the silent one, but Throil said, "None taken. Would likely be wise. Best of luck repairing the forge."

Once they checked back in at the garrison, the sergeant at the barracks desk instructed Asha to sign for a letter. She did so, surprised, then scolded herself. She had plenty of family who were likely desperate for news from her. The guilt of not even considering writing first tugged at her heart.

It was from her mother. She recognized the beautiful script over her family's seal pressed into the wax.

"First daughter,"

Her mother only used that title when it was something official.

"Fear not the devastation from the great beast."

What great beast? Then it hit her: This was a prophecy. Her mother's Spirit Sight had warned her of something.

"Blood given from a willing and knowing heart cries out to Ciirtas, and he will answer. He has seen the faithful sacrifice. He will sustain the blood bond; nothing will tear it asunder."

Then in the postscript,

"I search the post eagerly and daily for your reply with the goings on in the Capital and your new life."

Asha chuckled and shook her head. She supposed she deserved that.

"What is it, lass?" Thrarber asked her.

"It's from my mother, warning us of the troll. Might have been helpful a few days ago," she said, holding up the page.

"Not even a Seer can anticipate the lethargy of Imperial messengers." Enya chuckled, too, and looped an arm through Asha's as they turned to enter the female barracks. "But I think the Gods can smell our stench from their houses. To the bathhouse."

"To the bathhouse," agreed the others.

Asha would be glad to wash away the smell of the fighting and riding, and perhaps the disquiet in her mind would wash away with it.

Chapter 27

Mago

Mago steadied his writing hand with an outstretched finger against the rough, wooden desk, waiting for the deep roll of the ship to pass. He no longer got queasy with every rock, dip, or sway. It was also more rare that he stumbled as he walked on the deck. It had taken nearly a week for him to 'grow his sea legs' as the crew had put it. They had insisted he was inhibiting his growth when he took the opportunity to walk on the piers at each of the Trebri Islands where they docked along the way. They were likely right, but the allure of land had overcome him. He wasn't a sailor by heart nor trade. Nevertheless, he had adapted.

He still struggled a bit when writing, though. Perhaps he should have waited to do so. Writing his reports ahead of time would do him no good if they were illegible. This is why he delayed recreating his sketches. He examined the parchment and his ink marks thus far. Legible at least, though his mother would have thumped him solidly if she had seen the disarrayed squiggles that he passed as cyphered script.

Capping his inkwell, he began cleaning his quill while he waited for the ink to dry enough to place it inside the oilskin pouch. These instruments had been harder to acquire than the voyage itself, ironically. The fluid value of such items amused him. Scarcity and abundance ruled over all goods. Space aboard a ship in a port was abundant but writing utensils were scare once that ship was out to sea.

He left the small officers' quarters they had allowed him to use for his writing when they were on duty. Slowing his steps with the increasing sway of the planks, he made his way toward his rented quarters.

Sneaking aboard had not been necessary. In fact, in hindsight, it would have caused much more complications. He found that Sophi's arrangements had been solid and well-thought-out, despite the short time she had to make them. Had she made such an escape before? He had wished to ask her, but it felt too invasive of a question to ask in front of the others. Sharing a single room with multiple bunks had been necessary, but that meant he had very little privacy.

The press of bodies or silk bundles or wine barrels was as ever-present as the smell of the salt spray. It seemed no matter where he was on this little floating wooden bottle, there was always someone close by, whether that was one of his own party, a member of the crew, or one of the other merchants' parties who had also taken the opportunity to flee the southern continent.

He supposed it was not, in fact, a little wooden bottle. It was actually quite a large merchant cog, a deep-bellied longship with three tall sails. Sitting low in the water, its plentiful mixed goods bound for the Imperial coast.

As he muscled open the ill-fitted door to his shared quarters, the salt scent was overpowered by a far ranker one. Kanmi had not grown any sea legs and was retching again. Mago felt sorry for her. He had only lost his bile a few times on this journey, and each time had been miserable. However, he couldn't help being a bit relieved. The waves had been the only thing to silence her eternal yapping. That afternoon and night they had spent at the dock had made him consider driving his quill through his ear drums.

Sophi grinded a knuckle's length of ginger in a small mortar. She sat on the same bunk where Kanmi was hunched over a small wooden bucket. Gisco sat on the lower bunk of the pair he shared with Mago. Mattan was atop the upper bunk that she shared with Zamar, who was nowhere to be seen.

When the poor woman righted herself and wiped her mouth with a rag, Sophi held up the ginger to her. "Chew this slowly."

"Won't help." Kanmi's dark skin was tinted like ash, and her jaw twitched in anticipation of another retch. "Never had such an illness as this sea." She vomited again; bile and water flew into the bucket. "Nothing helps. When I see land—" she dry-heaved twice—"I shall kiss the solid ground." More dry heaving. "Never again will I set foot off of shore. Never. Not even dragon fire will drive me off the steady earth." She spat, then blew her nose on the rag. "A cruel Goddess is she who created this tossing, turning mass of waters."

"Chew it," Sophi said gently. "I know it doesn't fully stop the retching, but it did delay it last time."

"This is true." Kanmi took the ginger and tucked it in her cheek. "When we reach land, I shall dedicate myself to Iilusen. I never chose a patron, you know. My mother always said I should. But what good does a patron for a whore, says I? Better than a whore without one, says my mother. Well, I don't know, says I. Your patron has done little for you and nothing for me, your daughter—"

"Perhaps you should rest, Kanmi," Mago interjected. "Better save your energy. This will be our longest stretch without landfall. There are no more islands between us and the upper continent for you to rest on the docks."

Mago truly felt sorry for her then as she moaned pitifully, and tears welled up in her eyes.

"I won't survive to make my promises to the earth Goddess," she whimpered.

"You will. This won't last. Perhaps your oath is better given to Dynawach. She will look very well upon your endurance of this journey," Sophi said gently, rubbing her back.

Kanmi gave her a small, tearful smile and nodded. Then she lay on her side and closed her eyes to rest. Sophi stood and carefully picked up the bucket, doing her best to avoid where the bile had splashed onto the rope handle. "I'll go throw this over the side," she said.

"Let Gisco do it," Mago said, and Gisco rose and reached for the bucket without complaint.

"Still giving orders, master?" Mattan's voice was as cold and harsh as her stare. As Mago met her gaze, he realized this was the first time since the escape that she had spoken directly to him.

"I will do it," Gisco said. "I would like to walk the deck. I can toss this first."

"Such orders will be harder to enforce without dragons at your back." Mattan spoke as though Gisco had not.

"I never used dragons to enforce my orders," Mago said quietly, trying to understand her animosity. He didn't know her well, but surely, she didn't think he had any power over the dragons. "Our current accommodations aside, I am no longer your master if you no longer desire me to be."

"Ha!" The bitterness was thick in her tone. "I never *desired* any of this. Don't pretend you had no influence."

Then Mago realized why he didn't know her well. She wasn't part of his original group of whores. She had been one of the captives that he was given by Bomilcar.

Gisco slipped out the door with the bucket. Mago glanced at Sophi, hoping for her intervention. He had no idea what to do in this situation. She merely looked back at him, face as neutral as ever. He looked back at Mattan and met her large, dark, hate-filled eyes.

"I had far less influence than it may have appeared—"

"Don't lie and play victim to me!"

"I am not attempting to do either. I will not, however, be accredited for the Dragon Riders' crimes. I was a wine vendor who recruited a small brothel made of willing whores. I did not sack your lands, nor ravage your home, nor capture you."

"Perhaps not. But you accepted me, my sister, and many more. We were not willing, and yet you sold us to the very men who committed those crimes. Night after night, our bodies ravaged to fill your pockets."

Mago wanted to defend himself. To tell her that it hadn't been for his pockets that he'd allowed that. He wanted her to understand that he was protecting other women from her fate, even if he couldn't protect her. But he was still far from the Empire, and he wasn't sure he should reveal his true intentions. He might be needed to spy elsewhere.

"As I said, I am no longer your master if you do not wish. You may hate me if you wish, but I did save you from slavery to the Dragon Riders, twice. I think it is fair that you tolerate me politely until we can part ways."

"Saved me? " She leaped down from the bunk and advanced the meagre three steps to stand nose-to-nose with him. "What is forced whoredom if not slavery, *master?* What *exactly* is it that you think you saved me from?"

"You are alive. You were paid. You were fed and dressed. And you were never beaten. How many other captives can say the same?" He forced himself to keep an even tone, despite the frustration building.

"You think that you are so moral. So upright. You aren't." She hissed the words through clenched teeth. "You are no better than them. The Recorder sees your vile deeds, and he will avenge every one of them one day."

Before Mago could form a reply, Zamar pressed open the door, forcing both Mattan and Mago to move. She held up a small, lumpy cloth bag. "I got more ginger. A good-sized root this time."

"Thank you." Sophi finally spoke again. Mago felt a little betrayed by her previous silence. "That will last a few days, I hope. Will you sit with Kanmi? I would also like to walk the deck."

Zamar nodded her assent and sat next to the sick woman. She began humming a soft tune. Sophi stood and exited the cabin. Mago took the opportunity to follow her.

As they traversed the narrow walkway from the cabins, past the hold, to the ladder out on the deck, he asked, "Where did Zamar get ginger?"

"From the cook," Sophi replied, lifting her skirt just enough to ease her steps up the steep ladder.

"Yes, I assumed that, but how? We spent all of our coin on the passage north."

Sophi spared him a sanguine glance over her shoulder as he mounted the ladder. "The same way all whores get things, Mago. The cook is a simple man."

A bit of nausea returned, but this time, it wasn't the swaying of the ship. "You don't... She doesn't have to do that anymore. None of you do."

"As you said, master." She turned a quizzical eye to him as she walked slowly toward the rails of the ship, choosing a careful route that kept them out of the way of the crewmen who were hauling rope and trimming sails. "We spent all of our coin on the passage. What else are we supposed to do?"

"I can find you other professions when we get ashore."

"Whoredom is not a profession easily left. It has a way of following those who take it up. A whore master ought to know this. Besides, some don't wish to leave it."

Mago couldn't believe that to be true. He could believe that the shame and stigma followed whores who wished to leave, that it might even make it impossible to make any other living. But he could not accept that a whore would not want to leave it. "We are crossing an ocean. Surely, whoredom cannot follow us that far."

"You would be surprised," was all she said for a while. The silence stretched as they watched the endless deep blue of the sea meet the eternal pale blue of the sky.

Mago wasn't sure how much time passed, but his annoyance at Sophi for remaining silent while Mattan berated him slipped away. Truly, what could she have said? He defended himself as best he could without exposing himself. And Sophi wouldn't know his true intentions. He then turned to examining why he was annoyed at her in the first place. It seemed he had become entirely too dependent on her quiet assistance in all areas of his life.

"Mago," Sophi interrupted his thoughts in a whisper.

"Yes?" He matched her tone.

"What the Blind Seer said about you, it was true. You were working against the Dragon Riders?" Her eyes were still on the waves, and the evening wind stirred whisps of her thick, black hair.

"I was. I still am. But please don't ask anymore. I don't know yet how much I can tell you."

She nodded. "That's why you are so uncomfortable being a whore master. Why you resist Mattan's accusations so. Why you speak of other professions in the north." They weren't questions. She was merely verbalizing her conclusions.

"Yes." Mago didn't know what else to say.

"She will not be comforted. No matter what 'mortal blow' you strike, it will make no difference to Mattan."

Mago knew that was true. He wished it wasn't, though. Dido's words echoed in his head. Her prophecy was the first thing he had written down with his new writing utensils. He had repeated it a hundred times in his head to make sure he hadn't missed a single word.

It would be worth it. It would. Mattan would see that someday. Her suffering wasn't for nothing. It would ease or avert other's pain. She had to understand that. Someday, he would make her understand. He would find her and the others a proper place in the Empire, and then, when the Dragon Riders were defeated and everyone comfortably settled, she would see then.

Mago stood on the stern platform, enjoying the salty bite of the wind on his face as the ship entered the port. He stood off to the side of the officers shouting orders, overlooking the crew as they scrambled around, trimming sails and adjusting ropes. He still didn't think he would ever enjoy sailing, but it was fascinating to watch a crew work a ship, no longer individuals but parts of a well-functioning whole. This was how the Empire must run. All the citizens working at a small, singular task, under a master, sheriff, or lord. Then each of those would manage his or her tiny realm under a commander, bailiff, or governor, each of these estates managed under a prior, earl, duke, or some other aristocrat. And all of them would run his fiefdom for the best function of the Empire. The thought brought him comfort as the ship maneuvered to the docks of the Capital of the very same Empire.

Mago placed the quill back in the inkwell. He was too agitated to write, much less to draw. At least the ground beneath his chair no longer swayed, and he didn't need to steady his writing hand against the overturned wicker-basket-turned-lap-desk.

Kanmi had, in fact, kissed the solid ground when they had finally been permitted to disembark the ship. She had required assistance to stand again after doing so, she was so weak. Two weeks of near-constant retching had left her barely able to walk. Gisco had carried her off the ship and intermittently until they arrived at lodgings.

Perhaps that was his fault; he had insisted that they first visit the garrison of the Order of Holy Heroes. He intended to report directly to the Grand Commander. Two weeks of cramped sea travel had only heightened his need to warn the Empire of the growing threat.

Of course, that was highly unusual. The Grand Commander, the second to the Master of the most powerful military order within the Empire, was not often called upon by refugees from the south. Even his previous reports would likely have passed through several intermediate hands before they reached the Grand Commander. And, since he had not been able to send out his final reports, the Order had no idea just how urgent the threat had become.

He should have anticipated being turned away and sent Sophi and the others to find accommodations. The trip was not entirely wasted, though. The Grand Commander's secretary had accepted his identification cypher and scheduled a meeting for him. He had also directed them to the hospital arm of the Order, which had registered them as refugees and given them food, blankets, and a place to sleep.

This was much better than letting the women find other means of obtaining lodgings, as they were still without coin. All the funds acquired from the sailors had been spent on herbs and broth for Kanmi. Mago fingered Bomilcar's signet ring in his pocket. He would no sooner sell it than his dagger; it might be useful to the Order.

But five days! His reports could not wait that long. He needed to speak with the Grand Commander sooner. Logically, he should be grateful that the man would see him at all and hadn't refused or delegated down the meeting. How could he impress upon the secretary the urgency of his information? He would have to keep going there. Perhaps if he waited at the Grand Commander's office, he could find a quiet moment, a gap between other meetings and duties.

As he decided this, Sophi, Mattan, and Zamar returned to the large, open bay of the refugee quarters. Mago had offered to sit with the now sleeping Kanmi, partly to ease the guilt he felt from delaying her chance to rest. Gisco also slept on a nearby cot. As the women approached, Mago noticed the tall, well-dressed man walking behind them.

His features were angular and sharp. Mago thought his skin was pale, but then he was not so good at judging the shades of native Imperials. He had spent too much time in the south recently. Perhaps sand tan was more apt than pale? Mago had seen men of the far north who were far paler. His hair was close-cut but with gray sprinkled into the deep, nutty brown.

What stood out most to Mago was his clothes. He wore the Order's uniform: Brigandine cuirass with the Order's heraldry, sword belt, and boots. His arming doublet had expensive silk embroidery on the sleeves. The sword handle, cross guard, and scabbard bore intricate designs and some silver plating, and his boots were of the finest leather Mago had ever laid eyes upon. Even in uniform, following behind three whores-turned-refugees, this man's wealth and social standing was evident.

"Here he is, sir," Sophi said to the man when the group reached where Mago sat. Mago quickly set aside his writing utensils and makeshift desk, jumping to his feet to provide the man an Imperial salute. "This is our master, Mago. Master, this is Grand Commander Alonso Fernandez. Second in the Order of the Holy Heroes."

As was his right as social superior, the man did not return Mago's salute, but he did say, "Pleasure to meet you, Master Mago. Though, I think I have your reports under a different name." He smiled wryly. "I hope you will forgive my presumption at moving our meeting earlier than scheduled. I doubt you have left such an advantageous post to sail for weeks to speak with me if the matter were not of great importance."

"Yes, Grand Commander. It is of great importance. Thank you for meeting with me. It is most gracious of you," Mago said.

"Well then, come with me somewhere we can speak freely. I wish to know all that you do about these Dragon Riders." The Grand Commander tilted his head and turned, indicating Mago should follow him.

Mago did not allow himself to look at Mattan as he did, did not indulge himself to see if she understood his position now. No, his vindication would have to wait. He needed to warn the Empire so that Imperial women did not suffer the fate of her and her sister.

Chapter 28

Asha

The streets were blessedly light in traffic as Asha walked them at a clipped pace. She felt out of place but not trapped. The air was already warm and sticky, despite the early hour before dawn. Sweat droplets began to run down her back and legs. Gods, she hated this southern heat. At least the foul smell was greatly reduced. The street cleaners worked mostly at night, and the renewal of foul deposits had not yet begun.

It didn't take her long to arrive at the great temple complex. When she had arrived in Meditullio, the Order's garrison was the largest complex she had ever seen. Now, standing before the towering stone archway of the main temple in the Empire, the garrison seemed downright humble. To be fair, the garrison was structured for practicality and defense, function over beauty, ready and capable of being the last structure standing in the Capital, should the need arise.

This, rather, was a monument. She took a moment to breathe in the awe of the sheer height of the carved stone pillars. The prayers chiseled into the tightly fitted stone weren't legible to her, but they brought her a sense of comfort all the same. How could mere men build something so tall, so cohesive, and so intricate? What type of stone did they use? She shook her head and smiled to herself as she strode inside. *Thrarber would love to tell me.*

Inside the towering walls, the temple was, as most things in the Capital, split into seven. In this case, each of the Gods had their own temple, spread out in a semi-circle with a large, open courtyard in the center. Directly in front of her and furthest away was the seventh Goddess's. It was a giant, rectangular structure with seven pillars in the ancient style holding up the flat roof. An equally large statue of Dynawach carved from marble stood atop the roof, her arms outstretched like a mother welcoming a child home.

On the left there were three temples with the same general construction, but only half the size. Estesbryd perched atop the closest to the archway, cradling the moon in her right arm and holding a star in her outstretched left hand. Her temple only had one pillar, but the builders had compensated for this by joining her roof to that of Trunii's with an archway. The Twins' temples were separate buildings but placed closer together than the others and joined in a way that Asha thought was poetic. She marveled at how the sculptors had suspended the teardrops from Trunii's statue, running them down his face onto the tome in his hands. Despite knowing it was stone, she almost wanted to weep herself. Next to him, Iilusen smiled warmly as she knelt beside a lamb on a bed of painted marble flowers.

On the right, directly across from her dearest sister, Niiwyd had one arm raised as though she were casting the lightning bolt in her hand like a javelin. Her other hand was upturned near her breast, the carved stone tumbling out of it like a waterfall toward her feet. The skirts of her robes appeared to be whipping in a great gale. Beside her, Feorach was not atop his temple, rather his statute formed the fifth pillar, holding up the corner of his roof with his head as he carved the fourth from raw stone. Nearest the archway, Ciirtas stood proudly upon his temple. A somber, hard look upon his face, he held a scale in one hand and a jagged-edged sword in the other.

She could probably spend hours in the courtyard, staring at the impossibly lifelike statues, but she didn't have time for that. She turned and loped up the wide stone steps to Trunii's temple, not pausing to admire the mosaic of the formation of the Gods by the now dead Great Mother, nor to observe the wall carvings of creation of the world and races. Nor did she slow at the tapestries of the Great Judgment of Ciirtas, his release of fell beasts upon the wickedness of early humankind. The stained-glass windows showing the great resolution that averted the War of the Gods slowed her for a moment, but then the splitting of mana into affinities, the peace treaty of the Gods, and the creation of Voids had always interested her.

But she didn't allow herself to linger. She continued on, through the temple, past the archives and confessionals, and out the back doors to the memorial garden. Why it was called a garden, she didn't know; nothing grew in it. But she couldn't think of another word for an outdoor space designed for walking between exhibits, statues, and memorials.

It took her a few minutes to find the one she sought. Once she did, she sat cross-legged on the freshly swept paving stones in front of it. She had a brief thought that she would inconvenience other viewers, but she hadn't seen any other people in the memorial garden yet. Light peeked over the deep twilight in the east, and the cool stone felt lovely through her sturdy trousers.

She rested her elbows on her knees and let her forearms and hands dangle as she read the engraving silently:

> *Memorial to the heroism of Commander Lucius Titus Bellona and his outpost in the face of overwhelming odds in the Colde Tourmalet pass.*

It was strange to see Great Uncle Luca's full name spelled out like that; even stranger was thinking of him as the commander of an outpost.

> *Commander Lucius and his subordinates showed exceptional fortitude and bravery after being drawn into a narrow valley and trapped with an artificial rockslide.*

The inscription left out the part where he had gotten bad intel on the topography of said valley.

Cut off and outnumbered ten to one, these brothers and sisters turned upon the army of raiders that had trapped them and fought valiantly.

According to Great Uncle Luca, the numbers had been more like four to one, but the official story inflated the numbers to hide the inconvenient fact that the raiders were augmented by the men-at-arms of the local baron.

We remember their honor, dignity, and bravery in this life and entrust their souls to the Recorder, who shows kindness and compassion to all worthy souls. This memorial stands as a testament to their sacrifice, and a call to all who follow in their footsteps. Persistence unto death. Honor unto destruction. Holiness unto eternity.

A shiver ran down her spine at the final line: *Commissioned by Baron Colchester*. The very man who orchestrated the murder of an entire outpost was the one who'd made the report of their deaths and commissioned a memorial for them. It was vilely clever. He had eliminated his greatest political headache and removed himself from all suspicion in one fell swoop.

Of course, he couldn't know that Commander Lucius had survived, just barely, and made his way northwest through the Dwarf lands. That he was living to a ripe, if quite paranoid, old age in a glacier valley under a new name. Great Uncle Luca had risen to a high rank for his birthright in the Order of Holy Heroes. He had commanded an outpost, controlling and protecting the largest trade route in the region. All the manpower and equipment he had ever asked for was at his disposal, and none of it had protected him from one rotten aristocrat. How could she join the order that had failed her mentor? How could she trust them with her life, her body, and her soul? If they couldn't, or perhaps didn't, protect him, why would they bother to protect her? What chance did she have?

Her heart pounded in her ears. The ballast binding ceremony was in just a few hours. It had been moved up. She should have had a few more weeks to prepare. Something must have happened, not that anyone had told the recruits. The Order had rushed the last few training tasks and trials, all while gathering equipment for a long, hard march. She thought about the report she had read months ago in the Commandant's office. War was coming to the Empire, and the Order seemed to think that it did not have much time before it arrived.

She was on the precipice of swearing seven years of her life to the Order, not that she had an option to avoid that, unless she voluntarily revoked her citizenship to the Empire. But the ballast blood oath... She would bind her very soul to six others.

That oath was unto death. Blood oaths couldn't be broken by any other means. Even if she and all the others survived this war, survived the dragons, survived the political machinations of the nobility, their souls would be bound. When a ballast took their blood oath, they were able to cast more cohesively and draw strength from each other. Their mana didn't change or cross, but when casting as a unit, each member was stronger than before. As with all things, this had consequences. If the ballast ever separated, each Mage would find themselves weaker to the exact proportion that they had been stronger together. And if one of them was killed, every other member would feel the pain of the physical wound imprinted on their souls. A broken ballast was no small matter. Often, a Mage who survived such a break would be unable to access mana for weeks or months while their soul recovered. It drove some mad, others never cast again.

She couldn't do it. Her ballast were her friends. Maybe more than that. Letting her guard down, she had started to let herself enjoy being a part of something other than her family, to find contentment and even excitement in the commission of the Order. She had let herself forget that this was what the Order did to people. What it had done to Great Uncle Luca. It chewed them up and spit them out, not caring if it killed or maimed them in the process.

You have to do it. If you don't, they will take Dendra. Would you have her pay this price? She's just a child.

The Commandant said that she would be safe, she wouldn't be bound to anyone. They only summoned her as a precaution. She didn't even have access to her mana yet. She couldn't be bound in a blood oath for over a decade. This war would be long over by then.

Protect her? Like they protected Commander Lucius? And his outpost of soldiers? They aren't summoning her because they care about her. They want to protect their future asset. Are you going to let them indoctrinate a five-year-old? Because you're afraid? Grow up.

I'm not afraid.

Liar.

Hanging her head, she admitted she was lying to herself. She was afraid. Afraid of binding her very soul to others she barely knew. Afraid to swear to serve as a cog in a gigantic bureaucratic machine. Afraid to face Mages who had tamed dragons and conquered a continent.

She thought of her sisters. Of the day she watched her mother give birth to Dendra. Of the first time holding the tiny, red-faced baby. Of

Dendra's first steps and words. Of her sister's round cheeks and perfect curls. Of her other sisters, stealing her embroidered overdresses and silver hairpins. Of them rolling their eyes when she asked them to cast a cleaning spell that wouldn't char the floors or to recharge one of her runes. Of the deafening roar of their dinnertime arguments, of laughing at each other until her sides burned, of hiding under blankets, holding their breath as Mother came to shush them the third time since they were supposed to be asleep.

Would you shirk this duty onto them? Would you steal their innocence and give them your fear? You have to protect them. Protect your home. Stop the invaders and their dragons before they ever reach your sacred valley.

She stood and walked out of the garden, back out into the courtyard, still afraid. But the fear was now paired with quiet determination, with resolution. Pausing in the courtyard, she looked up at the statues of the Gods. She turned her gaze between Ciirtas and Dynawach.

"You didn't protect my uncle. It is not my place to question the Gods." She spoke the words aloud, not that there was anyone to hear. "But I will ask you to protect my home and my family. I will do my part. Please do not abandon me as you did him."

Then she turned and strode confidently back to the garrison.

The city streets were teaming on Asha's second journey to the temple complex that morning. Recruits swearing themselves as members of the Order of Holy Heroes was a public spectacle, it seemed. Asha had no idea that there would be so many witnesses until they received a brief (that sounded an awful lot like a threat) about proper behavior prior to forming up in ballast lines to march toward the ceremony. She felt as though the crowd were the true spectacle. Citizens lining the streets, elbow to elbow, children stacked atop shoulders, pale shades of blue, yellow, and green constantly shifting as feet shuffled, and the throng pushed and vied for a better view.

Stranger still was the calm that being in formation brought her. Her curiosity overcame her anxiety as they marched seven across and at least a hundred deep. The formation was not comprised of only recruits, of course. The entire training brigade was kitted, polished, and marching tall for the ceremony.

"Are there always this many onlookers?" Thrarber asked from her far left without turning his head. They had been arranged in height order for the parade. This put him on the left-most end and Asha dead in the center. Throil and Enya were between her and Thrarber. On her right marched Will, then Odo, with Mayumi on the other end. Asha thought it would make more sense to have the shortest one setting the stride, but the instructors seemed to think that this looked more professional. They were all supposed to be taking thirty-inch steps anyway, so perhaps that didn't matter. Both the Dwarves and Mayumi found the very specific distance awkward, but it was, after all, a human parade.

"Wasn't the first time I did this." Enya didn't turn her head either when she spoke. They weren't supposed to speak while marching, but the cheering and shouting of the crowd would cover their transgressions if they maintained forward posture and bearing. "I imagine that this is also our farewell parade. More people show for such things."

Thrarber only grunted in response. It was a stark reminder. The recruits had loaded all the gear they wouldn't be expected to carry onto the baggage trains before they formed up. They would leave immediately after their celebration feast. Her question of why the ceremony had moved up was answered. The Order had received intelligence that invasion was imminent. They would continue training on the march to the coast. Though there was still great confidence that the Order's Navy with royal support fleets would still stop the Dragon Riders.

It had felt good to wear her own boots again. She had gotten so used to the issued boots; she had almost forgotten what it felt like to wear a properly fitted pair. But regulations be damned, she wasn't marching all the way to the coast with pinched toes.

The arched stone entryway was every bit as impressive the second time passing under it, although she had much less time to gawk at it; marching left no time for architectural appreciation. Inside, the massive courtyard also brimmed with people, though this crowd was better dressed and far quieter. The cacophonous roar of the peasants was replaced by a reserved palaver. Flashes of the morning light catching on gems set in gold and silver made her eyes dance across the kaleidoscope of expensive shades of deep red, bright blue, and shimmering purple. The poor lined the streets, and the rich lined the courtyard.

Asha thought there might be a symbolism there, but the halt was called, and the formation compressed into the only open space left, directly in front of Dynawach's grand steps. An Imperial retinue was seated upon the veranda, whose vibrant silks and heavy jewels put all the others to shame.

Panic overcame curiosity as it struck Asha that before her was the Emperor and Empress, as well as the Grand Master of the Order, the entire High Council, and the High Priests of all seven Gods. Her head swam, and she couldn't draw in a full breath.

"Unlock your knees," Odo hissed through a clenched jaw. "Breathe in through your nose. Don't you dare take airs now."

"My revival remedy is rather unpleasant, Asha, darling. Can't put it in the mouth for fear of choking." Enya's tone was playful and menacing at the same time. Asha wasn't sure where else a revival herb could be placed, but she didn't want to find out. She followed Odo's command, and her vision became clear again.

Commandant Bernard Paynes left his place at the head of the formation and knelt at the base of the temple steps. "Gracious Emperor, Enlightened Empress, by your leave, I present my recruits as candidates to join our most prestigious Order."

"You have my leave," was all the Emperor replied.

The Grand Master rose from his thickly cushioned chair. He saluted both royals in turn, then faced the Commandant.

"Rise, Commandant. Join me to inspect these candidates."

The entire Council then rose and followed the Master and Commandant as they walked between each ballast line. Asha stifled an eyeroll. It was the nature of ceremonies to have such pomp and pageantry. As far as she was aware, the High Council had never rejected a recruit in such a ceremony. Any concerns or prohibitions were addressed privately by the instructors to the Commandant. A truly unsuitable candidate was never permitted to make it to the binding ceremony. But this was a remanent from centuries ago when the Order of Holy Heroes was small and not a de facto arm of the government, when joining was a far less formal affair.

Asha was, in fact, a suitable candidate, so she held her bearings as her superiors played out their part, walking slowly with disapproving faces among the ranks. She held perfectly still, not turning her eyes when they walked in front of her ballast line and murmured about the unusual nature of binding all three races together.

It wasn't their blood being spilled today, so she didn't know why they cared. Not their souls on the line. They wouldn't be marching south. They wouldn't be facing dragons. She supposed that wasn't entirely fair. The Order did require its officers to lead from the front of battlefield formations. It often cost the Order noble blood, but it had proven effective, war after war. Still, if she were willing and proud to bind herself to an Elf and two Dwarves, what right had they to question her decision? She certainly trusted Mayumi and the Tuasgs more than silk-clad bureaucrats.

Moments stretched to what felt like hours as the High Council continued inspecting the ranks. It dawned on Asha that her ballast rank was one of the first recruit lines after the instructors and various other members of the training brigade in the formation. She did a quick count, and only three ballasts would bind before hers. The first type of ballast, she did not immediately recognize, but the silk-collared gambesons and royal heraldry told her that all seven were high nobility. Couldn't have noble blood binding to lowborn. The next two wore the distinct half-plate of knights at march. She was surprised that they marched at all, but that was likely for uniformity. The Order of Holy Heroes was one of the only organizations that required its knights to march, most others would not debase themselves to dismount and walk in public, especially not for a ceremony or parade.

That is good, she insisted to herself despite the racing of her heartbeat. *Then I don't have to wait so long. Just get it over with. Just get this whole damned thing over with, so I can stop being a spectacle for highbrow, silk-clad, politicking dignitaries who have nothing to do with an invading force advancing across the sea. Get this ceremony over so I can go and deal with your problems while you dine on imported wines, aged cheese, and look down your nose at me.*

Warlords had tamed Dragons, conquered an entire continent, and were heading north with the intention of conquering another. Not to mention, they were murdering or enslaving the next generation of Mages as they went. And what was the nobility, presumably the most powerful and best-funded people in the whole world, doing about it? Sitting on cushions, wearing enough jewelry to fund a small army a piece, waiting on the chosen one to stop the threat. Pity for them that she was just a child, needing protection rather than ready to provide it. Pity that it was her older sister there to take her place. Not one of them. Her Asha, the little fool from the north. Powerful, sure, but young and anxious, and barely in control of the power she had.

Her anxiety retreated as the High Council made its way back to the steps before the Emperor; it was replaced by revulsion. Let them watch a lowborn, northern merchant girl do what they couldn't be bothered to. What had she to fear? This day would not change its course for their condescension, and neither would she.

"Most gracious Majesties." The Grand Master could really project his voice, but then the shape of the courtyard and placement of the formation in relation to the temples likely assisted him. "We find no unworthy men or women in the ranks. With your permission, the binding can begin."

"What of unworthy foreigners?" a voice called out, Asha knew not from where, and no one seemed bold enough to claim it. All the noble faces she could make out on the veranda remained as still as if cut from stone. But Mayumi became a fraction more rigid, and both Dwarves' faces reddened.

"I trust your wisdom and judgement, Grand Master." The Emperor could also project his voice, and it struck Asha as the tone that her grandmother used on unruly children—calm and unmoved, but with a hint of retribution to come. "As all who stand before us are worthy, please proceed."

Lesser priests appeared from somewhere outside Asha's field of vision, carrying with them an altar. They placed it at the base of the steps, while the ranks of instructors made facing movements and marched off to line the side of the smaller formation. A large, golden bowl with deeply carved runes and scroll work was placed on the altar. Next to it were placed seven silver knives, each with the name of one of the Gods laminated onto the hilt in gold. The Grand Master stood directly behind the altar, with the members of the High Council standing behind him in a single line on the first step, except for the Order's High Priest and the Commandant. They stood on either side of the altar.

She should have been paying attention to the movements and actions of the first three ballasts, but she couldn't bring her mind into focus. Her thoughts drifted to her home, her mother, her sisters, and all of her aunts and uncles who had sworn septum oaths before her, to the only two that she was aware of that had sworn an Infinitus oath, Great Uncle Luca and her father. It seemed to work out well for the latter; he was still intensely loyal to and proud of the Order. But it had been absolutely devastating to the former. Which path would the Gods lead her down?

Obligatory cheers for the second ballast of knights rose from the well-dressed crowd, cutting short her pondering. Her heartbeat jumped again as she realized there was nothing between her and the altar. Then Mayumi whispered the command to march, and the ballast moved forward as one. Asha commanded her body and mind to be calm as Mayumi halted them.

The Grand Master smiled in a broad but controlled manner. He had moved in front of the altar to accept their oaths. The Commandant's face was perfectly neutral. Was that a flash of disdain on the High Priest's? Whatever it had been, it was gone now.

"Brother Odo, your oath we accepted long ago. Who of your ballast will go first?" the Grand Master asked.

"I will." Heat flooded Asha as soon as the Grand Master's eyes snapped to her. He had addressed her Preceptor, not her. Undermining your first line commander was not the best way to start a ballast binding. But the Grand Master didn't seem to mind. In fact, his eyes twinkled with amusement as Odo said, "Our youngest and newest member will, Master."

"Excellent," was his only reply, but those amused brown eyes bored into her as though he could see her very thoughts.

Asha stepped forward, then knelt and placed her right hand on her heart to address the Grand Master, not allowing her eyes to waver from his. She would not balk, would not be weak now.

"Before these assembled witnesses—" her voice cracked, so she swallowed, then steeled her shoulders and continued—"I, Asha Pacatus, as a servant of Ciirtas, hereby vow and dedicate myself unto the Order of the Holy Heroes for no less than seven years." The Grand Master's brow twitched when she added the limitation of the septum oath, rather than leave it open-ended in the infinitum. "I, hereby, dedicate my strength and spirit to the defense of the weak, to justice for the injured, and to vengeance of the Gods.

"I pledge restraint in all of my deeds. I will not draw mana without forethought. I will not brandish my weapon without purpose. I will not accrue wealth without charity. I will not procreate without responsibility.

"I pledge obedience to the Grand Master, his successors, his representatives, and the rules and regulations of the Order."

She took a steadying breath and let her mind catch up to the words she had memorized. "I vow to keep myself in all Holiness before the Gods unto eternity. To persist against evil unto my own death. To uphold honor, even to my own destruction, so help me, Ciirtas."

When she finished speaking, she bowed her head and waited. The Grand Master bent down and clapped her on the shoulder. "Rise, Sister Asha! Welcome to the Order of Holy Heroes!"

She stood a bit stiffly and stepped back into the ranks. Enya went next, then Wilford, the Dwarves, and Mayumi. Will was the only one to swear an Infinitus oath. Asha wasn't sure why it struck her as strange. None of them had discussed it, but it was unusual for members of a ballast to swear different lengths of oaths. Then again, there was nothing truly usual about her ballast.

"Rise, Brother Wilford! Welcome to our glorious Order," the Grand Master boomed again. He didn't seem to tire of the ceremonial greeting. Was that an aristocratic mask, too? Did he welcome them? Probably, they would be very useful to his Order in the near future. "Now, for the binding, I yield to our esteemed High Priest."

The Grand Master stepped around the altar and took a place on the step behind it and off to one side. Then the High Priest moved to stand behind the altar, with the bowl directly in front of him.

"Before the Seven Living Gods breathed, the Great Mother held all of their mana within herself." The High Priest projected his voice surprisingly far for how nasally it sounded. There must have been some trick to the architecture that reverberated the sound. "But she was alone, and, in her wisdom, she knew that it was not good to be alone. She cleaved herself into seven pieces, and so created the Gods, but she herself perished. In the same way, it is not good for Mages to be alone. But this oath is not to be entered into lightly. If any among you are uncertain or unwilling to take it, let that person depart now, without shame or fear."

He paused and waited, looking hard at each of them for a count of ten. When no one flinched or stepped away, he said, "Brother Odo, please step forward. By now I'm certain you need no reminding of the way of binding oaths. You have always honored your oaths, even if it is at the expense of your duty to the Order." There was an edge in his tone that caused hairs on the back of her neck to stand on end, subtle but disdainful and belittling.

Odo bristled externally as he stepped before the altar. His hand had been reaching out toward the silver knife bearing the name of Ciirtas, but he paused his movement and spoke lowly to the priest. "You are too wise a man to show such imprudence as to denigrate my wife and our barrenness here and now. No, I must misunderstand you. Too wise, and far too poorly armed."

The two men stared each other in the eye, neither yielding until the Grand Master cleared his throat. Then the High Priest said, "My words were not as clear as they could have been. But let us not delay this procedure any further."

Odo picked up the silver blade and, with a flash, cut his right palm. He held his weapon hand over the golden bowl as the blood dripped slowly out.

"With this vow, I bind myself to those who bleed with me this day. I take them as blood of my blood, bone of my bone, soul of my soul. I pledge my fealty, honor, and strength to them as my closest kin, until death parts us." He replaced the knife and took a strip of linen from a basket beside the altar that Asha didn't remember seeing placed. Tightly binding the wound, he returned to his place in line.

One after another, all the ballast members did the same, except they didn't all use the same knife.

Mayumi used Niiwyd's. Will used Dynawach's. Enya used Estesbryd's, and the Dwarves used Feorach's. Asha, of course, used Ciirtas's. The High Priest did not make any more cryptic, snide comments.

Once they had all taken the vow and bled into the bowl, the High Priest dipped his finger in the mixed blood and drew a seven-pointed star on each of their foreheads. Then he said, this time loud enough for all to hear, "What the Gods so bind, let nothing in this life tear asunder!"

The resulting cheers and clapping were polite and modest, but it still felt deafening to Asha. Her skin under the rune grew warm, and that warmth spread down from her head, through her chest, and out to her limbs. Her finger and toe tips prickled with energy. She drew in a great lungful of air and, in the corners of her eyes, saw the others do the same. It felt similar to when they bound the troll, but deeper, stronger, and far more divine. In that moment, she swore her soul tugged and stretched and then wound into the others. It made her feel strong and restless. She suddenly had the urge to run and run, chasing the horizon to feel out her new strength.

Then her head swam again, but she had no time to dwell on it as they faced right and marched off to line the sides, letting the next ballast rank move forward to take their place. She breathed slowly and deeply while the other ranks took their vows. The surge of energy faded as the morning marched on, hours dragging slowly, standing in a loose formation, interrupted at intervals by cheers that never seemed to dull in their performative enthusiasm.

Eventually, blessedly, the ceremony came to an end. Then they reformed and marched back to the garrison where a feast had been prepared. They ate outside on the training field. The provision hall was filled with various dignitaries and aristocrats. It was by far the best food she had eaten since leaving home. Well, perhaps since she'd stayed at The Pretty Pike. There were roasted meats of several types, heavily spiced stews, glazed vegetables, bread still warm from the oven, and even sweet pies and candied nuts. Asha couldn't help wondering if the cooks had saved all of their spices and talent for this occasion. Not that she was going to speculate aloud for fear of washing duty.

A large retinue bearing various heraldry led by a representative of the royal court was weaving in and out of the ballasts seated on the grass, offering polite congratulations and accepting thanks on behalf of the Emperor. When they arrived, each ballast in turn rose and saluted. The retinue would acknowledge with slight inclinations of the head. Asha knew that it was not required of higher ranked individuals in the south to return the salute, but it still rankled her. Respect ought to be mutual.

Thrarber and Throil had already consumed an inhuman amount of food, several servings' worth piled in a way she was sure they would spill but they hadn't and were eyeing her roast pork loin and brown bread that she hadn't finished when the retinue reached her ballast. *Her ballast.* They were a proper ballast now. It still didn't feel real as she stood and saluted alongside them.

"Both of their royal majesties extend you congratulations." The lead aristocrat's face was perfectly even, smiling just enough. "Whatever other prejudice you may face—" this was addressed at the Dwarves and Elf—"remember that all three courts support this endeavor."

Something stung her left hand. A wasp? Now, of all times? She tried to wiggle her forefinger and shake the hand inconspicuously to displace it to no avail.

"Thank their majesties for their kind words and support. We could not succeed without them," Mayumi said. She seemed very much like her husband then. Was she emulating him on purpose?

Asha's hand still stung, and now her forefinger grew uncomfortably warm. Great, she was going to march to the coast with a massively swollen hand. She tried to be subtle as she brushed her right hand over the left to dislodge it. Maybe Enya had a salve?

"May the Gods guide you in all you do," the dignitary said again, glancing at Asha's hands but not commenting on her disrespectful movement as he accepted their parting salutes.

The stinging increased until her eyes watered as the last aristocrat passed her on their way to the next ballast over. Once their backs were turned and attention was no longer on her, Asha looked down at her left hand, preparing to swat it, but she stilled midair. There was no wasp. Her ring was glowing. She looked back at the retinue, her stepmother's voice in her ears.

It'll glow when there are evil creatures about, to warn you.

The stinging and warmth were gone, and the pale white light faded from the ring the further away the royal retinue got.

"Asha, lass, are you going to finish...?" Thrarber gestured to the trencher she had not yet picked back up.

"No," she said distractedly.

"Well, then if not—" He cut off abruptly as Mayumi snatched it up, her long arm far quicker than his. "Oi! I was gonna eat that!"

Mayumi winked at him as she stuffed the loin in her mouth.

Odo and Enya noticed Asha fiddling with her ring and exchanged a look. She put on a smile that she did not feel and sat back down, doggedly refusing to look at the ring or either of them.

Chapter 29

Matilda

Admiral Matilda Tewkes wiped the salt spray from her slate gray eyes with a small linen handkerchief, the delicate embroidery in stark contrast to the stiff starched wool of the uniform pocket it came from. The morning had dawned bright and clear, with a favorable wind. Thank Niiwyd, finally something was going in the Navy's favor. She shook her head. Her mostly gray hair with streaks of the original blond tightly braided and sewn up into a bun that did not budge with the wind or the roll of the ship. She scanned the sails crowding the mouth of the inlet. Not nearly enough.

One might think that the Imperial Navy would have been easier or at least faster to muster than an Imperial Army, not relying on dukes, earls, or barons to send for lords and gather men-at-arms and prepare baggage trains. Especially considering the nearly constant pressure on trade routes from pirates, but this had not proved true. Indeed, even now, the Emperor's representatives were out arresting merchant ships and crews and pressing them into service. The Imperial court maintained four ships and only two with crews at all times due to cost.

She had managed to find enough excess sailors from the Order to crew a third, but that was all the help her small fleet would get, at least for now. The Order maintained a small Navy to protect their vast trading assets and collect fees for protecting others'. They also kept the infrastructure to build it larger, regardless of cost. Did her Order have greater foresight? Or simply deeper coffers? She did not know but supposed both, and less political mire to muddy that foresight and spread the coffers thin.

Which would arrive to relieve her fleet of thirty-one battleships first? The impressed and repurposed merchants? Or the newly built and crewed Order? Either way, she didn't plan on being assisted in the coming battle. Perhaps it would be the Elvish armada that had been promised months ago. She scoffed at that. The Elves had been talking out of both sides of their mouths of late. Bernard had gotten a single, if incredibly powerful for her race, She-Elf for his 'experiment', but that seemed quite a different matter from the fast, lightweight galleys and double canoes that the Elves favored. She almost couldn't blame them. The Elvish islands were not along the route the Dragon Riders would take to the Northern continent. It was fair to assume they might be able to stay neutral. But if they wished to be neutral, they shouldn't have made promises of assistance.

The southern invaders would be within range soon; she was counting on the early afternoon winds for her tactical maneuvers. She had the urge to command the first mate to calculate the distance again, to be sure, but she repressed it. It was just the nerves. She trusted his calculations, and she trusted that her mind and body would cooperate and still themselves as they always did once the engagement began. For now, she needed to find something useful to do.

She stepped forward and swiftly down the stairs of the aft castle where she had been standing. Men and women paused their work at the ropes of the small aft lateen sail and the larger mid and fore square masts to salute her. As did the archers and marines who cleaned and sharpened weapons, among other prebattle preparations. She acknowledged them, but her gaze was set upon the forecastle.

It really is fine to have the castle permanently attached, she thought as her eyes swept over the sturdy new construction of it before mounting the steps. Most were removable so the ship could be used for things other than combat. She liked the idea of having permanently dedicated warships, though.

Another change, the one she was there to examine again, was the replacement of the fore cannons with a massive ballista. She had left the aft cannons and the outcroppings for the archers, but she had instructed all captains to make the best use of whatever ballista or harpooning rigs they could get a hold of. The forecastle gave it the most maneuverability. Or at least, it should. Her master gunner had never taken aim at a fell beast in the sky above him.

The gunners and archers in the forecastle also saluted her. But her master gunner did not turn from his argument with a grizzled old whaler, who leaned heavily on a cane sword. His permanent stoop and empty right sleeve, pinned out of the way to his shoulder, did not diminish his presence. *How much trouble were you a few decades ago, with two arms and a strong back?* The admiral suppressed the grin her thought brought to her lips.

"I told you once, you son of a port drab, I'll not be removing any more gunnery from this forecastle! The archers will stay right where they are, and may the Recorder take your soul, ye arrogant, wave-riding blubber chaser!"

"The Recorder will take all our souls before the sun sets if'n ye don't move them twig tossers ta midships and more harpooners here in their stead!"

"Master Gunner." Her curt address cut through as intended. "Master Whaler." Both men turned and offered her a respectful salute. "What is this carrying on about archers?"

"This old barnacle wants to remove all the archers off the forecastle," her master gunner explained with a rude gesture toward the other man. "I understand why we traded our guns for a ballista, but this is too far! Too far entirely."

"What exactly do ye think steel-pointed sticks are gonna do against a damned dragon?" the whaler retorted.

"Oh, what do you know about dragons? You don't even know if the arm-thrown harpoons will pierce its hide?"

"Me boys can pierce the hide of a sea snake." The whaler turned and addressed her. "Ain't that why I'm here and not chasing blubber? With all due respect, of course, Tapena." He used the Elvish word for captain, but she chose not to correct him to admiral. She didn't know the correct word for her rank in Elvish, and he likely didn't either. It was probably his best attempt at observing naval courtesies.

"The archers aren't targeting the dragons. They are for the enemy ships and the marines they carry. Perhaps the rider, if they get a clear crack at him. I acknowledge your concerns, but I will not leave my forecastle without any ranged weapons. Your harpooners will remain mobile about the deck, with the purpose of taking whatever vantage they can. However, I will give orders that the archers are to yield to them if they require it for a throw." She stared down each man in turn, making sure both knew not to push her. The master gunner was the first to yield and saluted her.

"Aye, Admiral. It will be as you command."

The whaler took longer. Not defiant, but he took her measure. She didn't blink or twitch, standing straight as a loading ram but with cool relaxation. Whatever he was looking for, he saw and touched a knuckle to his brow.

"Aye, Tapena."

"Trim back the sails," Admiral Tewkes called out, and her first mate echoed her. Only a few leagues now. The enemy's fleet was only about half the size of hers. That should have given her a massive advantage, but for two elements. One of which let out a bone-chilling, rattling roar, unlike anything she had ever heard. Then leathery wings spread from the decks of two of the ships. She couldn't hear them beat from this distance, but she saw the down draft cause the surf to churn as they gained altitude.

They planned to eliminate her ships before she was within range of theirs. They would be fools not to. *Your scout's intelligence had better be good, Alonso. We won't get a second chance to stop them.*

"Ready the ballista!" she shouted. "The harpooners may fire at will. And load the cannons."

A chorus of ayes and echoed orders rose around her, but her attention was on the sky. "Are your Mages ready?" she addressed the captain of the marines without looking away from the approaching fell beasts. Captain Pullium was young, but his illustrious father had taught him well. He was an excellent commander, and she was happy to have him.

"Aye, we will take a bit o' wind out of their sails." Out of the corner of her eye, she saw his grin.

The dragons were nearly above them now. Was that the wind from their wings or from the shifting air pressure of the heat of the day? Each beast let out another raspy bellow. One had recognized her flags as the fleet commander and banked toward her.

"Give the second line the signal," she said slightly louder than she intended. When her signal crew complied, the second line of ships let out their sails in perfect synchronicity, suddenly surging forward between the first line, taking the fight to the enemy ships at full tilt.

She hadn't taken her eyes off the fell beast. The saddle girth was visible under its belly, and the boots of its rider. Its chest began to glow red-hot as a forge, and it angled its wings to slow its forward momentum.

"Cut port! All she has!" Tewkes screamed, and her ship immediately obeyed, lurching and dipping the port deck rails dangerously low to the surf.

"Ballista fire!" The mighty arms of the engine twanged, and a bolt as tall as a man soared up. Several harpoons followed it into the air. "Cannons at will!"

The mighty beast belched fire, but it fell short of her masts as it tried to bank and twist away from the missiles.

Not fast enough. A bolt ripped through the outside of its neck, and a harpoon tore viciously through its port wing. The beast screamed, and somehow it was more frightening than the roar had been.

Her ship erupted with cheers as dark-red blood dripped off of green scales. The beast completed its bank and began to glow again. Volleys erupted from the aft cannons. Ball after ball whizzed by the fell beast. One struck its hindquarters.

The beast roared and pointed its nose up, climbing rapidly with mighty beats of its wings. It drifted slightly to port; she smiled to herself. That wing wasn't pulling its weight. Out of range of the cannons, it belched fire again. Flame and fury rained down, straight at her.

"Shields!" she shouted at the same moment as Captain Pullium. Red haze shimmered around the masts. Flame struck it and exploded back up toward the dragon. The beast screamed again, this time in anger.

Again, it climbed in the sky, out of range of harpoons and ballista, keeping the angle too steep for the cannons. It banked again, circling the ship's starboard.

"Starboard cannons load for volley!" she shouted. Her mate echoed it, but his face showed his doubts. She scanned her other ships. None were too close for her maneuver. Her stomach dropped when she saw nearly half the first line burning and drifting. She turned her eyes back to the fell beast just in time. The glow started in its chest just before it tucked its wings in tight and dove straight at her.

She waited for a count of four, confident in how fast her ship would respond. It was expensive to have weather Mages whose only job was to make a ship maneuver faster than should have been possible. Today would prove it was worth every penny.

"Hard port!" The deck dipped again, and she had to use a tiny wind spell to stabilize herself, something she hadn't done in years. "Starboard cannons fire!"

Again, flame erupted from the dragon's maw, and again, it fell short of the ship. Of the half dozen balls, only two struck the beast. They knocked it off its intended flight path, and it rolled and roared and flared its wings to right itself.

"That should have killed it. Why won't you die?" she asked herself aloud. "Vile creation of a vengeful God!"

"Drop the wind out of its injured wing!" Captain Pullium commanded his Mages beside her. "Archers, target the rider!"

A ballast of weather Mages was nearly obscured by violet mana as they complied. The dragon rolled and lost altitude suddenly as the air density under its port wing suddenly changed. A thicket of arrows flew at the rider, who was visible and in range for a brief moment. Then the dragon righted itself once more.

She wasn't sure if they did any good. Even if they struck, the wretched barnacle wore full plate armor. She hoped he was good and bruised, though, and whispered a prayer for a lucky arrow into a crevasse or lightly armored joint.

Smoky haze began to sting her eyes. She looked around again. Most of the first line was burning now. The water was filling with debris and lifeboats, and sailors swimming toward them. She was slightly comforted to see that the burning ships were not merely drifting but had sails and tillers set back toward the mouth of the inlet. Under normal circumstances, it would be outright idiocy to turn a fire ship upon one's own side. However, she had stretched a massive chain across the narrowest portion of the inlet. Any ships would catch there and ensure that if her fleet failed, the invaders could not access the Capital by sea.

The dragon veered off sharply. Was it disengaging? Perhaps its wounds were, in fact, severe. This led her gaze to the second line, engaging the enemy ships. Cannons boomed and arrows flew. Two ships had been boarded by her marines and seemed much worse off for it.

She turned back to the sky. The dragon was listing and struggling to keep itself above the water. Its injured wing was pulling it dangerously low and to the side. Where was the other dragon?

"Shields!" her mate screamed just in time to block most of the flames. Her rear lateen sail would need new yardage.

"Cut it free so it doesn't catch the rest." She wasn't too worried about the mast itself. All had been properly drenched prior to the battle, but she had no idea how hot dragon fire would burn.

The second dragon circled high above them, well out of any weapons range.

"What I wouldn't give for a tempest just now," Tewkes said.

"Your wish is our command," the marine captain replied and shouted commands to his Mages. Lightning struck out at the dragon, but the rider deflected it, pale blue haze turning to a wall of water around the beast, which, in turn, burned into steam and ate all the energy that should have stunned him. No shield could deflect the sudden change of pressure as the Mages stole all the air under the dragon.

The dragon plummeted straight down for a count of three before it thrashed its great wings. It avoided hitting the surf but was now in range. Cannons bellowed from the aft castle, the ballista turned and twanged from the forecastle, and harpoons whistled from midships.

How all of the balls and the bolt missed, she had no idea; it wasn't statistically possible. But the smoke grew too thick to see if the rider had used a shield spell. The dragon banked and climbed. Tewkes coughed and fell into the marine captain as the ship lurched.

"What the fuck?" they said in unison. She snapped her eyes to the tiller; it wasn't the navigator. Whooping and jeers from the whalers chilled her.

They were being towed. It seemed that one of the harpoons had not been deflected by the rider.

A wheezing chuckle paired with a rhythmic thumping came from her starboard. She whirled on the whaler.

"Your harpoons were supposed to be thrown without tethers!" she bellowed, stumbling again as the dragon hit the end of the line and changed direction, attempting to snap it.

"Aye, Tapena. It was thrown without a rope or chain." He smiled wickedly.

"You knew what I meant!" she snarled. "You want the lash, old man? Ballista fire down the tether as fast as she can be reloaded!" she yelled to the mate, then back at the whaler, "A tether spell is the same as a rope."

"It really isn't, ma'am. If yer ship survives this day, ye can give me as many lashes as ye wish." He had the audacity to follow that statement with a wink.

She drew mana to throw him from her deck but caught herself. As the ship lurched with another change of direction from the tethered dragon, she exhaled slowly, pouring her mana into the runes etched deep in the bones of the hull.

"We cannot take a dragon as a whale," she said, letting the coolness retake her mind.

"Nay, more like a sea snake," he said as the marine captain bellowed for shields. The dragon had ceased pulling and was chasing the tether with its flaming breath. Her ballista still fired, but the bolts were turning to puffs of splinters and charcoal before they struck.

The torrent of fire continued to buffet them. Marine Mages began to cry out and some collapsed. The shields shimmered and flexed but held.

Tewkes glared at the whaler. "Well, perhaps not quite like a sea snake," he admitted.

"Release the tether," she growled, then coughed and hacked in the smoke and heat.

Instantly, tension released, and the ship and dragon lurched, no longer straining against each other. The dragon beat its wings and began its climb.

A horn sounded from the enemy ships. She wove a quick spell and cleared the thick haze in front of her enough to see that her second line had boarded two more ships, and the others were turning tail and heading for open waters.

The first dragon was slumped upon the deck that it had arrived on. It didn't look dead, though; quite agitated, in fact. Grounded, perhaps.

The second dragon roared directly above her. It glowed and spewed flame down at her, but it did follow the horn and fly out toward the retreating ships. Her shields held until it was past her foredeck, but more marine Mages collapsed.

They did it. They held the inlet. The Capital was safe. For now, at least. She squared her shoulders, refusing to hang her head as the ship cut sharply to avoid a burning vessel off to her starboard side. Hers was the only ship from the first line that wasn't burning and drifting. The Capital was safe, but there were miles and miles of coast now unprotected. Their enemy would find a landing place. But that was the Army's problem to solve. She had done her duty and kept them out of the inlet. Her legs shook with exhaustion, but she would not fall now. She had sailors to rescue, ships to douse, and a fleet to resupply and reform. It wasn't over. Not truly.

Chapter 30

Asha

Asha didn't think she had ever been so warm in her entire life. Well, perhaps on the rare occasion that she had assisted an aunt or uncle in the forge, but never outdoors. Her face flushed red and sweat ran in rivulets down her back and legs. Despite this, she kept her head high, shoulders back, and her steps measured as they marched onward.

For six days, the Order's army marched from sunrise to one hour before sunset, with a twenty-minute rest every third hour in the heat of high summer. Yesterday, they had picked up a detachment from the garrison of Domum Commercia. The detachment was a mix of Order members and soldiers employed by the Marquis. They marched together, acting as rearguard, but even at a distance, that heraldry was obscured; their equipment differentiated them. Marquis Chester Pullium outfitted his soldiers in mail hauberks and conical helms. He also employed far more spear and billmen, with fewer archers and men-at-arms. There were also a respectable twenty-odd knights, but they would have lands to support themselves, at least somewhat.

Despite the equipment difference, the Pullium detachment marched with every bit of professionalism the Order did. Asha wondered if it was because the Marquis had something to prove. After all, he had been only a low-level knight thirty years ago, and a merchant marine before that, homegrown from his crew. He had married quite advantageously while freshly knighted for exceptional bravery in combat against pirates. By all accounts, it had been a rare love match among the nobility. The scandal had died down somewhat after he had proven to be an even better commander than he had been marine. Still, the shock of a social climb from port loader (or chesty) to lord of a march was great enough that even a northern shepherd girl recognized his name.

Asha was grateful when the halt was called at a cistern. Her throat and waterskin were bone dry. She, and her ballast, lined up for their turn at refreshment.

"Mighty convenient how these cisterns are constructed at just the right places for a rest, eh?" Thrarber grinned after draining the remnants of his skin.

"So convenient that one might think the engineers who built the roads placed them that way on purpose," Odo replied dryly.

"Now, what a thought." Thrarber chuckled.

"Much less convenient on a forced march," Enya added.

"Aren't all marches forced?" Will asked, taking the next turn filling.

It was Odo's turn to laugh at that. "Just you wait. One day, we'll really need to cover ground. Then you'll learn the true meaning of double-time."

Asha's legs ached just thinking of it. "Do you think we will need to double-time to reach the coast in time?"

"Depends on where they try to put in. But likely not." Odo refilled his skin, drained half of it, then refilled it again before continuing. "We should reach the coast by midday tomorrow. Since the Navy kept them out of the inlet, they don't have many options for good ports unless they sail far northwest or east. We're heading for the best location to land an army."

"They could always beach the armada in the shallows in the near east," Mayumi said quietly.

"They could, but intelligence believes that this is just a small advance force. They'll want to capture and hold a good port. Ados is the best place for that." Odo restrung his waterskin as they walked away, and the next ballast took their place. "If not, then we will have to push long and hard to intercept them."

The ballast fell back into line. It took a bit over the allotted time to water all of the formation. Asha had no idea how the baggage train would water all of the pack animals and still catch up.

Yet they did. As the beating heat of the day turned into a muggy twilight and the army halted to make camp for the night, they all fell into the duties Odo had assigned to make best use of the remaining hour of light. The Dwarves went to fetch their tents off the baggage train. Will searched for fuel for the cooking fire. Asha went to the quartermaster's train to retrieve the evening rations of bread, salted meat, and, since it was a third day, tobacco. Enya prepared the sleeping arrangements. She insisted on sanctifying their resting place to Estesbryd each night. Asha sometimes wondered if that really mattered, but she had to admit she did not wake up as sore as she was before falling asleep. Mayumi inspected and oiled all of their weapons. Odo went to the end-of-day meeting with the other preceptors.

Asha was lost in thoughts of a dip in the glacier river back home. She didn't often do it, but now when she was drenched in sweat and breathing air hot as a bellows, she scolded herself for not appreciating the frigid cold water.

Since she wasn't looking where she was going, she promptly tripped and fell flat on her face. Her inattention didn't explain the knots in her boot laces that caused her to trip again when she tried to rise. She cursed quietly as she tried and failed to untangle them. Something poked her hands as she did so.

Asha looked up and found herself face to face with a Gnome, who stood on the shoulders of another Gnome, holding a sharpened stick. This pair looked much the same as the Gnomes she encountered on the river barge, but their clothes and hats were woven grass and twigs. They had identical, unblinking fish-like eyes.

"Gift?" the top Gnome asked. Asha blinked in confusion. "Gift? Friend?" the Gnome asked again. When Asha didn't reply, it brandished the stick again, inches from her nose. "Not friend," it said, surprisingly menacingly for a creature only two feet tall.

"No," Asha yelped as a dozen more Gnomes appeared with small, twisted ropes and pointy sticks. She was fairly certain she could fight them off but was more worried about the 'strange type of magic' they controlled. She remembered the Dire Pike and its aborted charge. "I am your friend. You just startled me is all," she explained.

The Gnome dropped the stick and smiled, still without blinking, and held out its hand.

Shit, now what do I give them? Asha patted her pockets quickly. She pulled out the red river stone that the river Gnome had given her, glad she had obeyed the instinct to keep it close on hand for the march.

All the Gnomes gasped and recoiled. "No, no, no," said the one on the other's shoulders. "Silly friend. Something else."

"Uhm." Asha looked around her. The tobacco! She dug out the small pouch. Enya and the Dwarves would be disappointed. "How about this?" She held it out.

All the Gnomes clapped their hands and smiled. The leader Gnome took it and squeaked out something she didn't understand. Her bootlaces unraveled. Maybe her cousins were right, and the Gnomes' strange magic was just scamming travelers.

When she looked up again, all the Gnomes were gone. A small, gray pebble, chipped into a cube, rested where the leader had stood. Asha sighed and tucked it in the same pocket as the river stone as she made her way back to the ballast's campsite.

The rest of the evening and night passed quietly, except for Thrarber bemoaning the lost tobacco.

A red sunrise dawned, which felt like an unlucky omen, but nothing else seemed changed. By the morning's first rest, Asha imagined the air was a bit cooler and got a whiff of salt, but that couldn't be. The coast was still too far off.

An hour later, another halt was called, and the preceptors called to a meeting. The rest of the formation stood in an unnatural silence. Asha pondered the reasons for such an action. None of the answers she could think of were pleasant.

Odo always looked grim, unless someone cracked a good joke, but when he returned, he looked harder somehow. Maybe it was a tightening of his scars, like they remembered how they were earned.

"Scouts reported spotting the armada." He was brisker than usual. "They already took the port. They are still working on unloading their forces. The formation is going to rearrange into smaller elements and fan out. Try to hit them from multiple directions and provide less of a target for the dragon."

Asha suddenly felt a chill despite the growing heat of the morning.

"Just one dragon?" Mayumi asked.

"No, two. But only one in the air. The other is acting strange. It was still aboard the ships when the scouts saw it. They seemed to be having trouble unloading it. Scouts think it might be wounded, but we shouldn't count on that. It might have been hobbled for transport."

"So, a dragon ain't all that different than an unruly stallion?" Thrarber sniggered.

"If you don't count the fiery breath and ability to fly, sure." Throil rolled his eyes as he spoke.

"Are we going to learn the meaning of double-time now?" Will asked.

"No, they are already holding the port. No use showing up exhausted and unready to fight. We'll be moving over to the artillery though."

"Why?" It was a rude question, and Asha regretted asking as soon as it left her mouth.

"I figure that the siege engines and cannons are the greatest threat to the beast. Other than us, of course," Odo answered it anyway. Asha appreciated that he seemed to understand her questions were genuine curiosity and not rebelliousness. "The dragons will likely try to destroy them first then deal with the troops. It's our task to ensure they fail."

Everyone nodded, then followed him at a clipped pace out of formation and over to where the artillery split into three sections. Odo looked from the ballistae to the bronze cannons to the catapults, deliberating.

"Stick closer to the catapults, I think. But be ready to move quickly if I've chosen wrong."

They all acknowledged him. After a group of infantrymen arrived to form a bulwark for the artillery, their small element set out again. The only sounds were the creaking of wood, crunching of boots, the scrape of metal, and the thundering of her pulse in her own ears. *It is our task to ensure they fail.*

The weight of such a task had never felt more heavy in her mind. *No one else has, why do you think you will? Because you have mixed the races together? You oh first daughter? You are not the Gods' chosen hero, yet you would fight a dragon? Two perhaps?*

Asha set her eyes upon the horizon and squared her shoulders. *I am not the chosen hero; I am the willing one.* ***We*** *are the willing. All else is just an excuse for cowards. And we are not cowards. I will-we will-face the dragon, and all the fell beasts of this world if we must.*

Chapter 31

Asha

The port was nestled in a range of hills. As they approached, Asha knew the salt smell was no longer her imagination. She heard a rattling, croaking roar, and her mouth went dry. Reflexively, she reached into her pocket where she had tucked her ring with the medallion from Glormhar. She didn't need to be warned that there was evil about, they were marching to meet it, so she had taken the ring off. Besides, the stinging might distract her in battle.

The Gnome stones rattled against her fingers. Would their strange magic be of any help against a dragon? She remembered the Dire Pike in the river. Gods, that felt so long ago, and it had been merely one season. Two small stones against a God's judgement made flesh. Her lips twitched but failed to form a smile as fear gripped her heart again. *A God's judgement made flesh. A war of fire and blood. Fire and blood.*

Her fingers clutched the medallion in her pocket instinctively, grounding her thoughts back to the present. It was a foolish time to think of Glormhar, but far more comforting than thinking of the coming battle. Why couldn't she get him out of her head? Even now, when she was about to face a dragon, and possibly die.

He was a terrible distraction, but she finally allowed herself to acknowledge that she missed him. Missed his jokes and winks. Missed the casual way he discussed philosophy. Would she ever speak to him again? She had a feeling she would miss his prowess with a war axe soon, but she was grateful to be flanked by his cousins.

Their element had left the road about two leagues back and was slogging the catapults up to a ridge that overlooked Ados. The commander had seen no reason to attempt to hide the siege engines. Their projectile trajectory would be traceable back to them. She opted for the increased visibility and range the ridge would provide. Pulling beasts and artillery men struggled for what felt like hours to get the engine up before the signal flags were finally raised to alert the other two groups that they were in position.

Asha knew that these preparations were important. They were not counting on the element of surprise. They assumed that the invaders' scouts had spotted them, as surely as their scouts had spotted the invaders. But a good solid barrage before the infantry moved in should save lives. Holy Heroes' lives, anyway. But Gods above, how long did it take to maneuver? Manuals and training demos always skimmed over this part, stressing the importance of it but not the time it took. This anticipation, waiting, and finagling machines into just the right position, readying projectiles into queue, then more waiting...it had to be worse than actual fighting. It was certainly worse than her encounter with the pirates. Worse than the fight with the troll, too.

A signal from the front lines did not come. Instead, a great green shadow darted out of the clouds. It swooped downward and began to glow, then fire rained down on a company of spearman. They did not get their shields up in time.

The commander bellowed something. Asha heard it, but her mind reeled too much to interpret. Ropes cracked, wood groaned, and rocks whooshed overhead. Cannons belched flame and smoke. Their booming drowned out the screams of the men as they burned to death. Asha couldn't hear the ballistae twang from across the ridge, but the bolts arced into the air. She immediately felt shame for thinking the waiting was worse than fighting. Nothing could be worse than watching men burn to death. At least the dragon fire burned hot enough to take them quickly.

Projectiles struck the piers, sending one loading ramp with all souls aboard it into the water. Cannonballs shook the city gates, and the bolts narrowly missed the dragon as it banked gently southward.

The preparation time paid off. As soon as Asha had surveyed the damage by the first volley, another followed it into the air. The cannons focused on the fortifications and tops of the walls, the catapults on the docks, while the ballistae swiveled as fast as they could to lead the dragon. Massive bolts came close but sailed past it into the clouds.

Another volley gave cover to the soldiers bringing a ram to the gate. Asha lost sight of the dragon in the clouds.

"We need to get closer to it." She turned to Odo. "It isn't targeting the engines."

"It will," he said, his confidence as unnerving as his tone was soft. "We would kill mounts chasing it across the field. We wait for it to come to us. Or at least closer."

"Horses can run as fast as it was flying," she insisted. "We can't just watch while it murders entire companies of soldiers!"

"Horses can't use wind currents to rest themselves." He took his eyes off the sky for a moment to meet hers. "The companies have shields. Did you think we would stop an invasion without losing a man?" He turned back to the sky, then moved further away from the line of artillerymen who passed a shot with glowing destructive runes.

"That didn't help that first company—" She started but jumped when Enya placed a hand on her arm.

"We can't be everywhere doing everything, Ash," she said quietly, pulling a thin pipe from a pouch and beginning to tamp it. "Those spearmen are counting on us being right here, waiting to do something they cannot." She breathed in smoke and offered a puff to Asha.

"I don't smoke, and I don't know how you can right now," Asha whispered, frustration and embarrassment vying for dominance in her chest.

"Helps the nerves," Throil answered, holding his hand out for the pipe.

The volleys continued. How many? She had lost count already, though she didn't think more than ten. She scanned the sky. *Where in Niiwyd's creation did that dragon go?*

Green and a flash of something metallic showed against the dark gray clouds over the ballistae. Again, it began to glow, and Asha's heart stuttered. But this time, a patchwork of green and red haze covered the artillerymen and siege engines just before the flame hit them. Scrambling, the ballistae swiveled again and fired bolts upward, as the flame exploded back from the red haze and dissipated into the green.

The dragon roared, but she didn't think any of the bolts had struck it. Most had aimed along the torrent of fire and were summarily turned to char as a result. It banked and circled, looking for an opening in the shields.

"Do we relocate to the ballistae?" Will asked.

"We relocate but not there," Odo answered, stringing his bow as he spoke. He had removed the string during the march, as was customary for preservation of the wood and fibers. "The catapults will be its next target, I think. We're heading to that saddle there." He gestured northeast at a low point between the ridgeline and towering hilltop behind the engines. "I think it will use that to block itself when it fails to destroy the ballistae."

He didn't turn to see if the others followed when he started jogging down the ridge. Asha turned and saw a new torrent of fire raining down on the other ridge. A few spots in the patchwork haze flickered and extinguished under the onslaught. But most of it held, so the damage was minimal. The dragon was directly overhead, rendering the bolts ineffective. She then glanced at the docks where volleys were still striking. Most of the piers and several ships were in bad shape. She turned and had to run to catch up to the others.

When she got down into the position Odo had described, she didn't see the Dwarves. Then she heard heavy footfalls and whirled. Thrarber and Throil lumbered down the ridge with great chains wrapped around their shoulders.

"The arty men were kind enough to support our fishing endeavor." Thrarber winked at her.

"Fishing?" she exclaimed, Will echoing her.

"Aye, sky fishin'," Throil said nonchalantly. "Assuming ye can knock the air out from under it and bring it low enough, Mayumi, lass?"

Mayumi spoke for the first time since the last halt. "I can knock it low. Be sure your net is ready."

"Estesbryd preserve us all." Enya shook her head as she spoke. "When we have a dragon on the line how do ye propose ta kill it?" Her familiar northern accent got thicker, the only indication she was nervous. Perhaps the pipe she still puffed on was helping after all. "I suppose ye expect me ta keep its bloody fire mouth closed, aye?"

"I suppose that's the whole point of bringing you along." Odo's tone was flat, but his eyes twinkled as Enya's flashed angrily. She harrumphed and puffed heavily on the pipe before dumping out the ashes and placing it in the pouch. Her face grew stiff and lined, showing the age that was normally hidden by her round face and full cheeks. She formed her shield sign just before the soft rushing of great wings reached them. All eyes turned to the sky, scanning the clouds.

"I doubt your fire spells will be much use on it," Odo said to Will and Asha. "Try others. You three focus on keeping it out of the sky. I'll focus on killing the rider. If anyone gets a clean kill, take it, of course."

As everyone murmured acknowledgement, the green shadow dipped out of the cloud to the northeast. It banked slowly, leisurely dropping its altitude to use the hills to block the ballistae, as Odo had predicted. If it saw them below, it did not fear them. Why should it? Both it and its rider were quite confident in their superiority.

Enya raised her shield over all but Odo anyway. Asha grew nauseous as her mind flashed an image of Odo's fate if the dragon turned fire on them. Did dragons draw mana to breathe fire? Or was it formed like the venom in a snake's mouth? Could he shield himself? She didn't have time to keep wondering as the Dwarves moved outward and flanked the saddle, shaking out the chains like a rope to catch a cantankerous mule.

The dragon was nearly above them. Mayumi raised her spear and drew mana deeply. Asha felt her drawing. She had felt Enya's draw for the shield as well, but that had been much subtler, gentler, teasing the mana out like a tangle from a ball of yarn. The Elf pulled like she was drawing a heavy rope to herself. Will pulled mana, too, and it felt poisonous, sickening. Despite the imminent danger, Asha grinned. She didn't need to ask how he wove a spell. Now she could feel it. A ballast bond was a mighty thing, indeed.

Mayumi yelled and threw out her wind spell, purple haze swirling around her. Asha couldn't discern the type of mana or the spell, not like when Will pulled.

Air rushed in her ears and pressed against her skin; she struggled to breathe in for a moment. The taut membranes on the dragon's scaly wings went slack and the great beast fell from the sky. Plummeting straight down, it screeched and thrashed its huge wings. But Mayumi drew and threw out more spells, changing the air and shifting the pressure faster than the buffeting of the reptilian, fleshy wings could recover.

The air around the rider began to glow light blue. A natural? The Dragon Rider was a natural Mage? His light blue glow was extinguished by a sudden ball of shadow striking it. She hadn't felt Odo draw his mana, but perhaps that was for the best. Void mana being woven would likely feel as nauseating to her as the runed training pit.

Thick chains suddenly seized the dragon's wings, wrapping around and pulling down, first the right, then the left merely a heartbeat later. Hammers struck metal as the Dwarves drew mana to shape the chains' ends into deep stakes, driving them into the hard earth.

The dragon writhed in the air as Mayumi stumbled back a step. Her legs shook with fatigue, but she kept her spear in a ready stance. Asha felt Will draw more, and this time, she matched him. They threw a poison spell together, and it hit the dragon center mass as its chest began to glow.

That insidious glow stuttered and receded but didn't extinguish. The dragon still thrashed and writhed, but its movements were slower, and the green hue of its scales paled. Light blue haze formed around the rider, who was now in full view of the ballast. Asha drew and hurtled a fireball without thinking. But it bounced off the rider's runed plate armor. From the corner of her eye, she saw Odo retrieve an arrow from his quiver. It looked like a fire basket arrow. But instead of incendiary, Odo breathed a shadow into the basket, and the previously invisible runes filled with darkness. He drew it back in his bow, and in a flash, it stuck deeply into the gorget of the Dragon Rider. His runes fizzled out, and the spell he had woven died.

She felt Will draw more mana, and she snapped back to match him. They threw another poison spell at the dragon. The glow in its chest dimmed, then it roared and thrashed at the end of the chains. Suddenly, it tucked its wings and dropped straight down. They had it out of the sky. Now how to kill it? Poison helped, but it would take much, much more. Dragons were incredibly hardy, it seemed, even for a fell beast.

The ground beneath them shook when the dragon's feet struck. Immediately, the dragon stoked the fire in its chest and blasted it out. It swung its head and let out flame directly at Thrarber, who was still feeding orange mana into the chain, strengthening and reshaping the 'net'. The green mana shimmering in front of him solidified, and Asha felt Enya draw deeper on her mana as the flame impacted it.

Roots rose up from the ground and gripped Mayumi's legs hard enough that she shouted before turning her spear on them. Her spear blade was ineffective at hacking living roots. Asha drew a fireball but extinguished it in her open palm. It would burn Mayumi under the roots.

She turned her attention to the Dragon Rider as his gorget hit the ground with the Void arrow still embedded in it. Enya drew more mana, grunting as she did so, and tried to bend her shield closer around Mayumi, attempting to run it under her. But a healer's shield was preventive against intended harm, it could do nothing to stop the roots that already reached and climbed her. Will drew a rot spell and threw it at the point where the roots rose from the ground. Asha threw a fresh, larger fireball at the Rider, as the dragon's fire breath cut off.

It whipped its head around and tried to bite at Throil. But its jaws bounced off the green mana. Enya's humming was interrupted by a grunt. When had she started humming? The tune was vaguely familiar to Asha, but she had no time to try and place it.

She drew as much mana as she could hold and threw the poison spell at the dragon again. It staggered a bit and paled again in time for Mayumi to strike it with a lightning bolt. The dragon screamed and flailed again, throwing its weight back and forth against one chain, then the other. The Dwarves drew massive amounts of mana to repair the chain as the links strained and popped. They held, but Asha didn't know how many times the Dwarves could draw like that.

A thorn bush suddenly grew right before her and attempted to wrap itself around her. Enya's shield held it back a hair's breadth from her face. She scorched it, but it regrew instantly. This time, a branch got through and dug deeply into her right arm as the dragon attempted to roast Thrarber again. Even the best shields had their limits, and Asha felt a fatigue, a slowness, in Enya's draw this time.

She used a rot spell on the thorn bush, starting on the branch around her arm, and traced it down the roots all the way to the mother plant. That time, it did not regrow.

Will was pulled off his feet by a tree root as he drew in mana for another poison spell. Mayumi called down lightning again, but it was barely more than a thunderclap, and she dropped to one knee. Enya still hummed, but Asha could hear her ragged breathing, and she made no attempt to bend her shield spell along the ground to help Will.

The Dwarves continued drawing and hammering at the chains, keeping the dragon on the ground. Asha ran to Will, drew her sword, and began hacking and burning the roots choking him. Odo picked up a run in the corner of her eye, charging toward the dragon.

Chapter 32

Odo

Odo Bleolydd hated grappling. Unfortunately, he was good at it, and even more unfortunately, it was the best way to take out an opponent wearing plate armor. Plate armor, especially the runed plate that the Dragon Rider wore, was excellent at its protective function. Defeating the plate was almost impossible with handheld weapons. Someone strong enough, with a large enough bludgeoning weapon, could dent the plate and break bones beneath it. But, from tragic experience, Odo knew that dented plate and broken bones didn't stop a determined Mage from killing someone. And the Dragon Rider was determined to kill Asha and Wilford.

So determined, in fact, that the prick had dismounted and was focusing all of his spells on the two of them. That could only mean that whatever those two had been doing to the dragon was working. Mayumi was reeling and resting on one knee, exhausted from her casting that knocked the fell beast from the sky. Enya was doing a good enough job keeping the Dwarves from getting roasted or eaten while they kept the dragon tethered. And Asha had run to help Wilford and had been caught by the same root system. Odo had assigned himself to the Rider for just this reason. Now he had to execute. *Hell of a time for puns, Preceptor*, he thought to himself as he dropped his sword next to his already discarded bow and drew his rondel dagger.

He checked the distance. If he could run fast enough, he wouldn't tear too large of a hole in Enya's shield. He would just have to gamble that the dragon would continue trying to free itself and not turn its maw at him before he reached its master. If he lost the gamble, his Void mana would not save him from its fire breath, but at least his death would be quick. Incredibly painful, but quick.

Odo leaned forward and picked up a sprint. As he charged, he calculated his chances of surviving the grapple. His goal was to get in close, bind the opponent's weapon, and drive the point of his own through the small gaps in the chainmail that covered between the plates to ensure proper range of motion. The risk was that his opponent, once grappled, was equally close, and likely equally capable of binding his weapon or driving theirs into a gap in his chainmail.

He knew his risk was even higher because he was not wearing plate armor. That meant he had many more gaps for the Dragon Rider to exploit. Perhaps a slim chance was too generous, but he would not lose Asha or Wilford to the dragon-fucker. Odo had a better chance than any other member of the ballast, stronger than all but the Dwarves, more experienced than any but Mayumi, and, of course, he was the only Void. He had been confident that the rest of them could kill the dragon if he took out the rider. The Rider's actions confirmed his confidence.

Odo impacted the Dragon Rider, whose head was turned and left arm upraised, blocking a fireball Asha had managed to throw while still helping free Wilford. His superior body weight impacted the Rider from his quarter right, knocking him to the left and pinning his sword arm against his abdomen. Odo slid his rondel into the exposed armpit and drove as deep as he could. The Dragon Rider brought his left arm down first trying to block, then struck Odo's head. But the dagger in his axillary artery deadened the blow, and Odo had his chin tucked so the strike was ineffective. The Dragon Rider screamed in pain and dropped his sword. Pulling his right arm free, he used both hands to grab Odo's shoulders and threw him to the ground. Odo looped his left leg behind the Dragon Rider's knee and pulled him down with him.

When Odo's shoulders impacted, he brought his knees up and drove his feet into the ground, twisting the still impaled dagger and using it as a third purchase point to force the Dragon Rider to continue the roll and land on his back with Odo on top of him. As he did so, blood ran down his hand. Not enough blood. *Fuck.* He hit a vein, not the artery. It could still kill, but it would take several minutes, and that was a lifetime in a grapple.

A lifetime he didn't have, he barely had enough time to match the flick of a hand with the tensing of muscles as the Dragon Rider drew his own dagger and drove it toward his exposed neck. Odo released his dagger, leaving it right where it was, catching the Dragon Rider's gauntleted wrist and turned it back toward his own neck.

A blast of mana hit them as Asha yelled something he couldn't understand. She was trying to help him, no doubt, but Void magic didn't differentiate between friend and foe. His essence dissipated whatever magical assistance she had attempted to give him. The Dragon Rider was able to deflect his own dagger past his neck and now had his armored elbow locked in a triangle. Odo shifted his grip, pushing down hard on the Dragon Rider's elbow, while he reached around behind the man's neck with his left hand and grabbed his wrist from behind. He lifted his hips and twisted the Dragon Rider around onto his belly. The Dragon Rider got his feet and left arm under himself and lifted them both up a bit. Odo released his wrist and grabbed him under the chin, pulling back and up, keeping him off balance and exposing his chainmail-covered neck. Simultaneously, Odo reached across him and pulled his rondel from the Dragon Rider's left armpit and drove it up at his neck.

His rondel met its mark, driving between the flattened iron rings and piercing into flesh, severing the Dragon Rider's carotid artery. Bright red blood pumped out, dropping the Dragon Rider forward onto his face, then down into death. But Odo never knew this. By releasing the Dragon Rider's weapon to grab his own, he had left his face wide open. He collapsed on top of the fallen Dragon Rider, his opponent's dagger six inches deep into his left eye.

Chapter 33

Asha

Asha finally scorched back the last of the roots that were strangling Will and turned her attention to where Odo had the Dragon Rider in a grapple. She summoned the poison spell they had been using on the dragon and yelled for Odo to duck before she pointed her sword and fired the spell directly at the Rider's face.

It did nothing. Odo's Void mana was powerful enough that touching him protected the Rider from her spell. Her attention was split. Mayumi called down another lightning strike on the dragon. Indominable as ever, the Elf was back on her feet, chest heaving but looking less drained. And on the ground next to her, Will struggled to his hands and knees. Asha fired a rotting spell into the dragon; testing if it would do more damage than the poison spell seemed worth the effort. Then she turned and helped Will stand, only for him to stumble again.

He was spent. She could feel his exhaustion when he attempted to draw. It was far deeper than her own, and the muscles in her legs and arms burned.

"Sit." She panted when she tried to speak. "Rest. Join back. When you. Can." Will nodded, unable to catch his breath.

Asha turned and white-hot, blinding pain stabbed her left eye. She didn't know if it was an arrow or perhaps another thorn got through, but she screeched and grabbed at it. No blood warmed her fingers, and nothing protruded. She didn't have time to investigate further. The green haze had flickered and broken, and the dragon swung its open mouth toward Throil.

Charging closer in a stumbling run, Asha heaved at her mana. She drew more deeply than she ever had. Poison, rot, decay. She envisioned the dragon old and decrepit. Too sickly to fly or hunt. She imagined it collapsing and breathing its last breath as she drew in mana until she thought her chest would burst. The pain in her eye seared deeper, and every muscle in her body began to tremble. She imagined its corpse rotting and the flesh falling off the bone as she threw her decay spell at its chest.

Throil dove to the side, swinging his hammer at the dragon's open jaws that came within inches of him, but instead snapped around the chain and ripped it out of the earth.

Asha's spell hit it then. *Poison. Rot. Death. Decay*, she chanted under her ragged breathing, drawing and pushing out her spell until black haze edged her vision. She stumbled again and fell. But so did the dragon.

The fell beast staggered, dropping the chain from its mouth. It fell sideways, flailing its limbs, trying to rise, but it failed. All color drained from its scales, and its teeth cracked and fell out of its mouth. The halter and saddle turned to dust. It flared the glow in its chest, but the light died back, and only a foul stench emerged from its mouth as it rasped out a breath.

Asha felt Mayumi drawing mana again, and she drew once more as well. Leaning back to sit on her haunches rather than expend the energy to rise, she threw another decay spell, hitting the dragon at the same moment as it was struck by another lightning bolt. The dragon let out a croaking, moaning sound, then collapsed. Asha stared at it from her good eye and saw its chest rise once, twice, but not for a third time. Its scales withered, and the flesh receded until the dragon was nothing but a pile of bones.

She tried to open her mouth to speak, but only a gasping, heaving squeak came out.

Throil appeared in the corner of her vision, limping around the dead beast. "I'd call that a successful fishin' trip." He chuckled at his joke before gripping her arm and pulling her to her feet. "Ye alright, lass? No blood. Any pain?"

"Is. There. Something in. My eye?" She panted, leaning on his shoulder for support.

"I can't tell. Got some bit or bob stuck in my own, lassie," he said, shaking his head.

Thrarber approached, a hand over his left eye. "You, too? Maybe we picked a bad chain fer fishin', brother."

"No. No." Asha pulled away from them and looked around frantically. Three sore eyes were no coincidence. "Who fell?" she yelled, scanning both hillsides.

Her eyes fell on Odo and the Dragon Rider, still grappled. The sunlight dancing on a golden bracelet on the Dragon Rider's wrist was the only movement. She ran toward them as fast as she could manage, but it was more of a tripping walk.

Grabbing Odo's limp shoulders, she used every bit of strength she had left to flip him over. A dagger protruded from his eye. She screamed, dropping his body back to the earth.

"Enya! Enya, help him!" she cried out. "Help—"

"He's with the Recorder now, Ash," Enya said softly, breathing heavily out of her nose as she approached from the other side of his body.

"Do something! You're the healer! Take something out of your pack! That's the whole point of you!" she screamed. She reached out and pulled the dagger from his eye; hardly any blood came out with it.

"I can't help the dead," Enya said in a firm voice.

"Try." Asha sobbed. "Please."

Enya stepped around the body and wrapped her arms around Asha in a hug. "He's already gone."

Will stumbled over and knelt beside her, gripping her open hand. The Dwarves each wrapped an arm around the pair. Mayumi placed a large, warm hand on her head and said, "He will find peace with his patron. He was a good man, and it is an honorable death."

Asha had no more strength to cry out, so she only shook her bowed head. *This can't be the end. He can't be dead. Honorable death? No, this is not honor, nor peace.*

Chapter 34

Asha

Asha struck the flint together again, biting back a curse when the sparks scattered around her tinder and fizzled, again. She couldn't remember the last time she had tried to start a fire without mana. Her mother, Great Uncle Luca, and her father had all, for once, agreed she needed to know how to do it. Just in case she ever needed to be able to start a fire and couldn't use mana, like if she was hiding, or if her ballast was broken. The pain of loss squeezed in her chest, then stabbed her eye again. She had barely been part of a ballast. How could it be broken already?

Odo's death stare burned in her mind's eye. The strange, limp, heaviness of his body as they had carried him back to camp. The sorrow as they laid him down in the burial tent and had been instructed to strip him of all weapons and valuables. The nauseating guilt following that instruction felt like a violation in some way. The finality as they walked away from his corpse, carrying a bundle of belongings to return to his widow. The horrid stench of burning flesh as the burial corps had instantly cremated him as they walked away. Throil had stayed behind. *Had he gathered some ashes for the Clach Shin-the gemstone the Dwarves made from a loved one's body? Was Odo a loved one to the ballast?* He wasn't a relative, but they were blood bonded. Surely, that had to count, but what did she know of such things?

She looked down at her hands, flexing the fingers. How long would it take the spiritual wound to heal? How long until she could access her mana again? Panic mingled with the pain in her chest and formed into outrage. *How long until the Order tried to replace Odo? Or worse, scatter the remnants of the ballast amongst others?*

"Asha, lass." She jumped as Throil's voice came from behind her. "There's a gentleman here to hear our report o' what happened. 'e wants us all together like."

Asha set down the flint beside the still dry tinder. She stood and gestured for him to lead but couldn't form the words on her lips. He didn't seem offended, if he noticed at all.

She followed him back to the ballast tent. Each member was assigned a canvas section and frame. They each could pitch them individually or join them together into one large tent. This time they had opted for the single large tent, not that anyone had given a reason. The fact that Odo had preferred the individual tents reignited that strange guilt.

Inside, Will leaned heavily with his elbows on his knees as he sat on his bedroll. The others stood in a loose semi-circle around two men in grimy but expensive armor. Asha glanced over their heraldry and recognized them as Marquess Pullium and the regiment's Prior. She saluted them, and they returned it.

The marquess turned to Mayumi. "As the most experienced member remaining, I assume you have taken interim command?" he said, then, at her inclination of the head, continued, "I understand the dragon is dead, but the ballast was broken. Your summary of events, please."

Mayumi detailed the positioning and tactics they had used only a few hours before. It felt surreal, like she was talking about someone else, like Asha wasn't truly inside her own body as she listened.

"You used poison to kill it?" Pullium asked.

"The poison only weakened it," Asha answered, realizing it wasn't her place after she said it.

Everyone looked at her but didn't scold or frown, so she continued, "My final spell was one of decay. And Mayumi hit it with lightning at the same time."

"That explains the condition of the carcass," the Prior said. "Did fire have any effect on it?"

"We didn't try fire. It breathes the stuff, so we didn't bother."

He nodded at her reply as if it confirmed something. "Anything else we should know?" He scanned the rest of them.

"The Dragon Rider wore runed-plate armor," Asha added. "My fireballs bounced right off him."

"Yes, the other one does as well." The marquess nodded solemnly. "Though his dragon seems to have been too injured to fly. The pair have been doing a marvelous job keeping our infantry out of the city gates. But we have damaged the docks enough so that they will not be resupplied any time soon. Time and sappers. That's what always breaks a strong wall. Time and sappers." He smiled slightly and turned to leave.

"I will send a clerk to obtain a more thorough report," the Prior said to Mayumi, then turned to Enya. "And another healer to finish the consecration you have started. All of you are to rest and heal up. More instructions will follow once your ballast wound is healed."

They all echoed farewell as their superiors left.

"Well, how's the cook fire coming?" Thrarber asked her. "Can't speak for the rest o' ye. I, myself, am starving."

"Not well," Asha grumbled and turned away.

"Oh, lass, ye hurt me. Why my bellybutton is nearly touching my spine," Thrarber lamented as he feigned collapse onto his bedroll.

"I reckon ye've more than enough blubber around your middle to make that a lie," Throil retorted, but she shook her head and intentionally stopped listening to them as she walked back outside.

She knelt in front of her small fire pit and rechecked the stack of dry kindling and tinder. Picking up the flint, she struck it again. It missed, again.

"Oh, just fucking burn, will you?" she snapped.

The tinder glowed red and caught flame. The flint hung in her still hands. She hadn't struck it. Dropping the flint, she focused on her right hand. She drew a fireball in it. Pain prickled in her left eye, but the mana came to her, and the flames burned brightly in her palm.

That's impossible. And yet, the fire crackled and fizzled, burning as pain intensified in her left eye. Her stomach churned and she extinguished the fireball.

"Fear not the devastation of the great beast."

Her mother's prophecy rang in her mind. It hadn't been about the troll after all, and it had not arrived too late.

"Blood given from a willing and knowing heart cries out..."

Had Odo known he would die?

Boots scratched on the ground behind her and Enya spoke, "Asha, what did you just do?"

Asha turned slightly, tears filling her eyes as she looked up at the other woman. "He has seen the faithful sacrifice. He will sustain the blood bond. Nothing will tear it asunder," she whispered, and drew another fireball without looking at it.

Enya winced and raised a hand to her eye, feeling the same stab that Asha did when she drew the mana.

Both women shuddered as a bellowing roar echoed off of the besieged port's walls. The battle was won, but the war was only just beginning. The wounded ballast would fight it together.

The End

Epilogue

Odo

Odo had felt the cut of steel fairly often in his forty-six years, and he had plenty of scars to prove it. This made it even more ironic that his death had been painless. He supposed he should count that as a blessing. Sitting with the Recorder, recounting his life, blessings seemed few and far between.

He understood Trunii was the God of Sorrow as well as Death. Still, the weeping made him uncomfortable. His life had been difficult, yes, grim, at times. But it wasn't bad enough to cry over. Worse were the looks of pity and occasionally horror as he told his tale. What could horrify a God? Particularly the Recorder, the God who listened to all the stories of humanity? Maybe Trunii was just sensitive; he was the God of Sorrow, after all.

Odo had thought this part would be different. He had thought that they would be in an archive or maybe a library. Before his death, he had pictured the Recorder behind a desk, bent over whatever the divine version of parchment was, scribbling furiously with an enormous quill. Instead, they sat on a grassy knoll that looked just like his favorite place to sit as a child when he wanted to be alone, but it felt different somehow. The wind brushed his cheek, then flitted off to bob the unripe grains in the vast field before him. And the God beside him listened and wept.

Odo didn't want to weep. He wanted to lay back on the grass, close his eyes against the gentle sunshine, and slowly drift off to sleep, preferably with his wife resting her head on his shoulder, leaning against his side, so he could feel her body relax and her breath deepen. Then he could fall asleep to the sound of the soft snores she always denied. Could his reward for a good life be holding his wife and never having a stiff or prickling arm? He didn't want her to die, too, but he couldn't help wishing he wouldn't have to wait too long to see her again.

"Then I pulled the dragon-fucker's—pardon." Odo coughed uncomfortably; it had to be bad to curse in front of a God. "I pulled *the man's* neck back and stabbed him in the jugular. I don't remember anything else."

"That was the last action of your life," the Recorder whispered through his tears. "It was a good life."

Now that might be taking it too far in the other direction. Odo wouldn't call his life bad, but he wouldn't call it good either.

"I mean that you were good. In that life."

Of course, a God could hear his thoughts. *Fuck.*

The Recorder smiled for the first time since they had sat down. "You will go to the house of your patron, so it is not for me to decide. But I think that an arm that never grows uncomfortable while holding another is a very fine reward and well-deserved."

Another God approached the pair, seemingly appearing out of nowhere. Odo recognized his patron, Ciirtas. Not that that made any sense as he had never seen his patron, and he did not resemble his statues in the Capital. But there was strange awareness in the afterlife. Even if there hadn't been, the jagged sword on the God's belt would have made it clear a moment later.

"I agree with my brother, but your wife has a good many years yet to live. I have other rewards in the meantime, my friend. Come." At least the God of Justice wasn't weeping.

Odo rose and followed his patron. They had only taken a few steps, and the landscape changed. The rolling hills and green fields turned into a familiar courtyard. His courtyard. His wife sat on her favorite cushioned chair, doing some needlework.

As he gazed at her, he saw something else. Another soul, nestled inside of her body. It was tiny, barely there, it seemed.

Odo fell to his knees, hanging his head. His voice cracked when he spoke. "Not again. She can't lose another baby. This isn't a reward, it is torment. I have been faithful. She doesn't deserve this. I don't deserve—"

"She will not lose this child," Ciirtas interrupted him without anger or judgment. "But the children she lost before will need their father."

"The children?" Odo looked from the God to his wife, then surged to his feet, carried by that same strange awareness into his house. There, around the large dining table his wife adored so much, were seated ten small souls. Six sons and four daughters. His children who had never joined the world.

Then Odo wept, a lifetime of pain mingling with intense joy to overwhelm him. A moment later, the tug of Asha drawing mana broke his mournful detachment. "That's impossible." He said aloud. He knew the spiritual pain of a broken ballast, knew it intimately. Far beyond frustration and grief, Asha was cut off from her mana, from a piece of herself and from the Gods. Eighteen times he had suffered that pain, felt broken and divinely bereft until his soul had healed. Or at least she should have been.

"You would tell a God what is possible?" Ciirtas chuckled. "Come. Your children have waited a long time to have their father, and you have waited a long time to rest. What happens next is no longer your affair. Though I suppose you will always know when your ballast mates are casting, you have other far more important matters to shepherd."

Thank you so much for reading *The Chosen One's Substitute*! If you enjoyed reading it would you mind leaving a review? Reviews help authors more than you know. You can scan this QR code:

or leave it directly with your preferred retailer.

Book 2 of the *Jagged Sword Chronicles* is in the works. If you would like to sign up for updates the link for my email list in on my website as well as links to all of my socials. The email list is best as it is not subject to an algorithmic change. My website QR code is:

Pronunciation Guide

The Gods:

Estesbryd: Eh-stEEz-brid

Trunii: TrOO-nee

Iilusen: Il-OO-shen

Niiwyd: NEE-whyd

Feorach: FA-ohr-ack

Ciirtas: Seer-tAHs

Dynawach: Din-ah-WAck

Locations:

Ados: Ah-dOs

Carados: Kar-ah-dOs

Domum Commercia: Daw-muhm Kah-mer-shee-ah

Hadrumentum: Hah-droo-MEN-tuhm

Inglerho: EHN-gler-ho

Meditullio: Mehd-i-tOOl-ee-o

Names:

Asha Pacatus: Ah-sha Pah-cAH-toos

Bomilcar: BAH-mil-car

Bostar: BOh-st-ar

Dido: DI-do

Dofrik: DOF-rick

Flinok: Flin-OAk

Genoveva: Gen-O-vee-vah
Glormhar Tausg: GLOARrm-har Tahg
Krinrun: Kreh-rUHn
Krusur: KrOO-ser
Mago: MAH-go
Masnachwr: Mah-nahs-ACK-wher
Mayumi: May-U-mee
Sophonisba: SOH-fon-ees-bah
Thomas Iurgium: Tah-mahs EE-uhr-gum
Thrarber: ThrAHhr-ber
Throil: ThrOIl

About the Author

Suzie Nicks grew up in rural Michigan as a voracious reader and daydreamer. She joined the Army at 17 to be a Healthcare specialist. After 8 years of service, a deployment, and lots of cool guy things later, she and her husband moved to Alaska to work in civilian healthcare and raise their family. She is currently writing to give her imagination an outlet as a Stay-At-Home Mom.

Read more at suzienicks.com.

www.ingramcontent.com/pod-product-compliance
Lightning Source LLC
LaVergne TN
LVHW041145150826

845673LV00001B/71
9798994990407